Enchant

DARING EVER AFTERS

TEACUP
DRAGON
PUBLISHING

To David. You're my favorite, always.

BOOKS BY TAMERI ETHERTON

*Song of the Swords**

The Prince of Dragons

The Stones of Resurrection

The Temple of Sacrifice

The Ruins of Betrayal

The Veils of Deception

*The Fatal Fae**

Fatal Illusion

Fatal Assassin

Fatal Legacy

*Court of Stars**

Sunset in Shadow

*Chronicles of Eidyn**

Child of Fire

Dragon Mage

Short Stories

UnBroken

*Daring Ever Afters**

Enchant

*Books that are part of the Aetherverse: The fantastical realms of Tameri Etherton. Characters and storylines intersect within the books with magical consequences.

Enchant

TAMERI ETHERTON

Chapter One

Just one bite. Just one bite to enchant the king. If only the apple were poisoned. If only she didn't have to marry a man thrice her age. If only...the story of her pitiful life.

The plump red apple sat innocently on a cushion, as if mocking Eira's despair. Her stepmother paced the elegantly furnished sitting room, her hands gesticulating wildly as she lectured Eira on the exact moment she should give the apple to King Otto. The timing had to be perfect if he were to fall madly in love with her on their wedding night. A wedding she'd not consented to, and until just now, didn't know existed.

Eira ignored Regan's lecture and slid her gaze from the apple to the frayed edges of a once-expensive rug that covered a gleaming white marble floor. She'd been lured to the palace on the false pretense she was to attend a ball. Not just any ball, but her first. It was to be her grand coming out to the court, something every high-ranking maiden was afforded upon their twenty-first year, and Eira had spent a dazzling month preparing. A month full of excitement at the prospect she was to —finally—see more of the kingdom than their castle.

There were dress fittings and special tutors to instruct her in court manners, cobblers who measured her feet to get her slippers just right, and milliners who made exotic pieces of art that Eira fretted she'd ruin within minutes of wearing. At the time, she had wondered where the funds were coming from to pay for all of it, but now she knew. The king. She should be flattered, but how could she rouse herself to a state of euphoria for a man she surreptitiously had to enchant to love her?

Perhaps she was looking at this all wrong. The wedding was an unfortunate distraction, yes, but, she'd had her own reasons for coming to the palace. And, she reminded herself, the month of fevered preparation had been devoid of whippings. For that alone, she was eternally grateful. Lady Regan Banworth was many things, but a caring, loving mother was not one of them. Yet Eira still held a tiny spark of hope that her stepmother would one day love her as a daughter ought to be loved. Regan had married Eira's father when she was four, and after he died when she was six, Regan became Eira's sole caregiver. Poor little Lady Cannaid, she recalled her maid saying, an orphan at such a young age, thank the goddess she had Lady Banworth.

Over the years, that spark grew ever smaller as the offhand remarks and slight digs turned to hasher criticisms, and then to a slap once every often, to finally the physical assaults that became part of Eira's weekly schedule. Sometimes for infractions Eira hadn't made, but Regan found fault with all the same. After a time, it became easier if she simply accepted the abuse. After all, her stepmother wouldn't punish her for no reason. Pleasing Regan became her priority. If she was a better daughter, then Regan would love her.

It was that damn spark that kept Eira from running away. That, and the small, but homey castle that had belonged to her father, where Eira's mother had once rocked her to sleep—she couldn't leave the one last connection she had to her deceased parents. Besides, if she tried to run away...she shuddered at the thought of what her stepmother would do to her. She glanced at Regan, at the determination in her eyes, the way in which she held herself so tightly contained it was a miracle she didn't self-combust.

It shouldn't have surprised Eira that Regan would lie about something as important as a marriage but she had, and Eira was left reeling with the revelation. Instead of dancing at the ball with a handsome lord—perhaps even a prince, she'd be forced to sit by King Otto's side, pretending to be thrilled. Although she'd never met the king, his reputation as a tyrant and glutton hadn't given her much interest in ever doing so. Now she didn't have a choice.

She'd always known Regan desired status at court. She moaned about it so often Eira had stopped paying attention. With the tutors and fittings, Eira assumed they were to make certain she didn't embarrass her stepmother, but she'd never, not in her wildest potion-fueled nightmares, would've believed Regan could go this far.

A macabre thought wormed its way into her brain. Regan hadn't laid a hand on her all month to keep Eira's pale as snow skin clear. It wouldn't do to have His Majesty see lashings across her back, or bruising along her arms. Then again, if he was as bad as she'd heard, he might be tempted to do Regan one better and cover Eira's entire body with welts.

She unconsciously gripped her arms and then smoothed her sleeves as she stared at the floor desperately searching for a solution to her dilemma, but the only escape she could imagine was her death. Just one bite of a poisoned apple and she'd fall to the floor, her raven hair and ruby lips in sharp contrast to the white marble. Regan would rage that she'd ruined everything. And then what? Who would miss her?

A sob cut her throat and she swallowed hard. No one. Certainly not her stepmother. Eira was a nobody with nothing to offer except her looks. Regan had made it quite clear often enough that Eira would never, ever be worth anything of substance. And that she shouldn't dare hope to find true love because it didn't exist. Little did her stepmother know, Eira didn't crave true love or any of the fairytale romances she read about. She would've been happy to simply have the love of her stepmother.

As the years wore on, that seemed ever more impossible. Eira doubted Regan had ever loved anyone except herself and her godforsaken mirror.

The cursed thing gave Eira shivers and she stifled a shudder lest Regan be tempted to renounce her abstention from whipping her stepdaughter. Wedding be damned, it must've been driving Regan mad that she couldn't punish Eira as she wished.

And now she expected Eira to marry a man she didn't know. There had to be a way out of the arrangement—preferably one that didn't involve her death.

"Why must I marry the king? Certainly, it's improper with his latest wife having so recently passed." Eira hoped reason might subdue her stepmother's enthusiasm on the subject.

"Darling, I've waited too many years for this moment. You're twenty-one now. That's plenty old enough to take a husband. I was only twenty when I married your father and he was my second husband." A shadow flitted across Regan's eyes and they narrowed dangerously. Eira braced herself for a slap, but instead Regan stroked a strand of Eira's hair in a somewhat loving gesture. Quick as a lightning flash, Regan grabbed her jaw and squeezed hard enough she tasted blood. "You'll marry him because your king deserves the best and you're the fairest in all the land." She released her with a snort of disgust and held the apple an inch from her nose. "You'll be a queen, darling. What lady doesn't dream of being queen?" Her tone changed from menacing to sickly sweet.

"This lady." Eira pointed to herself before taking the apple, but it was no use.

Her stepmother had already turned away to gaze into her mirror and smooth the tiny lines at the edges of her eyes with the pads of her fingertips. "Darling, think of the power you will have." Regan pouted prettily to her reflection before blowing a kiss.

A greenish glint rippled across the surface of the looking glass and settled in Regan's brown eyes. A moment later, the green was gone, as if it had never been. If Eira blinked, she'd have missed it.

She arched against the trembles that slithered down her spine and looked away. She hated that mirror, but Regan refused to leave it at their castle. She claimed it was a family heirloom she could never be without. Eira knew the truth. It was no ordinary reflecting glass, but a magic mirror. Only Regan could control it, and if she knew Eira had discovered her secret—Eira stopped herself from imagining the beating she'd get. She knew all too well the power of her stepmother. And was equally powerless to stop it.

Why would her stepmother risk bringing a magical artifact to the palace? Regan's words drowned out as Eira's mind whirled. King Otto despised all things magical. Humans, creatures, even inanimate objects infused with enchantments were all victims of his hatred. It was known throughout the kingdom that he and his specialized group of trackers sought out anyone with magical abilities and executed them. Including people like Regan who needed spell books and magic mirrors to use their power.

Regan was a witch, but she hid it well, even from their servants, and especially from Eira. But she'd learned her stepmother's secret long ago and kept that knowledge locked deep in her heart. Right beside her own, potentially deadly secret. As with people, Eira assumed not all witches were wicked, but her only experience with them had been through Regan, and she seemed to revel in her vileness. Naturally, Regan was arrogant enough to think she could conceal her abilities from the king, otherwise, why risk her life for the stupid thing?

Regan winked at her reflection while suggestively licking her lips. The gross display wasn't for Eira's benefit. She had probably forgotten Eira was still in the room. Her stepmother excelled at making her feel small and unimportant. Regan patted the dark curls piled atop her head—a hairstyle she refused to give up even when fashions moved on to less elaborate stylings. Eira often wondered if Regan hid items in the tower of poufed and teased locks. She wouldn't at all be surprised if one day a squirrel leapt from the mess to bop Eira on the nose.

Not what Eira would call a great beauty, her stepmother was attractive in a fragile, bird-like way. Shorter than Eira, she held herself in a manner that made her appear much taller, more regal than she actually was. Her sky-high heels didn't hurt, either. Everything about Regan was cultivated to present a package of genteel aristocracy.

If Regan wanted Eira to marry the king, there was profit in it for her. Money or power or station—she had probably bartered her stepdaughter for all three.

"I expect you to enchant King Otto, darling. Utterly and completely until he's so smitten he would gladly give you the throne. He hasn't crowned a wife since his third, but you, darling, you will be queen. The goddess knows you have the looks and figure for it, but do you have the brains? The cunning drive necessary to rule a kingdom?" Regan looked at her through the mirror's reflection with a penetrating glare that left little doubt whether she thought her stepdaughter capable of such a task. She tsked and powdered her flawless skin. "At least you have the apple."

Eira's stomach tightened and her face flushed. She wasn't as stupid as her stepmother believed, and yet, she had so little experience with men, only what the servants gossiped about and what she'd been able to glean from certain books in their library. The shiny red apple cradled in her palm, innocent, alluring.

"How does it work?"

"If you have to ask, then perhaps you're not ready for such an auspicious life." Regan reached for the fruit, but Eira pocketed it. Her stepmother eyed her a moment before raising a shoulder in an elegant shrug. "Very well. I bought a potion in the market. It's nothing more than puppy love, but it'll do the trick. With any luck, you'll get with child on your wedding night."

So very foul. Utterly and despicably repugnant.

"I thought magic was banned."

Regan snorted. "Banned? Yes, I supposed you could say it is, but a potion made from herbs and supplements is hardly magic. With that thinking, cooking a stew would be banned and I doubt very much if Otto would outlaw food. It's ridiculous, really—he" Regan stopped herself and glared at Eira as if she'd said something offensive. "This isn't magic, darling. I would never presume to thwart the king's law."

Eira bit her cheek to keep from pointing an accusatory finger at the mirror. It would do no good to argue. Regan had made up her mind that Eira should marry the king. She flicked a glance at the smooth marble and let out a long, mournful breath. Her stepmother didn't view Otto in the same lens as she. Despite being well over sixty years old and heavier than two grown men, rumor had it he still enjoyed a lusty frolic. The thought of him naked roiled her gut so violently it made her ill. She refused to envision herself pinned beneath his sweating bulk as he grunted and huffed above her. Rutting his virginal bride like a disgusting pig.

Her stomach lurched and she swayed against the onslaught of sickness that swirled in her belly.

"I should like to see more of the palace." She needed air. Needed to clear her mind of the horrific images that lingered with terrifying permanence.

Her reason for coming to the palace seemed trivial now, even more treasonous than before. This was her new life unless a miracle saved her from the travesty that was about to take place. If she ran away, where would she go? She didn't know anyone besides Regan and the servants at her castle. She doubted they'd risked Regan's ire to shelter her, and besides, no matter where she ran, she'd be hunted by the king's elite squad. How could she ever hope to outwit them? Or her stepmother? Or even Otto himself? The time for running was long past, but there had to be another way out of her predicament. She needed a moment alone to think.

"After we meet with Otto, you can explore all you like. For now, drink your tea and settle your nerves." Regan patted her hair and rose. "There will be feasts each night before the ball. His Majesty is in a fine mood to celebrate, but don't be greedy. You wouldn't want to be pudgy on your wedding night."

Eira tried not to gag at the suggestion. "I'm not sure His Majesty would even notice given his bulk."

As soon as the words were out, she regretted them. Regan's eyes narrowed to dangerous little slits and she clenched her fists, but held them at her side. Eira's stomach pitched so violently, she tightened her jaw to keep from being ill on her stepmother.

"Do not destroy this opportunity, Eira. Haven't I devoted my adult life to you? The sacrifices I've made to ensure that you were raised to be a lady of good standing. I provided a warm home, an education, I kept you safe from the world. And here you are, about to become queen. The least you can do is show the tiniest appreciation and respect to me for all that I've done."

Another tsk, this one accompanied by a sneer. "But then, you always were a selfish child more interested in your books and fantasies. No worries." She waved a hand as if to brush aside the past, and then stroked a finger down Eira's cheek. "You truly are lovely. Skin as soft as a petal, and eyes the color of a summer sky at dusk." Eira leaned into the rare caress, longing for more. "You always were too trusting, though. That's why I'll be here, guiding you as I always have done."

"What do you mean?" the tempest in her belly gained speed, pinching and twisting uncomfortably. "You'll not go back home to Castle Falkoyn?"

"Heavens no, darling! Why would I return to that hovel when my place is here, with you at court? You should be grateful —" Whatever she was about to say was cut off by a knock at the door. Her lips thinned as she glared at the intruder. "What is it?"

A page held a silver tray with a sealed note laying in the center. "A message from His Majesty, my lady."

Regan snatched the note and waved the young lad away. He bowed to Regan, but his gaze lingered on Eira. Curiosity lurked in his eyes, and perhaps a question as well. Whatever it was, he didn't say and before she could ask, he scurried from their rooms.

"Fuck." Regan tapped a nail against her tooth. "Otto's been delayed and can't meet with us privately until tomorrow." Her narrowed gaze landed on Eira and she smoothed the front of her jade satin gown. Drop earrings of the same shade glittered from her ears and danced with the shake of her head. "Perhaps this is a good thing. It gives you time to acquaint yourself with life at court. Yes, go on, darling." Her voice trailed off as if she were deep in thought.

"Thank you, Stepmother." She hurried to the door, but Regan stopped her.

"Don't leave the palace proper. I've heard rumors of a man

murdered in the forest." Her gaze narrowed and pinned Eira to the spot. "Could even have been at the hands of a huntsman. Ghastly ordeal. Probably one of those disgusting magical creatures the king detests. Stay indoors where it's safe, darling. And don't talk to anyone. The goddess knows you could make a fool of yourself and ruin everything."

"Of course, Stepmother." She dipped a curtsey, barely registering Regan's insults as she rushed from the lavishly appointed apartment.

After all these years, Regan still believed Eira didn't know that she was a witch. The fact gave her little comfort. At least that meant Regan also didn't know Eira's secret, for if she did, surely she wouldn't have sold her stepdaughter to the king. A wave of panic washed over her and she paused in her steps to grab a chair.

Regan was going to stay at the palace. But why, truly? Was it out of duty to Eira or another reason? Did Regan think she would retain control of her stepdaughter once she was married to Otto? Question after question pinged against her skull, and through it all, one solitary dark thought wove its way to Eira's heart.

If she were as truly worthless as Regan believed, only one thing would give her value. If Regan knew Eira's secret, then she was in far more danger than she'd realized. A second, no less terrifying thought caused her to nearly trip—had Regan said a huntsman? Eira gulped for air and steadied herself against a chair. It was mere coincidence, that's all. The murder had nothing to do with her, or the curse placed on her as a child. The one that said a huntsman would carve out her heart.

Chapter Two

The cheek of that woman. A huntsman? Him? What a lark. Henri Callan, Crown Prince of Ventoux placed the axe atop a sturdy branch and covered it with brambles to keep it from being discovered. A gift from his father to their dear friends, he would deliver it to the dwarves later, when it wasn't so dangerous to be seen in the forest. King Otto's bloody laws chafed at him. Magic wasn't to be feared, but respected. The kings of old knew this, but Otto's obsession had run afoul of the other kingdoms and now Henri was sent to spy on the king of Jura, among other things. His priority was to ascertain if war was necessary.

There was never a good time for invasion, but on this, he was aligned with his father and their allies. Otto was ruthless and dangerous. Becoming even more so with each passing day. It had been at least a dozen years since he last saw the king and his two sons. He'd hardly recognized Otto's eldest as he strode through the palace like a ram prepared to battle for dominance. Guillaume had always been a bit of a bully, but now Henri saw the meanness that Otto had instilled in him. Henri only hoped Otto's youngest son Leon wasn't of the same cloth.

The kingdom of Jura needed a strong ruler. A compassionate king who would once again unite with the other kingdoms in peace. Otto's war on magic was sending fissures of angst through all seven kingdoms of Savinael. At this point, they needed more than a peace treaty to calm the coming storm.

Henri leaned against the old tree and whispered a few words of reassurance in the old tongue. There was a murder in these woods recently and even the elder hardwoods were nervous. The king was getting too brazen with his efforts to cleanse the lands of magic. He ran his fingertips over the rough bark and slid his own power through the tree's heartwood to the pith.

"Be well, my friend." He couldn't give blessings to all the growing things in the forest, but this grand sire could spread his magic to the others.

What was King Otto's plan? Sending trackers to hunt down those with magic, and then what? Did he kill them? There hadn't been public executions as far as his discreet questioning had uncovered, so what was the purpose of arresting magical folk?

And what the devil did the king need five hundred thousand silver for? It was a handsome sum, not to be trivially granted. Yet there was nothing in King Otto's request for the money that said what he would use the funds for. Hence, Henri's father was also keen to know if he should loan the monarch the money. Henri had his opinion on the matter, but had promised to keep an open mind.

Not something easily done in a court as wretched as Otto's.

Henri patted the old tree fondly and made his way through the meadow. Clear skies loomed overhead, expansive with possibilities. A soft breeze lifted his hair to cool his skin. Days such as this were made for lingering with friends, laughing over a bottle of wine, and enjoying their company. But diplomacy didn't rest and there would be time for indulgences when he was home once again.

In the distance, he spied a column of smoke coming from Madam Davina's place. He almost veered in the direction of her cottage, but then swung back toward the palace. He'd made a promise to Lady Banworth that he intended to keep. The fool woman had conscripted him to be her personal palace spy. Now, that was rich. She thought him a huntsman because he carried an axe. At least she hadn't confused him with one of Otto's trackers. The men and women who hunted magical creatures for the king's pleasure. That would've been a travesty far worse than her insulting behavior—as though she were doing him a great favor. Elevating his stature, she'd said.

As if a prince of Ventoux needed the help, but he had found her request too intriguing to argue. Nor had he corrected her. When she asked what he was called, he'd simply said, "Callan," for that was true in some circles. Mainly among his drinking buddies back home, but if the woman didn't recognize a prince from a neighboring kingdom, he wasn't about to prance around like a peacock trying to impress her.

She'd paid him in gold coins, a modest yet impressive sum to be fair. Had he been an actual huntsman, he would've been overjoyed at the windfall, especially in these sorry lands where Otto's rule had brought the kingdom to near poverty in every quarter.

Not that he could tell from the lavish parties Otto was throwing each day and night before the ball. Tristano flowed like an untapped font with as many servants as there were courtiers. It appeared the king had invited not only every high ranking noble in Jura, but other lands as well. The king sought to impress his guests, but why was the question.

Who was Otto courting so vigorously he would bankrupt his coffers to the point he had to beg the other kingdoms for loans?

Surely the vulgar display wasn't for his future wife. Otto had been married six times already, what was it about this latest installment that deserved such flattery? His interest in the new queen was indeed piqued. For several reasons, Lady Banworth among them.

While the lady had doled out his coins, she made it very clear that as well as being her spy in the palace, reporting back anything worthwhile he overheard or saw, he would have one additional duty. A small thing, she'd called it. Spy on her stepdaughter, the Lady Cannaid, soon to be wife of the king.

How he'd kept his face straight when Regan made the request, was nothing short of a miracle. Never in his life had he wished harm upon someone until that moment. But he'd agreed out of some macabre fascination with the pair. What were they up to? And was it just Lady Banworth who was a deceitful, lying, traitorous bitch? Or her stepdaughter as well?

Not only had Henri come to the palace to spy on King Otto, but had personal reasons for attending the hastily planned nuptials. He'd once known Lady Cannaid—when she was simply Eira to him. A child of three to his six, he'd spent wonderful summer afternoons chasing her through the gardens of her castle while their mothers drank tea and chatted.

The Eira he knew then was joyous and carefree, but a lot could happen in eighteen years. Dropping her royal title for a start. Although why someone would wish to go down in rank baffled him. Eira's mother Eloise was the sister to Morovia's Queen Marguerite, which made her and her daughter a princess. Though now, it appeared, she only went by the title of Lady Cannaid.

After the death of Eloise, Henri never saw Eira again, despite his begging and pleading. Lord Cannaid took a new wife— Regan, Lady Banworth, and she banned not just Henri, but his mother from ever visiting Castle Falkoyn. Perhaps she had something to do with the stripping of Eira's royal lineage. It was one of the mysteries he hoped to solve in his short time in Jura.

Henri's glare went to the palace and up to the rooms where he suspected Eira and her stepmother would be staying. Lavish, but not too elaborate. Eira would be spoiled only a little before the wedding, just enough to whet her appetite for more, and then she'd be trapped in King Otto's web of revulsion.

Or perhaps he had it all wrong and Eira desired this wedding just as much as the king. Why would a man—old, infirm, hateful of all magical beings—wish to marry Eira? He'd heard rumors of her beauty—the fairest in all the land, they said. But beauty would fade. He shrugged against the questions that could only be answered in time. He hoped that Eira was happy, and if she wasn't, well, that's why he'd come to the palace.

He dusted dirt off his trousers and chuckled to himself. His traveling clothes certainly didn't look princely. No wonder Lady Banworth had mistaken him for a huntsman. His all black ensemble was meant for comfort, not status. He'd left his armor and court clothing in his rooms with his trusted butler Bernard. In truth the outfit would suit his purposes perfectly. He could lurk in the shadows spying on Eira without servants bowing and scraping to him. Yet he wouldn't look entirely out of place in a palace filled with courtiers, servants, soldiers, advisors, and the king's trackers.

At the road leading to the palace, Henri crossed to a gate leading to the palace orchards. Locked from the inside, he easily unlocked the gate with a touch of his magic. It was dangerous to use his power in Jura, but if King Otto sought to arrest him, it would certainly expedite his mission and he would get all of his answers sooner rather than later.

He crept through the trees without drawing attention to himself. Years of creeping through his own palace to spy on his four sisters had taught him stealth. To this day, they hadn't discovered his hiding places. An accomplishment that gave him great pride. He hadn't been to Otto's palace in years, but he recalled with ease the back stair that would get him access to much of the rooms without being seen.

Lady Banworth's gold sat heavy in his pocket. He should inform Bernard of the new development in their plans. The old fool would be only too happy to oblige in whatever scheme Henri set. The man might be nearing his seventieth year, but he had the vigor and impetuous daring of a lad still in short pants.

A servant sneered at him as he made his way up the back stairs and he grinned to himself. Let them think they were better than him. Their arrogance blinded them to his true identity. He took the stairs two at a time, pondering the ramifications of his plan to remain anonymous.

He'd have to find time in his day for a few select meetings, but perhaps those could be put off a few days. Whenever members of royalty gathered, there were too damn many conclaves. If they could save it all for the summit held each year, that would remove a load of stress from Henri's already burdened shoulders. Naturally, King Otto hadn't attended a summit in more than a decade, hence the need for secret gatherings now.

The next summit would be held in Allanica, a charming kingdom near the sea with a benevolent king and queen. He blew out a breath and slipped through the plain wooden door, meant to be inconspicuous to the passing nobles, and strode with enough confidence not to be challenged, but not so much as to garner unwanted attention.

The hallway was blessedly uncrowded as he made his way to his rooms. A door shut to his right and he turned in time to see a woman move quickly in the opposite direction to where he stood rooted to the worn, but still lush carpeting.

His heart beat in his throat and if he'd tried to swallow, it would've been as dry as the deserts of Charbonnel. She'd blossomed into a great beauty since he last saw her, but Henri would know his sweet Eira no matter the time passed or location.

Her hair swished across her back in a sheath of midnight against the sky-blue gown she wore. In the quick glimpse he saw, her skin was the same downy alabaster he remembered with lips as red as a rose. He pressed a hand against his chest to still the thudding of his heart. She paused in her hurry to grip a chair and for that single moment, she looked frail, frightened, even. He longed to go to his friend and offer assistance, but then she settled herself and lifted her chin in defiance, a smooth mask of indifference covered her lovely features.

Would she remember him?

Disappointment dripped like treacle over his excitement. He didn't know Eira anymore. The little girl he'd used to play with at her castle would never have consented to marrying Otto. If she was anything like her wretched stepmother, then his friend was truly dead and he would do well to keep his emotions locked tight.

For now, he would play the role Lady Banworth had assigned him—that of spy and nothing more. He would follow Eira and observe. Once he knew for certain her intentions, then he could decide if he would reveal himself. The last thing he wanted was for her to set her sights on his crown if she decided Otto's wasn't a good fit.

Chapter Three

Eira ignored those in the hallway and pretended to appreciate a portrait on the wall that she barely saw through the nerves that made her breath come in shallow pulls. She kept her face placid as she struggled to slow her galloping heartbeats and took a long, steadying breath to regain her composure. Despite willing calm, Regan's favorite bedtime story played out in her mind. The one Regan took great pleasure in reciting to Eira even in the sharp light of the day.

According to her stepmother, when Eira was born, an aged beggar woman had asked Eira's mother for an apple. A meager meal to tide her over. But Eira's mother had refused even that small kindness. In retaliation, the beggar placed a curse on Eira. When she was of age, she'd be betrayed and would die by a huntsman's hand when he carved out her heart.

Regan was wicked, but she wasn't a monster. She wouldn't purposefully taunt Eira with the threat of a huntsman. It was a simple observation, that was all. Nothing nefarious for her to get upset about. Eira shook her head against the treasonous thought. Her nerves were getting the best of her. She was leaping to conclusions that would do no good.

Eira took a slow drag of stale air and admitted to herself that Regan enjoyed being cruel and might be toying with her, but she didn't have to take the bait or play the game. She would avoid any and all huntsmen she happened to see. Simple. Don't go outside the palace, and she would be fine.

As for the sudden wedding? Again, nothing nefarious. High ranking marriages were often negotiated without the bride or groom's knowledge. They were often for practical, business reasons, although at the minute, she was having a hard time understanding what the king sought to gain by marrying her, specifically. King Otto was vain enough to demand the prettiest girl in the kingdom, and she was the lucky maiden. Even if she didn't feel fortunate.

She reassured herself that Regan didn't know about the powers she'd inherited from her mother. Eira held the secret deep in her heart and had never told a soul what coursed through her blood. But she was no witch. Her powers were pure, passed down from generation to generation from mother to daughter, originating with the goddess.

There was nothing criminal or obscene about her powers, despite what the king would have his subjects believe. Her magic was precious. That's what her father had told her. Witches were born with natural talent, same as a sorceress, but they needed spell books and charms to help channel their power. A sorceress, on the other hand, could command nature and the elements without props or instruction. If only he'd lived long enough to tell her everything she needed to know. The thought of him made her heart ache for his gentle words and ardent strength.

He often would say to her, "One day, you'll grow into your birthright, and when you do, you'll be a powerful sorceress just like your mother. But you must respect this gift. If you abuse what the goddess has freely given, there are consequences. But I have every faith you'll use your magic for good." Then he'd kiss her forehead and snuggle her close to his chest. "This is our secret, Eira. You must never tell anyone about your powers."

And she never had. Nor did she believe he would've told Regan, even though she was his new wife. To this very day, she didn't know what her father saw in Regan, but wouldn't be surprised if Regan had enchanted him somehow. The timing of her mother's death, and Regan's subsequent marriage to her father was too convenient.

The mysterious illness that claimed her mother's life was never spoken of, nor was her father's premature death, but Eira had her suspicions. She dared not speak them out loud. Regan had ears and eyes everywhere, and not just from her mirror. The servants, who claimed loyalty to Eira, loved coin and were easily convinced to spy for the wicked woman. And so, she mourned in silence, kept to herself, and pretended absolute obedience.

Eira had kept her father's secret warning, comforted by his promise that what coursed through her blood was pure magic. He'd never explained when, exactly, she would come into her power, only that when her magic did manifest, she wouldn't need spell books or potions, or even an enchanted mirror. Those things would enhance what she had, but she wouldn't be dependent upon them like Regan.

Not that it mattered. It seemed her magic was as elusive now as it ever was. Several times she'd snuck into the silent depths of the woods near their castle to try to coax her magic from hiding. She'd never been able to produce more than a tingling in her fingertips. Not even a tiny flicker. It was there—she could sense it, but if what her father said was true, it wasn't time yet for her power to develop. Or perhaps she'd hidden it so completely from Regan, that now she couldn't reach it on her own.

She smoothed her gown and straightened her shoulders. She was being silly. Regan couldn't possibly know about her power. All her stepmother had to barter with was Eira's beauty and maidenhood. To those vain enough, the pair were worth the price of a marriage. Small mercies, indeed.

Eira wiped moisture from her eyes and said a small blessing to the goddess. The nameless deity had never answered her prayers, but as with her intangible hope for love from Regan, Eira believed the goddess watched over her. If she was meant to suffer, there was a reason for it. She just wished she knew what it was.

Fully composed and the very picture of a lady, she continued on, her silk slippers gliding across thick rugs as she hurried down the main staircase to the first floor. She'd agreed to come to the king's ball so that she could search the great library for more information on what, exactly, having pure magic meant, but with Regan's declaration, that would have to wait.

The question she'd asked her stepmother rattled her brain. Why would the king need another bride? With two full-grown male heirs, surely he could enjoy the many mistresses she assumed he had, and live out the rest of his life a happy bachelor. She was missing something important, and that bothered her.

A servant passed with a tray of fluted crystal glasses and she plucked one with a shaking hand. She did love a good mystery, although to be fair, she'd only ever read them in books, and had no actual experience when the outcome involved her survival. It would serve her well to listen, to pay attention when others thought her uninterested, and to learn all she could about this court. After all, unless she found a way out of the marriage, it was to be her new life. Not a better one, necessarily, but at least she wouldn't be homeless, or alone. Perhaps she might even make friends who could offset the unpleasantness of her situation.

She took a long sip of fizzy liquid. Bubbles tickled her nose and she giggled. The cool drink slid down her throat as she emptied the glass. A small belch escaped her lips and she pressed a hand to her mouth to hide even more giggles. Regan would be mortified. Giggling itself was unbecoming of a lady, but passing gas of any sort was reprehensible.

"What is this called?" She asked a servant with another tray of the delightful beverage.

"Tristano, m'lady. Sparkling wine made from the king's own vineyards. Would you care for more?" He took her empty glass and handed her a fresh one.

Before she could thank him, he'd turned away. The bubbles went straight to her head and she braced against a column to keep from tripping over herself. The pale liquid looked innocent enough, and the fizz certainly was fun, but she didn't enjoy the effects tristano had on her. She'd had wine on occasion, not nearly as often as Regan imbibed, but this was something altogether different. The room spun with a lazy wooziness that only added to her already upset belly.

The glass wobbled in her grip and she leaned into the marble column, soaking in its cooling solidity. A flush warmed her face. The damask gown she wore scratched at her skin and she cursed the tight bodice that made it hard to breathe. She eyed the tristano as if it were an asp about to strike. How could something so delicious and merry make her feel so dreadful?

A page from Regan's grimoire danced in her thoughts and she tried to catch it, but it was sly and escaped her grasp more than once. Finally, she settled her mind on it and read the elegant handwriting. It was a spell to counteract the effects of alcohol. Clever grimoire. Despite her powers being locked inside of her, the grimoire often showed her spells and cures that, if she focused hard enough, she could bring to fruition without actually using magic.

It boggled her mind that she was able to use Regan's

grimoire without ever having touched the leather-bound tome. But since she was tiny, she'd been able to at first, understand the words, and eventually read the finely written script. It was another secret she kept hidden in her heart. In some small measure, the grimoire gave Eira comfort. Despite it belonging to Regan, the grimoire was often the only friend she had in the castle. As far as she knew, it never told Regan that it shared its secrets with her, for surely, she would've been beaten if her stepmother knew.

She hadn't actively sought to discover Regan's secret about being a witch, nor had she ever searched for the grimoire. It had happened quite by accident one wintry afternoon when Eira was just a wee lass. She had found Regan's spell books tossed willy-nilly on a bottom shelf in the library. At the time, she hadn't realized the importance of the old, crusty books, but through the years, she came to understand the magnitude of what she'd uncovered.

At some point, they were moved to Regan's sitting room, where her stepmother took tea with Eira each day. The spell books spoke to her, of amazing and terrible things. They tried to entice her to learn the words written inside the leather-bound tomes, but she refused. None were more insistent than her stepmother's grimoire. If she was near, the book would open and reveal spell after spell. On too many occasions, Eira had found herself gazing at the pages without quite knowing how she'd gotten there.

Eira knew every beautifully handwritten word. All she had to do was think of a need, and an image of the exact spell would fill her mind as if she held the book open to that specific page.

She stumbled to a table and set her full glass on the gleaming wood. Fresh air would help clear the alcoholic haze from her thoughts. Her glance wavered across the elegantly dressed women in expensive velvets fanning themselves with feathered contraptions that matched the plumes in their hats. The men strutted in silk tunics that reached their thighs with matching pants hugging their calves. Peacocks, the lot of them.

Eira steadied herself as she strolled past the sneers and barely concealed barbs the nobles lobbed at each other. She winced at their narcissism and hurried to a room near the end of the hall. It was blessedly quiet as she stepped into the semi-darkness and she breathed a sigh of relief. The room was empty save for her with only the one door that she could see. Her gut was a hive of nerves and her knees threatened to buckle as she closed her eyes to concentrate on the words the grimoire had shown her.

She spoke low, barely above a whisper, and chanted the spell that would flush the alcohol from her blood. Eira repeated the chant, keeping her voice level and calm despite the thundering of her heart against her ribs. Even though she used no magic of her own, to be discovered now would surely mean death. How could she prove to the king she wasn't a witch if she was caught reciting a spell? It was a risk, but one she willingly took to offset the unbalance she felt from the sparkling wine. If Regan found her drunk, the king's punishment would be nothing in comparison.

The last word of her spell hung in the air and she blew softly to disperse the charm. Her blood quickened, whether with eagerness or anxiety, she was never sure, but then her heart rate settled and her body warmed with a sense of protectiveness as if the spell gave her invisible armor.

She didn't know why the grimoire showed her its pages, but she was grateful that she had the spell books' knowledge to help and advise. Otherwise, she'd be lost to Regan's whims even more so than she was. More often than she could remember, the grimoire had shown her how to heal the bruises left from Regan's lashings, or gave her a meditative spell that allowed her to cast her mind elsewhere when the abusive rants became too cruel.

Wooziness seeped from her mind and her skin cooled as the effects of the tristano dissipated. Even her gown felt soft against her flesh. She rested her head against the wall and heard the clicking of a clock somewhere in the room. It's steady ticking calmed the beats of her heart.

Voices came to her from the other side of the wall and she pressed an ear to listen. A draft moved the edge of a nearby tapestry, showing a glint of light behind the thick fabric. She checked the room again to be certain she was alone and crept closer. Her fingertips outlined a gap in the wall. When she pressed, a secret door opened slightly. She snatched her fingers back as if burned and stood frozen, afraid she'd be caught spying. Which was exactly what she was doing, but curiosity held her in its clutches.

When no one came, she opened the door enough to hear the conversation clearly.

"My love, you must rest." A woman's voice, full of care and concern, spoke low, but forcefully. "When the trackers return, then we can heal you, but until then, you must conserve your energy."

"Send for Madam Davina." A male's voice, gruff and in obvious pain, ordered.

"She cannot help you anymore. You know this. She's done all she can. It's up to the trackers now."

"How long now until the next full moon?"

"Two weeks."

"And you think it'll work?"

"Shhh, my love." The woman cooed softly as if to a child. "It has to work. We're running out of time."

A crackle of magic singed Eira's skin and she swallowed a gasp. The feel was similar to what she experienced when Regan worked her spells, an uncomfortable heaviness that wormed its way across her body. A witch was nearby. To be fair, it could've been a sorceress, yet from what she could remember of her mother, magic never hurt when it came from the goddess. It only affected her when Regan used her magic.

Eira's knees trembled as she opened the door just enough to peer inside the room. If it was indeed Regan, and she was working magic in the castle, they'd both be punished. A fire blazed in the huge fireplace, its warmth blowing softly over her even from a distance. Fur rugs scattered across the dark marble floor. Some of the skins she recognized, others she didn't. Her gut pinched at the number of animals killed just for this one room.

Even before her gaze slid to the enormous bed that dominated the cavernous space, she knew who would be sitting propped up on cushions. A sheen of sweat glistened on the king's brow and his red cheeks puffed with each breath. A damp nightshirt clung to his plump chest. Greenish yellow stains and crimson splotches covered the fabric. This was her groom-to-be. This was the man she was to marry in two weeks.

A fortnight.

What was to happen then that would save his life? She scanned the rest of the room, noting the heavy furniture and broken glass of something recently shattered. Liquid oozed down the wood, staining the white fur of a wolf skin rug a sickly ochre.

Eira backed away slowly and closed the door without a sound. She leaned her head against the hard wood of the paneled wall, her mind whirling too quickly for her to make much sense of anything. Her chest heaved as she sucked in air to clear her thoughts and calm her racing heart. In two weeks, she was to be married at a grand ball, under a full moon.

Her hand cupped the apple in her pocket. Puppy love to

make the king believe he loved her long enough to get with child, which Regan hinted should happen on her wedding night. A child would cement her place in Otto's court, but for how long? The princes' mother was long since buried and replaced. A child would secure nothing for Eira, of that she was certain. She pressed a hand to her pelvis and half-turned against the wall. In a fortnight, she would have her monthly bleed. Regan knew her cycle almost better than Eira. Unless the potion worked for more than a night, what was the use? And if he was dying, why would she need to trick him into loving her? What was Regan truly up to?

Eira wouldn't get answers from her stepmother, not honest ones at least, so it was up to her to discover Regan's plans on her own, secretly. Whatever was going on at the palace—with the king and her stepmother, it involved her, but to what extent? She pushed off from the wall and turned toward the door, steeling herself for what was to come.

Something firm and immovable blocked her path. Something that wasn't there a moment before. Her breath caught as her gaze traveled up a black tunic to a clean-shaven neck. Bile danced in her throat as she lifted her glance farther up to a strong chin, set hard enough she saw nerves twitching beneath his skin. She skimmed his lips, past his straight nose, to eyes of jet that bore deep into her soul. As if he saw past all of her defenses to the raw places she kept buried. As if he saw *her*, for who and what she truly was.

Chapter Four

Eira bit her cheek to keep from screaming and took a step backward. Her head *thunked* against the wall, sending a jag of pain across her skull. She was trapped. The dark and broody man stood not a pace before her, his black hair catching the candlelight as he bent toward her, a finger to his lips. She scrambled sideways, too terrified to think.

He didn't stop her from escaping and so she ran, hard and fast to the door. Her slick palms slipped on the brass knob several times before she grabbed a clutch of her gown and used it to twist the knob violently. The door sprang open and she dashed into the hall. Blood rushed through her hearing as she tried to recall which direction she'd come from. It was all a blur.

Yes, this way. She spun to her left and forced herself to slow not just her rampant heart beats, but her speed as well. It was unbecoming of a lady to run wild through the palace. Instead, she walked with purpose toward the sound of courtiers enjoying their drinks and refreshments. Twice she checked over her shoulder to see if the man followed her, but she didn't hear his footsteps, nor did she see anyone behind her. That didn't stop her skin from crawling with anxiety.

Who was he? And why was he spying on her? Why did he seem familiar when she didn't know anyone at the palace? If he was a guard, then why didn't he take her to the king? He'd obviously witnessed her spying on Otto, so why put a finger to his lips in warning? Was he one of the princes? Her overriding curiosity about the man dulled some of the panic that propelled her forward.

Strolling at a more ladylike pace, she fanned herself to dispel the faint coating of perspiration that covered her upper lip. Ladies did not sweat. They also weren't supposed to secret themselves away to cast an illegal spell in an adjoining room to the king's bedroom. She patted her lip with clammy fingers. What other rules could she break before dinner?

A nervous giggle tried to escape her mouth, but she swallowed hard to keep from making a fool of herself. The palace had emboldened her in a way she wasn't entirely sure she didn't like. Rule breaking? Drinking without permission? These were not activities Eira naturally engaged in, and yet, they felt liberating in the most delightful way. Tiny rebellions that gave her courage to...what? Self-preservation cast a shadow on any plans for shenanigans. Spies were everywhere, and probably only too happy for the coin Regan would pay to know Eira's every move.

A servant with a tray of the delicious but dangerous Tristano swerved at the last moment narrowly avoiding a collision with her. He mumbled an apology, but his eyes showed he clearly thought her an idiot for getting in his way. She paused to clear her mind and get her bearings. To her right, glass doors opened onto the gardens, with orchards just beyond in the distance. The day was pleasant with a gentle breeze, a delight to the courtiers who strolled through the formal garden mere steps from where she stood. This late in the year, fall foliage should cover the ground, but they were having a rare warm spell and everyone looked intent on taking advantage. Everyone except her.

Another glance down the dark hallway showed no one was coming for her. Or he was lurking in the shadows, spying. It annoyed her to always be suspicious, but it had become a survival instinct.

Who was he? If he was one of the princes, that would explain his being in the room. The only problem was, she didn't know what the princes looked like. Regan had been reluctant to show Eira any portraits of the king or his sons, despite the fact that she'd had to sit for many long hours to have her own portrait painted—a memento of this auspicious time in her life, Regan had said, but now Eira knew the truth. The portrait had been for Otto. Most likely so he could determine if she was pretty enough to be his bride. What a revolting tradition.

Her gaze went to the rooms on the other side of the great hallway. There would be paintings in one of them, certainly. She just had to find one with enough people to hide among until the threat of the stranger was passed.

She turned away from the gardens and kept her expression placid as she meandered through the corridors of the palace, happy for her anonymity and lack of chaperone. Several courtiers gazed at her with curiosity crossing their features, similar to the page who'd brought Regan the note.

It might've been they all knew who she was and were interested about the king's future bride, or it might've been just a passing glance, nothing of interest to their lives. She told herself it was the latter and smoothed the front of her gown with trembling hands.

Each of the grand rooms she toured were stuffed with delicately carved furniture covered in brocades and had high, painted ceilings with gold filigree around every door and window. On every tabletop, bouquets of fresh flowers were a riot of color. It was a palace that screamed wealth. Not subtly, but loud and voraciously. She'd grown up with luxuries, but this was too much. The ostentatious display of wealth unnerved her. Who was the king trying to impress? Certainly not her. She was a nobody in the kingdom. Raised far from court in a tiny village.

In the third gallery, she found her prize. An entire wall of portraits dedicated to the king, with a few of his sons placed strategically beside the latest painting glorifying the monarch in what she hoped weren't exaggerated brush strokes. She checked the broad doorway to make sure she hadn't been followed. Once satisfied the mysterious man had no interest in her, and that the room had a sufficient number of courtiers she could hide among their groups, she allowed herself to relax a little.

Of the four walls in the gallery, three were dedicated to King Otto's ancestors and it was these Eira studied first. She wanted a sense of the man, but also to see the lineage he came from. She could learn a lot about her future husband by looking to his past. What she immediately noticed was the lack of women represented. Of the several dozen paintings she saw, only two queens sat beside their kings, and even those she felt the woman was minimized. An afterthought.

She traversed to the wall of King Otto's portraits and studied the latest painting of the king. She reached out, stopping herself short of touching the frame. There wasn't a single woman featured on this wall. Would she be equally dismissed? Pushed aside? Eliminated? Could she make a difference in this court to be remembered for something good?

The answer whispered through her mind and her heart— no. She wasn't raised to be a queen, despite Regan's assertions and threats. Lawks, she wasn't even sure which wife she would be, but it was beyond the fifth, that she knew.

Her gaze roved along the gallery to the first portraits of King Otto when he was young and handsome. The years had not been kind to him. He'd long ago lost the gleam in his eye, the trim figure, and an air of joviality. His later portraits showed a man proud of his gluttony, with meanness in his dull brown eyes. There was no sense of mischief in this king, only an innate picture of pride. And anger. So much anger.

Eira flicked her gaze from portrait to portrait, from youth to present and back again. There was a startling shift in the king between one painting and another, as if something had happened that made him a different person. She almost felt sorry for the man who steadfastly glared at her from the canvas.

Beside Otto were two smaller paintings, neither of which resembled the man in black. A fact she was curiously relieved about, and at the same time caused great consternation about his identity. If he'd been one of the princes, she might be able to ask for forgiveness from him and thus, receive it from the king.

Even though she'd pulled her attention to the princes, she still felt the cold judgement of His Majesty bearing down on her. The unsettling sensation wormed its way down her back into the crevices of her flesh. He was a disease she feared she wouldn't survive.

A commotion brought her out of her macabre thoughts and she looked up in time to see a woman with hair the color of polished copper glide through the gallery. A flurry of courtesans orbited the beauty, spewing flowery compliments about her flawless complexion, her dress, her jewels. The woman didn't quite smile, but just there, in the corners of her lips, Eira saw the tiniest lift to her mouth. Whoever this woman was, she enjoyed the flattery.

As the group passed, the woman did the strangest thing—she kept her face perfectly straight and glanced at Eira without so much as a slight turn of her head. She felt the force like a physical blow. A myriad of emotions stung Eira's heart as if they were her own, yet they came from the woman. Confusion, betrayal, curiosity, jealousy, and, perhaps worst of all—pity.

Eira pressed herself against the wall as if to avoid the woman's glare, but it was useless. She was caught in a snare, and the woman knew it. The woman's hand curled ever so slightly and her fingers flexed a fraction. Panic, raw and volatile, rushed through Eira's veins. Before she could run, an invisible thread tightened around her neck. Pricks of light dotted her vision as she struggled for air. The woman grinned, her gaze feral and challenging.

One word pounded through Eira's mind—witch.

The group moved on through the hallway, the courtiers unaware of what the woman did to Eira. In fact, none of them noticed her at all. As soon as the group cleared the doorway, the thread of magic choking her released and she collapsed on the floor, gasping for breath.

Several people in the gallery eyed her with suspicion, but no one offered to help. Eira dragged herself to a sofa and sat as demurely as possible while willing her heart rate to slow, begging the panic to lessen.

What the lawks had happened? She felt violated in a way she'd never experienced—as if her soul had been dumped on the carpet for examination and then left to rot in the harsh rays of the sun. As she tried to scoop her battered emotions into a protective hold, she struggled to grasp how anyone besides Regan could hate her with such passion. Especially someone she'd never met, and did not know. But it appeared the woman knew her, and was keen to let her know they were adversaries. Her confidence wobbled and she sank deeper into the sofa. Not even an hour away from Regan and she'd already made an enemy. The how didn't matter as much as the why.

Her dazed eyes landed on the smaller portraits and she studied the faces of the princes to distract her mind from what had just occurred. She feared if she thought about it too much, she might soil herself, and that was the least ladylike thing she could do. If Regan heard about her unbecoming behavior, punishment would be swift and terrible.

Better to focus on the handsome men in the gilded frames. Best to forget the interaction had ever occurred. She didn't wish to make an enemy at the palace. But who was the pretty woman? And why did she attack Eira when she'd done nothing to her? It was obvious the woman hated her, why else would she use magic to choke the life from a complete stranger? And why use magic in a palace ruled by a king who despised anything having to do with power and spells?

She rubbed at her neck as anxiety prickled her skin. It would be best to avoid the woman, that was obvious. First, she had to find out who her enemy was. She stared at the portrait of Prince Guillaume as if he could help in her dilemma, but the eldest son and heir to the throne looked blankly at her from the canvas. Her mind tracked every detail, noting that he resembled his father in coloring and stature. Both with dark hair and brown eyes, Guillaume could've passed for the youthful king's brother. But now, they hardly resembled one another. She hoped the king didn't resent his son for being attractive and young. Although, in her experience, she suspected he most likely did.

Her gaze slid to Prince Leon. Unlike his father and brother, Leon was fair of face with light green eyes a shade she'd never seen before. His blond hair was worn short, with the ends sticking up as if in a perpetual fight with gravity. Kindness lurked in the shadows of his eyes, but sadness, too. She wondered what he had to be sad about, living in a palace, second son to a king.

The horrors that happened behind closed doors were only too well-known for her. What were Leon's nightmares? She cocked her head and studied the two princes' portraits. Guillaume had none of the softness of his brother, nor kindness in any of his features. She'd grown up an only child in a castle full of adults who were either indifferent to, or ignored Regan's treatment of her. Her thoughts went to the king in his great bed, suffering from something that caused him tremendous pain. Somehow, she doubted he wasn't much better than Regan as a father figure.

A shiver jostled her body into the soft cushions of the sofa. There had been a woman with the king—one who appeared to care greatly for him. Her fingertips stroked her neck and she glanced at the gallery doorway, but the beauty wasn't to be seen. She might've been the woman with the king, and if she was, that would explain her reaction to seeing Eira.

Did Regan know the king had a witch for a lover? Eira churned this new information in her mind. Whether she knew or not, either way, it spelled disaster for Eira. One woman who wanted to control her. Another who wanted to kill her. And between them both, the king. What did he want from her?

Chapter Five

A servant walked toward Eira, a tray of tristano resting on his splayed fingers. She eyed the drink with suspicion, debating whether the tipsiness was worth the effort. If the bubbly drink could make her forget that she was a pawn in a game of chance that she didn't know the rules to, then she would take an entire cartload. As it was, she would have to learn the game quickly lest she be used, and discarded, for someone else's gain.

An ominous thought pinged in her mind, but she refused to acknowledge it. To do so would put her in danger. She rubbed her arms and shook her head to dispel the traitorous notion, yet it persisted. The king hated magic. So much so, he imprisoned and tortured anyone with even a drop of magic in their blood.

People like her.

No, she told herself, not people like her. She'd hidden her power deep enough no one knew, not even Regan. Unless, of course, her stepmother did know about Eira's powers and she was bartering her stepdaughter's life to improve, nay, save her own.

Was it possible Regan could be that evil? As her stepmother

said, Eira was far too trusting. Was that a warning that she was a fool not to see what Regan truly was? She didn't want to believe her stepmother could be these things, but with everything that had happened this afternoon, she feared she had no other choice. Her desperation for a mother's love had blinded her and now she was in an impossible situation.

An anxious sort of panic knotted in her throat and she rolled her shoulders to alleviate the tension. If the man in black heard her cast the spell, it meant certain death. What an idiot she was, thinking she could use Regan's grimoire to cure her hangover without repercussions. So what if she hadn't actually used magic, she'd only spoken the words—the grimoire did the rest. But how could she prove her innocence? To whisper the spell was still using magic in a way, even if it wasn't her own.

Was the handsome man who'd warned her not to speak, at that moment, telling Otto? Her instinct told her he wasn't, but until she knew who he was, and if she could trust him, she'd have to be extra diligent to keep her magic hidden lest he or anyone else decide to report her to the king.

A tremor of dread slithered down her back. All too soon, Otto would be her husband, and then what? Then she'd continue doing what she'd done her entire life—smile pretty, pretend everything is fine, shove her magic as far as it would go so she wasn't discovered, and survive.

Whether she wanted it or not, the wedding would take place the day after the ball. Eira curled her hands into fists and hid them in the folds of her gown. No. That wouldn't be her fate. She couldn't allow herself to become a statistic—another faceless woman neither loved, nor acknowledged on the wall of portraits. How long before Otto tired of her, or worse, discovered he'd been tricked into wanting her?

Enchant the king. What a farce. Once the enchantment wore

off, Eira's life would be in constant peril. More so than she'd ever known.

There had to be some way to stop the marriage. Two weeks wasn't much time to plan an escape, but this was her life, and she'd be damned if she'd let her stepmother determine who she wed.

It was daring even to dream of such a thing, but for far too long Eira had simpered and bowed to her stepmother. How, exactly, she was to extricate herself from Regan's control and influence was the question. Her stepmother had already taken so much from her, she had nothing left except her bodily possessions. Even those were for sale, it seemed. Well, her body at least. Her mind and heart were her own, and she would fight to keep it that way.

She rose from the sofa and ignored the servants carrying trays of fluted glasses filled with the deliciously dangerous tristano and made her way to the hallway where the pretty lady had led her group of admirers. She shook out her fists and her fingers brushed the apple tucked safely in her pocket. She would stay alert to Regan's schemes—appear to go along with them until she knew what, exactly, her stepmother was after.

Darkness clouded her thoughts. If the marriage went through, Eira might wear a crown and be called queen, but she didn't fool herself into believing she'd have any real power. Nor would she be more than a brood mare while the king's mistress would claim his passion. The extensive list of benefits from this marriage favored Regan far more than Eira, a fact of which her stepmother was undoubtedly aware.

No, she was being too harsh. Where was the proof of Regan's misdeeds? Her imagination was running amok. She brushed off the melancholy and told herself Regan only wanted the best for her, a lie she'd tried to believe ever since her father died, and failed. She pressed a hand to her heart and lifted her chin against the onslaught of memories that filled her mind. Tears threatened and she blinked rapidly lest they fall and give away her grieving. Ladies did not show emotion publicly. Lawks, but she missed him. Missed his easy laughter and unpretentious ways. Most of all, she missed the way he would wrap her in her arms and she felt instantly safe, protected.

Sunlight warmed her face as she stepped through the wide doors onto the portico that led to the gardens. If her father were alive, what would he think of her now? It was a ludicrous question. If he lived, she'd not be a prisoner in her own home. It did no good to think of what could have been. Regan might have stolen her father from her, but she couldn't take Eira's dreams. Those were locked away deep in her heart and didn't include her stepmother or a wretched king she didn't love.

She wandered along the formal flower beds, surprised at the number of people in the gardens. Otto must have invited the entire kingdom to the ball. Her legs trembled slightly as she stepped around the hedges. They'd come for Otto's ball, but were they also invited to the wedding? She'd imagined it being a small affair with just close friends and family, but seeing so many courtiers inside the palace and in the gardens, she was afraid she'd been woefully wrong.

Snippets of conversations drifted on the breeze, most centering on the murder in the woods. Several courtiers were shocked by the death, but a fair few seemed intrigued with grisly details. She turned away from the gossipers and made her way toward the orchards. She nodded to a large group of courtiers she didn't know. They smiled and bobbed their heads, but she heard the whispers they pretended to hide behind the elaborate fans they kept close to their faces.

"Who does she think she is?" A gentleman powdered to within an inch of his life.

"Why her?" A woman who would benefit from some powder.

"*She's* the fairest in all the land? The king must be blind. My daughter is by far prettier." A handsome woman with more jewels than Regan owned sparkling from her dangerously high bouffant.

"At his age, and in his condition...really?" A sharp "Shush," followed the impertinent question, but Eira didn't see who spoke.

She kept her gaze steadfastly on the remaining leaves that were in variegated shades of rusts and golds, yet the courtiers' hurtful words punctured her hearing.

"Skinny bit of trash." A rather rotund man wearing a waistcoat three sizes too small.

She ignored them and continued to enjoy the sweet scent of late summer ripened fruit that came from the bounty of trees planted in neat rows. Kindness cost nothing, but these courtiers dealt in a currency she refused to accept. She wouldn't let Regan or anyone else kill her compassion.

Eira listened to birdsong as she continued through the garden and eavesdropped on the groups around her, compiling information to be combed through later, in the privacy of her room. Gossip about the murder overruled the rude comments about her, and interspersed were subjects as far reaching as who had the more fertile farmlands, who wore what jewels, and what food would be served at dinner, but nothing about witches or the cause of the king's illness, or his trackers.

It was almost as if the courtiers deliberately didn't mention them. Even the identity of the murdered man was debated without naming anyone specifically. These people, despite their frippery and sneers, were afraid.

When she was young, one of her maids, an older woman who had once served Eira's mother, told her stories of how, not long ago, there were hundreds, perhaps even thousands of women and men like Eira's mother whose powers were revered, but somehow in the past century, they'd become pariahs— hunted and slaughtered. Slivers of frost dug into Eira's heart as she recalled the day that Regan learned of the maid's treachery and fired every last servant, replacing them with people from a distant village who didn't know Eira's mother or father and were loyal only to Regan.

To honor that maid and all those who had been murdered, Eira was determined to find out why they'd been so brutally killed. Although, she feared she needn't look far. Otto and his father before him were tyrants who sought absolute dominion over their subjects. Power like Eira possessed was a threat to their rule.

Yet it made no sense. If he hated them so much, why did he have a witch living in the palace?

Her throat burned anew at the memory of the woman's magic choking her as if with her own hands. Eira stroked her neck and swallowed a knot of anxiety. Did the woman know about Eira's powers? Was that her way of professing her dominion over Eira? Her legs wobbled at the sheer terror the woman had instilled in her in only a matter of moments. A trifle, nothing more.

It was a dangerous game she played—at once wishing to learn all she could about her heritage while also suppressing all signs of her magic. She would have to be extraordinarily careful, especially with a witch wishing her harm. She mentally shuttled all her traitorous thoughts to a hidden corner in her mind. It wouldn't do to have someone pluck the dark musings as easily as snipping a rose from a bush. She smoothed her gown and skimmed over the apple. Perhaps the enchantment would work on her? If she could find it in herself to love the king, perhaps it wouldn't be so terrible.

And yet, it would. No amount of magic or potions could change that fact. She had to escape the marriage, and the palace. The how eluded her, but she would find a way.

A page hurried in her direction, and she stopped him to ask where the library could be found. The directions he gave made no sense without a map of the sprawling buildings. The palace was several times larger than her castle. She couldn't imagine the elegant rooms ever feeling like home. She turned in the direction the page indicated, but hesitated at the sight of the gossipy courtiers.

All her life she'd been whispered about, why should the palace be any different? In her deepest wishes, she'd hoped that perhaps this time she wouldn't be stared at or have to endure gawking. Yes, she was beautiful. The fairest in all the land, blah, blah, blah. But there was so much more to her than her looks, if only they sought to see past her outer beauty. If only they would give her a chance, get to know the real Eira, not just the woman doomed to marry the king. If only she knew who the real Eira was.

Who would she be if Regan didn't control her near every waking moment? Bolder? More confident? Or would she be just like those surrounding her—insipid and shallow? How many of those around her started out with hopes and dreams? How many of them were slowly beaten down by a tyrant king? And, most importantly, how many of these courtiers were spies for her stepmother?

There would be plenty of time to find the library. What she needed was a quiet spot and fresh air to clear the paranoid and morose thoughts gathering in her mind. Her gaze swept past the portico and a clammy chill rushed over her as if she'd been dipped in a frozen lake. The man in black darted from the trees to the side of the palace, his movements too stealthy not to be suspicious.

If he was trying not to get caught, he was doing a poor job. Or perhaps he meant for her to see him. She scanned the area, but no one else paid him any mind. When she glanced back at the stranger, he was staring straight at her. His dark eyes bore into her, past her defenses to that part of her she kept hidden from everyone, including herself.

A flutter of familiarity curled around her heart, followed by a sharp stab against her skull. She winced against the sudden pain and met his intense gaze.

He stared at her as if all her secrets were laid bare.

Chapter Six

Eira knew she should look away, to run as far and as fast as she could from the man. Run, and never look back. But her feet were rooted to the ground, her curiosity too stubborn to let her flee. His glare softened to a look akin to curiosity, and a delicious jag of something foreign tugged just behind her belly button. Not quite dangerous, but not safe either. Seductive, almost.

A small smile lifted his lips and she lurched forward with faltering steps. It was mad, this compulsion to confront him and ask what he was doing by following her. If, indeed that's what he was doing. Nerves flared in her belly, heating the chill that had dampened her skin. She quickened her steps, but was blocked by a group of courtiers sipping from metal goblets and laughing at some joke she wasn't invited to share. By the time she made her way around the circle of noisy revelers, the man had disappeared. She scanned the area twice, her gaze panicky, her hands twitching, but he was gone.

Disappointment stung and pulled her mood even lower. Raucous laughter boomed behind her, and she ducked beneath branches to put distance between herself and the courtiers.

They could laugh with gaiety, but she could not. They weren't being stalked by a mysterious, albeit handsome, man in black. They'd not been promised to a man they'd never met and did not love. They were free to sip drinks, wearing expensive frocks while she had her life dictated to her by those she despised.

She plucked at the velvet gown she wore. It was costly, but not ostentatious. Figure-flattering without being risqué. Regan had insisted all of her gowns be modest without showing cleavage or too much of her slim arms. Eira didn't hate the gowns, but she did wish her stepmother would let her wear clothing she preferred, including breeches. They were so much more comfortable and allowed her to ride a horse properly, not sitting awkwardly with both legs to one side.

One day. When the king was dead and she was no longer under her stepmother's control, then she would decide what to wear, where to live, and what she ate. The pit of nerves in her belly spun even faster. One day soon.

The scent of apples nearly made her delirious, and she plucked one from a branch. Her teeth bit into the flesh, and she moaned as she chewed the tart sweetness.

"I must say, I'm rather jealous of that apple."

Eira jumped at the sound of a stranger's voice, and she whirled around hoping to find the man in black, only to be disappointed by deep-brown eyes she recognized from the portraits. Prince Guillaume. The painting made him appear young, but the man before her was in his late thirties, at least. Tall and imposing, he wore the countenance of someone who knew their worth and had decided long ago that none other would ever compare.

"Your Highness." She dipped into a low curtsey and bowed her head. "I hope I have not offended you by eating from your orchard. It's just, apples are my favorite and I can't seem to resist them."

"You are welcome to as many apples as you'd like." He waved a hand to indicate entirety of the orchards. "Consider this your personal banquet while you're here."

Despite the arrogant posture, he was rather handsome, and would've been more so yet his lips were too tight, and his eyes too hard. The beige satin doublet he wore did nothing to soften his appearance. If anything, his outfit of black trousers and high leather boots only seemed to give him a more austere presence.

"Although, I do hope you'll share." The prince leaned forward and opened his mouth, showing her his bared teeth as he took a bite of her apple.

The moans he made sounded obscene, and a furious blush warmed her cheeks. His eyes lit with cruel delight and his fingers brushed along her jaw. She tried to turn away, but he gripped her chin with strong fingers. A whimper sat on the edge of her tongue, but she knew better than to show any outward signs of pain. That only brought more punishment. Years of conditioning had taught her to soften herself to be as small and meek as possible.

"You are even more enchanting than I was led to believe." His thumb scraped across her bottom lip. "Aren't you just the sweetest fruit."

It wasn't a question. More like a claim.

"All these months I've imagined what you'd look like, smell like," he nuzzled his nose close to her ear, "taste like."

"You must have me confused with someone else." Thankfully, her voice did not betray the tremble that lay just beyond his touch.

She pivoted to break his grip and moved toward the palace, but he stepped in front of her, blocking the way. Head cocked, his face scrunched as if questioning, and then softened.

"Don't leave now, little mouse. We've only just been acquainted, and I've been anxious to meet my new stepmother."

Her stomach twisted at the word. "Your Highness, I would never presume to take the place of your mother, nor any parental figure. I think you and I both know that would be foolhardy at best."

"Not quite as foolhardy as strolling the orchards alone." His gaze skimmed the neighboring trees. "Who knows what wickedness might befall a beautiful young woman beneath these branches?" A throaty laugh filled the air, but there was no mirth in the sound, only cruelty. "Haven't you been warned about the lasciviousness of my father's court? Fuckery abounds within these walls." He slid the backs of his fingers across her temple to tuck a strand of hair behind her ear.

She held as still as possible, willing her legs not to give out, her wail not to pierce the air.

"Please stop, Your Highness. This isn't proper behavior for a prince, or any man, really. I've not given you permission to touch me, nor have I asked for this attention. The least you can do is respect my position."

"Respect?" Another barked laugh that was as fake as his flirting. "If you want respect, little mouse, you must earn it."

Without warning, he grabbed her buttocks and pulled her close. A sultry moan rumbled from his chest.

Eira pushed against his chest and wriggled to free herself from his harsh grasp. "Let me go this instant."

"Or what? You'll scream? That'll get you nowhere. Not here, at least." He jerked her against his body, and she stiffened, terrified of what he might do. Something hard and tube-like pressed against her belly and a sickening feeling washed over her. Unless he had a dagger in his pocket, she feared what it was she felt. Her mind wouldn't allow her to name it, but she knew, and hated that he forced her to recognize that knowledge.

She'd overheard servants whisper tales of debauchery in King Otto's court, but at the time she'd thought little of them. Stories of sexual escapades and drunken parties were titillating, but had no bearing on her life so far from court. But now...now she was living the nightmare.

"What have we here?" Guillaume moved just enough to pull the apple from her pocket. "A snack for later? Why, Lady Cannaid, you do love your apples."

He brought it to his lips, and panic whipped through Eira's veins. It would be a disaster if he ate it. She snatched the apple from him and stashed it in her pocket with a squealing cry that sounded like a mouse caught between a cat's paws.

"That's not for you. Or me. It's for, um..." Her mind went totally blank. Who was it for? Oh, yes, the horrid king, but she couldn't tell the prince she meant to use the apple to enchant his father. Thousands of words and images flashed in her brain, but nothing came from her lips.

"For who, my little pet? Do you have a secret lover?" His granite eyes narrowed and his lips curled as he scanned the orchard.

"No! I mean, of course not. The apple is for my stepmother, as a way of showing my gratitude for her years of devotion raising me. I know it's not much, but she does adore apples almost as much as myself." The lies poured forth and with each one, Eira prayed she didn't sound like a lunatic.

"Ah, yes. We mustn't upset the formidable Lady Banworth. I've heard of her beauty, but it must pale in comparison to yours." Guillaume stroked her jaw with his thumb and pulled at her lower lip. "Lucky is the man you're promised to, even though promises, it would seem, are easily broken." His eyes narrowed and lip curled. "And to think, you're as yet unspoiled."

Eira swallowed, but her throat had gone dry. Her hands shook as she pressed them against his hard abdomen to make space between their bodies. No promises had been broken. Or did he mean Otto? It was difficult to think with panic nipping at her thoughts.

"Perhaps your father would prefer a more seasoned wife. As you said, my stepmother is indeed quite attractive. She would make a fine queen for your father." It was impertinent to even suggest such a thing, but Eira was desperate.

The prince's fingertips gripped her jaw and squeezed. "If you're trying to play coy, it's not working. You and I both know my father would enjoy something fresher, just plucked from the apple tree, as it were."

Despite her best efforts, Eira whimpered, and the prince chuckled. There was no fakery in his cruel little laugh.

"You're hurting me, Your Highness." Fear paralyzed her from screaming or crying or kicking out. Until that moment, only Regan had abused her, and she'd never considered someone else might be as brutal as her stepmother. Certainly not a prince. They were supposed to be charming. But then, with a father like King Otto, what else should she have expected?

"Don't tease me with promises you can't keep." He tilted his head as if listening for something, but all she heard was the blood rushing through her veins and her heart thundering like horses' hooves. "Do you know, there are men who can change into wolves? They hunt fair maidens and devour them with fangs sharp enough to tear through flesh. Be careful, my little mouse. You're a tasty morsel they can't refuse."

He leaned closer and breathed in her scent, trailing his nose from her collarbone to her lips. All the while, her legs trembled and dark thoughts pinged off her skull. If Regan knew he'd been familiar with her, the punishment would be swift and severe. What did the prince mean about the wolves? Was he jesting with her? Or did he tell true? Or, most likely, he was toying with her. Unbalancing her already rocky grasp on reality.

"So fucking sweet." Guillaume's lips were close enough she smelled apple on his breath. "He'll ruin you, my lady. My father will break you before you even know what happened and then what?" He pulled back, with a quirk to his mouth. "Perhaps I should save him the trouble."

The change in subject broke her paralysis. Mythical beasts were one thing, but the king was alive and real. Too real.

"I'd prefer not to be ruined or broken by anyone, thank you very much." Eira pushed through her fear and twisted out of his hold to take several steps backward.

Instead of running off like her mind screamed at her to do, she remembered her manners and curtseyed prettily, hiding her clenched fists in the folds of her gown. She was, after all, a lady. The prince might behave ghastly, but she'd not give him or Regan an excuse to abuse her further.

"It was a pleasure to meet you, Your Highness, but I really should be going. My stepmother will be worried about me. Good day, sir." Lies and more lies she hoped would keep her from punishment.

Without waiting for him to respond, she walked briskly to the edge of the orchard and shoved open a gate, hoping it led to the formal gardens. Her thoughts were a tangled mess of anger, confusion, fear, and impotent rage.

"The gall." Her muttered curses lifted with the breeze, and she took a long drag of air to calm her fractured nerves.

The gate slammed shut behind her and she found herself outside the palace grounds.

Alone.

Chapter Seven

Frosted panic chilled Eira's blood. Before her stretched a field of flowers, with a forest perhaps two hundred paces away. A dirt road, more a cart path, separated her from the meadow. This wasn't good. She turned back to the gate, but it wouldn't open. She knocked on the wood, calling for someone on the other side to please open the latch, but no one answered.

Her stepmother would be furious with her. Regan had warned her not to leave the palace grounds, but there was more. Eira pressed her fingertips to her temples to ward off the impending headache that threatened. What was it Regan had said? A man was murdered in the forest. Eira's glance slid to the trees in the distance. Forests were vast, it might not have been this part of the woods where he was killed.

Her gaze skimmed the emptiness of the meadow. If she died there, no one would know where to look. A rivulet of fear tangled down her spine, and she shuddered. Where was the grimoire now? Why wasn't it showing her a page to get her out of this mess? Perhaps she was too far from it for the magic to work. For the first time in her life, she was completely alone and dependent on only herself to find a solution to her present situation. The thought didn't fill her with the expected dread. Instead, a bubbly giddiness filled her belly.

On the other side of the gate, she could've sworn she heard low, mocking laughter.

A cart rumbled to her right, and her newfound excitement died swiftly, leaving her reeling in its absence. She banged on the gate, begging whoever was there to please let her inside, but only deep chuckling answered. If she was caught outside the palace grounds, even by a servant, she'd be punished severely. Her backside hurt just thinking about the whipping Regan would give her.

If she had thought to put on a cloak, then she could pull the hood up to hide her face, but the day was too nice and she'd been desperate to get away from her stepmother's scheming. The horses' hooves pounded the dirt to the beat of her heart, and she cast a furtive glance at the driver. He was too distracted by the woman at his side to notice her or anything else.

With one hand holding the reins, his other was buried deep in the woman's bodice. The maid giggled and stroked the driver's crotch before swinging her leg over the man to straddle him fully. Eira stared at the pair, shocked at their public display of fornication and also in awe that the man could carry on driving while utterly distracted.

The gate and mocking laughter now forgotten, she took a step toward the oncoming cart, too fascinated with the couple to care who taunted her from the other side.

Her breasts tightened and warmth pulsed between her legs. It wasn't the pair's lovemaking that excited her, but the freedom they had to do so whenever and wherever they liked. She'd wager neither of them had to deny themselves the pleasure of self-satisfaction for fear of being discovered. Eira's fingers twitched to caress the places that tightened with need. The woman's sultry moans pierced the air and Eira looked away, ashamed at her voyeurism.

Her vision was blocked by a square of black that rushed into her with such force she nearly lost her footing, but someone had picked her up. Her thoughts swirled with the movement, confusion and fear and desire all coalescing into a rush of emotion.

She cried out from sheer shock, but the sound was muffled from the man's black coat. Not just any man. The skulking man. Where the lawks did he come from? He hadn't been in the meadow, nor had he followed her outside the gate. Or, had he? She didn't recall seeing him, but then again, she'd been too distracted by the couple.

A moment later, she found herself unceremoniously dumped on the ground.

"How rude!" She scrambled to stand and face him, stunned as much by his attractiveness as she was by the mocking gleam in his eye. "You didn't have to drop me, you know. I'm perfectly capable of standing."

"Aye, I saw." His right brow lifted as if he doubted she had any sense at all. "You should watch where you're going. That cart doesn't care if you're a lady. It'll run you down all the same."

"Am I supposed to thank you for rescuing me?" She crossed her arms and knew that was exactly what she should've done, but he irritated her.

He blew out a breath and cast a sharp glare her way. "I don't really care what you do. You're dangerous and a bloody nuisance."

The garden gate opened, and she crouched low to hide in the long grasses.

"Get down, you idiot," she whispered.

He didn't answer. When she looked where only a moment before he'd been standing, he was gone. Again. If she hadn't felt the solidity of his body, she might've thought him a specter, haunting her for sport.

The tall grass and overgrown weeds hid Eira from Guillaume's searching gaze. He stood in the open gate, grinning, as if he expected to see her standing there. As his gaze swept the empty road, his grin turned to a malicious snarl. He looked left and then right, eyes narrowed. Finally, he scanned the meadow, but she kept still. His focus shifted to the forest and for a moment, she worried the skulking man had given her away.

The cart rumbled far down the road, and Guillaume squinted toward it.

As if she'd jump onto a moving cart, just to escape him. Her life wasn't much, but she valued it all the same. A life she now owed to a scurrilous man dressed in black.

"Gil, come back to the celebrations." A slender arm snaked from behind the prince and clasped his chest. "I have a friend I'd like you to meet."

One last glare and he turned to address the unseen woman. "If she is half as lovely as you, then lead me to your lady friend."

"What makes you think it's a woman, Your Highness?" Her laughter was cut short when the gate slammed shut.

Eira remained crouched for several minutes until she was certain no one else would emerge from the palace grounds. Slowly, she rose and shook out her clenched fists. Two trees dotted the meadow, and a short distance away, she spied smoke coming from the chimney of a small cottage. In the opposite direction, nearly to the forest, stalked a lone figure dressed in black. Despite herself, she was impressed he'd managed that much distance in so short a time.

Dangerous and a bloody nuisance, indeed!

For a full minute, she stood motionless, letting the meadow speak to her of its secrets. A breeze lifted her hair and she inhaled slowly, setting the moment in her heart to relive later.

Early fall blooms dotted the landscape, and she twirled between the dianthus and marigolds, jubilant at this tiny bit of rebelliousness. Birds darted across the cloudless sky, their chirps and calls echoing in the stillness. Muted sounds from the garden made their way over the tall walls, but Eira ignored them. Reality could wait.

Now that she was away from the palace and had escaped detection from the servants and the prince, her heart was emboldened to adventure further. Perhaps even to the forest, where the man had disappeared. Wolf-shifting men and murders be damned; it felt good to be free—if only for an afternoon.

Regan's warning pierced her brain with urgency and Eira slowed, not wanting anything to disrupt her peaceful moment. Regan mentioned a huntsman. Was he the victim? Or was it possible he was the murderer? She scanned the empty landscape once more. The longing to be free of the palace outweighed her anxiety over an uncertain, threat. She might never have the chance again and she wouldn't let her stepmother ruin it. Not this time.

Resolved in her purpose, she walked through the meadow trailing her fingertips across the flora. In her mind, a fantasy played out of a life very different from the one she lived. One where she was free to wander wherever she wished. Could wear clothing she'd chosen for herself, and eat whatever the bloomin' lawks she liked. She leaned against the trunk of the nearest tree and closed her eyes, imagining what it would be like to live a life unfettered. Unbeholden to her stepmother, puppet to no one. A life where her beauty wasn't bartered away like a wheel of cheese.

Beneath her flawless skin, her heart beat with ferocious excitement. What would it be like to love another and have them love her in return? She gripped her dress and sent a silent prayer to the goddess that one day she would be free to feel a man's touch without fear.

"One day." She sighed. The life she craved was out there, she just had to be brave enough to claim it.

But first, she had to find a way out of her present predicament. She pushed off the trunk and checked that the man in black hadn't come back, but he was nowhere to be seen. She was alone, and for once, not afraid as she meandered through the meadow. A sappy smile quirked her lips and for the briefest moment, she allowed herself to believe in happy-ever-afters. As she neared the cottage, her steps slowed and she peeked through the garden gate. It looked tidy from the outside, with a well-tended kitchen garden in the back and a small patch of turned soil closer to the forest. Eira glanced over her shoulder toward the palace, now too far away to see whether anyone spied her movements.

Which meant she could explore, but only for a short time. She bent over a low stone wall that separated the cottage garden from the encroaching meadow and admired the colorful foliage. Tucked between the flowers, she spied various plants with apothecary and medicinal uses. Several she recognized, a few she did not. One, she knew intimately. Emerald leaves with tiny white flowers. Valerian. It was Regan's favored herb to use in sleeping draughts, of which she often gave Eira.

She shuddered against the memories of being forced to drink cups of the foul tea made with the stuff. Regan preferred her stepdaughter sleepy and pliable and, after a while, Eira stopped fighting the nightly ritual. Sometimes it was easier to give in, and, truth be told, being in a state of hazy consciousness made the beatings more tolerable.

Eira turned away from the dreadful plant and peered into the cottage. At first, what she saw made little sense. A man, naked from the waist up, stood with arms wide. Jagged red lines crossed his chest, some dripping down his abdomen. Blood. The man was bleeding. She cocked her head and tried to imagine what would give him such injuries.

A woman with wild grey hair ducked beneath his outstretched arm and pulled a piece of cloth over his chest. The man's face was tilted toward the ceiling, hiding his features from Eira, but there was something familiar about him. A swath of wheat-colored hair swished when he turned his back to her. More of the bloody cuts marred his left shoulder. Three in all, same as across his chest.

Eira slipped behind a hedge to keep from being seen and continued to watch the pair until the woman tied off the bandage and the man eased into his tunic. He hugged the woman, his face pinched with pain, or was it worry? From where she hid, she clearly saw his lovely green eyes as he stared out the window, past her to the forest. His lips moved, but she couldn't hear the words spoken, and despite her best efforts, she'd never been proficient at reading lips.

Whatever he said caused the woman to pull away and shake her head. Her hand cupped the man's cheek in a motherly sort of way and he nodded. Eira desperately wished she knew what the conversation was about. To witness such an intimate act made her feel a pinch of guilt that she spied on them when she loathed being spied on herself.

The man left the room and a moment later a door closed at the front of the cottage. She crouched low, her mind a whirl of terrible possibilities if the man came this way and found her behind the hedge. Seconds ticked by slower than a snail crossing a salt trail. Her face flushed with worry, her skin became clammy as she debated her options.

The sound of a door closing for a second time tripled her anxiety. Would the woman come this way? Would she be found out? She risked a peek over the stone wall, but the cottage was dark. No one stood in the window, nor did she see anyone in the tidy garden. She eased from her hiding place and searched the meadow. Two figures walked away from her, one some distance in front of the other.

She leaned against the wall and sighed a long, shaky breath. Adventuring was fun and all, until the very real possibility of discovery became evident. As much as she wished to see more, she knew she should return to the palace before her absence was noted.

A thrumming started at the base of her neck and she twitched as if to relieve herself of the uncomfortable sensation. When it didn't cease, she rubbed her skin, but the vibration wasn't physical. It came from outside her body. As if she were being watched. Hunted, even.

Chapter Eight

Ever so slowly, Eira turned toward the forest, half expecting a huntsman to jump out at her any moment. No one stood between her and the thick copse of trees, yet she felt a presence. An uncomfortable shiver scratched across her skin and she took a step toward the castle. Her foot, however, shifted mid-air and moved her closer to the forest. Another step, not entirely of her own volition, and another.

It wasn't magic, at least it didn't feel the same as when the witch tried to strangle her. Nor did it feel in any way similar to the subtle manipulations Regan used. This was more akin to a compulsion, as if the woods needed to show her something. Or a huntsman were luring her to her death.

Conflicting emotions waged war within her: angst, anxiety, and there, lurking beneath it all, curiosity. The forest didn't wish to harm her, she somehow knew this deep in her core. Along with the tale of her curse, ever since she could remember, Regan had warned her away from not just the forest near their castle, but all thick woods, claiming all sorts of vile things could happen there.

They were terrible places full of rogues and miscreants

who'd like nothing more than to kidnap Eira and sell her into servitude. Of course, they'd only sell her after they'd ravaged her in every horrific way possible. On these details, her stepmother had been deliberately wicked, scarring Eira's young mind so thoroughly she still had nightmares.

Those terrors might be true of most forests, and this one as well, but as Eira took another step toward the firs and cedars, a sense of calm came blanketed her, the same as she felt in the woods near her home. The trees provided shelter, a place of solitude. She took several more steps until thick trunks filled her vision, and she looked up to where the canopy blocked out the sun, yet she still felt its warmth on her face. Why would Regan seek to deny her this?

The man from the palace had gone into the forest—was he a rogue or miscreant? Or possibly the huntsman? Although, why would he be in the palace if so? As much as she trusted the trees, people were another story and she didn't desire a grisly death. Nor did she fancy making herself a suitable victim for whatever else might be lurking behind the foliage. Just as she was about to turn from the forest, a group of six—four men and two women —emerged from the trees not far from where the man in black had slunk into the shadows.

Eira's imagination spiraled too fast to make sense of what she saw. Two of the men carried a long wooden pole, but it was what hung from the rod that had her gagging against bile that rushed up her throat. A man, naked and bleeding from many cuts, hung from the pole, his wrists and ankles bound with leather straps. His head lolled with the rhythm of the pole bearer's steps, his eyes closed. Light brown hair hung near to the ground.

That lone detail brought her no small amount of relief, a fact that confused her. Why should she care if they caught the man in black? He was nothing to her. Once again a sense of familiarity was followed by a sharp stab to her skull. She rubbed the back of her head and chalked the strange pain to her anxiety.

As the group neared, they laughed with one another, their conversation revolving around the naked man. Eira put a hand over her trembling lips and slipped behind a trunk.

"We showed him, didn't we?" A greasy looking fellow with a short, piggish nose chuckled. "The king'll be pleased with our progress, don'tcha think?"

"Don't be getting ahead of yourself. There's still two weeks 'til full moon. We gotta be discrete or the guards will steal all our glory." A woman with arms as thick as Eira's thighs responded. Her gaze swept across the meadow and then to the naked man. "Take him to the dungeons with the others. I gotta see to something." Without waiting for a reply, she sauntered in the direction the pair from the cottage had gone while the rest of the group went left, toward the back of the palace.

They grumbled about the woman, but their voices trailed off until Eira could no longer make out what they said. Her gaze went to the dark woods as if searching for the man in black. If he was injured, she could help. What a ridiculous thought. Hadn't the man saved *her*? He was perfectly capable of handling himself. Besides, if the group had found him, he'd be swinging next to the naked man. Her heart urged that she should go investigate, but then what? It wasn't as though she had scads of experience with blood or murder or, well, much of anything useful.

But what if the man was injured and needed help? What if he was the huntsman, a voice in the back of her mind warned. If he was, then why did he first risk his own life to save her from the oncoming cart, and then leave her in the meadow instead of killing her? She pressed a hand against her chest where her heart remained intact, albeit thumping wildly.

The magic hidden in her blood stirred, and she bit her lip to keep it from growing. Now was not the time. Besides, she couldn't get involved. As it was, Regan might not know she'd left the palace grounds, and helping the man would surely bring unwanted attention. No, she couldn't risk it. Instead of venturing further into the forest, she turned back toward the palace, where safety wasn't guaranteed but she understood the dangers.

"Hey!"

A gruff voice brought her out of her tumultuous thoughts and she yelped in surprise.

A long stick poked her middle, and she grunted with each stab.

"Stop it. That hurts."

"Are ye spyin' for that no-good king?" A shortish man with grey in his long beard and dark, almost black eyes glared at her. Even at full height, he only reached her belly button.

"Of course not. Why would you even think such a thing?"

A second man, equally as short, yet without the beard, peered at her from behind the first. In all, she counted seven of them. Dwarves. How could that be? Regan had told her dwarves were a myth. Of course she did. Eira bit her tongue to keep from saying a few choice, unladylike words.

If she lied about dwarves, what else had her stepmother lied about? The forest? Rogues? Heart-stealing huntsmen? Murders? Well, probably not that last one since she saw for herself evidence that something untoward was happening in the woods. Even so, a sourness burned in her belly. What if Regan's admonishments to stay within the castle walls were meant to intentionally limit Eira's knowledge? What a fool she'd been to not see it sooner or even question Regan's motives. She'd given over too much control and now, the binds Regan had clasped too tightly were starting to loosen.

"Are you dwarves?" Maybe she had it wrong and her stepmother hadn't lied.

"Aye, ye daft lass. Did ye think we be giants or summat?"

A soft giggle escaped her lips and she curtseyed to the man. "Apologies, kind sirs. I was told dwarves were fairytales."

"An ye prolly believe wolves be bad, too." He sniffed and spat something foul and black on the ground.

Guillaume's strange words about men changing into wolves vibrated down her back like an axe hacking at each vertebra.

"I've never met a wolf, good or otherwise."

"Used to live in these woods all peaceful like, I tell ye. Until the old king hunted them to near extinction and turned them into the enemy, just like he tried to do with us." He toggled his thumb to indicate his friends.

"But we hid from him, didn't we?" the beardless one said. "To this very day, he can't see us, even when we be standing 'neath the noonday sun right 'neath his soddin' nose."

"Shhh, Gorse. She don' need to be knowin' all our secrets." He stood on tiptoe and peered at her. "Do ye, lass?"

Couldn't see them? Intrigued, she made a cross over her heart and schooled her features into seriousness. "Your secrets are safe with me. Although, I am keen to know how you can make yourselves invisible." And how men turned to wolves, but one revelation at a time.

Whether they were telling tales or the truth, she couldn't say, but anyone who thought the king bad was a friend of hers.

The older one peered at her as if he were looking for something deep in her bones. "Ye not be ready, lass. Some knowledge kin heal, some kin kill. D'ye know the difference?"

"I, uh," she hung her head, "I don't." It was becoming achingly apparent she knew very little of the world. "But I'm a fast learner."

"I'm sure ye are." He glanced at the sky. "But time's runnin' out, innit?"

More than he'd ever know. "I should be getting back. Gentlemen, it's been a pleasure." The desire to look past the dwarves to see if the skulking man had emerged from the forest uninjured was great, but she kept her attention focused on the seven faces staring at her. "I seem to have been locked out of the gardens. Do you know if there's another way in?"

"Why not use the front door? Unless'n, of course, yer not s'posed to be there?" The elder squinted one eye and grinned.

"I wish I wasn't supposed to be there, but if I don't return soon, there will be trouble."

The one called Gorse pointed down the road in the direction the cart had traveled. "Follow this here road an' at the first fork, take the left. If ye follow it to the right, ye'll be heading out o'town an' ye don' want that." He pointed to the cottage with the tidy garden. "This here's Madam Davina's place. If'n ye need medicinal herbs, she'll set ye right." The way his face lit up made Eira wonder if perhaps he wouldn't mind escorting her to the woman's cottage. "If'n ye need summat stronger, there's the shop just yonder that's run by a sweet lass and her pa. Trinkets and whatnot. Potions, even a few poisons, too, if that's your measure. Can't think what a nice lass like ye might need with those, though, can I?"

He couldn't read her mind, she told herself. He was just being cheeky.

"Why are you being so kind? You don't know me."

"Kindness costs nothing, m'dear." A twinkle lit in Gorse's eyes. "I think ye could use a little right 'bout now."

"Thank you." She stretched her hand for Gorse to take and curtseyed again to show her appreciation. Indeed, she needed their kindness more than she could say.

Gorse held her fingertips as if she were made of glass. His eyes widened, and he glanced at the elder dwarf in alarm. Eira's heart thumped and tumbled in her chest. Did they know who she was and would they tell Regan?

"Dorton," Gorse said, and passed her hand to the elder with a silent nod.

Dorton's callused fingers gripped hers less gently than Gorse had, but the widened eyes were the same.

"What are ye called, girl?"

The galloping of her heart stuck in her throat and a lightness buzzed in her skull. Stars danced at the edge of her vision. How foolish she'd been to think she could escape her stepmother. They were probably sent to find her and bring her back—in chains if necessary. An image of the bound naked man pushed through her anxiety. That would be the ultimate humiliation. She could imagine Regan clapping with glee.

"We mean ye no harm." Gorse's sweet face entered her periphery. "Yer safe with us." He patted her hand and smoothed the skin beneath his short fingers.

"I have to go." She tripped on a root as she fled and swallowed a sob when she heard her gown rip.

Whether they told Regan or not, her stepmother would know she'd been outside the palace grounds. How else could she explain her mud-stained dress and the tear? Lifting the soft velvet, she ran down the road, fighting the flood of worry that threatened to overtake and drown her. Only once she was a fair distance away did she dare turn back to see whether she was followed.

The dwarves hadn't chased her, nor were they beneath the trees. She bent at the waist and huffed shallow breaths. Her ears pulsed with the sound of blood rushing through her veins and her vision was hazy. Never in her life had she run so far, so fast. In fact, she couldn't remember a time since she was a child that she'd ran at all. Her poor heart was the victim of her sedentary life and pounded its unhappy state.

After several minutes spent regaining her equilibrium, she straightened and dusted off her gown. The tear wasn't as terrible as she'd imagined, and hope tentatively took hold. In the distance, she saw the dwarves crossing the meadow. A lone figure emerged to meet them. She recognized the black hair and clothing of the skulking man from the garden. Relieved he looked hearty and hale, she started to smile, but her lips froze when he greeted the dwarves and one of them pointed to where she stood at the fork in the road. Even at that distance, she saw the man's head snap up and he stared across the meadow.

The intensity of his gaze struck her as if he'd been standing right in front of her, and she stumbled backward. A fresh jab tugged at her nerves, this time traveling to her heart, where it warmed and soothed rather than tormented. Whatever the strange man and the dwarves were planning, she wanted no part. Except, a tiny thought pushed forward, what if they could help her escape the palace and her arranged marriage?

But they couldn't. Not them. Not that man. Especially not him.In his hand, he carried a huntsman's axe.

Chapter Nine

Eira gripped her gown in her fists and ran, hard and fast down the road, her vision clouded by wild panic. Damn her stepmother and damn the dwarves and especially damn the stupid man. Damn them all. Even Prince Guillaume, with his seductive words and sadistic touch. She ran to escape them, but that was impossible. She was trapped and didn't know who to trust—herself included.

Her side pinched from the rabid sprinting, and she skidded to a stop on the hard dirt. Sweat streaked from her temple, and she wiped her brow with a sleeve. Her feet ached from the pebbles that dug into her silk slippers and tears she could no longer ignore cascaded over her cheeks. What a fool she was. Running like a madwoman from a destiny her stepmother said was set for her at her birth. No one could outrun Fate. Could they?

A destiny far more cruel than marriage to the king. But why now? Why here? She didn't believe in coincidence or serendipity. There was a reason the huntsman was at the palace and she desperately hoped it had nothing to do with her. Her imagination was running amok, that was all. There were woods, so it only seemed natural that there would be a huntsman. Who happened to have access to the palace, and seemed to be everywhere she was. Nothing unusual about that.

She squeezed her eyes shut against more traitorous tears and dragged her hands through her hair, back arched, her face toward the sky. Sounds pushed through her fear-fueled agitation. People chatting and smells—oh holy stars, the smells. Of stews on a cookpot, animal waste, fresh baked bread, and the acrid tang of body odors. She breathed in and out, absorbing it all and willing calm to soothe her tangled thoughts. A dog barked nearby and a child shrieked as it ran past.

She was in the town. Slowly, she opened her eyes, not quite wanting to believe that in her desperation to flee she'd missed the palace. This was bad. All around her were people dressed in dull shades of browns and greys. Their dirt-streaked faces peeked from beneath frayed hoods. Curious yet wary eyes watched her.

She whirled this way and that, unsure where she was or how to get home. A soft grunt drew her attention to a pretty woman who looked flustered. Eira apologized, but the woman was already rushing away, her chestnut waves flowing in her wake.

"You look lost, duckie."

Eira spun around to see a woman with a kind smile and grey hair that looked untamable.

"I was trying to find the palace."

"You can't miss it." She jutted her chin toward the looming building. "Come, let's get you home."

Eira shivered, and the woman wrapped a soft blanket over her shoulders. "Thank you." She pulled the corners tight against her chest and sank into it as if it were a cloak. There was something familiar about the woman, but her mind twisted this way and that too quickly for her to grab what it was.

"What's got you so befuddled you lost your way, eh, duckie?"

Eira's gaze slid toward the meadow. "I thought I saw a huntsman."

"A huntsman, eh? Not seen one of them today. All the same, it's not safe for you to be traipsing around on your own."

"Why?" She peeked at the townsfolk from beneath the blanket. They looked half-starved and poverty stricken, but not likely to murder her. She had nothing of value, except for the pendant her mother had left for her, but Regan had possession of that. In truth, she was as poor as these unfortunate souls.

"Never you mind. Come now, no dawdling."

The woman held her elbow as they walked to the main road that led to the palace entrance. Instead of escorting Eira through the massive golden gates, the woman hurried them to a small wooden door half-hidden by a large holly bush.

"They call me Madam Davina. If you need anything, you come to me, duckie. I live in the cottage just in the meadow there." She jutted her chin toward the cottage Eira found earlier and she blushed at the memory of seeing the woman bandage the handsome man.

Madam Davina leaned back to look right and then left down the road. With a satisfied huff, she then did the strangest thing —she ran a finger down the wood and breathed out a hum that set Eira's hair on end. When she finished, the door clicked open and swung inward. Eira's skin prickled with the woman's magic, and she rubbed her arms. There was comfort in her magic, a subtle touch of lightness that Eira was drawn to like a rose to the sun.

Madam Davina squinted at her and pursed her lips, but said nothing.

"Thank you." Eira removed the blanket and handed it to the old woman. "For your kindness and the warmth."

"You'll not be thanking me for what I'm about to say. King Otto is a brutal, bitter man. He cares for no one but himself, as you've seen of the townsfolk. If you're who I believe you are, do not let him consummate your marriage."

"What do you mean? What will happen to me?" Eira's hand fluttered at her neck and her knees wobbled with the unwelcome warning.

"Some say I'm just a crazy old woman and some call me a witch, both of which are correct, yet also not. But I'll tell you true—I see flashes of the future and yours plays a prominent role in my nightmares of late. Now, go before we're discovered." She practically pushed Eira through the doorway. "Trust the huntsman, Lady Cannaid."

The door slammed behind her, and Eira stared at the planks, trembling from head to foot. How did the old woman know her name? And why should she trust the huntsman? What was to become of her on her wedding night?

More questions, dark and insidious, swirled in her mind like a miasma. She placed a hand on the door and jerked when a shock ran up her arm. Magic—even more powerful than Regan's and not at all the same. Was it innate, like hers? Or learned? Did it matter? She shook her hand and rubbed the stinging skin as she made her way through the thick foliage. There was no way to tell whether Madam Davina was friend or foe, but she'd shown Eira kindness. If she had an ulterior motive, until it was exposed, Eira would trust the perplexing witch.

An overgrown path led away from the door in a part of the garden she didn't recognize, and she chose her steps carefully. It wouldn't do to fall and further damage her gown. She was in enough trouble with Regan already; there was no need to give her anything further to be angry about. At least she was within the palace grounds. Safe-ish for the time being.

A rustle to her left startled her, and she quickened her pace. Low sounds of laughter drifted through the leaves. Probably a courtier or three having a little fun away from prying eyes. The sound of slapping, not the violent kind, but softer, followed by moans and throaty cries, touched that place in her she had to deny. She'd never have lovers. Only a king who would take what he wanted and then ruin her. Her nipples tightened, and she clenched her legs together to stop the awkward pulsing at their apex.

First the couple on the cart and now this. Prince Guillaume had said it was a court of fuckery. She blushed at the word, liking the way it sounded in her thoughts. When she was queen, would Otto expect her to sneak off to the bushes for lustful play? An image pounded through her mind of another man, clad in clothing as black as his hair. They were the couple in the garden, and in her daydream, she enjoyed every moment.

A chill swept across her bare skin, and she glanced at the darkening skies. Moody weather and traitorous lust were the last things she needed. She turned from the illicit sounds and hurried toward an opening in the overgrown patch. Her slipper caught on a root, and she lurched forward with alarming speed. Just before she hit the ground, a hand snatched her arm and she was jerked upward.

The world tilted and she caught only a glimpse of a handsome face before meeting green eyes that watched her with an intensity that made her yearn to be free of his grasp and far, far away from those unusual, penetrating eyes. Eyes she recognized from his portrait in the gallery, and that, if she weren't mistaken, she saw gazing at the forest from Madam Davina's cottage.

"My lady." Prince Leon settled her upright and stroked his hands across her shoulders, causing her to shudder. "There now. That's better, yes?"

She steadied herself and nodded despite wanting nothing more than to sprint away. She had no desire to be accosted by yet another of Otto's sons. Damn manners. She dropped a curtsey and murmured, "Thank you."

Giggles came from the bushes and the prince's eyes narrowed. "I see. I do hope I haven't interrupted your fun."

Eira's cheeks bloomed red from mortification and burned clear to her chest. "Oh no, Your Highness, I wasn't, I wouldn't..." She fumbled for words, but only stuttered denials came forth.

"There now, I was only teasing. May I?" Without waiting for her reply, he tucked an errant strand of hair behind her ear. "What's got you so flustered? Stars above, this should be a joyous time for you."

A pit formed in her gut and she had the sensation she was being mocked. But why? What had she ever done to this prince or his brother that they should be mean to her?

"If you'll excuse me, I must change before dinner." She curt-seyed and turned to leave.

"Wait. I'm sorry." He stepped in front of her and bent at the waist, his golden hair catching the last of the afternoon sun. "I'm afraid I'm not quite myself lately and am being rude. Will you allow me to escort you to the palace, my lady?" He held out his arm and she eyed it suspiciously.

"I can't tell if you're making fun at my expense, as your brother did, or if you're sincere."

"My brother is an ass. Fortunately, I am nothing like him, but how would you know that by my actions? I'm afraid Gil would love nothing more than for you to sully yourself with him, but please let me assure you, I want nothing of the sort."

Sully herself? With that wretched man?

She faced Leon fully and lifted her chin. "I might be naïve when it comes to this court, but I assure *you*, I would rather have my eyes poked out by a falcon than debase myself with your brother."

Leon's chuckle was full of warmth and mirth. "And here I was told you were a child, unable to fend for yourself. I suspect there is mettle to you, dear stepmother."

Eira shuddered violently and Leon's features tightened.

"Please don't ever call me that. I'm hardly a child, and since you're at most six years older, let's not pretend this is anything except what it is." If only she knew what, exactly it was. "I don't wish to be anyone's stepmother, if the truth be told." She snapped her mouth shut to keep from saying any further traitorous remarks.

Another low chuckle came from the prince. "So, it's as I thought." He wrapped her hand around his arm and led her toward the palace. "You and I might be of use to each other, Lady Cannaid."

"How so?"

"We are both trapped where we do not belong."

Her blood quickened with his words. Perhaps she had a friend in the palace, after all. And someone from the royal family, no less. She was formulating a reply when Regan slid into view and dropped a clumsy curtsey to Prince Leon.

"Your Highness." Regan addressed Leon, her face a mask of congeniality.

Eira's grip tightened on Leon's arm and he looked at her with genuine concern.

"I've been looking everywhere for my stepdaughter. I do hope she hasn't been a problem." She moved beside Eira and took her free arm in hers with a death-like grip that promised future punishment.

"Not at all, Lady Banworth. Eira is a delight. I should like to accompany her through the gardens some more, if you don't mind." Leon kept his tone casual, yet authoritative. He was a prince, but to Regan, that meant nothing.

"I'm afraid I do mind. As you can see, Eira is a mess. We need to fix this disaster before dinner. We can't have your father seeing her in such a state, now can we?"

Leon kept his grip on Eira's arm. "I doubt Father would complain to have such an enchanting companion by his side."

"Does something ail the king that's affected his eyesight?"

Leon looked at Regan as if she were the stupidest creature in the kingdom. Eira nearly chortled to see him stare down her stepmother without an ounce of fear.

"Be mindful of your words, Lady Banworth, for they may be your last. Now, if you'll excuse me, I would like to continue my stroll with your lovely stepdaughter."

Regan stepped in front of them and met Leon's calm demeanor with an equally silent, yet terrifying glare. After a dramatic pause, she removed Eira's hand from Leon's arm.

"You'll stay away from Eira, if you know what's good for you, Your Highness."

"Is that a threat?" His green eyes became flecks of granite.

Regan's mean little glare didn't waver, nor did she flinch. "Yes."

The moment hung pregnant with weighted expectation. Leon's eyes narrowed as if a silent conversation was held between him and Regan. Was that even possible? She knew Regan could pluck thoughts from her mind, but an actual conversation? There was still so much she didn't know or understand. If she didn't learn quickly, she might lose the only friend she had, and any hope of escape.

Regan practically yanked Eira from Leon's side and pushed her toward the palace. Eira glanced back to apologize, but the words stuck in her throat.

Leon gazed after them, his face ashen. The smirk Regan wore told Eira all she needed to know—somehow, Regan had threatened Leon with something. From the tears that sparkled in his eyes, it was something he held dear.

Chapter Ten

Regan's fingers dug into Eira's arm as she hurried them through the garden. She wore a genial smile, but anger crouched in the tiny cracks at the corners of her tight lip. Eira dared not say a word lest she displease her stepmother even further. Whatever she'd done to Leon was enough to frightened him into submission.

"Don't dawdle you useless twit. We must get you to your room immediately." Regan hissed in her ear and gripped harder, causing Eira to wince.

They darted around a large group of courtiers, and in the distance Eira spied the king. He sat upon a large wooden chair with his heaving waist bouncing with his laughter. To his right, a serving girl bent to pour him wine and he casually pinched her nipple. The girl winced, and covered her discomfort with a forced giggle. Eira searched for the woman who'd magically choked her, but couldn't see more than a blur of fabrics in their rush.

"Do not let him see you. It seems he's well enough for a party, even though he denied our private audience. That worked out for the best, didn't it? I've promised that you will not cause trouble and from the state of your dress, I see you've failed in that respect."

Regan led them to a side door and up a narrow flight of stairs that were for the servants' use. When they reached their floor, Eira's thighs burned and her lungs wheezed.

"Stupid girl." Her stepmother swatted her head and pointed to their rooms. "Get in there and cleaned up before anyone else witnesses this despicable display. Look at you—dandelion fluff in your hair, flower petals stuck to your gown, you're positively a fright. Where the hells were you? Rolling around with the pigs?"

"Touring the gardens, Stepmother. There are some lovely apple trees in the orchard."

"The only apple you need concern yourself with is the one I gave you for the king. I'll not have you wandering around like a simpleton mooning over a pretty rose. Do you understand? You are to be queen. Start acting like it or—" Regan put a hand to her forehead and blew out a breath. "Why do I even try with you? Years, I've put into molding you into the perfect queen and this is how you repay me?" She waved a hand to indicate Eira's state. "You could've ruined everything." She looked away with a grunt. "You're as useless as your father."

The last was said under her breath, but Eira heard it and a swirl of cold wrapped around her heart. Regan couldn't physically abuse her while at the palace, but that wouldn't stop her from inflicting mental wounds. Not this time. Regan knew how much the words would hurt and Eira refused to believe she or her father were at fault. Not anymore. She'd courted ruin with her rebellious afternoon. Regan's retribution would neither be swift, nor free of misery.

Yet she wasn't afraid. Not as much as she should've been. Prince Leon could be an ally, as well as Madam Davina. Dare she hope, for the first time in her life, she wasn't alone.

After her stepmother ordered servants to run a hot bath,

heated to such a degree that Eira's skin would remain red for hours afterward, Regan turned to Eira with an evil glint in her eyes.

"You are not to leave this room for the remainder of the night, do you understand?"

"But the king—surely he expects me to be at dinner."

A sharp slap to her cheek burned hot with anger and indignation. Rivulets of alarm coursed through her nerves. The time of abusive amnesty was at an end. Eira dared not touch her face or show any sign of weakness, no matter how much the stinging of her skin ached.

"You aren't to speak to the king until the ball, do you hear me? I can't have you saying something asinine and ruining all of our plans."

Our plans? More like *her* plans.

Eira didn't argue. Not having to see or speak to the king was better than the alternative.

"Yes, Stepmother." She bowed her head, her mind spinning. If she didn't have to interact with the king, that left more time to plan her escape. And an evening alone would be heaven. She mentally readied her writing supplies. "Is the king, Otto, is he well? I thought perhaps that might be why he cancelled our meeting."

It was a risk to ask, but the man on the bed looked to be painfully sick.

"King Otto is as hearty and hale as ever. If you hear otherwise, it is slander, do you understand? I won't have you vexed over gossip." Regan flicked a long nail toward Eira's room. "Get undressed and bathe. I'll have your dinner brought up. I don't want to have to resort to extremes, but your behavior this afternoon leaves me no choice. I warn you, do not leave this room. If I hear of you even sneaking a peek out the door, I'll whip you until you can't sit. Is that clear?"

"Of course, Stepmother. I will stay in my room, reading, the entire night."

Regan sneered at her as if she didn't know whether to believe Eira or whip her right then and there. Her stepmother enjoyed punishing Eira a little too much, and her skin prickled with even the threat of the whip.

She rubbed her arms against the memories of the last beating she'd endured one moonturn past. Tears threatened, and she blinked to hide the traitorous emotions that surely crossed her features. Regan saw crying as a challenge—as weakness—and there was no place for weakness in a queen.

After several more threats, Regan left Eira to the servants. They scrubbed her hair and skin as gentle as they could, but even so, the water was too hot and their touch only served to irritate rather than soothe. The beginning of bruising where Regan's fingers dug into her skin flamed deep red as she sunk beneath the surface. She endured the torture huddled in the porcelain tub, her silent tears hidden from the servants behind a curtain of ebony hair.

In the deepest corners of her heart, she wished she could kill Regan, but a witch as powerful as her stepmother would counter an attack with one even more deadly. Regan had spent decades honing her craft, whereas Eira had only attempted the spells the grimoire showed her, and even then, it wasn't her magic being used. A dagger surely would suffice—just one stab to Regan's heart, but her stepmother's mirror would alert her to an attack. Eira squeezed her eyes shut against the familiar, yet unwelcome thoughts. She wasn't a murderer.

Hot water poured over her head as the maids rinsed the delightfully scented soap from her hair. Her skin had grown accustomed to the heat and barely registered the fresh wave of stinging.

Now that Eira knew the king kept a witch in the palace, did

that change her situation? The woman had shown no compassion to Eira, but what if she could somehow befriend her. Would she stand up to Regan? A harrowing thought scratched through Eira's brain. Regan might be trying to usurp the pretty blonde. Perhaps her stepmother's insistence she marry the king had more to do with her stepmother's ambitions than she previously thought.

Two witches, one king. Eira was a distraction neither of them needed nor wanted. How could she use this new information to her benefit? If Regan was distracted with the king's witch, she wouldn't bother with Eira. Yet, Regan hadn't mentioned anything about the woman, which meant she either didn't know the king had a witch in residence, or she didn't see the woman as a threat.

The question pummeled her skull once again—why did the king, who voraciously denounced magic in any form, allow a witch to live freely in the palace? Surely, he had to know what she was. Maybe his blustering was all for show. If so, then why? And what about the naked man the trackers captured? What was really going on in the palace? Not just the palace, but the whole kingdom?

And why did the king wish to marry her, specifically?

Eira flexed her fingers and struggled to reach her magic, but an invisible barrier blocked her the same as it had always done. Not even a spark lit beneath the water. If her magic were unleashed, would it destroy everything, including herself? Was that why she hadn't yet fully come into her power? And if so, then why did she feel it stirring at times? She let go the will to tap into her magic. Despite it all, the lies, the brutality, the deception, she wished to live. She yearned for freedom with every fiber of her being. A life unfettered. She might be a trapped bird, but one day she would soar above the clouds and touch the sun. One day.

Heart racing, she chanced a glance at the two women, but they had their backs to her. Dreaming was dangerous with so many eyes constantly watching her every move. She licked her dry lips and stood.

"I'm finished with my bath."

The young women jumped to attention, and she idly wondered what they'd been doing hunched together as they were.

A soft towel was wrapped around her singed skin, and she stepped from the tub with extra caution. As she passed where they'd been seated, she spied a clump of emerald-hued leaves and tiny white flowers half-mashed in a granite bowl. Her gaze went to the water, where more crushed leaves floated.

Varidian root. She clutched the towel and shuffled to her bedchamber. One of the servants handed her a cup of tea and bade her drink it. Eira lifted the cup to her mouth obediently, but didn't allow her lips to touch the liquid. The scent was off. It was varidian root, and something else.

Why would her stepmother put the sleeping draught into her bath? This wasn't the first time she'd drugged Eira, so why the added measure? Unless, somehow soaking in the herb made it stronger. She mulled over the ramifications and benefits as the servants readied her for bed. Regan's threats to not leave the apartment echoed in her thoughts. What possible motive could she have for keeping Eira away from the courtiers? Several, actually.

But which one was her main motive? Could she be trying to keep Eira from ruining herself with one of the princes? Possibly. Or did she think Eira couldn't be trusted in her present state to enchant the king? Most definitely.

"Finish your tea, miss." A cheery-eyed lass held the cup for Eira.

"Of course." This time she had to drink. The maid stood firm in front of her with an intense stare that said she wouldn't leave until the cup was emptied. "What about my dinner?"

She knew the answer before the second maid spoke. "The mistress said you won't be needing anything else tonight."

Fine. If Regan wanted her starved, drugged, and kept from court, she'd at least get a good night's sleep without nightmares. If she was lucky.

When she lay down on the soft mattress and curled beneath the covers, her mind circled through the events of the day from their arrival to the present. She thought she was coming to the palace for a ball, but in the course of one day, the entire trajectory of her life had changed dramatically. She'd made an enemy of a power witch, befriended one prince while denying another, learned that dwarves and wolf shifters were real, and met a healer who was also a witch.

Woven through them all, one face remained constant. The huntsman.

Did she dare trust him as Madam Davina advised? Was he her destruction, or her salvation?

Chapter Eleven

Bloody fucking hell, what was he seeing? Henri stood in the shadows, spying on Eira as she sashayed through the courtyard. She wore a midnight blue gown with a stunning ruby pendant he recalled had once belonged to Eira's mother Eloise. Otto and his mistress were in another part of the palace, but here, Prince Guillaume held court as if he were king. *Not yet*, Henri silently warned as he glared at the man, disgusted he would presume to rule, even this tiny courtyard kingdom, while his father still lived.

And what role would Eira play in this farce? His gaze went to where she laughed at something a courtier said, her hand fluttering delicately near her face as if she was scandalized by the comment. This emboldened woman bore little resemblance to the quaking lady he rescued earlier that afternoon. He really didn't know his Eira anymore, it seemed. She was either a skilled actress, or had dual personalities.

He stepped from his hiding place only enough to reveal himself to Eira, curious what her reaction might be. Her gaze lifted, as if sensing him near, and sought him out. Her eyes narrowed momentarily, and then a sly smile lifted her lips.

Equally as quickly, she took on a confused visage as if she didn't recognize him. Before he could slip back into the darkness, she'd already turned away and engaged a woman in conversation.

"Tis truly a puzzle, is it not?"

Henri jumped at the sound of Leon's voice, chiding himself for not being more aware of his surroundings.

"What is, Your Highness?"

"Oh, come now, Henri. We are old friends, let's not ruin it with titles and formality."

They spoke low, just above a whisper in the pitch-black corner where those in the courtyard couldn't see them.

"I would hope we are still friends. Though I confess, I hardly recognize this court from the one of my childhood memories." He felt Leon's warmth beside his right shoulder. Light lit the courtyard, but where he stood was shrouded in complete darkness. There could have been an ogre in beside him and he'd not see it. That was why he chose this corner, specifically, even with the understanding that he might not be alone in his spying.

"Nor do I, sadly." Leon's voice lowered even more and a hint of melancholy laced his words. "What do you make of our soon-to-be queen?"

"How do you mean?"

"She is not the shy innocent I met this afternoon in the garden. That woman was graceful, yet reserved. This version of Lady Cannaid is confident, still graceful, but there are hesitations in her movements as if she wears shoes that are two sizes too small. And her scent is off." The latter was said almost as an aside, not meant to be spoken aloud.

"I too noticed the differences in her countenance. Although, I am not close enough to decipher a change in scent." That Leon had been, chafed at Henri.

Jealousy wasn't an emotion he was familiar with, at least not until he'd witnessed the exchange in the garden between Leon and Eira. The gentle touch and encouraging words he'd said to Eira had brought about a beast of vexation that surprised Henri in its depth and voracity.

"Gil claims she promised herself to him, even says he has proof, but when she arrived here, Lady Banworth informed him Eira would be marrying our father instead." A note of disgust entered Leon's tone and despite the darkness, Henri nodded his agreement.

"They met in the orchard this afternoon. Perhaps they've made another arrangement without Lady Banworth's knowledge." Henri watched as Eira circled Gil, as if teasing him with her presence. The blood in his veins turned molten and he clenched his jaw to temper his ire. If Eira chose Gil, then she was truly lost to him.

"In this court, falseness is in plentiful supply. But tell me, Your Highness, why is it you're skulking around in the shadows instead of meeting with my brother to hash out a treaty between our two kingdoms?"

Why, indeed. Henri had enough of spying. He was wasting his time following his childhood friend in the hopes she would be the same sweet Eira he'd once known. His glance swept the courtyard one last time. Eira stood beside Gil, their heads bent in conversation. Enough of this farce. She'd chosen her fate, he would choose his as well.

Leaving Leon's question unanswered, he stalked away from the courtiers and entered the palace proper through a side door. To his dismay, Leon followed. He frowned at the prince, but Leon's affable smile was undaunted.

"What's got you in such a bother?" Leon nodded to a passing nobleman while Henri ducked his head, still playing the role of spy.

Ridiculous. All of this frippery and flappery, he should've stayed home and left Eira to live out her life however she saw fit.

He was done with her. In fact, he would tell Lady Banworth immediately his true identity and give up the intrigues. He pivoted toward Eira's rooms with Leon in tow.

"Why are you following me like a lost puppy?" his tone was harsher than he'd meant, but seeing Eira flirting with Gil vexed him to no end.

Leon pulled him aside to a partially secluded area. "We were once friends, Henri, and I'd like to think we still maintain at least a semblance of that affection. What's truly going on?" his gaze darted up and down the deserted hallway. "I'd like to help, if possible."

Henri clenched his fists, debating whether he could trust Leon. It was true, of the two brothers, he'd always had a fondness for Leon, but too much time had passed to be certain who was friend or foe. He would tell Leon of his arrangement with Lady Banworth and study his reaction, that could give him a clue if the man was to be trusted. He had little to lose by confessing that much.

"Very well. Lady Banworth hired me today to act as her spy —not just to report the goings on of the court, but to keep track of her stepdaughter as well."

Leon's eyes widened and a frown creased between his brows. "Why? And why you?"

"She mistook me for a common huntsman."

"Did she now?" Leon chuckled and shook his head. "That woman is a piece of work. I don't understand why she'd have you spy on Eira. Unless the innocent woman I met truly was an act and Regan fears Eira will cause a scandal with my brother." Leon rubbed his temple. "Gil might've been telling the truth this time. Something is not right and I am determined to find out what is happening. Who is lying, and why?"

Henri hid his shock at Leon's anger. "I didn't realize you

cared so deeply for Lady Cannaid. Is this perhaps jealousy speaking?"

"Not in the sense you mean. I only just met Eira this afternoon and have no desires on her. I am already spoken for, but that is another matter entirely." Leon cleared his throat and looked away, but not before Henri saw the faint sparkle of tears in his grass-green eyes. "I fear there is more at play here than a hastily planned wedding. I'll do what I can to keep Gil busy, but I'd also like to know the motives of our fair Eira. I doubt my father's mistress, Lady Annah approves of the marriage, perhaps she can provide answers."

Henri shook Leon's hand, grateful for the assistance. "I'm glad we are still friends after all these years. I shall go now to tell Lady Banworth I no longer desire to be her spy. As you've noticed, I can't be in two places at once. No do I wish to watch over our dichotomous Lady Cannaid any longer. She can have Gil or your father, it means nothing to me."

Leon's nostrils flared and he looked at Henri with an intensity that should've made him squirm, but he held fast beneath the scrutiny.

"You love her. Lady Cannaid, you have feelings for her—suppressed, but there all the same."

"No," Henri shook his head, "I loved my childhood friend, but this woman, I do not know her anymore."

"Hmm," Leon nodded as if he understood the meaning of everything and only waited for Henri to catch up. "Continue the farce. Spy on Eira as instructed, but do not limit your surveillance to only her. Discover what role her stepmother is playing. I will do what I can to keep Father and Gil from bothering you. There is too much at stake for us to leave anything to chance."

Henri chewed on Leon's words for a minute, knowing he spoke true, yet apprehensive all the same. What did he hope to uncover in his investigation? If Eira had promised herself to Gil and changed her mind, why should either he or Leon care? If it was as Leon said, and there was more at play here, then what? And whose game were they playing? Gils? Or Ottos?

"Fine. I shall continue spying. We shouldn't be seen together lest someone recognize me."

"If you truly wish to remain unseen, you should use the old servants' corridors. They're no longer used, and few people even recall them being there since my father cares little if servants traipse through the hallways with the courtiers. Of course, they have their own stairwells for ease of access to the kitchens and pantries."

Henri smiled at the memory of the three princes, himself, Leon, and Gil playing hide and seek in the hidden walkways. He bade Leon goodnight and snuck into the nearest stairwell. A torch sprang to life—a relic from the days when magic was freely used in Jura. He scanned the floor, but no footprints showed on the dusty stones. Now, to remember which way led to Eira's rooms. He should seek out Lady Banworth to give an update first, but the desire to learn more about his mysterious, confusing childhood friend was too powerful to ignore. With her busy in the courtyard with Gil, that left him plenty of time to inspect her quarters for clues as to her intentions.

The thought of rummaging through her belongings didn't sit right with him. He might be playing a spy, but he wasn't actually the sort who would paw through personal effects. Observe only, no direct contact, isn't that what Regan had said? In a way, he was only doing as commanded.

At the second floor, he paused to get his bearings. If memory served, Eira's rooms should be just down this next corridor and to the left. To his right was a tight stairwell that led to the dungeons. Definitely not a place he would expect to find a lady.

He counted his steps and stopped at a torch that lit with his passing. Three more paces and he could just see the outline of a door cut into the paneled walls. Blowing out a nervous breath, he pressed against the wood, unsure how much pressure was needed to open the secret door and not wanting to alert anyone should there be someone in the room.

This was ludicrous. He should use the front door like a normal person instead of creeping through the unused servants' corridors.

The door opened with a soft shush against a thick rug and Henri peeked inside. No fire burned in the fireplace, nor were any candles lit. Stillness hung heavy in the air. He listened for a moment, but heard no sounds of movement. Only a soft snoring that came from somewhere deep inside the apartment. He pulled the rest of his body into the large room and closed the door behind him. Scant moonlight gave him enough light by which to see and he frowned at the uncovered windows. Strange that the maids hadn't pulled the shutters closed and drawn the heavy drapes to keep out a draught.

In fact, where were their maids? Besides the snoring, which he determined came from a closed door to his left, the apartment was silent as a tomb. A shiver, not from the cold, but the unsettling oddness of his situation, slithered down his vertebrae to settle at the base of his spine. He stood in the sitting room with bedrooms on either side. Ignoring the left where clearly someone slept, possibly Regan, he crept to the room on his right.

He stood for several long heartbeats listening at the door, and contemplating the choices in his life that had led to this exact moment. Here he was, a prince not in his own kingdom, but a guest of another, about to enter a lady's bedchamber uninvited. He could leave. Pretend he'd never been in the apartment. Excellent plan. Go back to his room, reconnoiter, and begin again in the morning.

"No, please." Eira's voice came from inside the room and Henri gripped the door handle.

'Struth, what now? If she wasn't alone, he would certainly cause a scandal barging into her room. Another whimper, this time softer, broke his resolve. He clutched the doorknob and twisted gently until it unlatched. The room was dark and cold, too cold for a lady's bedchamber. He peered into the darkness, emboldened by the fact his eyes were accustomed to the scant light. He searched for a shadow, or a figure, but only a cold fireplace, some furnishings, and a moderate sized bed filled the space.

Eira tossed against an unseen enemy and cried out again, this time panting as if she were being chased. He went to the bed and placed his hand on her shoulder, making soft sounds like his mother used to do when he was little and needed reassurance the monsters under the bed wouldn't eat his face.

"Shhh, you're safe, Eira." He kept his voice low so as not to startle her awake. It was bad enough he was in her room, but should she wake and find a stranger beside her bed, she would surely scream.

She settled into the duvet and her breathing returned to normal. He stood beside her for several minutes until satisfied she would sleep peacefully. Icy shards of dread tore at his gut and his fingers shook where they lay on her shoulder.

He'd left Eira in the courtyard with Gil. She didn't possibly have enough time to pass him, prepare for bed, and fall into a deep sleep while he spoke with Leon and made his way to her rooms. His gaze went to her face, to the soft lines of her lips, the slight blush of her cheek. In sleep, she reminded him so much of the little girl he'd know all those years ago.

His heart thumpity thumped in his chest. Leon was right— he loved Eira. Always had, but told himself she had abandoned him. What if it wasn't as simple as that? He needed answers. One, in particular he desired to know above all others.

If this was his Eira, asleep in her bed, then who was in the courtyard?

The front door banged open and girlish laughter followed. Henri crept to the door and opened it enough he could see two figures locked in an embrace stumble through the sitting room. They passed beneath a window and the moonlight shone across Gil's profile. His lips curled as he bent toward the woman who writhed in his arms.

What the bloody hell was he doing in Eira's apartment?

A moment later, Henri had his answer.

The woman spun out of Gil's grasp and into a beam of moonlight that illuminated every inch of Eira's visage. He jerked his head toward the bed where his Eira still slept and back to the pretender.

"Do you want me like this, Your Highness?" A throaty chuckle came from the woman and she bent to beckon Gil closer. "You were superb tonight, darling. Now come here and fuck me."

"Lady Banworth, you are a devious minx." Gil's words drifted toward the opposite bedchamber where Henri could've sworn he heard snoring.

This made no sense. Why would Regan hire him to spy on Eira when she herself pretended to *be* Eira? A crawling sensation went up his arms to his neck, prickling the hairs along the way. To be that convincing, magic had to be involved. The spell necessary to impersonate someone was involved and dangerous, and also illegal even in kingdoms that allowed magic.

Regan wasn't just a witch—she practiced forbidden magic. He closed the door, wincing at the slight click it made. He now knew the measure of Lady Banworth, but what of Eira? Was she complicit, or innocent?

Until he knew for certain, he would continue the charade and treat both women with diplomatic indifference. Easily done for one, achingly difficult for the other. He pressed a fist against his chest where a jag of anxiety tore at his heartstrings. If Eira knew of her stepmother's schemes, then she was truly lost to him.

Chapter Twelve

The gentle whisper of a servant brought Eira out of a deep sleep that was neither restorative nor peaceful. She'd been plagued by nightmares all night—of huntsmen chasing her with wicked knives sharpened on a cutting wheel, and also by a handsome prince shredding her skin with long nails as he laughed at her suffering and mocked her pain-filled cries.

She pulled a pillow over her head and willed the awful images away. The prince's taunts rang through her mind and the hot prick of tears stung her eyes. Lawks, but she was getting soft. Never had she felt the need to cry as much as she did at the palace. Self-loathing for her weakness battered against her heart. She placed a hand on her chest and tried to shut out the awful nightmares, but what he'd said was true, all of it. She was a mouse caught in a game she didn't understand, surrounded by fierce, hungry cats.

"Git up, ye lazy arse." A stick poked her buttock, and Eira grunted against the pain. "Yer lady said ye needs to eats. Come on, I ain't gots all day fer the likes of ye."

Eira lifted the pillow to glare at a woman with wispy silvered hair and crumpled skin. "How dare you speak to me so informally. I'll have you reported."

"Eh, do what ye like. I dinnae care." The woman scratched at an armpit and spat into the fireplace. "Come on, food's gittin' cold."

This was no servant. Her clothes, tattered and worn, weren't in the king's colors. And her bare feet certainly weren't acceptable for a servant of the crown. Still, there was something familiar about her that Eira couldn't place.

"Who are you?"

"Not someone to be trifled with. Now git before I whoop yer arse."

Eira grabbed her dressing gown and slid it over her nightdress while sneaking a peek out the window. The sun had yet to make an appearance, but a thin strip of orange over the horizon promised its imminent rise. Soon enough the rooms would be a hive of activity, but a quick scan showed no signs of other servants. A pinching started in her belly.

"Is my stepmother still sleeping?" Regan rarely rose before midday, so why the early hour for Eira?

The odd woman huffed and waved a hand. "Sit. Eat. It'll give ye what ye need."

Eira sat with caution. The food looked normal, but after the sleeping draught the previous night, she didn't dare trust anything that she didn't herself prepare. And even then, she'd be suspicious of the ingredients.

"Here, see? It'll not kill ye." The woman grabbed a scone and took a rather large bite. Then she drank from Eira's cup and poked her finger in a custard. The sounds she made licking the cream from her fingertips made Eira's stomach churn.

"I believe you. Now stop it." She reached for her cup and

sniffed. It smelled like apples. A tentative taste confirmed that it was indeed warmed apple cider. A basket of apples sat in the center of the table, but when she reached for one, the woman batted her hand away.

"Not yet. These is for later." She put a protective hand over the fruit.

"You're not the beggar woman who put a curse on me when I was born, are you?" Eira jiggled her custard, her cheeks warming. "I'm sorry, that was rude of me. How could you be? That was ages ago. It's just, you being here, now, with a huntsman so close, is too coincidental to ignore." Her nervous rambling only added to the apprehension that puckered her gut.

"Ye been through a rough patch, eh? I tell ye true, I ain't the one whose ye needs worryin' about. I helps thems in needs, not hurts thems. Now, eat." Compassion lingered in her smile and in the depths of her eyes.

"I can have whatever I wish?"

The woman's face softened and she patted Eira's hand. "Git yer fill, lassie. Yer naught but skin'n bones. Half-starved kitten, no fire, what's that fool woman thinkin'?" The last was said under her breath.

Too hungry to argue, Eira tucked into her breakfast and devoured everything on her plate. When only a smear of egg remained, she slathered butter and jam on a scone and ate it in two bites. The woman poured more cider into her cup and she drank until her belly was full to bursting.

"I like seein' a good appetite. Now git dressed. Ye's got some time yet afore the mistress wakes. Explore the palace. Sees what's here. Talk to folks. These'll be yer subjects soon. Might as well get to know 'em. Take these here apples for later. They'll sustain ye, don't ye worry."

"I can't. My stepmother told me to stay in my rooms. If she

finds out I left," Eira rubbed her arms and shuddered. "I'm sorry."

"No need to 'pologize to me, missy. As fer yer stayin' in, that was only fer the night, wasn't it?" She pointed out the window. "Days a'comin', innit?"

She was right. Besides, Eira could explore before Regan woke. As long as she avoided the king, she'd be fine. She excused herself to change and when she returned, the table was cleared and the woman gone. Only the basket of apples remained.

She stood in the empty room and contemplated the strange woman's words. Explore the palace. Where to start? The library, if she could find it. As if in answer to her unspoken question, a light glinted at the far end of the room, and Eira snatched the basket of apples off the table before going to investigate.

A hidden doorway stood partly ajar, the timing too perfect to not have been from the woman. Still unsure whether she could trust her, Eira hesitated. She placed a hand on her belly and frowned. The food hadn't made her ill, or killed her, so perhaps a little trust could be placed with the stranger. And she did quite like the idea of exploring. From a young age, investigating every nook, crevice, and hidden passageway in her castle had kept boredom at bay. She'd discovered she wasn't afraid of spiders or mice, in fact they were sometimes her only friends, and she'd learned that nothing is ever as it seemed. Otto's palace most certainly had secrets. Possibly even some that could help her escape.

The rest of the apartment was still, the silence unnerving. Perhaps the woman sent all the servants away and was luring Eira into an elaborate trap constructed by her stepmother. Convoluted doubts and concerns warped and waned in her mind, overwhelming her into panicky inaction. Finally, she forced her shoulders back and stood tall. Whatever awaited her on the other side of the door, be it punishment or death, she would accept with the grace of a lady.

The door opened with a soft swoosh and without hesitation, she took a bold step through into a darkened corridor. The door closed behind her without a sound.

Breathe, she told herself and inhaled the musty air.

A torch blazed brightly to her right, and she grasped the handle with a trembling hand. In the other, the basket wobbled. She drew another deep breath and peered into the darkness.

Nothing moved, and if the woman had come this way, there was no sign of her passing. Eira took a tentative step forward, and another, until she was walking as if she strolled in the gardens. Her slippers shushed against the slate tiles. That and her ragged breaths were the only sounds in the dank space.

With each step, her fear subsided and her courage grew. When she came to a spiral stone staircase, she didn't falter before taking them down. She passed three smaller landings before coming to a large opening. The stairs continued their spiral downward, but she stepped into the murky darkness as if she knew where she was. Which, to be honest, she didn't. She could've been outside the palace with all the steps she'd taken. Yet, unlike the night before, her thighs didn't burn and her breathing had evened.

Ten paces in, the room ended abruptly with a slim arched opening leading to the left. The hazy light of a wall sconce burned somewhere in the distance, and she squinted to make out the open area she'd entered. Heavy bars went from floor to ceiling on either side of a straw covered walkway. Each cell had a gate with a thick lock keeping it closed. Through the still air, soft sounds of someone sleeping came from the shadows.

The dungeons. Had to be. She wrinkled her nose at the

smell of bodily waste, yet she didn't turn back. Just this tiny act of defiance made her heart flutter and gave her courage to be daring. Besides, curiosity burned in her thoughts. What would someone have to do to be thrown into the dungeons? Would she find the naked man here? And, selfishly, she wanted to know what sort of king Otto was. How someone treated those less fortunate told her more about them as a person than any oath or public declaration.

This was a rare opportunity, and she seized upon the chance to not only learn more about the man she was to marry, but about the poor souls locked away from their lives. Even so, taking that first step wasn't as easy as she'd imagined. These were criminals. Perhaps even hardened killers.

Her body automatically half-turned, as if to return to the stairs and the safety of the palace proper.

"No." She spoke aloud and the single word echoed in the silence.

No, she would not hide from the possible vulgarities facing her and return to the comfort of her room. Hers was a life of privilege, full of luxuries, true, but a prison nonetheless. She squared her shoulders and strode to the first cell, only to find it empty. A pit of disappointment lodged in her throat. For what, she wasn't sure. The next two cells were also devoid of prisoners. In the fourth cell, she found the source of the gentle snoring in the form of a huddled woman.

Greasy locks of brown hair swept over the slate bench that served as her cot, nearly touching the filthy straw bunched on the stone floor. The sharp angle of bones protruded from the cloth she wore. Eira hesitated to call it a shirt as it was nothing more than scraps. What kind of monster would toss someone into a smelly dungeon and leave them to perish?

The king. Of course, it had to be Otto who ordered such

harsh treatment. What would someone have to do to deserve being locked away and forgotten?

As if hearing her thoughts, the prisoner rolled over and stared at her for several moments before blinking rapidly.

"By the goddess, are you real?" The voice, raspy and cracked, held a note of such optimism it nearly broke Eira's heart. "Have you come to release me? Or kill me?"

"Neither, I'm afraid." She looked at the heavy bars with a frown. The woman didn't strike her as a vicious killer, but then, most people thought Regan was charming. Her pale face and huge, sorrow-filled brown eyes regarded her with wariness. "How long have you been here?"

The prisoner looked to the ceiling, her fingers tapping on the concrete slab. "I'm not sure." She swung her legs over the bench and sat up. "When is the full moon?"

"Not for a fortnight."

She nodded and chewed on a lock of hair. "Ten days, then. Possibly more." Her eyes narrowed. "What are you doing here?"

"I was exploring the palace." She held out the basket. "Take these. They will sustain you until I can return and bring more. I'm afraid for now, it's all I can offer."

"It's more than I've had in several days. I was beginning to think they'd forgotten about me." She scooped the apples into her hands and emptied them into a dark corner. "Have you seen any other prisoners?"

Eira shook her head. "Just you." She thought of the naked man and hesitated a moment before saying, "Although I did see another man yesterday. A group of trackers had him tied to a wooden pole."

The woman gripped the bars and growled low in her chest. Eira took a step backward to escape the feral threat.

"What did he look like?"

"I didn't see his face. It appeared he'd been beaten." A blush stained her cheeks at the memory of his naked body. "He had light brown hair and a fit body. That's all I know."

A long breath exhaled through the bars and her face softened as if in relief. "You shouldn't be here. If they discover you're helping me, then you might find yourself my cell mate, and neither of us wants that."

"Is there anything you need?" A fresh tunic for starters, and perhaps a flagon of water. Eira started a mental list of items she could bring the woman.

"There's nothing you can do for me, I'm afraid." Her fingers gripped the bars hard enough her knuckles turned white. "You're too kind for the likes of this place. Stay clear of the king and his eldest son. They'll surely ruin a precious thing like you."

Ruin her. There was the threat, yet again. Why must there be so much ruin? And why was it that a woman was ruined, but not men? Why couldn't a woman have lovers and cavort as much as her male counterparts? Why was her worth based on her chasteness? What happened after the king ruined her? Would he then dispose of her as easily as his last wife?

Anger blossomed in her chest, and she drew in a deep, steadying breath. She clenched the empty basket, lighter now without the apples, and willed her heart to calm.

"No one will ruin me, good woman. I shall not let them." And no huntsman would take her life, either. Somehow, someway, she'd survive this palace, just as this woman had survived the dungeons.

The prisoner's gaze took in Eira's face and a crooked smile showed lovely white teeth, the two canines came to sharp points. A tremble started in her belly and she looked away before the woman caught her staring.

"What are you called?"

"Eira, ma'am."

A flicker of recognition crossed her dirt stained face. "Ah. The one whose name means snow and is said to be fairest in all the land. Yes, I know of you and your stepmother. The gaoler was boasting just last week, or was it yesterday? Doesn't matter, he was pleased as punch the king found a new queen. I just didn't realize you were so young. A lamb for the slaughter."

"Pardon me?" Eira must've misheard her. A sacrifice? Her?

She moved away from the bars, her face half covered in shadow. "Rumor has it your stepmother is as wicked as they come. Is this your idea of a sick game? Show me false kindness to lure me into a sense of trust? Have you been sent by Gil to torment me? Well, tell him he can fuck off. I'll never willingly submit."

Eira's mind swished and the dungeon wobbled with a bout of vertigo that nearly knocked her to her knees. She grabbed the cell bars to steady herself.

"I assure you, I'm playing no game. If anything, I'm a victim of their whims as much as you."

The woman returned to the front of the cell and held Eira's gaze. The hairs stood on the back of her neck and she felt the familiar prickling of someone using magic in her presence, but this was an altogether different kind of power that she didn't recognize. Gruff, wild, dangerously seductive. Eira swooned toward the woman with a low moan that came from somewhere deep inside she didn't know existed.

"What are you doing to me?" Her words came out slurred and her mind felt deliciously woozy as if she'd drunk two glasses of Tristano.

"Deciding if I can trust you." The woman sniffed as close to Eira's face as the bars would allow, and along her fingers that grasped the bars. "I trusted someone once, and they left me here to rot."

"You can trust me." Eira pulled away from the cell and gently pushed the woman's magic away like the grimoire had showed her to do, long ago. "I know what it's like to be left all alone." She peered at the woman, at the single tear that cut through the grime on her cheek. "Are you certain they forsake you? What if they don't know where you are? I could get word to them."

"They know. How could they not?" She swiped at her cheek and growled. "Never trust a man who says he loves you."

"What's your name?"

A moment's hesitation, followed by another snarl. "Sacheen. It will do you no favors to mention my name to the king or his horrid sons. Best to keep this little interaction our secret—for your safety more than mine."

"I will. But Sacheen," Eira placed her hand over the woman's. "Don't give up hope."

Sacheen snorted and retreated to the back of the cell. "Thanks for the apples, snow girl."

Eira waved and retraced her steps to the spiral staircase. She altered her mental list to include finding the man who had forsaken his lover. Eira had never been in love, and part of her desperately wished to be, but even so, if someone said they loved you, that had to mean something. Or perhaps she was being too naive. She wouldn't say she loved someone unless she meant it.

She raced up the stairs, fueled with purpose. Hiding her meeting with Sacheen from Regan would take some doing. Her stepmother always seemed to know her thoughts despite her best intention to conceal them. Eira knew Regan used magic to pull information from someone's mind, she just didn't know how her stepmother did it. If she knew the spell, then she could use a counter spell from the grimoire.

Her mind was mulling over the pages of the grimoire, searching for the exact right spell, when she reached the landing on her floor. Just as she stepped into the musty passageway, a hand grabbed her wrist. The basket she held clattered to the floor and a second hand covered her mouth to muffle the scream that came unbidden from the depths of her sternum.

Terror paralyzed her as she stared into the ruthless, handsome face of the huntsman.

Chapter Thirteen

Eira slid along the dusty floor, her slippers useless to stop the strong pull of the huntsman. He'd not said a word, despite her wriggling to get free. He simply held her against his body and tugged her along after him. His strong, unyielding body that made her blood thicken despite the direness of her situation. So inappropriate. So dangerously seductive.

As the door to her rooms loomed, dread, cold and dark and foreboding pooled in her thoughts. Her mind grasped at pleas to utter, leniency to beg for, but she said nothing. Not that she could speak with his hand digging into her lips. The solemn promise she'd made Sacheen was too fresh in her mind for her to give in to weakness now.

Just then, her legs went limp and she dropped near to the floor before he stopped her. With a fluid, almost elegant twist, he pulled her to stand and she tumbled forward. His hard chest stopped her momentum, and she grunted against a stab of pain that went straight to her heart. She glared at his stupid handsome face. The eyes that regarded her weren't cruel, but filled with something close to confusion.

"You smell like apples."

"You smell like death." It wasn't true. He smelled of fresh air after a sudden rain. Of a single ray of sunlight on a cold winter's day. Of the woods. Pine and soil. All good things that weren't frightening at all. Yet his grip hadn't loosened, nor had his tight lips broken into a smile.

"Hmm. I suppose that isn't up to me, is it?" He jerked open the door and shoved her through.

She stumbled and braced herself on a leather chair that just the day before she'd envisioned herself snuggling into to read.

"There you are. Thank you, Callan, for bringing her back to me. Where were you, Eira?" Regan entered the sitting room and strolled close, her long nails outstretched as if she'd pluck Eira's eyes with them.

"I got lost in the darkness. Thankfully, this man rescued me." She curtseyed prettily to the huntsman. "Thank you, kind sir, for your assistance."

The calmness of her words belied the rapid beating of her heart. She licked her parched lips and tried to swallow, but the moisture had been sucked from her throat as well.

The huntsman regarded her with a cool, unreadable gaze before turning to Regan. "She hadn't traveled far, milady. Nor did she see anything untoward."

Why was he lying for her? Surely, Regan would know he wasn't telling the truth. Eira had to have been gone the better part of an hour.

"Leave us." Regan flicked a wave toward the door, and the huntsman nodded before taking a step forward. "Not you." She put a hand on his chest to stop him, and Eira saw his jaw tighten, his fingers curl into fists. "I meant the servants. Are you loyal to the king?"

He took a step back and lifted his chin. His near-black eyes studied Regan in a way that would've made Eira's legs tremble had his focus been on her. When the door closed behind the last servant, the huntsman narrowed those lovely granite eyes.

"What you ask is treason, Lady Banworth. If I answer in the negative, you could have me arrested. If I answer affirmative, what then?" His gaze slid to Eira.

Madam Davina's words grazed her thoughts. *Trust the huntsman.*

"Tell me true. Are you a loyal subject of the king? No harm shall come to you if you speak the truth. But know this, boy: I will know if you're lying."

Eira watched Regan's fingers with rapt attention. She was undulating them in the way she did when casting a spell. There was no way she could warn the huntsman without alerting her stepmother to the fact that she knew her secret, and so Eira kept quiet.

"I am not loyal to the king, ma'am." The huntsman stood still, his gaze locked to Regan's with an angry intensity Eira could feel from where she stood a pace away.

Did he know Regan used witchcraft on him? A slim blue light hovered between him and her stepmother for the space of two heartbeats, and then it dissolved. Eira's mind spun to the page in Regan's grimoire that held the truthseeker spell. She'd never seen it in action, but the light fascinated her, and she longed to say the words that would force her stepmother to speak the truth beyond what she'd confessed the night before.

"Very well, boy. You're telling the truth. Although there is a shadow lingering in your words, I will trust you. For now." A long nail scraped the underside of the huntsman's chin. "Don't disappoint me."

"What would you have me do?"

Regan snapped her fingers and took a step back, as if that

was a sign that the truthseeking was finished. Although, she doubted her stepmother would ever completely release a spell once cast. Whether or not the huntsman had chosen to work with Regan of his own free will, Eira wasn't certain. Regan had called him by his name, but that meant nothing. This could be yet another elaborate game her stepmother concocted to unsettle Eira. Invite the huntsman into their lives under a false pretense to gain Eira's trust. Why now? The timing was suspicious, to say the least.

And why here? What did Regan gain by taunting Eira with the huntsman's presence? Unless Regan truly didn't know who he was. For surely her stepmother wouldn't bring the prophecy of Eira's death to fruition in the king's palace? Or was that exactly the spectacle Regan wanted? Perhaps even at the ball.

Her legs threatened to shake violently as she took a step backward to hide her nerves. Where could she run? The huntsman had tracked her to the hidden corridor—he'd find her no matter where she went. How had he found her? The door had closed behind her, and she was sure she'd not made noise on her return.

"For now, keep an eye on Eira. Not too close, mind you. I don't want the courtiers gossiping and your presence would put them into a tizzy. Stay in the shadows, unseen. Watch. Listen. Then report back to me."

Regan wanted him to spy on her, and she wasn't even being coy about it. Whatever game her stepmother was playing, Eira had precious little time to learn the rules. Regan enjoyed watching Eira fret, but this was something else, something much more sinister. She curled her fingers into her palms and squeezed until the pain blotted out her anxiety. If Regan wished to see her stepdaughter quake like a terrified rodent, she'd not give her the satisfaction.

"Should I intervene if a situation becomes, ah, difficult?"

Eira kept her face blank, but surprise sparked in her thoughts. Had he witnessed Guillaume's threats the day before? Or had the dwarves told him that she was hiding from the prince in the meadow?

"You are not to approach, no matter what transpires." Regan turned to Eira and held her chin between her thumb and forefinger.

A long nail cut into Eira's lip, but she didn't cry out.

"You, my darling, are to avoid the king at all costs. I thought you mature enough to enchant him, but you're too raw, too innocent. I did my best to prepare you, but you're too dreamy, just like your father."

At the mention of her beloved parent, Eira's heart skipped, and she desperately wished to seize upon the moment and ask Regan to explain further how they were similar. Mentions of her father were rare, and similarities only divulged if they were thought to be weaknesses. But Eira didn't care. She adored being linked to him, no matter how trivially.

"Charm the princes, darling, but don't let them take advantage. They are rogues and see you as a prize worth claiming for themselves. I'm not inclined to believe they'd leave you alone just because you're promised to the king." An ugly snort punctuated her disgust at the princes' perceived behavior, but a sly lift of her lips and a glint to her eye confused Eira. "Go and change. You're dustier than a spinster's cranny. When you're presentable, you may do as you like, but heed my warnings."

Regan sashayed to the door and yanked it open. Two maids immediately stepped forward—most likely they'd been eavesdropping—and Regan bent to whisper to the women. They looked up in unison, their eyes squinted toward Eira, and nodded.

With a last glare for the huntsman, Eira strode to her room. If Regan wanted her to be charming, she'd beguile not only the king, but every last living soul in the godforsaken palace. Starting with the huntsman. What game was he playing? If he was to be her doom, she'd at least like to know her executioner better.

Chapter Fourteen

The morning sun struggled through ashen clouds to warm Eira's cheeks as she paced beneath the fragrant scent of the orchard's apple trees. A quiet hum came from inside the palace where servants hurried to attend their charges, but the dappled leaves and dew-tipped grass provided a solace that was a balm to her frazzled nerves. She'd managed to avoid both princes and even though the huntsman was near, he kept out of sight, which left her to her thoughts.

Charm the princes, but don't let them take advantage. How, precisely, was she to do that? She flexed the fingers she'd been fisting and shook out her hands before wiping them on the brocade gown she wore. A fur cape hugged her shoulders and kept the chill at bay while her fur-lined boots snuggled her feet in warmth.

She ran her hands over the luxurious fabrics—gifts from the king—and frowned. The muted golds and ruby might've been his colors, but they felt foreign on her. Wrong, even. She much preferred the lush eggplant and brilliant gold of her father's colors, even though Regan rarely let her wear them.

A hive of anxiety buzzed in her gut and tears filled her

vision. She swiped at the offending drops and admitted to herself the truth she'd rather deny. Since her father's death, her life had been planned, one seemingly unimportant decision at a time. She once heard a parable about a frog being boiled alive without realizing his impending doom, and it rang true for her now.

Like the frog, had she been thrown into scalding water, she would've immediately jumped out to save herself. Regan was sly and ever so clever. She'd put Eira into a metaphorical pot of water and gradually raised the temperature until she realized too late that she was slowly boiling to death. That's how she now found herself a pawn of the most powerful man in the kingdom. Or was she still Regan's pawn and the king also caught in her stepmother's trap?

Her gaze drifted to the huntsman. One seemingly unimportant decision at a time. What choice could she make right now that might upset Regan's plans? Did she dare? Most of her life had been spent obeying her stepmother. Breaking that particular habit wouldn't be easy. And yet, she'd smashed Regan's rules yesterday, and even this morning had explored clear to the dungeons. She glanced at the turrets of the palace and the flags that snapped in the breeze.

Regan's control of her wasn't absolute here. She wasn't the caged bird she as at Falkoyn. Here, she was the king's future bride and that probably angered her stepmother more than any slight Eira might've given. She had to be wary, to not play her cards too early, lest she trigger Regan's rage. She'd not squander the freedoms she was allowed at the palace, but she wasn't about to pass up an opportunity to improve her situation.

Starting with the huntsman. She took a deep breath and steadied her nerves. Before she charmed the princes, she'd practice with him and in the process, she'd learn why he was in league with such a horrible woman. Yes, excellent plan. That's precisely what she'd do. Charm the rather handsome fellow whose very presence made her blood warm and face flush.

The grass squelched beneath her boots, and she winced at the sound. As she'd feared, it drew his attention and he stared at her from the shadows of a fountain about thirty paces away. Flustered that she'd lost her element of surprise, she pivoted away from him and ducked beneath a low branch. What an idiot, cowering at the first obstacle. She would regain her composure and try again, this time employing stealth.

A booted foot protruded from behind a tree, and she drew herself up with a gasp. The foot splayed at an awkward angle and her heart hammered at the base of her neck. From the style of the shoe, and the fabric that pooled at the ankle, she feared it was a woman's body she'd discovered. Her thoughts spun to Regan's warning that a man had been murdered, and then to even more horrible, macabre scenarios, even while she told herself it was simply a servant who'd fallen asleep. Desperately, she hoped it was someone unharmed, but Guillaume's behavior and her own experiences thus far at the palace made her doubt. No one was safe here.

She crept around the tree to see a lovely young woman slumped against the trunk. Her glorious blonde hair hung over her shoulder like a blanket and her pink lips quivered with sleep.

Alive. Bless the goddess, she wasn't dead. There was no visible blood or signs of an attack, yet that didn't mean she wasn't in danger. Eira scanned the orchard, fear gnawing at her belly. The woman would make a convenient victim for the horrid prince. If she wasn't already.

Eira drew a shaky breath and gently prodded the woman's shoulder.

"Wake up."

The woman murmured and her head lolled to the side.

Sounds of courtiers entering the gardens came to her. Soon, there would be others in the orchard and questions she couldn't answer.

"Please," Eira begged, her fear growing with each passing moment. The imagined horrors that went through her mind could easily come true if the woman remained where she was. She was too vulnerable to be left alone. "Wake up."

The woman blinked and gazed at her surroundings, her features scrunched with confusion. "Where am I?"

"In the orchards." Eira kept her tone cheery so as not to alarm her. A twig snapped nearby and she touched the woman's forearm. "Can I help you to your room?" She peered through the trees at a pair of tall black boots. Boots she recognized from the day before. They were advancing in her direction far too quickly. "You'll catch a chill if you stay here."

The woman nodded and Eira helped her stand, but not quickly enough. Prince Leon ducked beneath a branch and smiled when he saw Eira. His gaze flicked to the other woman and a frown dipped his brows.

"There you are. I had hoped to find you here and look, my wish has been granted." He cocked his head to the side and studied the woman a moment. "Bryn? Is it really you?" A wide smile cracked his features. "When did you get in?"

The woman called Bryn blinked at the prince as if she were still half asleep. "Leon? Little Leon, it's good to see you."

They embraced with a familiarity that gave Eira a twinge of jealousy, even though she had no right to be jealous of the prince or anyone else. It was the way Bryn folded into his arms, as if hugging were as natural as breathing. And the way Leon gripped his friend, as if at long last they met again. She was happy for the pair, truly she was, and at the same time, a little sad she couldn't remember ever being embraced with such loving care.

"You're chilled right through. What are you doing out here?" Leon held Bryn at arm's length, his gaze taking in the woman's frothy pink gown and mussed hair. "Did you sleep in the orchard?"

"I'm not sure. I've been dozing off in the most inopportune places lately. To be honest, I don't remember much, just that this lady woke me." Bryn indicated Eira and she blushed.

"I found her just there, Your Highness. Asleep." She tried to impart meaning into her words so that Leon wouldn't be alarmed, yet understood there was need for caution.

"I see. Come with me, we'll get you sorted." He took Bryn's arm and turned to Eira. "I should like to speak with you. Will you wait for me?"

How could she say no to the prince? "Of course, Your Highness." She dipped a curtsey and stood beneath the apple tree, rubbing her arms not to keep warm, but to keep her nerves under control.

What could he wish to speak to her about? Regan's threat the day before? Whatever it was, she was eager to hear what he had to say. She paced a small circle, aware that now she was completely alone in the orchard, easy prey should Guillaume decide to harass her again. Minutes ticked by with her nerves jangling with each passing second. She bit her nail, a terrible habit she was trying—and failing—to stop. She'd go inside and send word to Leon to meet her there. Yes, excellent. No, terrible idea. There were courtiers everywhere in the palace. That's why she'd come to the orchard, to be alone. She smoothed her gown and breathed slowly for several heartbeats.

Boots crunched across the ground and she crouched to see who might be approaching. At the sight of Leon's legs, she released the tension coiling in her gut and sighed with happy relief.

"I sent her to her rooms with a servant and will have Madam

Davina check in on her. I don't believe there was anything...
inappropriate." His intense gaze held meaning she understood.

"Thank you. I was worried something might have happened.
She's not safe here." Eira rubbed her arms again. "None of us
are."

She hadn't meant to say the last out loud and put her fingers
over her lips.

"You're not wrong, Lady Cannaid." He bent to look beneath
the trees. When he stood, his eyes were clouded. "Although
perhaps it's best we keep those thoughts to private quarters."

"Yes, of course. I'm sorry, Your Highness. Seeing the woman,
I was so frightened for her. They say there was a murder..." She
left the rest of her thoughts unspoken.

"One of my father's trackers. Vile man." Leon shook himself
and cricked his neck. "Please, call me Leon. There is no need for
formality between us, if that's acceptable to you."

"I would like that. Aren't," she bit her lip, unsure if she
should be so bold. "Aren't you afraid of what my stepmother will
say if she finds us talking alone?"

Leon arched back and planted his fists on his waist. "Ah, yes.
The formidable Lady Banworth." He stared at the sky a moment
before indicating the palace and she walked beside him through
the orchard. "That, my fair maiden, is a story for another day.
For now, let's say I believe the risk is worth it." He smiled down
at her and her insides warmed at the gentleness in his eyes. His
nostrils flared and he sniffed the air, but she didn't smell
anything other than the sweet fragrance of fruit. "That scent,"
his gaze traveled to her and he shook his head. "I must be
mistaken."

"Sir?" Eira smoothed her gown and rubbed her arms. "Am I
offending you somehow?"

"Not in the least. You are a burst of sunshine in this gloomy
old palace and I am happy for your company."

Gaiety bubbled from her belly and she wrapped her hand around his arm. "Let's not bore ourselves with talk of that which displeases us. We should do something fun. We are young, Prince Leon, we should not be burdened with such seriousness." She put a finger to her lips in thought. "You have a library here, do you not?"

"Yes." His skeptical look made her giggle.

"I should very much like to see it."

"A library? That's your idea of fun? Of being less serious?"

She shrugged. "I had a sheltered childhood. Libraries are a world of adventure between leather-bound covers."

"Then we should make our own adventures." He poked her in the ribs. "Catch me if you can."

Before she could speak, he darted off. She stared after him, not knowing if she should follow. Her gaze raked over the near-empty orchard to the fountain where the huntsman had been watching her, but no one was there.

A few courtiers meandered through the gardens, with the ever-present servants nearby holding trays burdened with heavy goblets.

With a delighted little squeal, she ran after Leon, giggling at the sheer idiocy of his game. He ambushed her from behind a tree, and laughed when she squeaked like a caught mouse.

"Your turn. I'll give you to a count of ten, then I'm coming after you." To see the look of joy on his face was something she'd hold in her bosom forever. She couldn't disappoint him.

"You might be surprised how quick I am." It was a lie, and she was fairly certain he knew it was, but he nodded in agreement all the same.

She trotted in the opposite direction, toward the palace. Wind rushed past her face and she grinned like a fool at their silly game. A lightness carried her forward and she sped up in the hopes she might actually outrun him. A quick glance over her shoulder killed that hope immediately. Leon was gaining on her.

Without warning, he skidded to a stop. His eyes widened and his mouth opened, but no words came out.

Eira looked forward and barely glimpsed the beast of a man before she ran smack into him. She bounced off his rotund belly and stumbled backward, losing her footing, but not enough to fall completely on her face.

"Scumbering idiot!" She meant the oaf who'd stepped in her way, but equally the prince for not warning her.

"Pardon?" A male voice sneered above her, and Eira kept her head bowed. "Stand up so I might see the churl who so violently attacked us."

Us. He used the royal us. Blood and fucking ashes. The king.

<h1 style="text-align:center">Chapter Fifteen</h1>

King Otto. She was supposed to avoid him at all costs. Regan was going to kill her. Bile rose up her throat, and she swallowed hard to keep it at bay, but her mouth was too dry. She rose slowly, her hair making a curtain over her face. As she reached to part her dark locks, cold stung her skin and she sputtered against sticky liquid. A second blast of icy goo hit her face and she bit her lip from using another swear word on the king.

"Leon, what is the meaning of this?" the king bellowed. He sounded nothing like the anguished man she spied upon a day earlier. In fact, he stood resolute and proud, hearty and hale, as Regan had said. Perhaps she'd been mistaken about the seriousness of his illness, or about the woman's words. She must've misheard. Yes, that's what it was.

"Apologies, Father. I was bringing you a goblet of mead and tripped on a root. You should have your gardener look after that. What if you had been the one to have a mishap?"

Dark fabric covered Eira's sodden head, and she was propelled forward by strong arms.

"I'll see to the lady. You carry on with your morning, Father."

Then, lower so that only she could hear, "Keep quiet. I don't think he recognized you."

The king called out his son's name, but Leon ignored him. The prince drove them onward until Otto's voice no longer chased them. Eira's boots thudded on hard slates, and she slipped from Leon's grasp. She took a beat to control her riotous emotions and take stock of the situation. Soggy hair covered her face and she pushed it to the side and glared at Leon.

"Was that really necessary?"

His shrug was sweet. "I panicked. If Father saw you, we'd both be in trouble with your stepmother, wouldn't we?"

They stood in an alcove, away from prying eyes, but she still felt exposed. She plucked at her ruined dress. "I'm afraid I won't escape her anger. Thank you, Leon, for being considerate of me." Her belly twisted and she sucked in a breath. "I can't believe I called him a scumbering idiot. What was I thinking?"

"Brother!" Prince Guillaume greeted Leon before scrunching his face at her appearance. "Aren't you looking rather wretched. Don't let Father see you like that." Before Eira could defend herself, he turned back to his brother. "Have you seen Prince Ventoux? We were supposed to meet this morning, but he's nowhere to be found."

"No, I haven't seen him. Now get out of my way. As you can see, Lady Cannaid had an accident and I must escort her to her rooms."

Leon took her elbow in his hand and she schooled her features to appear as ladylike as possible despite the swarm of nerves pinching her skin. She hated that she was a damsel that needed rescuing.

A vicious snarl marred Guillaume's features. "Careful, brother. Remember Father's warning. Her untainted quim will cost you the half a million silver Father paid for the privilege, and a solid beating for your impertinence." He chuckled and slapped his brother on the shoulder. "Might as well wait a fortnight until the old bastard's done with her."

Gil's mean little eyes met hers and the snarl deepened. Her legs buckled, but she held herself steady, desperate to not show weakness. The king had paid half a million silver? For her virginity? Sickness swirled in her gut and revulsion pulsed through her veins.

"You're vile of the worse sort. How dare you speak to me so. I might not be a queen, but I'm still a lady and deserve to be respected as such."

Guillaume glared at her hard enough it felt like slivers of ice pushed slowly through her sternum. Her head pulsed and vision blurred.

"Respect? You? A lying, deceiving whore? Your worth's already been determined by the coin my father paid, slag. I predict less than a week. That's how long the king will be interested in you before he moves on to someone else. Do you really believe you're charming enough to keep his affection for more than one fuck? Once he realizes you weren't worth the disgusting amount he paid for the pleasure of your quim, he'll toss you aside like the others. Then you'll be fair game." A low chuckle rumbled up his chest and he roughly pinched her cheek. "I'm a very patient man. Why pay for a whore when you can get her for free?"

How dare he. How very dare he. All-consuming anger made her mute, and so Eira did what every lady dreamed of, but would never, ever do—she made a fist and slammed it into Guillaume's twisted, gloating face.

Ringing started in her ears and the palace noises dulled to a low cacophony. Time moved in fragments of a clock's ticking. What had she done? She hid her throbbing hand in the folds of her gown and buried her deceitful glee equally as deep. It might cost her a crown, but punching Prince Guillaume felt good. So fucking good.

The surprise in his eyes matched her own, and even Leon gasped. Guillaume whirled back as if to return the punch, but his brother held out an arm to stop him.

"Gil, don't. Your words were cruel and deserved much more than what you got. It's not Eira's fault that she's been manipulated by those with more cunning and experience than she." Leon faced his brother, which put his back to her, and she debated smacking him as well. "She's an innocent pawn in these machinations."

Was he defending her? Or mocking her innocence? His flip-flopping loyalties were dizzying.

Impotent rage whipped through her veins, but he was right. How could she argue against the truth? She'd allowed Regan to coerce and manipulate her so thoroughly she hadn't even realized what was happening until it was too late. The pot had already boiled over. Her time to jump for safety was long past.

"Fine. I'll leave it for now." Guillaume glared over his brother's shoulder to Eira, and that chilling sensation washed over her again. To Leon, he said, "If you see Ventoux, tell him he's an ass for missing our meeting. I'll draw up a new treaty if necessary and punish his insubordination." Guillaume took Eira's hand and squeezed her fingers a little too hard as he bowed. "You'll pay for your impertinence, slag. I never forget an insult."

She would've worried about his words, but where her fist had connected with his jaw there was a slight reddish bloom that made her rather proud. She glanced at her hand and hid a grin at the bruises forming on her knuckles. She enjoyed punching the insolent jerk too much to let him rob her of that small victory. It was a feeling she'd savor for the rest of her days.

"That was a very brave, yet stupid thing to do." Pride undercut Leon's words.

"I don't know what came over me. He's infuriating."

"Not half. Try growing up with that arrogant prat." Leon bent low to whisper in her ear, "You've made an enemy of my brother, I'm afraid. You're lucky I was here. No one else will save you. Not in this forsaken place." He motioned to the courtiers who milled about, but paid the two of them little attention. "They are shallow, grasping, sycophants who only use each other to gain favor with the king."

Her stomach pinched and churned with each word he spoke. And she was to be their queen only as long as she could enchant the king. Less than one week—if even that. She wasn't charming or enchanting or entertaining enough to keep the attention of her own maids. Even with an enchanted apple, she'd be lucky if Otto gave her even one night before tossing her out. And then what? Return to Regan? There was little chance her stepmother would take in a disgraced one-time queen. She couldn't let Guillaume have his way with her, either.

If no one else would save her, she'd have to find a way to save herself.

A dangerous idea began to form in her mind. What if the game wasn't to keep Otto's affection, but rather, let him take what he paid for, and then bargain to be set loose? If she could secure funds from the king, he could publicly displace her, and she would be free to live her own life. It was mad to even consider such a ludicrous idea. Otto didn't let his wives leave. They all died of mysterious illnesses.

Yet, she refused to be used and discarded, only to then be defiled by the king's son. He thought nothing of tormenting her —publicly, even. She could only imagine his brutality once Otto was done with her. And that punch she'd given Guillaume would surely earn her viciousness in the cruelest forms.

Guilt sliced through her worry. A vision of the townspeople flashed in her mind, and she berated herself for being so selfish.

Her plight wasn't hers alone. The money Otto paid Regan had come from them. The king robbed his own subjects to pay for Eira's virginity.

Repulsive. Disgustingly arrogant and narcissistic. What made him believe she was worth such a vulgar sum? No, what made him believe he was worth her time, naked or otherwise? Anger flared in her veins. She twisted out of Leon's grip and stormed to the palace entrance. His clipped footsteps kept pace behind her.

A commotion came from the open doors and Eira slipped into the shadows, her anger swiftly turning to panic. Leon stood in front of her, half covering her with his broad shoulders. The same group of courtiers Eira saw the day before swept onto the portico, buzzing around the beautiful blonde with their false flattery.

A derisive snort came from the prince and Eira grinned in their camaraderie.

"Who is that?" She whispered to his back.

"Lady Annah. The king's mistress. Be very wary of her, she —" he paused and Eira saw his shoulders stiffen.

When she peeked to his side, Lady Annah glared at them in that strange way she had the day before, without her head turning. It was utterly disturbing and made Eira's stomach clench. She looked to the woman's fingers, and her heart quickened when she saw them twisting as they had when Annah tried to strangle Eira in the gallery. She gasped and took a step back, bumping into the wall.

Her breaths came in shallow drags and her gaze darted all around the wide portico for an exit. The dreaded magic didn't strike. Then she heard it—the low growl, raw, primal, animalistic. It came from Prince Leon.

Chapter Sixteen

Eira cowered behind the prince, unsure what she heard. The growl didn't sound human, yet she was sure it came from Leon. She was delirious from her encounter with Guillaume and now Lady Annah. Must be. As she passed, Annah sneered at them, but her hands relaxed and she carried on into the garden with her magpies chirping happily around her.

Leon's shoulders shook and she realized he was trembling. She placed a hand on his back for reassurance, but he twitched as if her touch burned. Rage vibrated from him and pummeled into her. Even though she knew it wasn't meant for her, she felt its power and shuddered to think what it could do if unleashed.

Words came to Eira, to soothe, to comfort, but she stared dumbly at Leon's back, unsure what he needed. Finally, she managed a tiny, "Thank you."

"Stay away from her if you can. She makes your stepmother look like a kitten." Bitterness edged his voice.

How was she supposed to avoid both the king and his mistress if she was to marry the man? With each passing moment, her predicament seemed even more impossible. Especially if what Leon said about Annah was true. The need to escape just rose beyond urgent. It was critical that she get away from Otto, Annah, and especially her stepmother.

As if her morning couldn't get any worse, Regan breezed through the open doorway, looking remarkably fresh and youthful. She must've spent the last hour in front of her mirror casting spells to give her the illusion of beauty. Years of bitterness had lined her features and only with the help of her magic mirror was she able to temporarily hide the cracks.

When she spied Eira and Prince Leon, storm clouds gathered in her features, only to immediately be replaced by a look of indifference. "What the hell's going on here? Why do you look affright?"

"Your stepdaughter had a run-in with the king, but all is well now, my lady." Leon bowed slightly to Regan, but she didn't notice.

Her attention was fully on Eira.

"You saw the king? Did you speak to him? No, don't answer. We must get you cleaned up before anyone else sees you." To the prince, she said, "Tell me all, Leon. I must know every detail, from words spoken to glances given. Come."

Eira followed Regan to the stairs they'd used the previous night and kept silent while they climbed the interminable steps. Along the way, Leon told a highly edited, and sometimes purely fictional tale of what happened, with Regan tsking every so often. He omitted any and all details that involved Lady Annah, or his brother. Each time he changed the story, she felt a soft poke in her ribs.

He needn't worry about her betraying him. She was too tired to play this new game and sought only the solace of her rooms, where no one would bother her and her life wasn't constantly threatened. If she could spend the remainder of her time until the ball hiding in a dark corner, she'd be grateful for the peace and quiet.

They stepped into the main corridor as if there was nothing unnatural about two ladies and a prince using the servants' stairwell. Regan smiled and nodded to passing courtiers with an air of confident snobbishness that Eira admired. She held herself straight and walked as she'd been taught ladies should, but internally she was a hive of bees swarming at the nest.

The moment Regan set foot in their private rooms, the smile disappeared. She ordered every servant out and, once the door clicked shut behind them, turned on Eira with violent curses.

"You insolent twit! What were you thinking? I told you under no circumstances were you to interact with the king."

She lifted her hand as if to strike Eira, but Prince Leon stepped between them.

"Let's not be hasty in anger. Leaving a mark on our precious would-be queen might be frowned upon."

The derision in his voice sounded to her ears quite convincing. Eira did appreciate his intervention, but this other side to his personality produced more questions than answers.

Regan hissed at him and pivoted to pace the room, her hands flexing in that unusual way they did when she was about to cast a spell. Eira braced herself for a blast of magic, but none came. Not even her stepmother would tempt fate by blatantly using magic in front of the prince, apparently.

"Once again, you could've ruined everything. What possessed you to approach the king? What did you hope to gain?" Regan rubbed her temples and looked to the ceiling for answers, mumbling beneath her breath.

Eira knew better than to answer the rhetorical questions, but she was too tired to care anymore what happened to her. Constantly watching her words and measuring her actions, always on alert to what might set off her stepmother, and now having to avoid the very man she was supposed to marry was the tipping point.

"Despite what you'd like to believe, I didn't intentionally approach the king. I was running away from His Highness, if you'd really like to know." She decided to play Leon's game and up the stakes. "He and his brother have treated me abysmally and I sought to escape their cunning words and cruel gazes. They've made it quite clear what they'll do to me after the wedding when the king tires of me, and I'll tell you true—I want no part of it. Return the half a million silver to the king and let him find another woman to debase."

Eira paused to take a breath and fought off the light-headedness that came with her rant.

"He told you about the silver, did he?" Regan glared at Leon.

"Not him. His vile brother." Eira crossed her arms over her chest as if to protect her heart from betraying Leon. He didn't deserve her angry words, but his actions were confusing, to say the least. At least the part about Guillaume was true.

"That idiot." Regan tossed her hair and paced a circle, her hands writhing at her sides. "Return the money? Are you mad?" She cast an angry glare in Eira's direction. "You will marry the king and once wed, it's up to you to enchant and titillate him. I haven't worked your entire life raising you to be a queen for you to quit now. I've always known you were dull, but I never dreamed you were truly this stupid. What else did you think you were good for?" Regan stormed to within a pace of Eira and stabbed a pointed nail at her chest. "You will marry the king. If you destroy this opportunity, I'll kill you myself."

Even though she'd heard the threat many times before, this was the first time she truly, in the depths of her being, believed it.

"Do it," Eira challenged. "Then I can be free from this miserable life."

Regan shook with rage, her face turning four shades of red before she opened her lips. "Go to your room. You are not to leave unless I give you permission. I shall forget this conversation happened and I suggest you do as well."

Her tone, low and measured, terrified Eira in its intensity.

The fight left her and, defeated, Eira shuffled to her bedchamber without even glancing at Leon. Was he an adversary or an ally? At the moment, he played the role of both, but which was true?

Once the door closed behind her, she stripped off the expensive clothing she wore and rinsed her hair with the pitcher of water meant to be used for washing her hands. It wasn't nearly enough to get all the wine out, but it would do for the moment.

She scrubbed her face as if to rid herself of Guillaume's taunts, but his words pounded through her mind.

"Your worth's already been determined by the coin my father paid, slag."

She'd been bought and paid for like a common cow. Not a cow—a whore.

A slag. The prince was wrong to accuse her of being a slut. If she was, then at least she'd be having a grand time bedding most of the men in the palace.

She stared at her reflection and ran a hand over her naked breast. What made a person's worth? Surely more than a quim. A shudder ran the length of her. She hated that word. It defined her as nothing more than a sexual object to be abused and used. Discarded, not worth a mention.

She was a woman with desires and needs, same as everyone else. Needs that sometimes made her womanhood ache, especially lately when she thought of a certain mysterious huntsman. Her hand slid over her flat belly to the patch of black hair between her legs. Warmth flared beneath her fingertips and she hesitated before moving them lower. Regan had forbade her from touching herself in private, and the few times Eira had risked punishment, the pleasure had been bittersweet. Just once, she'd like to know what a release felt like without threat of repercussions.

The feeling of being watched itched along her skin and she tilted her head to peer at the room through the mirror. Nothing moved, but beyond a small table, shadows cloaked the corners. The curtains had been drawn and the cold fireplace gave no light, nor were any candles lit safe for the few beside her bed and on her dressing table. She turned slowly, untrusting of what she couldn't see, even less trusting of what she could. The cool air felt good along her heated skin. Her nipples hardened and gooseflesh prickled her skin.

Desire, rampant and needy coursed through her veins. There, in the shadow, was what she craved. Yet she saw nothing. Only sweet blackness like the hair on the huntsman's head. Why she would think of him at that moment, she couldn't fathom, and still his eyes were the ones she sought. He was danger and death and desire wrapped in darkness.

He was her escape from this life. She took a tentative step forward, alert to any motion or sound.

A knock at the door jerked her into action and before she could grab her nightdress, one of the maids from the night before entered with a tray. On it was an apple, bread, cheese, and a cup of tea.

"Eat before your tea, miss." The maid kept her eyes downcast, but Eira saw the furtive glances at her nakedness. "Let me help you." She set the tray on the table and tugged Eira's nightdress over her soggy hair. "Sit and I'll brush out these tangles."

Eira was too exhausted to argue. She sat in front of her dressing table and ate while the maid ran a brush through her long hair. Every so often, the maid's fingers would caress the bare skin of her neck and a strange flutter would start in her belly. The quivers weren't for her maid's touch, but someone else's. Someone dangerous and seductive. Her gaze went to the shadows again and again, but still there was nothing there. She was hallucinating from lack of food or sleep or both.

By the time the maid finished, Eira had eaten all the food and picked up the teacup. One sniff told her it was made with a sleeping potion, and she sighed. A sharper scent followed the valerian.

"What's in this? Besides valerian, I mean."

The maid flicked a glance at the door, her lips trembling.

"You can tell me. I promise I won't say anything."

"It's a mixture of valerian, mint, and betane. Please don't tell her." The woman's gaze settled on Eira's breasts and a flush colored her cheeks.

"Thank you for your honesty." Eira didn't know the herb, yet she absolutely understood if Regan ordered it, then it wasn't for any altruistic reasons.

"I'm sorry, my lady. The mistress insists." The maid held the cup until Eira emptied it. "You need to sleep now."

It wasn't yet midday. She should be in the gardens or game room, flirting with young men and gossiping with the other ladies. Instead, she was sent to her rooms—drugged to sleep the day away.

Eira glanced one last time to the shadows before sliding between the blankets and closing her eyes. When the door clicked shut, she heard the gravelly sound of a key being turned in the lock. An elegant cell, but a prison nonetheless.

Chapter Seventeen

A face materialized in the haziness of Eira's drugged sleep. Bluish-black hair framed pale skin, and dark eyes watched her intently beneath drawn brows. Beneath his straight nose, the most kissable lips she'd ever seen teased and beckoned.

Eira pressed her palm against her heart. The huntsman would be the death of her, not Regan. Wasn't that how the prophecy went? Then why was she dreaming of his tender kisses? Her blood turned molten and a soft moan rumbled up through her chest. He was dangerous, perhaps even more so than her stepmother, and although she tried to push the thought aside, she couldn't resist the promise of his lips.

Gentle fingertips traced along her forehead to her jaw, and she arched into his touch.

"Please don't take my heart."

"It is not mine to take, but yours to give." His warm lips pressed upon her brow, and she sighed with absolute contentment.

Hers to give.

They were all hers to give—body, soul, mind, spirit, virginity, laughter, anger: everything belonged to her and no one else.

She was not to be bartered and sold.

When she opened her eyes, a lone candle flickered on the fireplace mantel, giving scant light to her room. The smell of pine lingered, and she inhaled to imprint the scent on her memory. She rose on unsteady legs and wobbled to the chamber pot, where she relieved herself.

Sounds came to her from the other side of the door—curious noises not unlike fighting, yet softer, more muted. Moans and cries.

Eira's heartbeat quickened and she swallowed the fear that sprung up with an awful vision of the huntsman with Regan, their naked bodies entwined. He wouldn't. Couldn't. Would he?

She shoved the thought from her mind and reached for the doorknob. It turned easily and for a moment, confusion halted her movements. The maid had locked the door; she was sure of it. When was that? Today? Yesterday? Was she still asleep and this was only a dream?

If it involved the huntsman and her stepmother rutting, that was a nightmare she truly hoped wouldn't come true.

The sitting room was quiet, with only a few lanterns to light her way. More cries followed by a growl hastened her steps. She didn't want to know, but had to see for herself who was with Regan.

A sliver of moonlight stretched from where the bedroom door stood slightly ajar. Eira crept slowly toward the door, her trembling knees knocking so hard she was half convinced her stepmother would hear the awful clatter.

A quick peek inside the room gave her a glimpse of two naked bodies. It wasn't the huntsman, thank the stars. Relief, cool and sweet washed over her. To know that he hadn't betrayed her brought confusing, yet welcome solace to her battered heart. The same couldn't be said of the sight before her. Prince Guillaume, in all his naked glory, splayed beneath a writhing woman. Eira pulled away from the small opening and clapped a hand over her mouth.

What her brain thought she saw couldn't have been what she actually saw.

She leaned forward again, her focus entirely on the woman.

Not Regan, but at the same time, definitely Regan. Her image flickered and waned, bouncing between her stepmother and —herself.

"Is this what you'd prefer, Your Highness? A tight little pussy, yet no experience?" Regan pouted and wriggled her ass atop the prince. "I could giggle and flutter my lashes if you'd like."

Guillaume reached up and squeezed Regan's breasts. She gave a little cry, but the smile on her face said she enjoyed it.

"When I fuck that slag, it'll be none of your business, as agreed. Now stop with the games." He flipped their positions with such speed and skill, Regan yelped in surprise. Guillaume placed his hands at her neck and leaned forward. "Don't make a sound or you'll be punished severely."

Regan's eyes bulged, and Eira's heart rammed against her chest. Should she help? What if the prince hurt her stepmother?

A low chuckle came from the prince, and he arched away from Regan. "Although, I did promise you a resounding spanking, didn't I?" His hand whipped across Regan's breasts and she cried out, but not in fear.

Her hips bucked, and she grabbed the prince's waist. "Harder."

Eira covered her gasp and backed away from the door. It wasn't a dream. It was much worse than a nightmare. A horror that would scar her memory for eternity. She hurried to her room and closed the door behind her. Chest heaving, ears flooded with the sound of blood rushing through her veins, she tried to fathom what she saw and heard.

Yet it made no sense. Regan and the prince. Was it just a palace affair or something more?

She crawled into bed and fought off the images of Regan pretending to be Eira. Her mind spun with whispered words and spells, but none of them gave her what she needed. Perhaps it was the mirror that was affecting her stepmother's appearance. It was a nightmare, she told herself over and over again. Just a bad dream. Not real. Couldn't be real.

She pulled the duvet over her head and curled into herself. These games, these intrigues were far beyond anything she could comprehend. How deep the lies and betrayals went, she couldn't possibly know, but if what she saw was true, she was in far more danger than she'd originally believed. If Regan and Guillaume were in league together, why? The obvious answer was to overthrow the king. If that was their ultimate plan, how did Eira fit into the scheme? She snuggled deeper and tried to block out the sounds that drifted through the walls to torment her. Did Leon know his brother was bedding Regan? If so, did he care? Did she care? About any of them? Unease enveloped her and the question went unanswered.

Sweet, blissful sleep pulled her under, but it was not to last. Women's laughter woke her and she rolled over to face the wall. She didn't want to care, yet damn her stupid heart, she did. More laughter broke through the walls—sultry, seductive, confident. Regan had no friends back home, who would she be laughing with at the palace? Curiosity tugged at her until she found herself walking barefoot to the door to spy once more.

Through the small opening she allowed, she saw Regan's dark curls piled high, and bent close to a head of copper curls. They whispered and giggled like two maids caught gossiping about a boy. The lady with russet hair leaned back in laughter, and Eira caught a glimpse of her pretty face. Lady Annah.

A chill slithered down her throat and she closed the door quickly before she was discovered. On shaky legs, she clambered into her bed and begged her heart to slow, her nerves to steady. This nightmare was even worse than the one with Regan and the prince. Between their laughter flickered images of the two women fighting over a glass box with something bright red inside. In the next moment, it was Eira herself being torn by the women. Why was her mind betraying her so? Why show her images of such horror? Tears she couldn't stop, nor did she wish to deny, wet her pillow as she slipped into the darkness once more, but this time she feared it wouldn't be blissful, only that terrors awaited her.

Voices brought her out of her sleep a third time, and Eira pulled the pillow over her head. The sound of a heated argument pierced through the down and she hummed to block it out. One voice lifted above the other. The huntsman.

No. Please, not him.

Valerian never gave her such vivid dreams, it must be the betane disturbing her sleep with these seemingly waking nightmares. The first with Guillaume was bad enough, but now, she loathed the idea of seeing the huntsman with Regan. Once again, she was compelled to know. Begrudgingly, she slid from the comfort of her bed and traipsed to the door. She turned the knob slowly and peered through a tiny opening. In the sitting room, Regan paced behind a sofa, wearing her dressing gown and an irate expression. Before her, fully clothed and looking equally as vexed, was the huntsman.

"You're telling me Leon lied about Eira's encounter with the king?" Regan raked her nails through her hair, upsetting several pins.

"Embellished. Eira's version was the truth. She was running

away from Leon and accidentally bumped into the king. Leon threw mead on her, for what reason, only he knows."

"I don't believe you. She's enchanted you to betray me. Admit it."

"You asked me to spy for you, and I have. Whether you choose to believe me is not my concern." The huntsman picked at a cuticle, a bored expression on his handsome face. "I do find it curious that Prince Leon omitted the part where Eira punched Prince Guillaume, don't you? It was a thing of beauty to behold, I tell you true. And the prince deserved it."

A certain amount of pride laced his words, and Eira placed her hand over her heart. What game was the huntsman playing? He was obviously on Regan's payroll—did he get paid in coin? Or fornication?

"Have you asked Prince Guillaume why such a meek little thing as Eira would be compelled to accost him in public?"

Regan stopped her pacing and glared at the huntsman. "Are you mad? Of course not. Honestly, I could care less why she hit him, only that she caused a scene. We don't need gossipers giving Otto any reason to mistrust his new wife." A look of knowing crossed her features, and she pointed to Eira's bedroom. "Guard her. She's not allowed to leave our apartment. I have business to attend to."

With that, Regan swept from the sitting room toward her bedchamber.

Eira closed the door with excruciating precision so as not to make a sound. The last thing she needed was for the huntsman to find her eavesdropping on their conversation. It was obvious to her that he was loyal to Regan; she didn't need him reporting this breach of trust to her stepmother.

Yet the pride in his voice when he spoke of her hitting Guillaume hinted at something other than loyalty. Eira yawned and pulled the blankets up to her chin. These nightmares were strange, indeed. Even stranger if they weren't dreams at all, but real.

In the morning, she'd know the truth of them.

Soothing quiet overtook her, and she relaxed into the twilight of sleep.

"Fear not, princess. All will be well." The huntsman's voice whispered in her dreams. The gentle touch of his fingertips stroked along her cheek, and she murmured her agreement.

All would be well...as long as he didn't carve out her heart with an axe.

<h1 style="text-align:center">Chapter Eighteen</h1>

Soft, feminine voices came to her and she rolled over, afraid of yet another nightmare. No more. Please, dear goddess, no more visions of Regan with her lovers. But the voices she heard weren't her stepmother. The sound of cutlery being placed on a table cut through the women's quiet words. Her maids. Not Regan. A rush of relief swept over her and she exhaled a shuddering breath.

"M'lady," one of the girls shook her gently. "Wake up."

Eira blinked against the brightness of her room and put a hand up to shield herself from the light. It must be nearly midday. A fire blazed in the fireplace, warming her bedchamber to an uncomfortable degree.

"How long have I been asleep?" The last dregs of her dreams slithered from her mind and her thoughts became clearer.

"Since two mornings past." Uncertainty edged the maid's words. "You were not easily woken."

Eira sat up, fully awake now and stared at the maid who had locked her in the room. A look of contrition twisted her features and Eira almost felt sorry for her.

"Where's Regan? My stepmother?" She slid from the bed and reached for her dressing gown.

"Out for the moment, but she left word that you're to eat and then bathe. Further instructions will be made available to you once you're presentable." The maid dipped a small curtsey. "Ma'am."

After a hearty breakfast that did nothing to lessen the sourness in her stomach, Eira bathed as told and sat silently fuming as the maids dried her hair. Another gown from the king was brought forth and she wriggled into the heavy fabric, sighing when the maids pulled her corset too tight. She much preferred less structured garments and could only guess why Otto would send her something so constraining.

Her thought traveled to Lady Annah and it all made sense—the king's mistress most likely oversaw the construction of Eira's gifts, making sure they were as uncomfortable as possible. The horrible woman should've put poison in the seams and saved Eira the trouble of having to wear them all day.

Her head ached and she was exhausted even after having slept for so long. Something about Annah lingered in her thoughts, but like a bee, buzzed away before she could fully appreciate it. Although, she didn't have the sense it was a good memory, more likely one that would sting.

Just as the girls were putting the final touches on her hair, an elaborate style with gems and curls that she would never, ever, choose for herself, a servant entered with Prince Leon not far behind.

He bowed to Eira and held out his arm. "I'm here as your escort for the day. And might I add, you look exquisite. Truly lovely."

Eira blushed at the compliment and looked to the maids, hating herself a little for seeking confirmation from servants, but Regan had yet to return and she didn't fancy being drugged for two more days as punishment. They nodded in unison that Eira should go with the prince, and so she did just that.

Once outside her suite, she released her arm from Leon's hold. "So, are we friends now? Or will you turn into an arsehole again?"

"I'm sorry for that, Lady Cannaid. I am your friend, truly, but I've given you reason to doubt my intentions." He reclaimed her arm and bent low. "Which I assure you, are honorable."

"Where are you taking me?" Anxiety whipped up her spine and she swallowed a morsel of panic.

"Somewhere safe." He grinned and squeezed her hand. "The library."

"Oh. Well, yes, that does sound delightful. But, why?"

"Your stepmother bade me look after you today. She thought I could keep you out of trouble, although I have a feeling you have a talent for finding mischief." Another squeeze. "To be fair, I did play a rather large role in your last disaster."

"That you then lied about."

"I did. People like Lady Banworth don't care about the truth. They want to believe the story in their head and I only sought to give her what she desired. Thanks to you, that utterly backfired."

"If you'd told me the plan beforehand, perhaps I wouldn't have been blindsided. And I would've known I can trust you." She smiled at a courtier who glanced away as if he was ashamed to be in the same hallway as her. Strange. Several other courtiers also looked away, some outright hiding their faces behind elaborate fans. "Why are they acting as if I have the pox?"

"It's not you. Father is livid with me because I refuse to give him the name of the minx who called him a scumbering idiot." He chuckled low in his chest. "You're welcome."

"And Regan didn't give me up? Shocking."

"What? And risk my father's anger, putting the marriage in potential jeopardy? Never. I hate to admit it, but keeping you away from court for two days was actually brilliant. It gave Father time to find something else to amuse him." Leon directed her down a dimly lit corridor and she shuddered at the memory of her first day at the palace when she'd snuck into the king's antechamber.

"I'm so lost. How do you remember where everything is?"

"I grew up here. I know all the hidey holes. You will too, soon enough."

Bile slithered up her throat. "If I live that long." She glanced down the empty hallway. "Your brother's words were more than mere taunts, weren't they? Your father will soon tire of me and find something else to amuse him, as you said. Then what? Do I mysteriously die like the others?"

Leon stopped and turned to face her. "You live, Eira. However you see fit. I hope to help you in that regard."

Her eyes widened and a wild thrill whipped through her veins. "You do? But how?"

A shadow passed over his features and he glanced around them. "When the time is right, I shall reveal all. For now, trust that you have friends here. You are not alone."

He returned to her side and gripped her hand in the crook of his arm. What did he mean she wasn't alone? Who were these unseen friends? She wished to ask him all sorts of questions, but danger lurked in all directions.

They turned down another long hallway and at the third door, Leon opened it to allow her passage. Inside, her dream world spread out before her. Three stories of floor to ceiling bookshelves stuffed full of volume after volume. The dark wood and limited lighting gave the space a cave-like feel and Eira adored it. She skipped to the center of the room and spun like a little girl.

"Oh, Leon, it's glorious. And it's all ours?"

"For as long as you'd like. No one ever comes in here

anymore, so you don't have to worry about any prying eyes or gossiping mouths. I'll be over here, if you need me." He plopped himself into an overstuffed chair and picked up a book.

Eira skipped to him and kissed him on the cheek, her exuberance and gratitude too much to contain. Leon chuckled and pulled away just enough she noticed his discomfort.

"I'm sorry, I shouldn't have taken liberties." Fool! She kissed the prince, even if it was just an innocent gesture. If Regan's spy was anywhere near, he'd surely divulge her indiscretion.

Leon rose from the chair and took her trembling hands in his own. "Don't apologize, Eira. One day, when all of this is settled, I hope we can be as brother and sister, but that's all it can ever be." His eyes searched hers. "I'm promised to another."

Eira smiled up at him with genuine joy. "Then I am happy for you, and shall be glad for your friendship."

He twitched beneath the silk court jacket he wore and it reminded her of the other morning when she'd touched his back. She wondered idly if he still wore the bandages Madam Davina applied in her cottage, or if the wounds had healed.

"There is so much I wish I could share, but now is not the time. I promise you, all will be revealed in due process. For now, please know if I say cruel words, don't believe them. There are intrigues afoot that don't concern you, yet I worry you will be dragged into the drama nonetheless."

"Is there anything I can do to help?"

He gazed at her with something akin to sympathy. "Stay sweet. Stay innocent. Do not let this court ruin you."

"You mean your brother." A shiver snaked down her spine, one vertebra at a time.

"Especially him, but your stepmother, too. She's up to something, I just don't know what."

Eira remembered her dream and revulsion roiled in her gut. Despite Leon's declaration they were friends, she couldn't trust him. Not yet. If she told him about her dream, and it turned out the dream was in fact real, then she'd have confessed to witnessing Regan use magic with the crown prince. She couldn't risk it.

"You could always ask the huntsman. She has him spying on me."

Leon cocked his head, confusion clouding his eyes. "What huntsman? I've seen no one besides my father's spies tracking your movements."

More spies? Her gaze went to the far corners of the room. "Are they here, now?" Had they seen her in the king's antechamber? More importantly, was the huntsman really one of Otto's spies only pretending to work for Regan? Her belly pinched and head spun.

"Not in this room, but most likely lurking outside." He shook his head sadly and shrugged. "You get used to it."

That, she understood. Every butler, coachman, even the cooks were potential spies for the king or one of his many courtiers. Whoever had coin could by information. No wonder Regan had been so brazen in telling the huntsman to spy on Eira right in front of her. It was accepted in Otto's court, even expected.

Leon returned to his chair and she drifted between empty desks waiting to be useful and the tall bookshelves built against the walls. With spies possibly skulking in the shadows, she would have to be careful in her search. That is, if Otto had kept books about magic and artifacts. It hurt her heart to imagine him burning the beautiful pages because of some misguided belief that magic was bad. Magic was beautiful when used for good.

Row upon row of books disappeared into the distance and she concentrated on those closest to the desks. Many of the spines had titles in the old language, a tongue she'd not been taught and so she skipped those. If they were the books she sought, she'd need a translator and good luck asking for that in Otto's court. She might as well strip naked and shout to the entire kingdom that she had hidden magic in her blood.

She drifted between the stacks, her frustration growing with each section she searched. It was as she'd feared—either Otto had destroyed all magical books, or they were held somewhere else. On the second floor, toward the end of the row, she found an entire section devoted to fairytales and romances. They weren't what she truly wanted, but at least she could lose herself in another world for a short while. She pulled a green cloth-bound novel from its place, being careful to turn the neighboring book so that she'd know where to return the one she read.

A door opened and she went to the balcony to see a pair of servants carrying trays of tea and food. Leon instructed them where to place the trays and thanked them before they left. A prince thanking his staff. It wasn't unheard of, but she doubted Guillaume would be so kind. And she couldn't recall Regan ever thanking anyone, for anything, least of all bringing her refreshments.

Leon waved to her and she held up her book with a nod that she'd be down in a moment. When she turned back to the shelf, the huntsman stood silhouetted in the window. A finger to his lips.

Chapter Nineteen

Eira nearly jumped out of fright and stifled a shriek as she glared at the man who came and went like a shadow, without sound, and seemingly, without presence if the prince had not seen him skulking after her. Maybe he wasn't real and she only invented him as some form of mental anguish. But she had stood beside him in front of Regan. Had witnessed Regan use a truthseeker spell on him. That wouldn't matter, especially if her stepmother were conjuring the man to torment Eira. It was possible. Regan had done far worse over the years.

She glanced over her shoulder, unsure if she should call to Leon or not.

"Follow me," the huntsman's low whisper came from her right, several steps away from the window.

He was truly a demon to not make a sound as he moved. Where the lawks had he come from, anyway?

Against her better judgment, she followed the retreating man to a corner where he pushed open a secret door and ushered her inside.

It was absolute darkness in the cramped hallway, but when

he entered, a candle flared in his hand. She stepped back from the dancing flame, anger rising to match its heat.

"Are you mad? What's the meaning of this?" A cobweb caught in her hair and she brushed it away.

"I had to be sure you were well. You slept an awful long time."

That took her aback. "Regan often gives me a sleeping draught, but I don't know why you should care." She poked a finger at his chest, his very solid and real torso, and tried to ignore the tug behind her belly button. Or the warmth that spread to her womanhood from his close proximity. "Are you working for Otto? Are you a double spy? Is that why you were in the king's antechamber that day?"

His chuckle was deep and throaty and goddess help her, sexy as hell. "I assure you, I am not working for King Otto, or his sons, if that's your next question. As for the king's antechamber," he cocked his head and sort of shrugged, "I was following you."

"It doesn't really matter if it's Otto or my stepmother who is paying for your services, you're spying on me all the same, and for that, you aren't to be trusted."

"Trust has to be earned, by both parties." An ominousness shrouded his words.

"That sounds like a threat." She lifted her chin in defiance. "What could I have possibly done to make you distrust me?" The nerve of the man!

His dark eyes flicked toward the library. "You tell me."

Her laugh came out more of a snort and he scrunched up his face. "Prince Leon? Please. He's trying to be kind to me in a palace full of people, half of which wish me dead, you included, and the other half wish to ruin me." She poked him again and moved closer to his dark gaze and damn kissable lips. "If I didn't know any better, I'd say you're jealous."

"You're right, you don't know any better." His jaw tightened and nostrils flared.

"Then why are you so bothered? Does my presence offend you?" She tilted her head and his gaze went to her neck. That close, she heard the low moan rumble in his sternum. His short breaths brushed against her skin, singing her with his heat.

He took a step back and licked his lips, his eyes locked to her forehead. "There are some things you should know, Lady Cannaid. Prince Leon, he's—"

"Promised to another, yes, I know." The moment snuffed out and she regretted losing their closeness. "It's not as if I had affections for him anyway, but I don't need to be reminded every five minutes that someone isn't available should I actually wish for something more. Which I don't, not with him. Or the king, even if it's treason to say as much." Why was she rambling like an idiot? And what was that delicious aroma she smelled?

Cinnamon and apples with a hint of pine. Lawks, it was coming from the huntsman. Why would he smell so good? She nearly swooned into him to inhale his scent, to mark him. She took a step back to distance herself from him and the rampant need culminating at the apex of her legs.

"I didn't ask about your feelings for the prince." A slight hint of irritation made jagged edges of his words. "Your romantic entanglements are of no concern to me. I felt the need to warn you that Prince Leon is being blackmailed by your stepmother. I thought you would be comforted to know I believe his professed friendship is true. He risks much by showing you too much loyalty. Do with this information what you will, but understand there are others whose lives you alter just by being near them."

"Blackmailed? Why?"

"That is his story to tell. Trust him, but know he will protect himself first and foremost."

"And you? Who will you protect?"

Anger and sadness mixed in his dark eyes. "If you have to ask, you're not worthy of the answer."

What an ass. What determined someone's worth? Knowing the answer to a simple question seemed like a silly measurement. Besides, it was an honest question. Was it though? Or was it a trick to see if his feelings were as complicated as her own? She knew the truth and didn't like the answer. If he felt the same, he would've said as much, would he have not? Lawks, she was too new to these games. Too innocent to understand the meaning of a glance or pretty phrase. Regan had schooled her in everything but affairs of the heart. Eira nearly snorted. The woman had no heart, no wonder she left Eira lacking in that area. She'd have to educate herself, then. Perhaps even with a willing pupil.

An overwhelming urge to smooth away the huntsman's ire thrummed through her. Her hand raised as if to stroke his face, just one touch of his perfect skin against hers and she would be satisfied. Her breathing shallowed and she stood impotent, unsure what was happening to her body, but not altogether disliking it.

No man had ever made her feel the way this man did, and yet she didn't know him. Couldn't trust him. That didn't stop her from wanting him with a need so deep and strong she feared she couldn't deny it.

It was magic. Had to be. What other reason could explain her reaction to him? Yet she didn't feel a prickling or tingling against her skin. Didn't feel any sort of magic, benign or hostile.

He turned to leave and she stopped him. "What's your name? I can't keep referring to you as the huntsman."

"Why do you think I'm a huntsman?"

Eira held the book in front of her heart as if it could protect her from what he'd eventually do. "I saw you with an axe, and—other reasons."

His dark eyes regarded her and her insides went melty. Whatever this was, she wanted more. Even if it meant certain death, she wanted the danger and for her pulsing ache to be soothed.

"My name is Henri Callan. You may call me Henri, but now, you need to get back to Leon or he will get suspicious." He reached for the door.

"Why all the cloak and dagger? Why bring me to a dusty passageway?" She was stalling. Just one more minute, one last glance, one sweet kiss, that's all she needed. Goddess help her, she was insane.

"The prince's hearing is very good. Even now, I'm sure he knows we are hidden away here, but can't quite make out our words."

She bit her lip in thought. "Can I trust you, Henri?"

He brushed a thumb over her cheek and warmth followed where he touched her skin. She nearly burst from his tenderness. "I'm probably the only one in this palace you can fully trust. Now, go."

The door opened and his candle snuffed out. Eira squinted into the darkness, but only his enticing scent remained.

How did he keep doing that?

Chapter Twenty

Eira breathed deeply, inhaling the sweet scent Henri had left behind when he disappeared, as much to remember him by, as steeling herself for what was to come. Regan blackmailing Leon, a prince of the realm? There truly was no limit to her stepmother's schemes. She slipped through the door, her heart thudding in her ears. Confirming Henri's declaration would be simple enough. Understanding why her body responded to the man would not be as easy.

What had caused her to react in such a manner? It wasn't like her to poke strange men and sniff them as if she were a bitch in heat. She wiped her clammy palms on her gown and ran the back of her hand over the perspiration on her forehead. Her nerves pinged and zinged with wild abandon and she willed herself to calm.

"Eira?" Leon called from below and she hurried to the stairs.

"I'm on my way." She ran down the steps, hoping he would mistake her rush as the cause of her overheated appearance. When she skidded to a stop a pace from him, she forced a smile and held up the book. "I found something to read."

His gaze went from her to the second floor, a frown dipping

his brows. "I heard talking. Were you with someone?" He plucked a strand of cobweb from her hair and let it drop to the floor.

The pulse at her throat quickened hard enough she fought to swallow. She could lie, but Henri said Leon had excellent hearing. Henri, she smiled at the name and a flush rose up her chest.

Stop thinking about the man in black. Calm. Cool. Collected.

"Yes." Eira answered and lifted her chin in defiance. "I was speaking with the huntsman you've not seen. He told me something remarkable."

Leon indicated she sit and reached for his tea. "Oh, and what is that?"

She noticed the slight tremble to his cup and took her own seat. Her fingers tapped along the gilded edges of her book, her mind spinning. She leaned forward to close the space between them.

"He said you are being blackmailed by my stepmother." She held up a hand at Leon's angry glare. "He also said your friendship is true, but you are divided in your loyalty by this devious act on Regan's part." She lowered her voice to the slightest whisper. "I saw you in Madam Davina's cottage the other day. Does this have anything to do with why Regan is blackmailing you? Perhaps if I know what she holds over you, we can stop her malicious schemes."

Leon's lips thinned and he glanced at the walls surrounding them. "It's not anything you need concern yourself with. I can handle Lady Banworth." He paused and sniffed the air. "Your scent is off." His gaze went to the corner of the room where she'd hidden in the passageway with Henri. "Does this mysterious huntsman have a name?"

It would be such a simple thing to name Henri, but she

couldn't. Not that she held any loyalty to him, but her heart wouldn't let her betray him to the prince.

"I'm sorry, but I'm not at liberty to say."

He leaned toward her until their noses almost touched. "You would deny your prince information he seeks, just to protect a man who is spying on you for your stepmother?"

"And possibly the king, but yes, I would. Are you going to throw me in the dungeons?"

The dungeons, lawks, Sacheen must've thought she'd abandoned her. As soon as she could, she'd gather the items on her list and take them to the poor woman.

Leon barked a laugh that actually sounded more dog than human, startling her out of her thoughts.

"No, my sweet captive. I'll not do something so depraved. The dungeons are no place for a lady."

He indicated the food and her stomach gave a hearty rumble. Two days without nourishment had left her famished. She picked up a sandwich cut into the shape of a flower and ate quickly, but as demurely as possible. Sometimes, she wished she could gnaw on a great turkey leg, manners be damned.

They kept the conversation light while they ate. Leon regaled her with tales of his childhood and of the antics he and Gil would get up to—especially the pranks they would play on their nanny. Each time he mentioned his mother, his eyes would cloud and lips thin. Her heart ached for the prince for she understood the loss of a parent all too well.

When she'd stuffed herself full, and had an entire pot of tea, she smothered a belch and looked at the prince with anticipation.

"Did your mother love your father?" It was an impertinent question to ask, but somehow, she felt that if his mother had loved Otto, then perhaps there was hope for her, too.

"Their's was a love match, albeit, not in the traditional

sense." He patted his mouth with a napkin and set in onto his empty plate before he stood. Not a crumb was on his doublet, yet he'd eaten twice as much as she. "I'll tell you all, but not here. Follow me."

With narrowed eyes, Leon surveyed the library, his lips pursed. Seemingly randomly, he pivoted and strode toward a far corner she'd not explored. She grabbed her book and trotted after him, eager to learn more about the man.

They meandered through colonnaded walkways, haphazardly turning right, then left, and even doubling back in the direction they'd just come. By the time Leon took her arm and pulled her close, she was quite dizzy and discombobulated, not knowing which direction was what, or where they were, entirely. Or if he would ever tell her the story. If he didn't want to share, he only had to say so, walking her in circles was an unnecessary distraction.

Leon kept his voice low and began his tale. "My mother, bless her soul, was young and beautiful when she met Father. He was only a prince then, but already full of promise for a benevolent rule. He was spirited and athletic, that's what caught Mother's eyes, or so she claimed." Leon winked at Eira. "Father was once a kind man who fought against my grandfather's laws forbidding magic. When he met Mother, he saw in her an inner strength that challenged him in all the right ways. They made a formidable pair. It wasn't long after they met that Father asked Mother to marry him."

"Did your grandfather approve of the match?"

Leon's features darkened and his grip tightened on Eira's hand. "I believe so, but there were...difficulties. My mother denied father thrice before she finally said yes. Despite her rejections, they had a happy marriage that I, for one, am glad of. Without their union, I wouldn't be here to regale you with my sad little tale."

"It's always sad when a child loses a parent. Even more tragic when they lose both."

His grips softened and his fingers stroked hers. "I'm sorry, Eira. I should've been more careful with my words."

"No apology necessary. I've learned to make do with the only mother I've ever known."

"At least you've only had one to contend with. Gil and I had to endure nearly a dozen."

"That many?" she grossly underestimated the king's appetite for new brides.

"Aye, and through most all of them, Annah as well."

"I suppose I was lucky then. Still, I wish I would've known my mother and father, or at least had more than fleeting memories of them." She bit her bottom lip, unsure if she were crossing a boundary, but curiosity won out. "Was your mother's death natural?"

Leon's gaze narrowed and brows dipped, but he didn't lash out or smack her impertinence. "I see you've heard the rumors. Yes, my mother died of natural causes, and before you inquire, it was a long before Lady Annah graced us with her presence."

"I'm truly sorry for your loss." And she was. To lose one's mother when young was a wound that never fully healed.

"When Mother died, Father mourned her for two years. It broke my heart to see him alone on his throne. A few years after that, he had his accident and hasn't been the same since. Gone was the jubilant smile and easy laugh. A succession of step-mothers followed and that's when I knew my father—the man I grew up admiring and wishing to emulate—was gone. In his place was an angry stranger that terrified me."

"In that, our childhoods are not so dissimilar. There has to be a happy ending for us though, right?"

"Only if we make one ourselves." He led them to a fountain in the center of a small courtyard and bent low. "I don't think I fully understood your situation until this moment, Eira. And for that, I apologize. I was led to believe you wished for this marriage, but that's not true, is it?"

She lowered her gaze. "Regan wants this marriage. She doesn't care if I agree to it or not, she'll make certain it happens." She smoothed the front of her gown and met his gaze. "Truly, I don't understand why your father wishes for yet another wife when he has Lady Annah, and two heirs."

"Yes, curious, isn't it?" He took her hand and squeezed. "Thank you for being honest with me. And now I shall do the same. Do you wish to know why your stepmother is blackmailing me?"

Did she? Would it matter? They were getting along so well, what if he told her something that changed the trajectory of her feelings toward him?

"Only if you desire that I should know. I wouldn't want to put anyone in harm's way with the knowledge."

"Believe me, it wouldn't be you that's put anyone in danger. Only myself or your stepmother. Perhaps knowing will give you reason to trust me." Leon lowered his head until he was close enough she could smell bergamot from the tea they drank. "My mother refused my father because she had a secret she needed to hide from him and his tyrant of a father, the old king. A secret that could get her killed—she was part of a pack of shifters, men and women who could take on the shape of a wolf."

Eira shuddered when he said the last, her gaze darting across the courtyard, expecting the trackers, or even Otto himself to jump out and have them both executed for treason, but Leon didn't appear as concerned, even though his glances also looked to each corner and shadow.

"My mother never told anyone at court. She took her secret to the grave, and had hoped her sons would be spared. She was fair haired and green-eyed, like me. When my brother Gil was born, he resembled our father and Mother was relieved he didn't show any signs of being a shifter. My birth, however, filled her with joy and despair."

"You're one of them, aren't you?" A slight tremor filled her voice.

"I've hid it all my life. Even after Mother died and I was left alone to figure it out, I didn't tell a soul. Then, I met another like me, my mate as it happened."

"Mate?"

"For my kind, a mate is someone you're destined to be with. Not everyone finds their mate, but I'm one of the lucky few."

"Perhaps it wasn't luck, but Fate that brought you together." She pressed a hand to her abdomen to stop the fluttering. Destined by Fate to be together, against the odds. What a remarkable love story.

"And where are they now? Your mate?"

Leon shook his head, his eyes brimming with unshed tears. "I don't know. She disappeared nearly a fortnight past and I've been searching for her ever since."

"I'm so sorry. Do any of the others know what happened to her?"

"I don't know. I never met the others. She wanted me to, but I was too afraid. The promise of gold often loosens even the tightest of lips."

That, she understood. "I won't tell anyone. You have my word."

"Your stepmother already knows. I'm not sure how, but she's threatened to tell my father unless I help her. Sacheen would be disgusted with me if she knew I debased myself with that horrid woman." He looked at Eira with a lopsided grin. "No offense to you, but Lady Banworth truly is despicable. I just don't understand why Gil or my father can't see it. Even Lady Annah is besotted with her, and of the three of them, I always thought she was the sensible one."

Eira reeled with everything he'd said, her mind trying to pick out the most important piece of information and failing. One name thrummed through it all—Sacheen. It couldn't be the same person, but then, of course it had to be. And he didn't know she was in the dungeons, possibly beneath their very feet at that moment.

"Leon, I think I know whe—"

"Shh." He stiffened and looked over Eira's shoulder. "How the devil did she find us?"

Eira followed his gaze and there, standing between two arches on the other side of the courtyard, was Regan. She looked equally as flustered at their presence. A moment later, Eira understood why. Guillaume strolled into the walkway, tucking his shirt into his trousers. His tousled hair and sloppy grin told her everything she needed to know about what they'd been doing.

Leon faced her with a grim look settled in his features. "You can trust me, I give you my word, but please, ignore any harsh words I might say, promise?"

Words froze in her throat. Her dreams were real. There, in the bright light of day, she saw Regan and Gil—together. What else in her nightmares was real? Leon mistook her silence for acquiescence and strode away before she could stop him.

"Leon, wait." She whispered, but the words died on empty air as he took off across the courtyard.

She thrummed the book against her thigh and debated her choices for half a heartbeat before following. Dark thoughts tumbled through her mind, of wolves and cruel kings, of a man in black who was dangerous, but made her heart beat with desire. She had to tell Leon his Sacheen lived, and that she thought he'd forsaken her. But first, she wished to hear her stepmother's lies as she explained the situation with the crown prince.

By the time she reached the small group, Guillaume was already berating Leon for spying on them, a complete falsehood, but Leon didn't refute his brother's claim. Eira seethed internally as she listened to Gil threaten Leon. It was Regan who stopped the tirade with a raised hand.

"Obviously, there has been a misunderstanding. The prince and I were simply enjoying a stroll in this fine weather. Had we known you were nearby, we would've invited you to join us. Seeing as it's been an exciting day, Eira and I need to rest before we ready ourselves for dinner."

"But I'm not tired, Stepmother. Leon and I haven't yet finished our tour of the palace."

"Oh, but you have, darling. Come now, no arguing." Rebecca took Eira by the elbow and steered her away from the princes. "I should like to know why you secreted yourself away in a deserted courtyard." Regan's voice, low and threatening, hissed near her ear.

"We weren't secreted anywhere." She held up the book. "We went to the library and then through the palace, in plain view of anyone who wished to see us." Unlike some people, she added mentally. The hypocrisy was ridiculous.

Regan took the book and flipped through the pages as they rushed through an expansive hallway. They were in the palace proper now, in the areas where courtiers would see them. Eira was slightly taken aback that Regan would parade her through the galleries and not take them up the servants' stairs. Then she remembered the expensive gown and fancy hairdo. She reached a hand to the ornate style and sighed.

Regan thrust the book at her with a snort of disgust. "Lovely, yet another fairytale to fill your mind with fluff. You're to be queen, Eira, you should be reading something more profound."

"Like what?" She didn't recall there being any great tomes of literature in the castle. If there had been, she would've read them all.

"Never mind." Regan rubbed her temple as they ascended the grand staircase.

Neither spoke the rest of the way to their rooms. Upon entering, Regan made a signal to one of the maids who stood to attention beside the sofa. She immediately rushed from the room without a word. The second maid, the one who had brushed Eira's hair the other morning and seemed sympathetic to her situation, waited with hands folded across her abdomen.

"Ready her for bed. I'll be in my rooms. When the other girl returns, let me know."

"It's too early for bed, Stepmother. Besides, won't the king begin to wonder what happened to me if I don't show up for dinner?"

"Don't you worry about Otto, darling. He knows you're here and is happy to wait to meet you on your wedding day. I think he likes the thrill of the unknown." She winked and it made Eira's stomach twist.

"But what if I'd like to meet him first? He will be my husband, after all."

Regan half-turned and regarded Eira with a look of venom. "What you want isn't important, darling."

"Yes, it is." Eira stood firm, her arms crossed over her chest. "I don't want to marry Otto and I have no aspiration to be queen."

In a flash, Regan stood before her, hand outstretched. Eira braced herself for the blow, startled all the same at the power behind the slap. She fell sideways and lost her footing. The floor came up to meet her with astonishing speed. Her head bounced on the marble, sending sparks of light behind her eyes, and a ricochet of pain throughout her body.

The door opened and Eira saw the maid's booted feet shuffle to where Regan fumed above her crumpled body.

"Hold her down."

Two pairs of hands grabbed her roughly and she cried out for them to please stop, but was ignored. A heavy body lay over hers to prevent her from kicking out. Panic, raw, intense, and all-consuming raged through her. She tried to thrash, to free herself, but whoever pinned her down was far stronger. The bulk of their weight pressed down on her, stealing the air from her lungs. She gasped and wheezed as if she were a fish caught out of water.

Regan's face filled her vision. "If you aren't going to behave, then I'm afraid you need to be punished. Now, drink your tea, darling."

A cup was held to her lips and she closed her mouth against the steaming liquid. She jerked her head from side to side.

"No, don't." She kicked and struggled to get out of their hold, but it was no use.

Regan gripped her cheeks, forcing her mouth open. "Do it. Now."

Liquid poured into her open mouth, choking her. She gagged against it, but Regan shut her lips and held her hand over Eira's mouth until she swallowed. Bitterness stung the back of her throat as the drugged tea slithered to her belly. Immediately, her body went limp, her mind woozy. From the tea, lack of oxygen, or her own defeat, she wasn't certain.

Regan's mocking laughter flooded Eira's ears. "See? I told you. She's too meek to fight. Like a lamb to the slaughter."

Eira chilled at her stepmother's words. She'd heard them before.

Her thoughts warbled, moving in hazy undulations that made no sense. Prickling crept up her skin. Regan's magic. What more could she take from Eira that she hadn't already destroyed?

More tea was forced into her mouth and she didn't fight. There was no point.

Henri, Eira cast the thought, hoping beyond hope that he hadn't betrayed her and could help. Then her mind went blank.

Chapter Twenty-One

Wolves chased her, their powerful jaws snapping at the fringe on her sleeves. Their terrible snarls promised a painful death, and Eira ran faster. It was to no avail. One more step and they'd tear her flesh. Her blood would cover their paws and they'd howl their excitement.

Breathless and spent, she surrendered to her fate. Yet instead of wolves chasing her, when she turned to face her killers, it was the huntsman. In his hand wasn't an axe, but a slim dagger. Regan goaded him to rip out her heart, her wicked laughter ringing through Eira's mind, stinging through her blood.

"Wake up, princess." Henri's sweet voice taunted her, and she squeezed her eyes closed. "Eira, please."

What was that in his tone? Desperation? Determination? Death?

"You'll kill me."

"I promise you, I won't."

Was it a dream? Another nightmare? Another callous reality she wouldn't remember? Her head throbbed and body ached as if she actually had been running through a forest. The softness of her bed clouded her judgement. What was real? It was becoming harder and harder to know.

Warm breath tickled her cheek, "Come back to me. Please forgive me."

Forgive him? For killing her? But he said he wouldn't. He couldn't be trusted. This was another nightmare, more cruel and devious than all the others. Why would he be kind to her if he was going to carve out her heart with a dagger?

Lips, warm and firm pressed against her closed mouth and a firework of desire lit in her blood. Sparks flared from her nerve endings and for one glorious moment, she knew the absolute truth of everything, but then her mind snapped to Henri and his sweet kiss. Her lips softened, accepting and trusting. Her first kiss. Somehow, it was only fitting it should be with Henri.

She suppressed a moan and opened her eyes, half-afraid of what she might find. There, gazing at her not with death in his impossibly midnight-hued eyes, but affection, was the huntsman. Her Henri.

"You kissed me."

"I did."

Her fingertips traced along her lips where he'd left a trail of heat. "Why?"

"To wake you from your deep sleep." His eyes filled with worry and he stroked her face. "I was desperate and didn't know what else to do."

As much as she craved more of his touch, she didn't know what to believe. "Am I dreaming? They've been so...realistic of late, I hardly know what is true." She rubbed her temples to relieve the headache that throbbed against her skull. "Beasts, and the princes, lies and betrayals. Before that, you and Regan were talking. She was with—" Eira cut short the memory of Regan with Guillaume. When was that? It seemed so long ago, and yet as if she'd just dreamed it before the wolves attacked. Time was blurring one moment into the next until events were melded together. "They were horrible."

"You're not dreaming now." He stood at the side of her bed and gazed at her as if she were a riddle he'd not yet solved. "Although, you do seem to sleep quite a lot."

"Not by choice." She mumbled and blinked into the brightness of the sun's rays that streamed in through the window. "What time is it?"

"Not yet breakfast. Your stepmother is still sleeping, so we must be quick. I've convinced her to let me take you riding and we can't risk her changing her mind."

"Riding? Where?" A thrum of anxiety rippled through her veins. *Please don't say the forest.*

"It's a surprise. Now, get dressed quickly."

She didn't like surprises. They usually ended with her getting beaten and locked in her room. Yet the chance to leave the palace and her waking nightmares, if even for a few short hours, was too tempting. She'd not had time to plan much of an escape, but riding would give her a chance to work out a scheme, perhaps even with Henri's help.

She tossed the covers aside and immediately covered herself, realizing too late that she only wore a thin nightdress.

"Turn around. Or better yet, wait in the sitting room." She waved her hand toward the door, but he shook his head.

"I'm not leaving you alone. You've proved you're a master at disappearing, and I'll not be chasing you through hidden passageways all day. It seems I always find you here, snoring as loudly as Hamlin." He leaned against the door and crossed his arms to make his point.

"I do not snore!"

The throbbing in her head made thinking unbearable. She

gingerly felt her skull, unsurprised to find a small lump on the left side. She vaguely recalled falling and her stepmother's laughter. Before that, a library, or was she misremembering? No, she definitely went to the library to search for something, but... what? Everything jumbled in her mind, frustrating her with amorphous thoughts.

"My head aches."

"I know the perfect cure, but you might want to dress first. Riding naked isn't all that comfortable. Or so I've been told." Henri grinned and her belly flipped at the sweetness of his teasing.

"Fine, but I'm not changing with you watching."

"I have four sisters. Do you think I've never seen a woman's body before?"

"You've never seen my body, and I'd like to keep it that way." Although, the idea of him seeing her naked didn't alarm her as much as it should. In fact, she felt a peculiar little thrill at the thought, especially when those thoughts led to her seeing him unclothed. A memory of a night not long past, tickled her mind. She'd thought he might be in the shadows, and had done nothing to cover her very exposed body. Lawks, why did he have to look at her in such a way that made her breasts tingle and legs wobble?

"Would you rather I was Prince Leon? Would you mind him seeing you undressed?"

"Don't be ridiculous." Why was he jealous? She tried to recall what she might've done to make him think she fancied the prince, but nothing came to mind. "At least cover your eyes."

He put a hand over his face. "Better?"

It would have to do. She struggled into a pair of stockings, trying her best to keep her nightdress from slipping, and then tugged a sensible gown over her head. The nightdress would have to act as a chemise for the day. Sturdy boots, a wool cape, and she was ready.

"Done."

He peered at her from behind his hand and grinned. "I don't think even my sisters could dress as quickly, nor look as fetching. Shall we be off?"

He held the door open, and she sashayed toward him, pride swelling in her bosom. Compliments were few from the sullen man.

As she passed the table, she caught sight of a basket filled with apples and paused. A pit of guilt made her belly leaden. Apples to sustain her. No, not her, but who? Who was in the dungeons that was so important? She wracked her brain trying to come up with an image or a name, but there was...nothing.

"What is it?"

"I need to take these to the dungeons first."

"Is that where you were the other morning when I found you creeping up the stairs?"

"I think so. Yes, definitely, and I wasn't creeping. I was being stealthy." Why did she need secrecy? Faces and places rushed through her skull, overwhelming her. She put a hand to her forehead in an impotent effort to slow her thoughts. "Everything's all jumbled and confusing."

"What's the last thing you remember?" His voice lowered to a serious tone.

She scrunched her face, thinking, grasping at puzzle pieces that wouldn't fit. "Leon, in a courtyard?"

"Yes, then you left with Regan. What happened once you returned to your rooms?"

The attack came back in a flash of memory that made her stagger. Henri caught her before her legs gave way fully.

"I've got you. Here, sit for a moment." He put her in a cushioned chair and poured a glass of water before returning with an admonition to drink.

She hesitated, not trusting the clear liquid. "They forced me to drink the drugged tea. I tried to fight them, but they overpowered me."

"Who? Regan and Gil?"

"The maids and my stepmother. I told her I didn't want to marry Otto." She raised the glass with shaking hands and took a sip of the cool liquid. Her stomach recoiled, but she forced herself to swallow.

"I'm sorry, Eira. I should've been here. When you left with Regan, I remained hidden in the shadows, believing erroneously that you would be fine for the few minutes I wasn't trailing you. I was wrong and for that, I beg your forgiveness."

"There's no need for an apology. Regan isn't your problem."

He sat in the chair beside her and took her hand in his. "She is now. When I did arrive here, to your room, you were slumbering peacefully. Again, I erroneously thought you'd decided to retire early. But then you didn't wake and I feared the worst. Eira, you were asleep for three full days this time."

"That long? But how?" She felt the injury, wincing at the sensitivity on her skull. "I fell and hit my head before they drugged me."

"You had me worried you'd never wake. In fact, there were moments I believed you'd passed, your breathing was so shallow, and heartbeat near-nonexistent. I doubt that came from bumping your head."

A sleeping death. She spun through her memory for a spell from the grimoire, but came up empty. If it wasn't in Regan's spell book, then perhaps her stepmother wasn't behind the long sleep. If not her, then who? And again, why? Her gaze went to her vanity, but no teacups were there. What had the maid given her with the viridian? The name slipped her mind, but she was certain it would come to her.

Henri watched her with a worried frown. Genuine emotion flitted across his features and settled in his eyes. She hoped she hadn't confessed too much and he felt the need to cancel their lovely outing.

She cocked her head and considered Henri anew. "Why are you concerned about me? I thought you were hired to spy on me, not care for me."

A curious look crossed his features—not quite anger, but certainly irritation. "The reasons for taking the job are my own, as are my feelings. I would think you'd be grateful for some compassion, but if you prefer I not show concern, then I shall remain stoic and uncaring."

"You're terribly confusing."

"Only when around you. Shall we?" He picked up the basket and headed for the door.

Sacheen. She was the woman in the dungeons. Lawks, she probably thought Eira had abandoned her. The name swirled through her skull, a lingering need drifting just out of reach. What was she supposed to remember?

"Wait." She dashed to her wardrobe and grabbed a warm coat, chemise, and a pair of thick socks. It wasn't much, but perhaps would keep Sacheen from freezing. Was that all? What else was there? On the way to the door, she snatched a comb from her dressing table and slipped it beside the apples before taking the basket from the huntsman.

With compassion once again softening his features, he shuffled her out the door. "We'll need to be quick, and there won't be any skulking through the palace. I know another way into the dungeons."

Naturally, he would. He probably knew of every secret place perfect for spying.

Henri led her through the wide hallway where her room was located, and past about a dozen closed doors before he turned and motioned for her to follow him down a nondescript stairwell. The bare stone steps and limited décor hinted that these were public stairs meant for upper servants' use. Valets and personal maids, perhaps even a private cook, but not for scullery maids or stable boys. By now, Eira was used to sneaking along servants' corridors, even expected it.

What she didn't expect was to be directed to the kitchens.

"This way. Why do you do it?"

"What?"

Henri pointed at the basket. "Why risk punishment for a prisoner?"

"They're people, too. Just because they ran afoul of the law doesn't mean they should be treated poorly." She passed a pair of servants and lowered her voice. "I met a woman, wretched thing in scraps that looked like she hadn't seen a meal in weeks. The king might forget about her, but I cannot."

His eyes narrowed and jaw tightened, and for a moment he simply gazed at her with a look of confused wonder.

"How are you so good when you've been raised by a woman so vile?"

Eira's shoulders lifted in a shrug. It was a conundrum she'd often asked herself. "I suppose I never wanted for others what I experienced. It's not fair, but then, life rarely is."

In the quiet of the hallway, they stood a pace apart, separated by nothing more than their prejudices and positions. Henri reached a hand to stroke her hair and she willed her heart to slow, for time itself to stretch to infinity for this one moment. His fingertips blazed across her forehead to cup her head and she leaned into his touch, yearning for more, needed more. Craving everything he would give her.

His eyes sought hers and she held his gaze, afraid to look

away lest the moment end. Those lips, the ones that had brought her from her deep sleep, curved in the smallest of smiles and he bent forward as if to kiss her again. Thrumming pulsed low between her legs where an ache so strong and deep threatened to drown her with desire. His grip tightened on her head and gently pulled her close, so close, until their lips nearly touched. Yes, please. She closed her eyes with needy expectation. Just one more kiss.

Chapter Twenty-Two

A door opened and the serenity of the moment was broken by the cacophony coming from the kitchens. Henri pulled back, his features sliding into a mask of indifference within a heartbeat. Eira reeled from the loss of his touch, the promise of his lips.

A servant rushed out, snickering as he passed. Henri glowered at him and she could almost read his thoughts. They played a dangerous game, showing affection even here, in the bowels of the palace, where servants and staff loved to gossip. If word got back to the king that she was seen snogging the huntsman, they both might lose their heads.

She pulled herself up and put on a haughty expression to ward herself from the chaos in her heart. With a sigh, Henri led her to the doorway and pushed it open, escorting her to the tumultuous realm of the kitchens. Cooks shouted at their charges, and sweaty-faced youths scurried from one meal station to another. Henri nodded to a large man with forearms the size of a sapling. He cocked his head to the left and bellowed an order to a ragged-looking thing Eira wasn't sure was male, female, or even human.

It had to be human. King Otto wouldn't tolerate a magical being in his kitchen, would he? And what sort of creature might it be, if not human? If dwarves were real, and men could shift into wolves, then certainly faeries and elves had to be real, too. Possibly even trolls. What about mermaids? Or ogres? Suddenly, a plethora of possibilities opened in her mind, of strange and wonderful worlds and creatures that she'd only read about in supposed nursery tales.

Eira snuck a furtive glance at the being, but its shaggy brown hair hid most of its features. Her gaze shifted to the floor, and she was disappointed to see regular, distinctly unfurred, feet sticking out from beneath cotton trousers.

"Stop dawdling. We've not much time."

"Time for what?"

She hurried after Henri and slipped into a cool pantry. The smell of flour surrounded them and she was instantly filled with happy memories of baking. She hoped they were of her mother and father, but how could they be when her mother had died when she was only three. Henri clucked at her to hurry and she didn't linger, despite wanting to stay and relive more memories.

"Wait here. I'll only be a moment, I promise."

She gripped the basket and watched him skirt around the shaggy being to snatch a loaf of bread off one table, and a hunk of cheese off another. The large man ignored Henri, even though she was sure he saw everything Henri took. One more grab, this time a bottle, and he returned as promised.

"If that's for us, I'd rather it go to the prisoner." She didn't want to appear ungrateful, but knew Sacheen needed the food more.

"There's plenty for all of us."

He hustled her past bags of grain to a small wooden door at the back of the pantry. It creaked when he opened it, but instead of being worried about the sound, he yanked harder until the door hung wide. He bent low and shuffled through, indicating she follow. She crouched through the opening and rose into a cramped space lit by a single torch.

She sidled beside him, aware of their proximity, and tried to ignore the scent of freshly laundered clothing. Why did he always have to smell so damn good? And where would a huntsman wash his clothes? In a forest stream? That might explain the subtle hints of pine and, oh, goddess she really needed to stop breathing through her nose where scents tingled and teased.

Henri pulled the door closed and she was left in semi-darkness with the man who, despite smelling like heaven and possessing lips she dreamed of kissing, could quite possibly lead to her death just by being seen with her. And certainly he'd be executed as well.

And yet, she wasn't frightened. Her stomach grumbled its unhappy state, and she reached inside the basket.

"Where did those come from? I don't recall them being on the table earlier." His hand covered hers—warm and strong, protective.

"I don't know. My first morning here a strange woman gave me a basket of apples and said I should explore the palace. I ended up in the dungeons and shared them with the prisoner." She looked up at him and tried not to notice the tilt of his lips and how they were entirely too seductive.

Her breath caught and chest tightened. They were indecently close and without anyone there to spy on her. Well, except for Henri, who was literally paid to spy on her. Would he tell Regan of their adventure? Of their near kiss?

Trust the huntsman.

He had promised not to kill her.

"You're staring." One dark brow arched over his even darker eye and his lips quirked in a grin.

She glanced away, a furious blush warming her cheeks. How could she not stare at him? He was rather handsome when he wasn't being terrifying. He took a bite of apple and offered her the same. A memory of Guillaume in the orchard soured her stomach, but she refused to let him torment her time with Henri. She leaned forward and sunk her teeth into the apple's flesh. Juice ran down her chin and Henri's eyes glazed with a feral kind of hunger.

Every fiber in her body willed him to lick the juice from her skin, but he left her wanting. They finished the apple in silence, Eira too afraid to speak lest she beg him to kiss her again. He wiped his mouth with the edge of his sleeve and delicately dabbed at her chin. It would have to do.

He eased himself into the cramped tunnel and she followed close. Within a few minutes, they entered the same part of the dungeons she'd found the other day and she sighed with relief. Not that she hadn't believed him, but trust came reluctantly with her.

At her approach, Sacheen emerged from the shadows with a bemused smile on her face.

"I was wondering if I'd see you again, Lady Cannaid. I wouldn't blame you for forgetting I exist, that's what you royals are good at. And looky here, you brought a friend." Her gaze went to Henri and her brow rose, her lips curled. "By the goddess, if it isn't—"

"Henri. Just, Henri." He took the basket from Eira and broke off half the loaf of bread and a sizeable chunk of cheese. These he placed in the basket, along with the sealed bottle and handed everything to Sacheen. "We brought more apples and other foods to sustain you. I would recommend you don't drink the wine too quickly."

Sacheen nodded, the corners of her eyes crinkling against

the grime. She placed the food in the same corner where she'd hidden the apples previously and returned the basket to Eira.

"I brought you some clothing, and there's a comb with the apples," she glanced into the back of the cell, "somewhere."

"A comb? I'm stuck in a shithole and you think I want to comb my hair? Fucking royalty." Sacheen shook her head and glared at Eira. "I suppose you think your charity makes you a better person. You're probably fool enough to believe there's such a thing as true love, too. Well, don't be deluded. True love is a myth and I don't need fucking apples from a dimwitted royal. What I need is to escape, so unless you have a key stashed in that basket, fuck off."

"There's no need to be ungrateful." Henri warned. "Eira is taking quite a risk by coming here."

"It's all right, Henri. Sacheen's anger is coming from a place of hurt and isn't personal."

"Sacheen?" Henri looked at the woman anew, his gaze scrutinizing her features as if he might recognize her through the filth.

Eira's mind buzzed with a thought—a memory—but it wouldn't settle long enough for her to fully remember why it was important.

Sacheen scoffed and snatched the proffered clothing from Eira's hands. "Thank you, m'lady." She bowed low, a sneer on her lips.

Eira gripped the bars and stood as close to Sacheen as the cell would allow. "Why are you in here?"

"Ask him." Sacheen tilted her chin toward Henri with a low growl.

Henri's fingers brushed hers as he held the bars. His lips moved and he spoke words, but she couldn't hear them for the pulsing in her veins. In addition to the warmth spreading through her blood, she felt the sweetest tinge of something elusive, something she'd been blocked from for most of her life. Her magic struggled to break free, but it was...trapped.

Images flooded her mind—of Leon and sandwiches, wolves and crowns, wounds and books, of Leon striding toward Regan on a sunny day near a fountain. And of Gil's sneer.

"I remember." Eira grabbed Henri's sleeve. "Guillaume and Regan, the other day when Leon and I went to the library, he told me about his mother."

"Queen Issa?"

She nodded and glanced at Sacheen. "Prince Leon is your mate, isn't he?"

Sacheen glared at her. "You mean that spineless coward who's left me here to rot? Don't remind me."

"You've got it all wrong. Leon doesn't know you're here." Eira held the bars and met Sacheen's angry gaze. "The way he spoke about you, if he knew, he would rip this palace apart to free you, of that I'm certain."

Sacheen's eyes softened and her features went slack. "How could he not know? I've been missing for two weeks at least."

"And he's been searching for you just as long." Henri offered. "Every forest, every cell, he must be unable to enter these dungeons if he's been unsuccessful in his quest."

"He's injured." Eira blurted before she could stop herself. When the other two looked at her she blushed and wrung her hands. "I saw him being bandaged that first day when you unceremoniously dumped me in the meadow."

Henri winced. "Would you believe me if I said it was an accident?"

"It was intentional, don't deny it. Though, I don't know why —I hadn't had a chance to vex you yet."

"Well, you've certainly made up for it since." His grin gave her delicious flutters across her skin.

"Hello? Prisoner here. Need answers about Leon." Sacheen

snapped her fingers in front of their faces. "You can argue about who's more irritating later, when you're far from here. Leon's injured and doesn't know I'm locked up. Why?" She bit her thumb and paced a small circle. "The king's whore, possibly, but when has Leon ever been a threat to her? Henri, how many others have been captured?"

Eira ignored the familiarity with which the two conversed. If she let her mind wander into that particular direction, she might lose herself for good.

"I'd say half a dozen. They're being held in the common dungeons."

"Together or separate?"

Henri looked to the ceiling, eyes narrowed. "Not sure, but I'd wager together. I'll see what I can find out and report back."

Report back? Was Sacheen some sort of general among the wolves?

"Can't you pick the lock or something to release her?" Eira was tempted to touch the heavy iron lock that hung on a chain securing the cell door closed. Her heart thrummed with the need to help.

"It's possible, but knowing King Otto, he had a spell placed on this whole cell to prevent his prisoner from using magic to escape." Henri explained and Sacheen nodded.

"Already tried that. Got a nasty shock for my efforts." She rubbed the underside of her wrist and grimaced.

"I don't understand why a king that abhors magic has a witch for a mistress and unabashedly uses magic to do his bidding. Why the hypocrisy?"

Sacheen and Henri looked at her as if she were the dullest child in the kingdom.

"What better way to hide something than to have it out in the open? Pretend to hate the very thing you need. And trust me, the king needs our magic. So does his whore witch." Sacheen spit into the darkness and Eira's stomach roiled, but not from her gross display.

Her fears about the marriage were becoming all too real. A lamb for the slaughter. More likely, her pureblood power to feed the ailing king. She hadn't been mistaken in what she saw—Otto was dying. If the court knew about his illness, they hid it well. What else did they conceal behind their feathered fans and expensive frocks? What other hypocrisies did they ascribe to?

A chilling rivulet of dread swirled through her veins to that place where her magic remained dormant and she knew the awful truth of why she'd been brought to the palace and bartered for a disgusting sum of silver.

She wasn't meant to be a bride for the king, but a cure.

Chapter Twenty-Three

Two saddled horses awaited them in the stables, and Eira gleefully stroked her mare's muzzle. It had been so long since she'd been riding, she hoped she hadn't forgotten how to stay astride. When she saw the saddle, her excitement doubled. There wasn't a top pommel in sight, only flaps and stirrups on both sides of the horse. It would take some finagling of her skirt, but she was determined to make it work.

The stable boy approached to help her into the saddle, but Henri extended his hand to assist. When their fingers met, a tremor sparked between them and jolted up her arm. His cocked head and raised brow was enough to tell her that he'd felt it, too. Sacheen's odd behavior popped to mind. Something had happened to soften her edges, but what? And why suddenly did Eira feel a tremor when Henri touched her? She hoisted herself up and concentrated on situating herself without giving away her modesty.

The stable boy took the basket from Henri and handed him a cloth sack to hold their food. This was secured to the back of Henri's saddle and Eira's stomach growled its unhappy state. They'd eat when they stopped, she told herself, hoping it was true—and soon. The apple they shared would only satiate her for so long.

Once she was comfortable in the seat, with her skirt and cape draped demurely around her, he easily swung himself atop his own horse. Show-off. Although, seeing his ease with the animals delighted her, even if she couldn't say why.

They left the stables and palace grounds through a gate to the north of the palace. By the look of it, only supply carts used the gate, and she scanned the road for the randy pair she saw on her first day at the palace. At that early hour, the courtyard was empty, save for them and a lone wagon laden with barrels.

After passing through the gate, Henri urged his horse into a canter and her mare followed suit. Wind rushed across her face, tugging at her loose hair. Laughter bubbled up from the depths of her to burst forth with unexpected force. It had been so long since she'd laughed, she'd almost forgotten what it felt like. Joy, pure and unrestrained, flowed through her, and she urged her horse faster until she passed Henri.

His gelding galloped ahead, his laughter booming over the pounding hooves. They raced for what seemed a league before he turned them toward the forest and her gaiety snuffed out like a candle. He glanced at her, his lips pursed and eyes narrowed.

"What is it?"

"The forest. Regan forbade me from going into the woods near our home, but I would sometimes sneak away to a little spot that I claimed as my own. But this place..." A shudder scratched down her spine as she recalled how the forest had beckoned her that first day. "I don't know these woods, and there was a man murdered here not long ago."

Henri reached over to clasp her hand. "I promise nothing will harm you here."

Another promise. Was he only being kind to lure her into a trap? She shrugged off the thought and nodded.

"If you say you'll protect me, then I believe you." Now who was lying?

It was too nice a day, and she was finally free of the palace, to worry about betrayals and dying.

They walked their horses through the tall trees and immediately they were surrounded by the soft hush of the woods. Birdsong came from above them and the squelching of hooves below. She pulled her cape tight and searched the trees for anything untoward. Despite his declaration, Henri didn't wear a sword, nor any other weapon she could see. Not even an axe.

Several rabbits darted from the path to the undergrowth and in the distance, she saw a doe flick her ears before dashing away. It was calm beneath the canopy. Serene. She found it hard to believe anything awful could happen here, yet that was only wishful thinking. Thieves and murderers were just as likely to be hiding behind the next bush as they were to be found out on the roads. Or in a palace, disguised as a benevolent spy.

The farther they rode into the forest, the greater her unease grew. They were long past the point where she could call for help if anything should happen. And this far in, it would be easy enough to hide a body. Lawks, the animals would make quick work of disposing of her corpse, leaving nothing for the king to find.

Stop it. She shook her head and forced the terrible thoughts from her mind.

By the time they approached a charming cottage with thatched roof and timber beams, she was equally relieved and terrified. Trust the huntsman. Madam Davina's words pulsed through her skull with every beat of her heart. She wanted to— the goddess knew she desperately wanted to trust the man in black who was no less a stranger today than he was a sennight earlier. Had it truly been a full week since she arrived at the palace? She counted backward, allowing for the days she slept and came to this being her seventh day.

That meant her marriage to the king was skipping ever nearer, quicker than she'd like, and she was no closer to finding an escape than she'd when she first heard Regan utter the horrible words that Eira was to marry Otto. Her gaze went to Henri. He looked at the cottage and wore a smile so serene it made her wonder at the occupants of such a sweet home.

"My friends live here. Why don't we stop to let the horses rest and have a cup of tea?"

"Tea sounds lovely." She shunted her doubts and disbelief. If Henri wished her to sit for a cuppa and chat like old friends, then she would play along until she knew his real reason for bringing her leagues away from the palace.

They left the horses to graze in the overgrown garden and entered through a back door barely tall enough for her. Henri had to crouch low, which brought a welcome giggle to her lips. The dark thoughts she'd allowed to crowd her mind lingered, and she didn't at all like where they led.

Inside, the high ceiling allowed Henri to stand and while he heated water on the little stove and then made up a fire in the too large for the room fireplace, she explored the tidy cottage. The occupants took great care with their possessions, displaying treasured rocks on the mantel, and lining their spices proudly on a shelf near the hob. Nothing was out of place, except three distinct markings above each doorway.

She traced one of the scratches with her finger, but nothing came to her of how they were made or what they symbolized. Protection, perhaps, but for what? Henri watched, yet said nothing as he left the tea to brew and stoked the fire. He was comfortable in the cottage, enough so that he thought nothing of making himself at home while the owners were away.

Eira didn't have to guess who lived there. The seven plates

and seven tankards set neatly around the table, not to mention the seven little beds crowded to one side of the room, indicated this was the home of the dwarves she'd met in the meadow her first day. She wandered among the beds, imagining who would sleep in each. They were all made, with corners tucked and pillows plumped. Except the last one. The turned-down duvet wasn't as crisp as the others, and sitting atop the pillow was a felt toy.

"That's Gorse's bed. He suffers from nightmares and that wee dog gives him comfort."

She reached for the stuffed animal and paused. "May I?"

"I don't see why not. He was quite taken with you the other day."

The felt covering was scratchy beneath the soft pads of her fingers, and she sensed the love put into making the toy.

"Dorton made this for him, didn't he?" What would that feel like? That much love shown without restraint, without fear? Unconditional love given and reciprocated. Love she'd never know.

"He did." Henri handed her a steaming mug, and she breathed in the scent of spiced apples.

"This isn't tea."

"Don't tell Hamlin that. He swears by his special brew. Says it'll give you stamina and heal that which ails you."

"I don't think this small amount will help me." A sad little chuckle punctuated her words. She'd need an entire vat to heal her wounds.

Henri's dark eyes didn't leave her as he took a long swig. When finished, he smacked his lips. "I feel much better already. Come on now, drink up."

With a soft shrug, she sipped the fragrant tea. What did she have to lose?

Besides her life.

"Did you bring me out here to kill me?"

"What is it with you and death? No, I didn't. I told you, I won't harm you." He set his cup on the table and picked up the bag with their food. He meticulously laid it out without disturbing the dwarves' cutlery. A pause, and then he glanced at her with narrowed eyes, lips pursed. "Did your stepmother say something about me?"

Eira snorted a laugh. "Only every day of my life." She drew in a deep breath. Now was as good a time as any to tell him her real reasons for fearing him. If he was truly the huntsman come to take her heart, at least he'd know she wasn't fooled by his innocent act. "When I was born, it was prophesied that I'd die at the hands of a huntsman. Quite brutally, as it were. The prophecy said he'd take me to the forest and hunt me like a fox. When I was too exhausted to run any longer, he'd take his jeweled dagger and rip out my heart."

There. Now he knew.

Anger flashed in his gorgeous eyes. "That's horrifying. Did your stepmother tell you those lies? No wonder you have a hard time trusting people." He stood near the fire, right hand pressed to his chest. "I give you my word, I will not hunt you to exhaustion only to toy with you, nor will I, or anyone else, rip out your heart. Or any other important bodily organ. I simply won't allow it."

Despite herself, she chuckled. It was such an asinine claim to make. She set her tea beside his before joining him near the fire and held out her hands to warm them. Despite the wool cloak, a sudden chill snaked its way into her veins.

"You don't know Regan. She's—" Eira stopped herself from saying too much.

"A witch? Yes, I know."

He moved close enough she could smell the apples on his breath and she forced herself to stay in the moment, to not let fear or nerves or his sweetly seductive body scare her off. Since he'd promised not to kill her, then perhaps she could allow herself to trust him a little. She could use another friend in the palace.

He held her gaze, intensity burning to her core. "She tried to use a spell on me. That made it quite obvious."

"Tried to? What do you mean?" She kept her focus on his eyes, not trusting herself to look at his lips. They were utterly kissable. They were her doom.

Henri lowered his head, and she froze in place, unsure what he would do next. Wishing, willing him to do the forbidden. Being here with him, allowing kisses and sneaking moments were sheer bliss, but they were also treasonous.

"The power that flows through your veins also flows through mine. We are more alike than you'd ever guess, Lady Cannaid."

His whisper struck fear in her heart, and she turned away from his words, but he gripped her arm and held her firm. Unlike Regan's grasp, Henri's didn't hurt.

"Don't run. Please."

Panic raced through her blood, making her lightheaded and she shook her head, still desperate to hide her magic. "You're wrong. I'm not like that." Then, barely audible: "She'll kill me if she finds out."

"And that's why we're here, far from her spies and that bloody mirror. She won't find out from me, of that I give you my word." He wiped her eyes with a thumb and held her face between his hands. "I'm not the enemy, Eira. I would very much like to be a friend. That trust you are so reluctant to give, I would like to earn so that you truly believe the words I speak."

His eyes searched hers, and she felt him penetrating her defenses. Slowly, deliberately, and with such care it almost made her weep, he was breaking down the walls she'd built and rebuilt over the years. She had to stop him. Couldn't let him in—

couldn't allow herself to be vulnerable. And yet...and yet she was so very tired of hiding. Of denying herself even a morsel of happiness.

"Why do you think I'm at the palace?" he whispered, his face close enough she could almost taste the apple tea on this tongue.

Lawks, but she wanted to kiss him, to taste every inch of his body, to feel his weight upon hers. She couldn't. Shouldn't.

"I don't know why you're there, only that Regan's paying you to spy on me. I want to know, but I'm also afraid this is some sort of elaborate trap. I don't know who I can trust or what horror awaits me in the next minute. I want to trust you—to know who you are, but I'm scared." Scared she might like who he is, might even feel more for him, but then he'd be taken away and she'd be alone again.

"I'm here to protect you, Eira. Among other things."

Her breath caught, and she stepped backward, out of his hold. The loss of his touch was almost as unbearable as his words.

"Protect me? Why would you say such a thing? You don't know me."

He didn't reach for her, and she ached for his strength. Why would a stranger, a huntsman, protect her?

He raked a hand through his hair and blew out a breath as he stared at the ceiling. "I know you're kind enough to take food to a complete stranger. I know you risked your own safety to guarantee that of another woman. I know you have a helluva right hook." His lopsided grin tickled her belly. "And I know you are so much more than what they'd have you believe."

The way he looked at her—as though she mattered, and with desire skirting the edges of his dark eyes—made her almost willing to believe his words. Yet Prince Guillaume's taunts lingered in her mind. Her worth was already determined.

Or was it? Henri had brought her out into the woods, far from the palace and Regan's mirror so that they could have privacy. So that she could think without the distraction of her stepmother looming overhead. What if he also brought her here so that he could seduce her?

Her heart did a giddy little flip and she licked her dry lips, not altogether disliking the idea. Her mind spun with thoughts, wild ideas, and images of Henri that emboldened her to look past the palace to an entirely new reality. One fraught with the unknown, but one she controlled.

The last she checked, she was in control of her body: not the prince, not Regan, and certainly not the king. She alone could decide who she loved, who she shared her bed with. What if...? No, it was too dangerous to even think it. But then, why not? Why wait for some man she despised to ruin her? She was more than capable of doing that herself. Then they'd have no choice but to cast her aside, her worth valueless.

Eira unclasped her cloak and lay it over one of the chairs. Henri watched her as if he tracked a hawk on a cloudy day. And who better to ruin her than the man who professed such lovely promises of friendship and protection?

She unbuttoned the first two buttons on her gown. "Make love to me, Henri. Here, now."

He reached a hand toward her, and her heart skipped several beats. Yes, this was right. She'd remove herself from the games by destroying her virginity.

Henri's hand covered hers, and he looked at her with such sadness she couldn't bear it. She knew what he'd say even before the whispered word tortured her ears.

"No."

Chapter Twenty-Four

Eira stared at Henri a long time before she was able to corral her cacophonous thoughts into words. Shame poured through her veins and her cheeks reddened from humiliation. Every other man in the palace, or so it seemed, was eager to ruin her. Every other man except this one. The only one she'd trusted the tiniest bit to help. He said he'd protect her. What kind of protection was he providing by denying her?

The fire cracked and she startled at the sound. She had to leave, to get as far away from him as she could. What a fool she was. She thought he shared her feelings, but she truly was an innocent when it came to love. Regan would mock her until her dying day for being so stupid.

"I'm sorry—I thought—I didn't mean—" It was no use. Her stammering excuses only inflamed her embarrassment more. Unwelcome tears slipped over her cheeks and she angrily swiped at them. "I should return to the palace. I'm sure my stepmother and the princes will be worried."

"Eira," Henri took her hands in his and stared deep into her eyes, "I would love nothing more than to spend the entire day making love to you, but because you desire me, not because I'm convenient."

Lawks, she did desire him. More than she'd realized. More than she had any right to. More than desired, but the word stilled on her tongue. To speak it aloud meant it could be taken from her.

Her chest tightened, and she sucked in air. "You would give up the chance to fuck the woman with a quim worth five hundred thousand silver?" A bitter laugh scratched her throat.

"I would deny that chance because I don't see you for the worth of your maidenhead, nor should you. You mustn't believe the lies your stepmother and the prince told you."

Confusion ripped through her anger and it faltered, but nearly two decades of conditioning were difficult to ignore. "I've been bought and paid for, Henri Callan. You were hired to spy on me, so let us return to the palace and you can tell Regan all about my mortifying failure at seduction. I'm sure you'll both have a grand laugh at my expense. Hells, she might even share some of the silver she earned from selling me like a common cow."

"I can assure you, the king hasn't made good on that bill." A flicker of rage flashed in his eyes.

As if she'd believe that lie. Regan would be fuming if it were true. "You spout pretty words about seeing my worth, is that just an elaborate excuse to hide the fact that you're too frightened of what might happen when the king realizes I'm no longer a virgin?"

Henri's jaw clenched and he inhaled deeply, his nostrils flaring. "I do not fear Otto, nor his horrid son." He took another long breath and exhaled slowly, as if to calm his heart.

She mimicked his actions, needing to clear her fury, to quiet her pounding head. Henri reached for her and despite her harsh words and hurt feelings, she leaned into his touch, inviting him to stroke her face with the back of his hand. The rage that swarmed like a tempest in her belly eased.

He looked at her with eyes full of compassion, his lips soft. "Eira, you—all of you—is worth far more than silver or gold or precious gems." He placed his other hand over her thumping heart. "I wish you could see that who you are, what you are, is priceless."

"You mean my power?" A terrible vision sliced through her mind of Otto surrounded by her magic, a scepter in his hand, his mouth wide with maniacal laughter. She pulled away from Henri and rubbed her temples. "Tell me true—is my magic what Otto is truly after? He can bed any number of virgins. Surely, I'm not all that special in that regard. At least, the prince has insisted as much many times." She turned and pointed an accusing finger at Henri. "You saw it in me. How? And the dwarves—in the meadow—they saw it too. I've hidden it for so long, but now, I fear it's trying to break free. Is that how Otto knows?" Her legs trembled, and she steadied herself against the wall. The cool of the stones were soothing despite their rough texture. "Regan, oh holy hells. She knows, doesn't she?"

Henri shook his head and approached slowly. "The dwarves sense things even I cannot. They are of a magic far more ancient and powerful than you could ever imagine. As for the king, I doubt it, but never underestimate him, he is as wily as a fox caught in the hen house. As for your stepmother, again, I can't say for certain, but I would think most likely." Although he didn't reach for her, his hands flexed at his sides as if he wanted to touch her. She willed him to reach out—needed his touch, his calming strength.

"But the king has no magic of his own." Her eyes widened and her cheeks flushed with fresh ire. "His lover, Lady Annah, she's a witch. I once read about people with little inherent power who stole others' magic. Is that their plan?" she looked to him, beseeching, "Please don't let Regan or Annah take my power from me."

"Only you can prevent that, Eira. Your magic exists in you. It's not external, like witchcraft. Yours is a gift that only you can give and protect."

"I never learned how to control it."

"With your permission, I can help with that."

"Will it hurt?"

"Not if we do it right."

He took her hand and pushed her sleeve up to expose the soft underside of her forearm. His gaze was questioning and she nodded her consent. Whatever he sought to do, at least his touch didn't hurt. Slowly, he ran a finger down the length of her bare skin, leaving a trail of bluish shimmering light. She gasped and stared, fascinated by his magic. Where his touch lingered, her skin warmed and vibrated, the blue turning a brilliant golden.

If that happened with just a gentle stroke, she could only imagine what would happen if he caressed her entire body. Would their attraction to each other enhance the magic? It wasn't something she ever considered, but now desperately wanted to explore.

At the thought, her blood warmed and she bit her bottom lip to keep from moaning. A pulsing need grew between her legs and perspiration dotted her forehead. She desired him, and not just because he showed her kindness, but for the trust he placed in her, and the trust he earned in return. He'd known about her power, and yet hadn't told Regan even though he knew having that knowledge was a threat to them both. He hadn't lied—he had been protecting her all this while.

He hadn't brought her here to seduce her, but to allow her to explore her power freely, without fear of reprisal. Once loosened, would she be able to conceal it again? Did she want to?

No, she didn't. She imagined herself walking into the palace, magic flowing from her in radiant waves. No one would dare drug her to sleep, nor would they use her power for their own nefarious schemes. As much as she wished that could be true, she also knew she wasn't ready. Not yet. But with Henri's help, and the goddess willing, she would be soon.

Her breath came in shallow drags as she imagined a future free of her abusers—to live as she wished, to love whom she chose. Henri wasn't convenient or an afterthought, but how was he to know that she truly desired him?

Without permission or waiting for him to initiate, she slipped a hand behind his head and stood on tiptoe until her lips were even with his. His eyes widened with suppressed lust. Their lips met, tentative and unsure. This wasn't a stolen kiss in a darkened corridor, or a gentle brush of lips to wake her from a deep sleep. This was truly her first kiss, on her terms.

His hand pressed against her back and cradled her close. The scent of pine and apples drifted around them, cocooning her in a haze of protective comfort.

A soft sigh escaped her mouth and he kissed it away, his lips capturing hers with a fierceness that ignited her blood, and she rocked her hips forward. His erection pressed against her hip, teasing, tantalizing.

All of her doubts dissipated, and she gave herself to the moment. Here, with Henri, their tongues entangled, their bodies pressed together. Ripples of desire fluttered across her skin, and she delighted in every single sensation that overtook her body. This was what she'd imagined her life could be, and the reality was so much sweeter, more fulfilling than her fantasies could ever have been. After just this kiss, how could she possibly go back to her life? She couldn't. Wouldn't. But how, that was the question?

His lips left hers, and she whimpered at their absence. They settled on her jaw, and he nipped her skin with his teeth, eliciting even more flutters and a spike of need. She playfully growled and lifted her chin to offer the softer skin of her neck.

"In a pack, wolves protect their neck as its one of the most vulnerable places on their body." His tongue, hot and wet and oh so deliciously wicked, flicked across her jaw to the pulse point on her throat.

Her breathing slowed and she barely heard anything beyond the beating of her heart and his low moans. The fire crackled. Or was it her skin where he left a trail of blazing kisses? He sucked on her neck, and she would've melted into a puddle had he not been holding her aloft.

If this was what he did to her after a few kisses, she half feared what came next.

His lips nuzzled over her collarbone to the bodice of her dress, and she arched wantonly, offering her breasts with eagerness. Henri didn't disappoint. He rubbed his lips over the fabric of her gown, his hot breath seeping through to torment her taut nipples.

She fumbled with the buttons on her bodice, nearly ripping the damn things free in her haste to be rid of any hindrance between his lovely mouth and her skin.

He slid the unfastened gown over her shoulders and cocked his head at her nightdress. She shrugged with a crooked grin.

"I was in a hurry and had a rather rude gentleman watching."

"Yes, well, that rude gentleman is now rather eager to get you out of this contraption." He took a step backward, and she wriggled free of the gown and nightdress, and started on her stockings.

Henri stopped her. "I can handle those."

She clasped and unclasped her hands, unsure what to do with herself. Maids had seen her naked many times, but never a man. Lawks, even just that morning, she'd made him turn away. But the way his gaze lingered on her, the way he licked his lips as if she were a treat he'd gladly devour, it shifted her uncertainty. Almost made her believe she was beautiful, worthy.

Henri smoothed his hands over her thighs, rolling the stockings until they bunched at her feet. He knelt in front of her, not more than a hands' width from her privates, and looked at her with such devotion she stood taller, taking pride in her body.

"You're beautiful, Eira. Your skin is flawless, like freshly fallen snow." He leaned forward and inhaled. "Your essence sweeter than any fruit. May I?"

Confused by his question, she hesitated. What was he asking permission for? If only she'd been schooled on what to expect when alone with a man. The servants' gossip didn't include step-by-step instructions, only vague terms and gesticulations. No wonder Regan had given her that enchanted apple for the king.

Her confidence faltered. Regan might've made certain she left Eira's skin unblemished, but she inflicted plenty of scars emotionally and mentally. Unfortunately, those couldn't be smoothed away with salves and magic-infused herbal teas.

"Will it hurt?"

His chuckle went to the core of her desire, and she felt giddy at the sound.

"I promise you, it will not."

He flicked his tongue and licked at the patch of hair between her legs. A sharp snap of heat caught her breath. His hands cupped her buttocks and brought her closer to his face, where his devilish tongue waited.

She swooned into him, too caught up in the myriad sensations swirling through her body to care about much of anything besides Henri. If he'd asked her to run stark-naked through the forest, for the promise of his illicit kisses, she would have. Goddess forgive her, she would do whatever he asked.

But he didn't make demands. Instead, he buried his face between her legs. Her instinct was to cover herself, to turn away from him in shame, but curiosity held her fast and she stayed in the moment. Never in her wildest imaginings did she think someone would want to kiss her there, but holy stars—she gasped and shuddered at the pleasure that streaked through her body.

By turns, Henri slid his tongue along her womanhood and sucked the little bud that made her legs tremble and breath stutter. More please, and just there, ooohhh, this was paradise that she never wanted to leave. To know that her body was capable of this much pleasure surprised and delighted her. She ran a hand up her thigh to her abdomen, fighting off a bout of shyness. She cupped her breast and moaned at the sensations swirling through her blood.

With each lick, Henri broke down her defenses, leaving her vulnerable and exposed. With each nip, he built up her confidence that she was more than a pawn to be sacrificed to the king. With each moan, he unlocked her heart and allowed her to believe in the impossible.

She could love and be loved. She was desirable. She pinched her nipple and cried out, wanting more, needing a release before the molten lava that was her blood consumed her from the inside.

When her legs trembled and were set to give way, he lay her down on the soft rug in front of the fire and removed her boots before rolling her stockings off one by one.

"It's not fair. I am now fully undressed and you are not." Her voice came out low and husky with a slight tremor she didn't try to hide. She reached for his breeches and unsnapped first one, then two buttons while he shimmied out of his shirt. His bare chest was fit and muscular, with a seductively defined abdomen that beckoned her touch. She traced her fingers from his waist to the curve of his chest and a shudder of desire racked her body. "You are beautiful."

She glanced at his eyes and saw in them not just lust and devotion, but a wild strength that made her tremble. The memory of her nightmares scorched her mind and she shut them away. Not here. Not now. Please don't ruin this perfect moment.

"What is it?"

"It's nothing. Just a bad dream."

He kicked off his boots and breeches, making him as naked as she. She stared at his manhood, erect and engorged. A shiver of excitement and apprehension slid over her. Surely, something that size wouldn't fit in her small body. A moan, low and full of aching desire came from her sternum. Her mouth watered at the thought of licking that gorgeous cock. A blush rose up her neck to settle on her cheeks. What a strumpet she'd become in only a matter of minutes. But how could she not with Henri so near, and so naked?

She arched upward and reached for his erection, shocked at her boldness. The need to stroke him, to taste him, was too great. He didn't stop her when she wrapped her fingers around his cock and the rumbling groan he made encouraged her to explore further. She flicked her tongue over the little slit at the tip and salty sweetness tingled in her mouth.

Her hand stroked the base while she licked the bulging head. A flurry of emotions ran riot through her body. An impatient sort of achiness throbbed between her legs and her heart rammed against her chest, urging her to take him fully into her mouth. To claim him.

Another groan, and Henri gently pulled away before directing her to lay on her back. Afraid she'd done something wrong, she looked away, but her held her chin between his fingers.

"Your lovely mouth will give me much pleasure later. Right now, I want to hear about your bad dream."

"Now? Surely it can wait. I'd much rather continue what we were doing."

His hand slid up the inside of her thigh as he lay beside her.

"And we will. After you tell me what haunts you in your dreams." He kissed the tip of her nose, and she half-turned toward him, pressing her mound into his leg.

Infuriating, frustrating, sexy as sin man! Tingles covered every inch of exposed skin, but she knew he wouldn't satisfy her until she told him of her nightly terrors. With a sigh, she rolled onto her back and shut her eyes. "Wolves chased me. When I turned to face them, it wasn't a wolf, but you holding a dagger. The huntsman, come for my heart."

"It was a dream, nothing more. You're safe with me."

She opened her eyes and faced him. "Are you one of those men who can change into a wolf?"

His lips covered hers and his tongue invaded her mouth, filling her with heat and desire—and the taste of her own juices, which should've scandalized her, but didn't. Nothing about what they did was wrong. Everything felt too good for her to doubt. The hand between her legs moved, and she arched into his touch. Her legs fell open, inviting whatever sweet torment he might give.

"I'm not a wolf shifter, although I do envy their tracking abilities."

The scent of her sex pierced her nostrils. Henri growled against her mouth and flicked her sensitive nub with his fingertips. She yelped at the sudden flash of pain and ecstasy that shot through each and every nerve ending in the entirety of her body.

His gaze never left her as he inserted a finger into her aching channel. Her breath stopped and for the space of a moment, her mind went blank. Then her breath exhaled and inhaled again;

her heart continued beating, her slick heat clenched around his fingers.

A moan, low and sultry, came from deep in his throat, and she swallowed it with one of her own. He released his lips from hers and pulled back slightly, a smile making small crinkles near the edges of his gorgeous eyes.

Another flick of her bud, followed by another. She squirmed beneath him, her blood thick, her nerve endings sparking. It wasn't possible her skin could hold in the fireworks building in her body. They would burst through, rending her flesh to bits and she wouldn't care. For this sweet, sweet torment and even sweeter jags of passion, she would gladly surrender.

His devious fingers quickened their pace, a second adding to the one inside her, sliding in and out while his thumb rubbed her button. She thrashed beneath him, never wanting the pleasure to end, yet eager for what came next.

A strangled cry escaped her open mouth as the fireworks exploded and a waterfall of delightful sensations cascaded over her convulsing body. Never, not once in all her years of forbidden self-exploration, had she brought her body to this aching crescendo. Never would she have thought it possible to feel so much pleasure from simple touch. Euphoria bubbled in her belly and a miasma of emotions swirled through her heart.

Years of feeling unlovable fell away as she gazed at the remarkable man who'd given her this gift. Her heart swelled with love. For Henri, yes, but for herself, too. What an extraordinary thing her body was. What other delightful secrets did it hold, and would Henri coax them from her? For once, the idea didn't frighten her.

Henri's eyes softened, and he licked his lips before lowering them to her. She sucked on him as if he were her only hold on reality.

Another wave, smaller yet equally as lovely, caused her

channel to pulse around his fingers. He covered her mound with his palm and warmth flooded her senses.

"I think you're ready." He kissed the tip of her nose and moved his body to hover above hers. "I promise to do all in my power to keep you from harm, but this might hurt a little."

Whatever pain it brought would be worth it. This was her choice, and whatever consequences came, she would face with grace and bravery. This tiny act, huge in its repercussions, was the beginning of her claiming her power. Not just the magic swirling in her blood, but her power as a woman, and as a being that deserved more respect than Regan, Gil, or even Otto had ever shown. She wasn't sure how, but she understood that from this moment onward, her life would never be the same. She would never be the same.

She moaned into him and wrapped her hands around his back as his rigid cock pressed between them. For just a moment, he hesitated, but then she widened her legs and rocked her hips to take him into her. She was more than ready to be rid of her virginity. On her terms, she gave it to the one man who didn't demand it of her.

Chapter Twenty-Five

It didn't hurt. At least, not as much as Eira had feared. A slight pinch, less than one of Regan's slaps, and it was done. She was free. She was happily worthless.

And yet, she wasn't worthless, not anymore, never had been. Perhaps this was what Regan feared more than anything—that Eira would understand her power as a woman. Not for her beauty, or for her meek servitude, but for the intelligence and inner strength she'd always had, but suppressed the same as her magic.

Relief, cool and sweet washed over her and she said a silent prayer to the goddess for putting Henri in her path. A man she at first feared had freed her in more ways than he'd ever know. She was grateful that it was Henri, and not Otto or Guillaume who had been her first. They certainly wouldn't have shown the care and attention that Henri had—and for that, she would always hold a special place in her heart for him. Come what may, no one could take this moment, this day from her.

She'd removed herself from this game, but there were still many others in play. Although nothing would ever be the same, she couldn't ever allow herself to be manipulated again. Trust wasn't a word she was on comfortable terms with, but she chose to trust Henri.

Eira marveled at the man above her, at the veins that strained in his temple and roped along his neck. She ran her hands over his back, delighting in the feel of muscles shifting with each movement. His strong arms kept him aloft and she stroked those, too. Everywhere she could reach, she caressed and committed the touch to memory.

If this was the only time they were together, she didn't want to forget anything. Even though she knew it was fraught with danger, she made a wish that this was the first of many days of happiness for them both. Now that she knew what was possible, she wanted more. Not just for herself, but for Henri, too. She dared to dream of a future filled with languid days of making love, and adventure with Henri by her side. An equal in all things. She tucked that wish deep in her heart.

Henri bent his head and sucked in air as if he'd run a league in pouring rain. When he lifted his face, it was red and crumpled.

"Are you in pain?" She started to shift from beneath him, but his guttural moan stopped her.

"The best kind. Don't you dare move, you vixen."

He thrust deep into her and held for a moment before pumping hard and fast. The delirious feelings she'd had with his fingers didn't return, and she feared she'd done something wrong. The look on his face reassured her it wasn't something that would inhibit his pleasure.

He cried out with his release, and she reveled in the look of bliss and torture that crossed his features. Yes, she understood those feelings well. Had felt them only moments earlier.

"Damn, woman. Just...damn." He rested his head on her shoulder, his own heaving with labored breaths. "You are...

Eira...I never thought..." He looked into her eyes, and she saw the faint glittering of tears in their depths. "Thank you."

"It is I who should be thanking you, kind sir." She brushed his hair off his face so that she could see all of his beauty. "Although, I am sorry I didn't release with you."

"It's not as easy for you in this position. There are other ways, and I will teach you all of them."

"More than this?" Her heart quickened and a smile bloomed across her face. She hoped that meant not just today, but for many days to come.

He chuckled into her neck. "Yes, there are more. Let me catch my breath and the lessons shall begin."

"Perhaps you need some of Hamlin's special brew." She wriggled out from beneath him and walked, stark-naked, to the little stove.

"I've created a monster. Where is the shy lady from this morning?"

Eira poured them more of the apple tea and returned to her lover. She nearly dropped the cups from giggling. Her lover. What a scandalous thing to say.

"She's here, if that's what you'd like." She knelt and batted her lashes while gazing demurely at the rug.

"I'm more than happy with this new, emboldened Eira." He indicated she finish her drink while he downed his in one long gulp and then he set both cups aside. "Lesson one."

Henri grabbed her around the waist and spun them both until she was straddled atop his erection.

"Ahhh, I think I'm going to like this lesson."

She did. And the others that followed. By the time shadows streaked across the floor, she'd touched, tasted, and titillated every inch of his body and he hers in return. As much as she adored the way his body moved with hers, it was his face upon release that she loved the most. With each spilling of his seed, she captured the image in her mind to replay again and again in the quiet, lonely parts of her days.

They lay on the rug, the remnants of their lunch spread across the hearth where two teacups sat side-by-side. She marveled at the simplicity of the scene, but the enormity of their situation.

"Have you ever felt as if you've known someone your whole life, even though you only just met them? That's how I feel when I'm with you." She sighed and trailed her fingers over his torso. "Being with you reminds me of sun-filled days spent chasing butterflies in a meadow. I know that sounds silly." A blush rose up her chest to rest in her cheeks.

"Not silly at all. I believe our souls know when we've met the person who is our equal in all things."

"Like a soulmate?" She didn't dislike the idea, but she didn't dare hope for such a thing. Her mind spun to a less pleasant topic and she turned to face Henri, her breath catching at his attractiveness. "Regan gave me an apple to enchant Otto. She didn't believe me capable of attracting his affections." A shudder wormed its way into her heart. "I can't marry him, Henri. Certainly not after today, but for so many other reasons, the least of which is that I don't love him."

Henri's fingers idly brushed from her thighs, to her buttocks, and circled the small of her back before repeating the loop. "We'll sort out a plan, but we have to be careful. I know it seems simple, as if we could just run away, but you and I both know that would put a death warrant over our heads and we'd be hunted by Otto's trackers." His lips grazed her shoulder and she swooned into his warmth. "I have a few ideas and will share them with you once I've confirmed a few things, but for now, know you aren't alone and that you will not be marrying King Otto. Or anyone else for that matter, unless you choose them."

She glanced at him, unsure if he mocked her, but his face

was devoid of mirth. "That's a bold statement coming from a rumored huntsman and spy. But I do like the way it sounds. Know what I like even more?" He grinned and she took his finger into her mouth.

"I shall never tire of your seductions, my lady." He nuzzled her nose and sighed. "Message understood. No more talk of the king. For now."

This was Henri's day. His and hers alone. She reached for his cock and lowered herself between his legs. He moaned something about what a vixen she was, and she loved every single syllable. Eira the timid mouse was dead. Long live this new, brazenly confident Eira.

After they made love, they lounged on the rug, with the fire warming their bare skin. Henri held up his hand, his thumb and middle finger pinched together.

"Now, snap, but when you do, think of a small flame, like the flicker of a candle." He watched her hand intently, patiently urging her success.

She snapped, and nothing happened. Again, and again, still nothing.

"I feel," she put a hand to her chest, "like someone is pushing against me. It's hard to breathe."

Henri kissed her fingertips and scowled. "I was afraid of that. I believe you've been warded. Possibly by Regan, or by someone else."

"I don't understand. What does that mean?"

"It means your power is there, but suppressed." He looked away, and she had the impression there was more to it yet he held back.

"I used to hide in the woods and try to coax my magic forth, but it was always elusive. I knew it was there, though. My father said one day I'd grow into my power, yet I fear that will never happen. Perhaps I've spent too long suppressing it and hiding it from Regan for it to ever fully manifest." She snapped her finger again, unsurprised when nothing happened. "Regan's grimoire talks to me, you know."

He lay on his side, elbow bent, one hand cupping his head, the other stroking her breasts and she never thought she'd seen a more beautiful sight. "It what?"

"The grimoire—it shows me spells that I might need and somehow makes things happen. When you found me in the king's antechamber, I was casting a spell to rid myself of the alcohol that I'd drunk. I don't know how it happens, it just does."

He opened his mouth to speak, but paused at the sound of singing.

Eira sat up, fear chasing the pleasure of their day to the far reaches of her heart.

"What is that?"

"Nothing to worry about, but you might want to get dressed. I do believe we've overstayed our welcome and the dwarves will be coming through that door in a few minutes."

"They'll see me. They'll know what we've been doing. This is a disaster." Her mind raced with what needed doing, but was too scattered to land on one thing first.

"They'll be happy for us, Eira."

Easy for him to say. He wasn't—she stopped the thought. She refused to allow the mortification that nipped at her heart to take root. Even so, shame skirted her thoughts as she wasted no time pulling on stockings and her underclothes. Henri helped her with the nightdress and her gown before dressing himself far too leisurely. It was as if he cared not that the dwarves saw him indecently exposed.

Nor should she care, she realized. There was nothing indecent about their lovemaking. They were two consenting adults, which was more than she could say about her predicament with the king.

At the thought of the tyrant, her mood soured and she stomped into her boots. Their idyllic day was over. Telling herself she was a different person was all fine and well in the safety and comfort of Henri's arms, but would it be so easy to continue when faced with her stepmother? All too soon she'd have to confront the reality of her future, and what it looked like now that she was no longer a maiden. Yet it was more than just the loss of her virginity. It was the understanding and knowledge that there is pleasure to be had in life. Pleasure she'd been denied. She made a silent vow to do everything in her power to remember how she felt today, and to bring that sense of hope and fulfilment into each day.

She went to the window and debated opening it to air the room, but seeing Henri relaxed and unbothered gave her the courage necessary to face the dwarves without shame. She glanced out the window, hoping to see the dwarves, but the singing had stopped. The entire woods grew quiet, and her skin prickled with apprehension.

Just beneath the window ledge, two great wolves lunged and snarled at her with huge fangs covered in slobber. She screamed and backed away from the glass, losing her footing on the rug. Her arse hit the floor with a hard thump, and she cried out from the jolt of pain that shot up her spine. A moment later, the dwarves entered through the front door, weapons drawn, their faces serious.

"Get inside, you idiots! There's a pack of hungry wolves outside and you'll make a tasty snack." She sprang up, ignoring a second bolt of pain, and ushered them inside before instructing Henri to lock the door.

Like a mother hen, she corralled them as best she could, her arms spread out in an impotent barrier.

"Bless," one of the dwarves said as he beamed with a ridiculous smile that lifted his cheeks, making them look like ripened apples. "Bless, Henri. Bless, Lady Cannaid."

"Stop with the blessing and get away from the windows." Eira tried moving them closer to the kitchen, but they slipped from her embrace, one by one.

"Eira, there are no wolves out there." Henri took her hand and held it, his gaze indecipherable.

"I saw them."

Dorton blew out a breath and glanced at Henri. At his nod, the dwarf said, "You saw us." He toggled a thumb between himself and the others.

"But they were wolves." Then it dawned on her and she blushed a furious red. "You're shifters?" Was that even possible?

"Aye. We be of the oldest pack in Jura." Gorse said proudly.

"We caught a scent we didn't recognize. Were afraid someone had squatted in our place, weren't we? What with the smoke from the chimney'n all. But if'n we'd known it was yous, we wouldn't have scared ye like that." Dorton stroked his long beard. "Can't be too careful nowdays with the trackers 'n all."

"Trackers? Here?" Eira was spinning from what she'd heard. Could they track her and Henri? Would they tie her to a wooden stake and parade her naked through the town? Would she be thrown in the dungeons? Question after question pinged against her skull, causing a headache that would last for days.

"You saw 'em. Back at Madam Davina's. A whole squad of thems just itching to put a dagger in our hearts," another dwarf with a bushy red beard and crimson curls added.

"Prolly all on the king's payroll, too." Gorse moved closer to Henri, and Eira reached a hand to him. He took it with an impish smile. "He's ain't got a kind bone in his gobby body, unlike ye."

Henri looked out the windows with a frown. "It's getting late and I don't like riding in the dark."

"Ye kin stay here." Gorse beamed up at Eira and she wished for all the gold in the king's treasure that she could.

"What about them?" Eira indicated the seven cherubic faces watching her.

"We be all right. Ain't got killed yet, have we?" the redhead said.

"Just, promise me you'll be careful." Eira squeezed Gorse's hand before retrieving her cape. "I couldn't forgive myself if the trackers found you because of us."

Henri helped her shrug into her cape, and she fastened the button with deep sadness. Her perfect day was over. In a short while, she'd be back at the palace, where intrigues and machinations awaited her.

The ride back was quiet and heavy with tension. The saddle chafed in places tender from her day of lovemaking, but it was a tolerable pain compared to what she'd suffered in the past. She slumped under the weight of her obligations to her stepmother and the king. Would she tell Regan outright that she was no longer worth the gross sum the king owed her? Or would she continue the game, knowing full well it wouldn't end the way Regan had planned? The latter presented far less punishment in the immediate future, and would keep Henri from harm, too. Possibly even death if Otto discovered it was Henri who had taken what he believed was rightfully his. Disgusting pig. How she would love to gut the greedy man and see how he liked being treated like a farm animal taken to slaughter.

"Say nothing to your stepmother. Act as if nothing has changed." Henri said, startling her out of her reverie.

"Can you read my mind? I was just thinking what would be best."

His grin shone in the scant moonlight. "I promise you, we'll make a plan for your future, but for now, we must pretend you are committed to the marriage. If we give away our hand, Gil will pounce and ruin everything."

"He seems to excel at ruining things." She agreed reluctantly that it was for the best, but she relished the image of Regan's face when she realized she'd lost. Soon. Hopefully, very soon. Time was running out and the ball crept ever closer.

By the time they reached the stables, she was emotionally and physically exhausted. Her stomach growled as two stable boys took their horses, and she placed a hand over her belly.

"Someone needs to eat. You head to your rooms and I'll arrange for food to be brought up." Henri stood close, but didn't touch her. The distance caused an ache in her heart that surprised and delighted. "I doubt Regan let it be known you went riding with me, therefore, we can't be seen together or we'll draw suspicion. The last thing we need is anyone questioning your intentions."

She hated that they had to pretend indifference. Fortunately for them both, it was the one thing she excelled at. She nodded and strode away from Henri, in the direction of her rooms, her face set in a haughty expression she hoped scared off anyone hoping to make conversation.

As she rounded a corner, she caught a glimpse of dark hair before a hand reached out and grabbed her by the throat.

Chapter Twenty-Six

Stars danced in Eira's eyes and pain ricocheted across her skull where her head slammed against the brick wall. All the air in her lungs whooshed out with a rush, leaving her breathless and blinking through her hazy vision. Breath that reeked of wine assaulted her and she kicked out, but her legs hung in the air, useless against her captor. His vile chuckle sent ripples of dread through her nerves.

Prince Guillaume.

A strangled cry came from her pinched lips as she struggled against his tight grip on her neck. Her vision cleared and she stared into Gil's savage eyes, as if he'd lost all reason.

"What are you playing at?" His gaze took in her plain gown and cape. "Going for a starlit ride? Or are you meeting a lover?" To her horror, he pressed his nose to her breast and inhaled up to her jaw. "I'll find out if you are, slag, and cut off his dick. You've already broken one promise. The king is not as forgiving as I." The sour smell of Regan's favorite wine filled her nostrils.

"Let me go." Her words came out a muffled wheeze. He was choking her and didn't care. More than that, he seemed to like it, if the gleeful sneer he wore was any indication.

She lashed at him and her nails caught the flesh on his cheek, raking the skin and leaving bloody slashes in her wake.

"Bitch" Faster than should've been possible in his drunken state, he gripped both of her hands in his left and pinned them above her head. His right hand thankfully left her throat, but just as quickly lifted her skirts and shoved between her legs.

"Stop it." She cried out, but he bent low and hissed in her face.

"Shut your fucking mouth, slag. Cry out or scream and I'll slit your neck." He withdrew his hand and sniffed his glistening fingers. "Well, well, what have we here? You're already wet. I knew you desired me, despite your childish pretense otherwise."

He wiped his fingers across her lips, and she tasted hers and Henri's juices. Panic, raw and electric, raced through her veins. She couldn't let him know what she'd been doing all day. Couldn't let him find out she wasn't a virgin. Couldn't let him discover it was Henri who'd ruined her first.

She had to protect Henri at all costs. Guillaume could do what he wished with her, but she wouldn't let Henri be punished for her actions.

"Guillaume, don't. Please."

"Begging? I like it. And you like being bound, don't you? From how wet you are, I'd say you're gagging for it. By rights, you should be mine anyhow. I shall give you what you want, nay, what you deserve and I won't be gentle."

He reached as if to unfasten his breeches and her mind screamed at her to think, to come up with something that would prevent the inevitable.

"What of your father? He'll know you assaulted me and took what he considers rightfully his. I swear to you, I haven't broken any promises, but if the king learns of this, he won't be pleased."

"He'll be dead." The traitorous words were said low, with

enough venom that she feared he wouldn't care if Otto learned of his betrayal.

She clung to his words. "Is that what you want? Your father dead so that you can ascend the throne?" The traitorous words could get her executed, but she was desperate to keep Henri safe. And there was a part of her that wished to know what ailed Otto, but she feared giving away too much. All she had to do was stall Guillaume long enough to give Henri time to get far from the stables.

His hand left his breeches and rose as if to strike her. She didn't cower, instead she lifted her chin, defiantly daring him to do his worse. She'd been raised with abuse, what was another slap from him?

"You shouldn't speak of things you don't understand. I should teach you a lesson and shove my cock in your mouth to shut you up. Think you can tease and torment, do you?" He licked his fingers and she swallowed the bile that inched up her throat. "You're fucking delicious."

"I haven't teased you, Your Highness. Please, don't do this. Your father still lives and will strip you of your title and then what? I'm not worth losing a throne." She kept her voice low and measured, despite the fear lodged in her heart.

"Your worth, as I've said, has already been determined. As for my father—do you honestly think he cares what happens to you? Then you're duller than I thought."

An image thrust its way to the forefront of her mind—of Regan squirming atop Guillaume, her visage that of Eira. She almost cried for the ludicrousness of the situation. That Regan thought so little of her stepdaughter—no, of herself—that she had to pretend to be a much prettier, much younger woman just to get the prince to fuck her was so pathetically sad.

And Guillaume had gone along with the ruse enthusiastically. But that was just a dream. Or was it? Regan surely made a poor substitute for the real thing, which was probably why the prince now felt the need to take advantage of Eira, here, in the dark where horseshit and stale piss were a few steps away. A far cry from the luxurious mattress and soft sheets of Regan's bed.

He and Regan could abuse her likeness, playing their games, hells, Guillaume could even violate her physically, but neither he nor her stepmother would ever destroy her. Not unless they killed her, which at the moment, Eira didn't take for granted.

"He just wants your tight quim, you little tart. I'm sick of waiting for his scraps." Guillaume tightened his grip on her hands and grabbed her breast, twisting hard until a cry escaped her closed lips.

The magic she'd hidden her whole life, and that Henri had tried to stoke with kind words and gentle caresses, swirled beneath her skin and with all her might, she wished it would break free. But it remained as elusive as ever, which was just as well. She couldn't let Guillaume know that part of her existed. Keeping her magic buried was even more important than masking the loss of her maidenhood. So many secrets. So many lies. She hated it, but concealing these two things would keep her and Henri alive.

Guillaume spread her legs with his knee, and she bit her lip to keep from screaming. She didn't doubt his threat that if she cried out he would slit her throat. A noise came from her right, and he glanced over to see two stable boys staring at them. Behind them, Henri strode in the shadows. He glanced up and a look of rage passed over his face. He took a step forward, nearly knocking the stable boys to the ground.

No. No, no, no. Henri couldn't get involved. Her mind whirled and she did the only thing that came to mind.

She brought her knee up as hard as she could and struck the prince's crotch, hoping she smashed the hells out of his balls. Guillaume shrieked like a scorched scullery maid as he doubled over, swearing and calling her names that would make a hardened criminal wince. His grip slipped from her wrists and she wriggled free of his grasp. Before she could escape, he managed to grab her cloak and jerk her toward him. A flash of fist was all she saw before the crack of her jaw reverberated in her head. The impact knocked her backward and her head bounced on the stone wall. Darkness edged her vision and her ears rang loud enough she could barely hear the prince's taunts.

Blood filled her mouth, and she pushed away from the wall. Guillaume reached for her again, but she ducked beneath his arm and pivoted quickly to slap him hard across his cheek. White hot pain flared from her palm. Surprise lit his eyes and she sneered in his face.

"If you ever touch me again, I will castrate you like the filthy pig you are." She shoved him with all her strength, her foot squarely set behind his, and sent him flailing backward. She would've laughed at the picture he made, if not for the fear and rage that roared through her.

Arms wild, face a storm cloud, he landed with a thud on the dirt.

"I will fucking end you, slag." He flailed against the ground like a turtle on its back.

From somewhere deep inside, she found the strength to stand over him, her expression one of pity. "No, I don't think you will."

She turned her back on him, ignoring his threats.

At the other end of the walkway, Henri raced toward her, but she put up a hand to stop his approach. The prince couldn't see them together. She willed him to understand. Thankfully, he stopped and disappeared into the shadows.

Henri was safe. That's all that mattered.

Chapter Twenty-Seven

Henri glared at Guillaume as he struggled to right himself. He'd kill the man. Prince or not, Gil would pay for the assault. As angry as he was at Gil, he was even more furious with himself for leaving Eira alone. Never would he have thought Gil would attack her. Stupid, stupid, stupid. When he saw Eira pinned against the wall, he didn't care that he was a prince and must maintain peace between their kingdoms. All he knew was that Eira needed him.

But she'd stopped him with that one glance. The glance that said she would suffer Gil's assault to keep Henri safe. He rubbed his chest where he'd felt her fear for Gil, and slashing through the anxiety, her need to protect him. Even in that awful situation, she sought to keep Gil from seeing him because she knew that if Gil had, he would hunt Henri down.

His gaze went to the two stable boys and he quickly ushered them away. He pulled two silver coins from his pocket and handed one to each. "Go now. Do not return until after the ball, do you understand? The prince would have your lives if he recognized you."

The two grubby faces nodded up to him, understanding

clear in their youthful eyes. He waved them away and they scampered into the night. He had to make himself scarce, as well. There was no guarantee that Gil hadn't seen him. He peeked around the brick wall to see Gil dusting his frockcoat and trousers, mumbling obscenities to himself all the while. The desire to confront him, to plow his sword up that arrogant bastard's arse straight through to his gobby skull was too great. Henri took a shuddering breath and forced himself to think clearly. To think of Eira and what was best for her.

Pride swelled in his chest at the fierceness she'd shown. Who's to say if Gil would've gone through with his assault if Eira hadn't fought him off? An icy jaggedness cut at his heart. He told himself he was protecting Eira by insisting they not be seen together, but was that fear of his identity being discovered clouding his judgment? He needed to confess all to her—to tell her his true identity and purpose for being at the palace. And yet, he hesitated. Not that he was worried what she'd think or say to him, but rather, because he'd not yet uncovered what was truly happening in King Otto's court. What an ass he'd been.

He vowed to protect Eira, and then abandoned her. He hoped she could forgive him. And that maybe he could forgive himself.

Gil stormed from the stable yard in the opposite direction Eira went and Henri debated only a moment before following her. Gil would be dealt with in time. For now, he must make certain Eira was unharmed. Their situation was all the more tenuous because of their time at the cottage. It wasn't his plan to seduce Eira, but when she offered, and then kissed him, he was lost to her. He could only pray it wasn't to both of their peril.

They played a dangerous game. She was betrothed to the king, and Henri was beholden to the treatises of his kingdom and Jura's. Treaties that Gil was trying to usurp.

What a fine tangle he'd created. Yet if he hadn't taken

Regan's coin, someone else would have and where would Eira be now? He curled his fingers into fists and beat back the voice that said she could possibly be in a better position than he'd left her. The past was done, it was what he did going forward that mattered.

Eira was all that mattered.

He slunk through the darkened halls, clinging to the shadows and avoiding the courtiers and servants who lazily walked the pathways. It wasn't late, perhaps four hours until midnight, but the palace seemed to have a sleepiness to it this night. Otto must've been in fine revelry while he and Eira were away.

Which meant Regan most likely was pretending to be her stepdaughter again. It hadn't taken much to convince her to let him take Eira away for the day. He had to come up with a plan to convince Regan he should hide Eira until the ball. Play on her ego, yes, but the words had to be just right, the reason absolutely believable. And she had to believe Henri too simple to even think of seducing Eira.

If not for his position, he would take Eira away this night and never return to Jura or Otto's court. But that would bring war and he couldn't risk the lives of his kingdom's people for the woman he loved. By the goddess, he was sorely tempted.

He raced up the back stairs and crept to the main hallway of Eira's floor in time to see her hurry to her door and disappear inside. She made it safely. A huge weight lifted from his chest and he could breathe again. She wasn't out of danger, but at least Gil hadn't followed her to finish what he'd started.

At the thought of that ruddy prince, Henri's stomach convulsed and he nearly slammed his fist into the paneled wall. Breathe. Calm. Smash Gil's face on the morrow. Yes, excellent plan.

He snuck into the servants' corridor and hurried to Eira's

room. He heard her order the maid to run a bath and then entered her bedchamber with a shuddering exhale.

"Eira." He stepped from the shadow, berating himself for not giving her warning when he saw the stark fear light in her eyes. "Are you hurt?"

"You gave me a fright, Henri." She clasped his outstretched hands and folded herself into him. "You're safe. Thank the goddess." Her arms wrapped around his back and she squeezed tight enough the air wheezed from his lungs. "I was so worried about you."

He stroked her hair and held her close. "As I was you. Why didn't you cry out? I would've come immediately."

"And that's why I didn't. Gil threatened to slit my throat if I did, and I knew if you intervened, he would've—" She stopped herself from saying more and pulled back to look at him with such intensity he felt it in his marrow. "I don't want to speak of it now. Or ever, actually. I won't let Gil ruin my memories of our lovely, perfect day."

"But Eira, he nearly raped you."

"Yes, and he might try again. But I can't keep living in fear of what others will do. Not after today. Not anymore." She turned away from him and took off her boots, followed by her stockings.

The memory of removing them himself only a few hours earlier sent flutters through his veins. "He must be punished."

"He's the prince. Who's going to punish him? Otto? Regan? I doubt they care." She removed her cape and tossed it over a chair before she started on the buttons of her gown. His fingers itched to help, but she had that same look as in the stable yard that said she needed to do this herself. "Don't you find it strange the king hasn't once asked to meet with me? I've been here a sennight and slept through most of it, yet he doesn't seem to notice or care. No one does except you."

"Which is why we must make a plan to get away. But we

must be smart about it to leave no suspicion or clues for Otto's trackers. He might appear to be indifferent, but if you suddenly disappeared, he'd spend every cent in his treasury hunting you down. His pride wouldn't allow him to appear a failure. No one leaves Otto unless he decides it be so." An ominous tone entered his voice and he cleared his throat, afraid he'd given away too much.

Eira shook her hair as the dress lifted over her head. "Be that as it may, I won't marry him."

"You won't. May I?" He reached for the gown.

"I thought you'd never ask. You must take my garments and have them cleaned. Regan will have her maids in here sniffing around and I'm certain there's evidence on my clothing to suggest we weren't just riding horses." She grinned that saucy vixen grin and it took all of his will not to ravage her once more. The king and Regan be damned, he couldn't get enough of her.

Instead of spreading her on the bed like his heart and cock hoped he would, he helped remove her chemise and balled it up with her gown and stockings. "Is there anything else I can do for you?"

His gaze took in her naked body, relief rushing over him that she was unmarked, though he knew wounds weren't always visible. He didn't agree with her about not discussing Gil's assault, but would respect her wishes. If this was how she wanted to deal with the situation, it wasn't his place to tell her she was wrong.

She pulled a dressing gown on and he mourned the loss of her gorgeous nakedness. She was right—their perfect day of lovemaking was at an end, but he wouldn't let it be their last.

She stepped in front of him, her eyes shining with a strength he'd not seen before. "You have done so much already, Henri. You showed me that I'm not disgusting or worthless. In each of your gazes, even now, you look at me and I see myself through your eyes. I see beyond the surface beauty to my value as a woman. Not just in what pleasure I can give you, but in knowing who I am. It's new, and to be honest, terrifying, but I can't ever go back."

"No, you can't. You are so much more than you know." He lifted her chin and she winced. Upon closer inspection, he saw redness along her jaw and the faint beginning of a bruise on her cheek. "I can heal this. Take away your pain."

"Leave it. I'll need proof for Regan. Not that I think she'll believe me even with evidence, but she needs to know who she's in bed with. Literally."

He wasn't surprised she knew, but didn't expect her to mention it so casually. She truly wasn't the same Eira from that morning, and for that, he was glad of anything he might've done to give her confidence.

The maid knocked on the door to alert Eira that her bath was ready. She rose on tiptoe to brush his lips with hers and put a finger to that lovely mouth that he longed to kiss.

"Do not confront Gil. When he's punished, it shall be my doing. Promise me."

"I promise." The words nearly stuck in his throat, he hated saying them that much.

"One day at a time, Henri. That's how we'll survive this." She waved him away and went to the door.

He backed away to the shadows, her clothing nestled in his arm. Once she'd left her bedchamber, he hurried to his own rooms where his butler Bernard was seated at his desk, hands cupping his head. Upon Henri's entry, he glanced up and made a sign above his head. It was from the old days when they worshipped gods and goddesses, plural, and meant to bring luck.

Bernard spied the bundle in Henri's arms and rose with a grimace. "Don't tell me now you plan to dress as a woman to continue your charade? Your Highness, you must end this farce and deal with matters you were sent here to do. Namely, this treaty." He pointed to the table where papers were laid out in a tidy manner.

"And I shall. Have these laundered, will you?" Henri glanced over the papers and blew out a breath. "Gil tried to rape Eira this evening." He jabbed a finger on one page in particular. "She's forbidden me from punishing Gil, but I think I know a way to make the crown prince pay for his crimes." He snarled and looked to his butler. "We must get word to Father immediately."

Otto and his horrible son had terrorized Jura for far too long. He removed his black cassock and replaced it with a dark eggplant tunic. Not as simple as his cassock, but equally unremarkable.

"I've seen this look before." Bernard stood in the doorway, arms crossed. "It usually ends with me having to explain to your father why you'd been impulsive and rash. Will you at least tell me of your plans before I have to defend them?"

Henri gripped his butler's shoulders and grinned. "Why spoil the fun? I'm off to see the younger prince. There are intrigues to be plotted. I imagine I'll be back rather late, don't wait up."

"Sir," Bernard's eyes softened and his mouth quirked. "Be safe. This place is a den of vipers. I shall see to the young lady's clothing. Is there anything you wish for me to discover while I'm out?"

"You'd make a fine spy, my friend. For tonight, stay safe. There's no guarantee Gil didn't recognize me at the stables and I'd hate for you to pay for my indiscretions."

"I've raised you since you were tiny. I do not fear a spoiled prince with a wounded ego."

A better friend Henri could never have. He left his butler and nearly ran to Leon's apartments. It was time for the mouse to become the cat.

Chapter Twenty-Eight

Eira inspected her face in the mirror, relieved the swelling had gone down. Patches of purplish-blue dotted her jaw, and it still hurt to talk, chew, or smile, but at least nothing was broken. When Regan had returned to their rooms the previous night and saw Eira, she'd shouted and railed against her stepdaughter—more concerned that she'd marred her beauty than anything else, which Eira argued was entirely unfair.

It didn't matter that Guillaume had come perilously close to raping her. Regan blamed Eira for tempting him in the first place. No amount of explaining would change her stepmother's mind, and when Regan had finally stomped her foot and ordered Eira to her room, she'd gone without complaint. When the maid brought her tea drugged with valerian, but thankfully none of the betane, Eira drank the entire cup in one long gulp. If for no other reason than to forget the whole ordeal.

Henri was safe, and for the moment, Regan didn't know what had transpired at the cottage. Whatever happened, or not, with Guillaume, she didn't wish to dwell upon any of it. She willed herself numb to the situation, just as she'd done most of her life with Regan's beatings. The pain would pass, the scars would heal, if she could just get past one night, then she could survive the next.

She'd welcomed the blessed oblivion of sleep. Hells, she would've been happy if the tea had been laced with betane. At least then she could've slept through the horrendous ordeal of facing Guillaume again. Perhaps even sleep through the next week and the ball. Henri promised a plan, but Guillaume's actions told her the only plan that would free her once and for all, was the death of not just Otto, but Regan and Guillaume as well.

As much as she hated her stepmother and the crown prince, she was no murderer. They had to come up with a viable solution, they simply must. But what? And how? How was a huntsman and a sheltered woman supposed to outwit devious minds such as her foes?

Perhaps it was as simple as one misdirection at a time. If she could keep Regan's attention diverted, then she wouldn't discover the truth.

At least she'd had time to bathe before Regan returned, a small mercy. As it was, Regan was too angry to suspect Eira of anything other than grossly provoking Guillaume's perverse nature. If she hadn't been so shocked at Regan's rage, she would've thought her stepmother jealous. Disgusting. She could have the prince, and his horrid temper.

Thoughts of Guillaume twisted her gut and she shunted images of his arrogant face from her mind. If she allowed herself to relive the attack, she would cower into herself and lose the tiny bit of confidence her day with Henri had given her. One day, when she was no longer a prisoner and didn't fear the repercussions, perhaps then she would fully deal with what happened, but until such a day, it was easier to shove it aside and remain numb.

Besides, why waste perfectly good thoughts on the awful prince when she could spend her time recounting her day with Henri. She smiled to herself at the memory of his gorgeous naked body lying next to hers, and winced at the slice of pain it caused her jaw. He'd come to check on her even knowing doing so could be dangerous. He was right, she wasn't the same timid girl she'd been yesterday morning.

Something inside her awakened with their lovemaking, and it wasn't just her magic. A need to defend herself, to stand up to tyranny flowed through her veins, tempered only by the fact that she was woefully unprepared for such rebelliousness. But like anything else, could be learned. One small step would lead to bold leaps. If only she had enough time. And allies.

Her gaze went to the basket of apples on the table. Each morning that they showed up, she looked for any evidence of the old woman, but there was nothing to suggest anyone had been in her room—just a basket filled with red, ripe apples.

Eira rose from her chair and reached for an apple, knowing it would hurt to eat, but loved them too much to pass up, and could use whatever energy she suspected the old crone had spelled into them. Her gaze flicked to the wardrobe where the enchanted fruit Regan had given her to use on the king was tucked inside a wooden casket. She cocked her head and glanced at her breakfast that sat untouched on a gilded tray. She'd not had an appetite when she first woke, and now she was too pent up to eat, but knew she needed to keep up her strength.

Her gaze rested on the lone cup, full of what was surely now cold tea. Almost imperceptible flakes of green settled on the bottom of the cup. She poured the tea into the fire, unsurprised when it snapped and sparked. She poked at the bowl of porridge and saw tiny white flowers and more crushed green leaves. Not many, but once she really looked, enough to make her woozy, malleable.

Regan must've drugged Eira's food, too. Although, she did a piss-poor job. She must be getting desperate—it wasn't like her stepmother to leave evidence behind. She scooped half the porridge into the fireplace, hoping it would be enough to convince Regan she'd eaten the foul stuff.

An idea bubbled in her mind, one that would need expanding upon and careful planning. It was risky, with no guarantee it would work, but even in its infancy, she started to believe she had found a way out of her predicament. Hers and Henri's. She could free them both if the plan succeeded.

Unfortunately, the answer was in Regan's grimoire, and Eira was banished to her room for the entire day. She closed her eyes and willed the grimoire to show her a spell or incantation, anything to help, but nothing came. She'd never actually asked the grimoire for anything and was disappointed when only silence answered. She'd hoped it would work both ways. The information she needed had to be in the grimoire, how else had Regan known to enchant the apple?

She checked the door again to see whether Regan had left yet, but her stepmother still paced a steady circle around the sofa. Every so often, she'd cock her head, as if listening for something and then go back to walking in circles. If the damn woman would leave, then Eira could sneak into her rooms and look for the grimoire. While she was at it, she'd search for the silver the king allegedly paid her stepmother, too. To offset her impatience, she distracted herself by trying to work out how large a trunk Regan would need to hold that much money.

A servant entered the sitting room, and Eira straightened. She dared not open the door more than a slight crack, but that little bit showed enough that she was satisfied.

The girl nervously set down a tray and bowed to Regan before hurrying from the room. Regan watched her for a moment, her lips tight, but then she picked up the teapot and poured the contents into a delicate cup. Her stepmother wore an attractive gown of rust velvet and several strings of pearls that Eira didn't recognize. A gift from the king, perhaps? Or another suitor?

The servant returned and Regan snapped at her for intruding, but stopped her recrimination when Henri entered. He kept his face gruff, his eyes focused on her stepmother, and even though she knew he mustn't, Eira wished he'd glance her way, just for a quick smile.

"What news, Callan?" Regan wrung her hands and picked at a nail, a sure sign she was vexed.

"It is as your stepdaughter reports, my lady. The prince tried to take liberties with her, but she fought him off."

Interesting. So, Regan had asked for corroboration to her story. But did that mean Regan knew Henri had been there?

"If Eira's safety was in jeopardy, why didn't you intervene?"

Henri shuffled and looked properly circumspect. "I was seeing to the horses after our long ride."

Regan scoffed and waved a hand in his direction. "Naturally. Your kind always seem to gravitate to the muck. Although, you can't help it, can you? It's in your nature to love all things smelly and full of shit. Enough twaddle. Tell me about the prince. How close was he to defiling my stepdaughter?"

At this, Henri stiffened and curled his fingers into fists before flexing them and rolling his shoulders. "Too close. He not only had her hands firmly secured above her head, he nearly exposed his manhood and her modesty."

"Did the prince confide this to you himself?" Regan's non-reaction chilled Eira. Either she already knew the horrid details, or she was enjoying hearing Henri tell them.

To hear them speak of the attack so casually brought all of the emotions she'd tried to quell to the surface and her breathing deepened, her skin crawled with a sickly clamminess that made her twitch against her clothing. She didn't wish to relive those terrible moments when she didn't know if Guillaume would go through with his assault, or if Henri would be harmed. Bile swirled in her empty belly and sickness that she'd thus far kept at bay threatened to heave forth. She choked on her fear and reminded herself she was safe for the moment, as was Henri. It did little to diminish the anxiety that loosened with each passing moment of her stepmother's indifference.

"Madam, I have found when dealing with royalty, never ask the source. Apparently, the prince bragged about it to his valet, who then told me."

"Were there any witnesses?" Regan reached for her tea and then changed her mind. Eira studied her every move, trying to decide what angle her stepmother was playing.

"There were two stable boys, both of whom have mysteriously gone missing. I was grooming the horses, as I've said. It's believed there was someone else, but the prince didn't get a good look at him. Apparently, if he finds the lout, he'll make sure to cut out his tongue."

Henri cleared his throat, and Eira smothered a worried gasp. Certainly, Guillaume had recognized Henri. Or perhaps he hadn't in his rage-fueled flopping on the ground. Either way, for Henri to stay so calm while recounting the vile business was remarkable. He was remarkable.

"Yes, this witness must be found and dealt with." Venom laced Regan's words, but Eira didn't think her stepmother believed the witness was Henri.

Odd, to be sure. But the way Regan was reacting to Henri's tale made Eira believe Regan had more than one source of information regarding the assault. Who else would she consult? Another spy? Leon, perhaps? Eira made a mental note to ask him the next time they met.

Regan sniveled and her entire demeanor changed. Her

shoulders slouched and her face crumpled in helplessness. Eira had witnessed Regan's pitiful me performance before, and curious where she would take this game, shoved aside her discomfort to focus solely on her stepmother.

"What should I do, Callan? I can't very well leave her locked in her room until the ball, but with those randy princes prowling the halls, I have no choice." Regan grabbed his hands, startling Henri and infuriating Eira. "You must stay with her. Day and night, you must be her constant bodyguard."

Yes, please! Eira nearly clapped to hear the declaration.

"But take her away from the palace. Somewhere the princes won't find her." The simpering act continued, but Eira wasn't buying it. She knew her stepmother didn't have a feeble bone in her body.

"What about the king? Won't he miss her?" Henri played his part well, too. He wrung his hands and contorted his face with just enough doubt to be convincing.

"That's none of your concern." Regan tapped a tooth with a long fingernail, her lip curled. The façade of weakness waned as she plotted her next move. "Yes, this will do the trick. Take her somewhere safe where no one will recognize her and bring her back at two strokes before the ball is to start. Not a moment before, do you hear me?"

"Understood. Shall I send you updates?"

"Only if there's trouble. I expect you to leave within the hour. Now, go." She shooed him away, but Henri didn't move. "What is it? Do you need money?" She sighed and took several coins from her purse.

Eira doubted it would be enough to cover their costs, but Henri took the money and counted it like a true servant would.

"Why do you trust me with your stepdaughter? Aren't you afraid I'll take advantage of her?"

Regan laughed out loud, a brash laugh that was as fake as

her heart. "You? Seduce my Eira? Please. She has more sense than to bed someone of your position." She shook her head as if that was the most ridiculous idea she'd ever heard. Then, her face hardened and she grabbed Henri by the jaw, quick enough it startled him. "Besides, if you do, I'll cut you into little pieces and feed you to the king's mongrel beasts. Better yet, I'll let you loose in the forest where the king's trackers will hunt you down and gut you like a pig. And Callan," she pulled him to within a breath of her face. "Should you not return at two bells to the ball, both of your lives will be forfeit. Do you understand?"

Henri gaped at her with just the right amount of contrition and fear. He swallowed hard and nodded. Regan released him with a grunt and wiped her hand on her gown before waving him off.

As he turned, with his back to Regan, he glanced her way and winked. Eira swallowed against her heart pumping in her throat. She'd nearly soiled herself when Regan grabbed Henri, yet he played the role perfectly.

This was working out much better than she could've dreamed. Although, this meant she couldn't search for the grimoire or silver unless Regan left their rooms. That could wait, and hopefully by the time she and Henri returned, she wouldn't need the spell. This little gift Regan was giving them meant they had plenty of time to come up with a viable plan—one that didn't end in her death, real or fake.

She rushed to her wardrobe, but couldn't start packing until Regan told her about the change in plans. She bit into the apple and smothered a cry, forgetting about her injured jaw. She chewed gently while mentally planning her temporary escape. Damn Regan for thinking to warn Henri against running away. Even though she knew it could never happen, she'd secretly hoped somehow, they could.

Would Henri take her to the dwarves' cottage again? Or did

he know of somewhere else? Excitement bubbled through her thoughts, and she found it hard to concentrate on any one thing.

The apple finished, she tapped impatiently on the table. What was taking Henri so long? A bell chimed and Eira rushed to the door to see Regan stop her pacing. Several choice words dripped from her unnaturally crimson lips. It was a shade of lip pomade that Regan adored and Eira hated. Regan huffed and headed toward Eira's rooms with a look of hellfire upon her face.

Eira leapt to her bed and covered herself with the soft duvet, instantly feeling the pull of sleep. Damn varidian. It must stay in her system longer than she'd thought.

The door opened and Regan called softly, "Eira, darling, are you awake?" When she didn't move, her stepmother snorted. "Perhaps you're the one they should call sleeping beauty and not that wretch with golden curls." Regan snorted at her little joke. "Wake up." She pushed Eira hard enough she rocked forward and bumped her head on the wall.

"Ouch. Is that you, Stepmother?" Eira blinked sleepily and rolled over to look at the face she'd feared, loved, loathed, and mistrusted since they first met.

Regan sat on the edge of the bed and stroked Eira's face almost lovingly. "Tell me true, where were you yesterday?"

"In the forest. We had a lovely picnic." Eira rubbed her eyes and yawned loudly with a full body stretch. "Thank you for allowing me to have a day out."

"And Callan? Did he...do anything inappropriate?"

Eira widened her eyes, as if shocked her stepmother would ask such a thing. "He's a servant, he wouldn't dare." It was the truth. Henri hadn't done anything Eira didn't want and besides, she'd initiated their lovemaking, not him.

Regan's crooked grin confirmed she'd given the response her stepmother was looking for. "In that case, sleep a little more, my darling, and then you're going on another adventure."

She snuggled into the duvet and pretended to sleep. That was too easy. Even the excitement of going away with Henri couldn't take away the sense that Regan was planning something. The door snicked shut and Regan's low, throaty laughter flowed in her wake.

Chapter Twenty-Nine

Eira waited several minutes before she slunk out of the bed and opened the door just enough she could spy Regan sitting on the sofa enjoying a cup of tea. Despite her appearance, Eira could tell she was nervous, but why? What else was her stepmother planning? And where was Henri?

Regan barely blinked when a servant brought a fresh tray of tea and biscuits. It was only when they returned a few minutes later with Prince Guillaume that she stirred. She stood to greet him and stroked the pearls lovingly, her features a mixture of apprehension and irritation.

Eira couldn't breathe. Even though she knew it would happen eventually, she wasn't ready to see his smug face. Several thoughts crammed into her skull: of running away, of finding the nearest dagger and plunging it into his dead heart, of crumpling to the floor and sobbing. She curled her nails into her palm and focused on the pain she intentionally caused. Her nostrils flared with each tight breath and her chest heaved with the thrum of her heart. Where was Henri? She'd hoped he would arrive before she had to see Guillaume again. She thought she could handle it, but it was too much to bear.

Yet she must. She'd lived through Regan's abuse, she could overcome this. She pulled herself up and straightened her shoulders. If she weakened, the prince won.

Guillaume bowed to Regan, his brown eyes sparkling in the candlelight. "You look lovely as ever, Lady Banworth." His body pressed against Regan's and his mouth covered hers as if he were about to consume her whole. They writhed and thrust against each other for an indecent amount of time. Their moans could probably be heard all the way in the forest.

Eira stifled a gasp and watched the couple through the crack in the doorway. How could they behave so indecently after what he'd done to her? The sourness in her stomach burned straight to her throat and she gagged at the gross display happening only twenty paces away.

"What were you thinking? You could've ruined everything." Regan took a step backward and slapped him across his ruddy cheek, much the same way Eira had the night before. "I told you to frighten her, not fuck her."

Eira's heart stuttered. She'd heard wrong. No, her step-mother wouldn't have condoned the prince's appalling behavior.

"You dare?" Guillaume rubbed his face and glared at Regan. "I will ignore your attack on my person and remind you of what you've promised." He waved a stack of papers in his hand. "Eira certainly plays the part well enough. I'm surprised that you were able to school her in total innocence." His gaze lowered to Regan's breasts. "Who would've thought you capable of such a feat. I must say, she excels in her acting prowess. Even I am convinced she's a virgin."

"Of course she is, and that naivete you mock is genuine. Even so, she knows what's at stake, the same as you. And she's not about to throw it all away over some ridiculous idea of ego." Regan stabbed him in the chest. "Stick to the plan. Flirt with her, but don't you dare touch my stepdaughter again. Once your father is dead and you're king, you may do whatever you wish when she's your wife, but until then, she's off limits. I'm sure there's more than enough women to satisfy your urges for a few more days."

His wife? Never. Was she to be bartered to first his father, and then to the prince? What was Regan playing at?

"As long as you keep your promise." Again, he waved the papers.

They were too far away for Eira to see what was written on them.

"I'm a woman of my word. You do as we agreed and I will see that you're well-tended, my lord."

Guillaume grabbed Regan's buttocks and pulled her close. She made a delicate little squeak that would've sounded believable if she wasn't such a scheming witch.

"Come to my rooms. Satisfy my urges in the way only you can."

"Naughty, naughty, Your Highness. If you're a good boy, I'll think about it." She rose on tiptoe to lick the scratch Eira had given him and brushed her lips quickly against his. "So it's true, she truly did fight?"

"Our mouse has grown some claws, it seems. Rein her in, Regan, or she'll be the ruin of us all."

"I've already taken care of it."

Guillaume growled in Regan's ear. She giggled and fanned herself, but the moment he turned his back to sit on the sofa, Regan wiped her mouth with the back of her hand.

The deception went deeper than Eira had ever imagined. Why would Regan promise her to the king *and* to Guillaume? His threats cycled through her mind and she began to suspect they weren't threats at all, but foreplay. Sick, twisted, and demented, that was Guillaume's true self.

By the time Regan poured them tea, Eira had imagined six

ways she'd like to kill them both. But that was fantasy, nothing more. To take another's life wasn't something she should ever wish for, no matter how devious and decrepit the person was. She simply wasn't a murderer. And yet, she wasn't a mouse, either. At least, not anymore.

She flexed her hand and allowed herself a moment of pride that somehow, she'd found the courage to stand up to Guillaume. It was a small step, but one closer to standing up to her stepmother, too. Although, a silky thought curled down her spine, if Henri hadn't shown up, she wasn't sure she would've had the nerve to knee the prince in his privates. But she couldn't allow Guillaume to harm Henri.

A flare of anger shot through her, and she clenched her fists. Cut out his tongue. Indeed. If anyone deserved something cut off, it was Guillaume. Cruel didn't come close to describing him. He'd make an even worse king than his father. How had Leon remained kind in a palace full of tyrants? She knew the answer without having to think about it—the same as her. It was their form of survival.

"Tell me, have you news of your father? Is he still ailing? I admit, Lady Annah does a remarkable job making him appear healthy." Regan said nonchalantly, her finger tracing the edge of her cup, her tongue roving over her lips. "Moreover, does he believe our little ruse that Eira longs to be his wife?"

Otto was indeed ill, and Regan knew. Dread circled her thoughts. What if Regan was the one responsible for Otto's illness? Her gaze went to the wardrobe where the apple was hidden. Or did Guillaume play a role in his father's situation? Neither could be trusted and with the revelation that Eira was intended for the prince, she had to be extra cautious. Henri needed to know this new development.

Guillaume shrugged and guzzled his drink. "My father is a fool. Of course he believes Eira desires him. He told me himself that he looks forward to his wedding with unbridled enthusiasm." He held his cup in a toast. "To the happy couple." His dry laugh was like daggers to Eira's nerves. Sickness swirled in her gut and she swallowed against it.

"Excellent." Regan tapped a nail to her tooth. "He mustn't learn of your little incursion last night. We can't risk him souring on my stepdaughter."

"Quite the contrary. I told the old badger myself. I think he enjoyed hearing how she fought and looks forward to breaking in his new filly. Truth be told, the fact she resisted I think emboldened him to her affections. Poor sod. He still thinks himself attractive after all these years."

What was she hearing? Guillaume boasted to the king about the assault? She truly wasn't safe in this palace. Where the hells was Henri? She had to escape. If even for a few days, she needed to get away from these terrible people who cared nothing for anyone but themselves.

Regan regarded the prince cooly and Eira's muscles tensed as if it were she who would receive the lashing Regan was about to unleash. "Since you can't control your *urges*, I've decided to send Eira away until the ball." She adjusted her hair and sat half-sideways, which made her breasts bulge above her neckline. The pearls lifted and lowered with her measured breaths.

Guillaume noticed, as she was certain he was meant to do. What she didn't expect was for him to lean forward and pinch Regan's nipple. Her stepmother swatted his hand away without much conviction.

"Not now. With Eira away, we won't have to sneak around anymore."

"How will you convince her to leave?"

Regan rolled her eyes and waved a hand as if it didn't matter. "She'll do whatever I tell her to. I've arranged for that halfwit servant I hired to spy on her to hide her someplace safe. I'm sure he'll take her to his parents' farm, or wherever he comes from, and she'll stare moonily at the flowers the entire time. The goddess knows she can't stay here. She looks ghastly from the bruise you left, I can hardly look at her without retching. In any case, I can't risk having her roam the halls looking less than perfect. She is, after all, the fairest in all the land. Besides, she hates being here. I hate having her here. Ideal solution."

Unbelievable. Guillaume attacked her, and they were discussing how uncomfortable it made Regan. If only she could reach her magic. If only she could run away without fear of being hunted by the king's elite trackers. If only—no. She stopped herself from letting the negative thoughts spiral. She and Henri would come up with a plan that would free them both. She had to believe in that. Believe in them. They had to have faith in more than the goddess now.

"What about Father?"

"What about him? He still owes me payment and until I see my silver, he's not getting anywhere near my stepdaughter."

"So, you'll continue the farce?"

Regan leaned forward, exposing even more cleavage. "Oh darling, *we* will continue the farce. I love seeing your father red with jealousy. Just the thought that you might steal that which he believes to be his makes me wet."

"And the night of the ball? Have those plans changed?" Guillaume rubbed the front of Regan's bodice, and Eira looked away.

"Not at all. By the stroke of midnight, we'll both be free, darling."

Eira leaned against the wall, her heart pounding in her ears. What did Regan mean, free? And why hadn't the king paid the gross sum he'd promised?

She turned back to the door and swallowed her revulsion at seeing the pair practically rutting on the sofa.

Guillaume lifted his head from Regan's bosom. "How long until she's gone?"

"That halfwit should be here soon. If you're worried that she might overhear, don't be. I put valerian in her tea this morning. Just a touch to affect her mind, but not completely wipe her out. I enjoy her company so much more when she's...pliable."

"You devious woman."

"You love it." Regan's throaty laughter slammed against the paneling of the door.

There was a word for what her stepmother was, but Eira was too much of a lady to say it aloud.

The empty teacup and half-eaten food sat on the gilded tray. Regan was orchestrating an elaborate game, pitting one player against the other, including the king. If there was one thing Eira knew to be true—Regan would make certain she won in the end. But what did that mean for Eira and Henri? Why send them away for nearly a week? Whatever Regan's reasons, Eira didn't believe they had to do with her best interests. The ruse her stepmother and Guillaume spoke about, it was at the heart of the game, but what was it? Regan thought her stepdaughter stupid and Eira was happy to let her believe she was, but she was done being manipulated and coerced. She'd not wed the king, or his arrogant, malignant, psychopath son.

She'd die before she let that happen.

Chapter Thirty

Eira followed Henri through the quiet corridors of the palace with her hood pulled low over her face. It kept her from being recognized, but the scumbering fabric made it hard to see where she was going. Henri had helped her pack, choosing only clothes that were sensible and nothing with beads or expensive lace. The one pair of shoes he allowed were the sturdy boots she wore. He hadn't even let her take her fur-trimmed cloak and matching muff.

In her mind, she pictured they'd find a bucolic setting somewhere away from the palace with a meadow and, yes, pretty flowers she could enjoy for hours. Not stare moonily at, but definitely savor their sweet scents and delicate touch. And naturally, there would be plenty of time for savoring Henri's exquisite body. Several days of nothing but Henri was paradise. If Regan knew how much Eira looked forward to being banished, she was certain to have fits.

Eira stopped suddenly. "We have to go back. I forgot the apples."

"We can get more after we're settled." He urged her forward, but she shook her head

"I can't leave the basket there, or Regan will know someone's been in my room. What if she discovers the old woman? I can't risk her getting whipped because of my forgetfulness." Eira worked her jaw, surprised there wasn't more pain. "I have a feeling those apples are enchanted to give strength and stamina. Tell me, do you see bruising on my face?" She held her chin at an angle for him to appraise.

His eyes narrowed and his lips curved downward. "I do not. You think this is from the apples?"

"I do. I fear what will happen if Regan discovers magical fruit in my room. Besides, they're meant for Sacheen. We must go back."

He chewed a cuticle and gave a curt nod. "Very well, but we must hurry."

They rushed through the halls to her rooms. When they turned a corner, Eira spied Leon walking toward them at the other end of the hallway. Henri steered her away from the main entrance to her suite to an alcove she'd not noticed before. She watched silently as he pressed a decorative knob and a hidden door swung open. He ushered her inside while scanning the hallway.

A torch lit when he entered and she suspected they were all magically enhanced. She gathered her thoughts and realized this must be the same walkway she'd used on her first day when she found Sacheen in the dungeons. She hurried forward, unsure which door led to her room, but Henri stopped her at the fourth door.

He placed a finger to his lips and she shivered at the memory of him in the king's antechamber. So much had happened since then, she wasn't the same meek, vulnerable creature she'd been, yet there was still so much more she could be.

Henri pushed open the door and peeked inside. After several long, agonizing moments, he beckoned her forward and they slipped into her bedchamber unnoticed. The door to her room stood open, with the gilded tray still on the table beside the basket of fruit. Her gaze went to the fireplace where the fire had burned low.

There was no sign of the porridge she'd tossed into the flames. Relieved, she reached for the basket, but the sound of Leon's strong voice stopped her. She shared a glance with Henri and the two of them crept closer to the door, but kept out of sight.

"You summoned me, my lady? How may I do your bidding?" Sarcasm dripped from Leon's lips.

"Don't be so sullen, Your Highness." Regan grinned demurely, her head tilted at just the right angle, her lashes fluttering at just the right tempo. "I've decided to do the right thing and keep your secret."

Leon's chest heaved. "And why is that? Why now?"

"Do you know what your brother was up to last night?"

"No, and I don't care to. Gil and I have differing ideas of... entertainment." His jaw clenched and unclenched several times and he ran his palm over his trousers. He was lying. Did Regan see the signs, too?

"He thought to take it upon himself to ruin our dear Eira. A little too much wine emboldened him to seek her out and, according to my spies, he came too damn close to carrying out his attack."

"What does that have to do with me?"

"Everything, darling. Do this one thing for me and I'll release you from any further obligations to me." Regan picked up a glass box small enough to fit three apples at most, and handed it to Leon. "I want you to kill our precious would-be queen." She tapped the glass. "Bring back her still beating heart."

Eira smothered her gasp, biting the soft flesh of her hand to keep from crying out. Regan was mad, completely, if she thought Leon would do such a thing. She looked to Henri, but he was staring intently at the pair in the sitting room, his jaw clenched, brow furrowed.

She should've been appalled her stepmother would so blatantly command a member of the royal family to commit murder. And not just any murder, but her own stepdaughters. And not just in any fashion, but as Regan had told the prophecy for all those years. It was entirely possible she'd made up the whole thing just to frighten Eira and keep her from venturing into the forest.

Eira breathed through the rage that tormented her belly and gripped the basket with trembling fingers. Revenge could wait, she pressed her face closer to hear Leon's reply.

"You go too far, Lady Banworth. I refuse." He pushed the glass box toward Regan.

"Oh, come now, we both know murder isn't beneath you. What's one more? She's just a stupid girl who means nothing to you. Unless you've grown fond of her. Have you, Prince Leon? Do you have desires for my Eira?"

His nostrils flared. "We are friends, nothing more. But she is innocent. She doesn't deserve what you're asking me to do."

"Think of her as prey. You love a good chase, do you not?" Regan made little running motions with her fingers. "Hunt her through the forest until she's quite exhausted. Once you've had your fun, carve out her heart." Her delirious laughter boomed in the elegant room. "And when you bring me her beating heart, I'll reward you with a nice belly rub."

"You're mad."

"Oh yes, quite so. You'll do this for me because you couldn't live with the alternative."

Leon's shoulders drooped and Eira knew Regan had won. "Why do you need her heart?"

"That's not important. Oh, and darling Leon, make sure it appears as though the huntsman is responsible. Your kind have been persecuted enough."

Leon's knuckles turned white and Eira feared he might shatter the glass. "Am I to murder him as well?"

"Of course. Consider it my gift to you. Another killing to satisfy your savage passion." Regan slid her hand up his tunic and stroked along his jaw. "You could've been my adversary, Your Highness. Then we wouldn't have had to deal with such vulgarities."

Leon pushed her hand aside and glared at Regan. "Do not touch me, witch."

Henri backed away from the door and indicated that they leave. Instead of going the way they came, Henri turned them to the left outside Eira's bedchamber, toward the dungeons. At the spiral staircase, he continued onward, his face set in grim determination. Eira followed, lost in her own thoughts. Was this the original plan, or had it been altered? If so, what changed so that now Regan wanted them both killed? In a way, it made sense. Leon kills them, the huntsman—Henri—is blamed. It looks like a murder and suicide, no one is to believe any different, so there's no inquiry. So simple. So easy. So devious.

That was Regan. Using others to do the dirty work and absolving herself of any guilt. Would Leon go through with it? He already admitted he'd do anything to hide his secret. But murder?

Her mind went to the day in the meadow when she saw Madam Davina bandaging his wounds. They were jagged strips that could've come from another wolf. Had he fought someone? Another shifter, perhaps?

At last Henri opened a door to the outside and she breathed as if she'd been holding her breath the entire time. She bent at the waist, gulping fresh air.

"We must hurry, Eira. Our plans have not changed, but we must be more vigilant now than ever."

"Do you think he'll go through with it?"

"I don't know what to think anymore." He pulled her hood low over her head. "Keep your pretty face out of sight. We have no friends here, only enemies, it seems."

And they were multiplying by the minute.

Chapter Thirty-One

In their rush, Eira had quite completely lost any sense of direction and had no idea where they were. By the sounds around them, they'd passed the stables and were walking on packed dirt paths. The sound of a gate creaked, and she chanced a glance in that direction, only to see Henri's broad chest blocking her view.

Her thoughts were a jumble of half-formed ideas, escapes, pleas they might use, but nothing made sense anymore. She'd known Regan resented her, but to the extent she'd have her own stepdaughter murdered so savagely, it was beyond anything she might've imagined Regan capable of, and yet, here she was, running for her life. That life, and her trust, now rested with a man she'd only known a short while and who had started their relationship as a spy for her stepmother.

Regan's actions upended everything she thought she knew, especially her newfound feelings for Henri. If Leon could be so easily manipulated, who was to say Henri wasn't playing Regan's game as well?

She had to believe he wouldn't harm her. If he turned on her, then she was well and truly lost. The apples bobbed in the basket and the dangerous plan she'd begun forming in her bedchamber resurfaced. It was too risky to share just yet. Once she knew she could trust Henri explicitly, she would tell him her idea.

As she hurried beside him, Eira shuffled puzzle pieces into place. That Regan was manipulating them all was a simple fact, but what she couldn't understand was what Regan meant when she said she'd be free by midnight the night of the ball. *How* would Regan would be free? Free from what? If her stepmother's scheme with Leon succeeded, Eira would already be dead by the time of the ball. There would be no wedding, no silver from the king, no nothing.

She chewed the ends of a lock of hair and replayed Regan's conversations with Henri, Guillaume, Leon, and herself. So deep in thought was she, that she didn't notice Henri had stopped until she ran into him.

"Careful, princess."

"Why do you call me that?" She smoothed her cape and adjusted her hood.

"You're pledged to the king. Doesn't that make you a princess by default?"

"Not necessarily. Although, I haven't seen the betrothal papers, so it is possible, but I doubt it." She narrowed her eyes and pursed her lips. "If not for everything else I've learned, that alone would explain Guillaume's hatred of me. I mean, why would he care if his father weds again? Otto's had many wives in Gil's lifetime. I shouldn't be special."

Henri cupped her cheek. "You are extraordinarily special. At least, you are to me."

She warmed at his touch and longed to kiss him, but hesitated, doubt took root where only a day before hope had blossomed. Undeterred, he bent his head and brushed her lips with his own.

"And you deserve to be treated like a queen."

"Thank you. For everything." If his friendship was true, she owed him a great deal. But, what was real? And who could she trust? Moreover, who around her wished her dead? She lifted her chin so that she could see better beneath the hood and looked around in confusion. Long outbuildings, each with several doors lined three sides of a courtyard. "Where are we?"

"The perfect hiding place. Come." He opened a door and led her into a plain room outfitted with two cots, a cooktop, and a small wooden table with two chairs.

"A ground-level dungeon?"

Henri's laugh echoed off the bare walls. "It's the barracks. I spoke with the captain of the guard and he agreed to let us stay here. These buildings haven't been in use for some time, so no one will disturb us here. We have complete privacy." He pointed to a cupboard behind her. "We'll dress like the king's guard, so no one will recognize us. This way, we can spy on your stepmother without her knowing."

Sludge-like disappointment pooled in her belly. "So, no meadow? No flowers? No making love all day and night?"

His chuckle cut through some of the murk. "We'll see what we can manage on those cots. As for the rest of your fantasy, I'm sorry, but no. As much as I'd love to spend my days making love to you, there are games afoot and until we know what else your stepmother is planning, we can't react accordingly."

"Well, pooh. What you say is true, and what I've been telling myself as well, but a girl can dream."

"As you should. In the next few days, we'll find a way to make those dreams a reality."

"Won't Leon find us here? You said it yourself, wolves are excellent trackers." She liked the idea of being close to the palace to keep tabs on her wicked stepmother, but not being so close they made it easy for Leon to carry out Regan's kill order.

"I have an idea of how we might thwart his efforts." Henri winked at her and put her bag atop the cupboard. "I can use my magic to alter our appearances. That won't eliminate our scent, but hopefully it will confuse him enough to give us the time we need."

"I don't suppose there's a way I can help?" Lawks, but she hated that she couldn't reach her magic.

"Stay out of sight as best you can. What I propose doesn't come without its risks."

She took the guard's uniform he offered and changed into it without much enthusiasm. A meadow and stars was much, much preferable. So was staying alive. The wool uniform scratched against her skin, but at least she was allowed to wear trousers. She stretched her legs and bent low, enjoying the freedom of movement pant legs allowed.

"How does a huntsman know the captain of the guard? And for that matter, how are you able to roam the palace at will? Are you friends with the king?" Her stomach coiled at an image of them drinking together, laughing about how innocent she was.

Henri's eyes darkened even more than usual, and anger flashed in their depths. "I am not, nor will I ever be, friends with that repulsive man. When your stepmother asked if I was loyal to the king, I wasn't lying when I said no. As for the captain, he's a friend of my father's." He brushed a speck of dust from her shoulder. "And I never said I was a huntsman. You assumed I was and I didn't correct you."

She mulled over his words. "If you're not a huntsman, but you know the captain of the king's guard, and are friends with dwarves, what is it you do?"

"I do a little bit of everything. It's my job to know who's coming and going in the kingdom, and what their intentions are."

"You're a spy."

"Not a spy, either. For now, it's best you don't know, but I promise you—if we survive until the ball, I shall tell you at the stroke of midnight six days hence."

"I need to trust you, Henri. Tell me who you are."

His jaw clenched and little crinkles formed at the corners of his narrowed eyes. She sensed his apprehension and almost regretted demanding to know, but she spoke true—she needed his trust.

"I am an ambassador of sorts. Please, Eira, I think I've proved you can trust me implicitly, and on this one thing, I must beg you to wait less than a sennight."

"An ambassador?" A slow smile lifted her lips and she chuckled. "Why would Regan think you a huntsman? I confess, I haven't known any ambassadors, present company excluded, but I imagine they are ruffled and stuffed show ponies who crave the attentions of the nobles and king."

"Your stepmother saw me with an axe and made an assumption. I chose not to correct her. One day, I will share the whole sordid story." He grinned as if he were a cat who'd finally caught a wily mouse. "But right now, I am your teacher. Come."

"More lessons?" Her heartbeat tripled and blood warmed.

"Not those kinds of lessons. Later, we will work with your magic, and after that we can try out the cots, but right now, I am going to teach you how to defend yourself. That move you used on the prince last night was impressive, but clumsy. I'm going to make sure if he ever approaches you again, you can get out of any hold he uses on you."

Excitement coursed through her at the prospect of defending herself with more than plucky courage and luck.

An hour later, that excitement had long passed. Sweat rolled over her temples and down her back to pool in the crack of her arse. Breeches seemed like they'd be good fun to wear, but they didn't allow her legs to breathe the way skirts did.

Everything hurt. Even her eyelids ached from blinking against the midday sun, and yet Henri's enthusiasm never waned, despite the terrible names she called him.

"One last move. Remember, the goal isn't to overpower me. It's to regain control so you have a chance to escape." He grabbed her wrist like he'd done in the secret passageway the first day they'd met. "Try to break free."

She jerked her arm and twisted this way and that, but his grip never lessened. "I can't. You're too strong." As soon as the words were out of her mouth, she regretted them.

He let go and held out his arm. A disappointed tut came from between clenched teeth. "You need to use their body weight against them. Grab my wrist."

She did as told and in a single move, he had her on her knees. It was too quick for her to see what he did, but the way he held her arm behind her, she recognized that even someone larger than her would have a hard time retaliating if she held them thusly. With more patience than she deserved, he showed her, step by step, how to take control if someone grabbed her wrist. She practiced it several times until she felt confident that if surprised, she would remember what to do. With so many defensive postures roving through her mind, the trick was to recall quickly which one was needed in different scenarios. An impossible task, to be sure.

She bent at the waist and huffed her exhaustion. One more day of this might kill her and then she wouldn't need to know how to defend herself. With so many wishing her death already, she should be grateful Henri took the time to instruct her how to protect herself. The thought sobered her, and she rose to find Henri watching her with a curious expression on his face.

"You're terribly unfit. What do ladies do all day? Embroider?"

She wiped her brow and shrugged. "A little, but truth be

told, I'm rubbish at it. Let's see, my day usually starts early—much earlier than Regan's. A tray with my breakfast is always waiting for me. I like to read a little before I begin my studies. Then I spend several hours with my tutor, learning my letters and numbers. I like to think I'm not a terrible pupil, but since I'm the only one she tutors, I really have no idea. Regan is constantly telling me I'm thick, so perhaps I am not very bright."

"Don't believe your stepmother's lies. You are incredibly smart. She's convinced you, and herself, that you're dimwitted so that she can control you. Surely you must see this?"

"I didn't before, but I am starting to now. As for the rest of my day, I play games with the servants or read."

"But no physical activity?"

She shook her head. "Unfortunately not, but I can tell you practically anything you need to know about the kingdom."

"What about the other kingdoms?"

"What other kingdoms? There's only Jura."

He stared at her as if she'd lost her mind. "Only Jura? What about Ronce? Morovia? Charbonnel? Trevana? Allanica? Ventoux?"

Again, she shook her head. "I've never heard of them."

He kicked the dirt and paced a hard circle, swearing low enough she could make out enough sounds to know he spoke a foreign language.

"You just admitted I'm not stupid. I've seen a map before and there was only Jura." Granted, at the time her tutor showed her the map, she'd inquired about other kingdoms, but was told she need only worry about Jura. After the lesson, Regan had beaten her badly enough she vowed never to think of anywhere but her kingdom ever again. But she shared none of this with Henri. He was already acting as if she'd betrayed him in some way.

"Follow me." He stormed off, and she jogged to catch up.

Two hallways down, and several turns later, he ushered her

into a room crammed with books, and papers overflowed from desks onto the floor. On the wall were several maps. Only one she recognized.

Beyond Jura's borders were many kingdoms: some small, some large. Even a few that were bigger than Jura by quite a lot.

"My history lessons never mentioned these kingdoms." She traced a finger along a mountain range in a tiny kingdom to the south. "Do you think their rulers are as harsh as King Otto?"

"Most of the kings and queens of these realms are benevolent. They take good care of their subjects and don't overly tax them for trivial fancies."

Guilt cut through Eira, and her hand trembled. "Like Otto paying for me."

"As the king has for many things, only one of which is you, although I would argue that you are anything but trivial." Henri waved an arm to indicate the palace beyond this room. "He wrongly believes all of this makes him look like a strong and powerful ruler. It only serves to make him appear the fool."

Her finger roved over the mountains to the sea. "Charbonnel. Is the king here good?"

"The king is wise and kind, yes, but his son Alaric is not so charming. Granted, he pales in comparison to the princes here, but he is vain and arrogant all the same. And here, in Allanica, I've heard rumors that the crown prince made a bargain with a sea witch to capture the heart of a mermaid."

Eira gasped at the absurdity. "You're jesting. Mermaids aren't real, are they?"

"Did you believe in dwarves before you met my friends?"

"I've been sheltered and deceived." She sighed with suppressed longing. What other wonders existed beyond the borders both mental and physical that she'd always thought made up the whole or her world? The books she'd read mentioned places with names similar to what she saw on the map. If she had to guess, she'd say Regan magically manipulated the pages to keep Eira from getting wanderlust. No more. She was in charge of her education from this moment forward. "Now that I know these places exist, I want to visit them all. Especially those by the sea. I've always longed to see the ocean in person."

"Then I shall take you to see them all. We'll start with Ventoux and work our way clockwise until every kingdom has been conquered. Once we've dealt with our situation here, and assured your freedom, we'll set forth."

"I honestly don't know if you're teasing and I don't care. It sounds divine." She tapped her chin, "Ventoux...I've heard that name before. I thought it was a person, not a place. Guillaume mentioned it, I believe."

"He's keen to make a treaty with that kingdom. One that benefits himself, I would wager."

Eira eyed him skeptically. "Friend of dwarves, knowledge-able about palace politics...you are quite the enigma, Master Callan. Or should I address you as Ambassador?"

"Just Henri, please. As for my abilities, I find it's easier to survive when I'm aware of the dangers. A trait you would do well to embrace."

"I've been thinking." She kept her gaze on her clasped hands, not yet confident in her musings. "Just after I left you in the antechamber that first day, Lady Annah tried to strangle me with magic. I believe she desired to go through with it, but she stopped short of me passing out. Since she's the king's mistress, what if Otto does know about my power and is seeking to use me somehow for his own gain? I'm afraid if Otto or Annah get control of me, I'll be unable to stop them." She breathed through her nose, her chest heaving. "That day, I overheard them say something would happen the night of the ball to save him, or heal him, I'm not entirely sure."

Henri rubbed a finger along his jaw and stared into the

distance, his eyes glassy. "Interesting. They very well could be planning something, and if so, we need to know in order to thwart their plans. There's only one way to find out. It's time the mouse outwits the cat." He winked and headed for the door. "We shall spy on them all and the best part is, they won't even know it."

Dressing like a guard was one thing. But play fighting with wooden swords and learning self-defense moves wasn't enough to make her appear authentic. This was a terrible plan. Unfortunately, it was the only one that would get them answers. If it didn't get them killed.

Chapter Thirty-Two

King Otto bellowed for more wine, his stained lips glossy with drink. To anyone who didn't know he was sick, they would see an inebriated monarch, but Eira saw beyond the wine to the tremble of his hands, the slightly jaundiced skin, and the perspiration on his forehead. He hid his illness well, or rather, she suspected Annah hid it with her magic.

A nervous serving girl shuffled close, her face set in a genial smile. Eira watched the scene from beneath the feathered cap she wore and winced when the king grabbed the girl's buttocks. She giggled and tossed her hair, but the look of dread in her eyes didn't escape Eira's notice.

They'd been spying on the king the entire afternoon and were no closer to solving their riddle than they'd been when Eira had first arrived at the palace what seemed a lifetime ago. Henri floated from one pillar to another, making affable conversation with the other guards in between surreptitious glances at Eira. Beads of sweat gathered on her forehead and she longed to release her hair from the wool cap, but she had to look the part, if not exactly play the part.

She studied the real guards and mimicked their posture, their walk, even the way they spoke to each other, and she still felt like a fraud. Because she was. The splotches of dirt Henri had smudged on her face to hide her beauty itched and she needed to relieve herself. How did the guards manage? Standing for hours without a break was sheer hell, but these lunatics seemed to enjoy it. She tried to act interested, but she'd been raised in a castle far from talk of battles and which weapon was more effective at a distance and which to use in close combat.

What she admired most was the comradery. The guards, made up of men and women, formed a tight family and even in the short amount of time she pretended to be one, she felt that sense of brotherhood. They protected each other like a family should.

Her gaze went to Henri, and she idly wondered about his siblings. He said he had sisters, but didn't mention any brothers. Did they get along? She couldn't imagine them not. He probably played peacemaker. An image of him romping through the woods with a toddler clutching his back went through her mind, and she grinned. He most likely had not only his siblings, but a dozen cousins back home—wherever his home was.

His cagey answers didn't go unnoticed by her, but eventually, she'd suss out his secrets. Why he felt he needed to be obtuse was intriguing, if also irritating.

A commotion at the other end of the courtyard where the king was presently ensconced drew her attention, and a dread-filled chill scraped along her neck. Escorted by the elder prince was an exact replica of—her. Guillaume beamed as he held the false Eira's elbow and wove between the courtiers. Behind the pair, Leon scowled and clenched his fists, his jaw flexing.

She flicked a glance at Henri, and his expression looked as troubled as she felt. What the scumbering hell was going on?

A flash of nightmare played out in her mind, of Regan

looking like Eira as she straddled a very naked Guillaume. Her mind whirled and a second image broke through, of a page in her stepmother's grimoire with a spell to cast yourself as another. Raw fury battled against her beliefs. Regan had gone too far this time. No wonder she was only too happy to drug Eira and then remove her from court as if she was being benevolent. She needed the real Eira out of the way so that she could perpetuate her charade. It made Eira sick. And angry, and also sad.

Henri watched the false Eira as she demurely curtseyed and giggled at something the king said. She batted her eyelashes and cooled herself with an extravagant lace fan that Eira didn't recall owning. Around her neck she wore the only item Eira owned of her mother's—the ruby pendant. Rage burned through whatever vestiges of love she'd had for Regan. The spark she'd nurtured for so long snuffed out, leaving a pit of darkness in her gut, an emptiness in her heart. It was long overdue, and she was happy to be rid of her affections for a woman who deserved nothing from her.

From somewhere deep, she felt a calling to her, as if the pendant reached out to whisper something in her ear, but she was too far away. A low simmering warmed her insides and she rubbed the place where Henri had brought her magic forth. If she wasn't certain it would ruin everything and perhaps end with her hanging, she would've raced to the false Eira and ripped the pendant from her neck. She took a step back to put distance between her and Regan, but the whole of Jura wasn't far enough to keep her from seething with hatred for the woman.

The king leaned forward and placed a sparkling bracelet around the false Eira's wrist before kissing along the soft underside of her forearm. That Eira swooned and made all the appropriate sounds, which the king lapped up as if it were an expensive wine.

The display disgusted her, and she absently rubbed her wrist against her trousers as if to remove his taint. Staying was torture, but she remained where she was, eager to learn more. Henri skulked closer to Otto, keeping to the shadows. Eira stood still as if at attention, not wanting to draw attention to herself and expose their disguises.

The more she studied the false Eira, the wilder her stomach churned. Each mannerism, while appearing to be the real Eira's, was stuttered. The moves weren't as fluent as they should be if they were innate to the person. When the false Eira chatted to a courtier and stopped to ponder his question, she tapped a nail to her teeth.

Bile crept suspiciously close to the back of her throat, and Eira dug her nails into her palm to keep from screaming. How dare Regan betray her this blatantly? How dare those courtiers believe the lie! Yet they'd never had a chance to meet her, or to know the real Eira. Regan saw to that quite efficiently.

Yet this new information only added to the conundrum and took Eira leagues away from finding an answer. To what end did Regan hope for with this farce? And, thrumming in the back of her mind, an ever present threat, why did Regan need her still-beating heart?

"We'll learn nothing more tonight. Let's get dinner and retire to our rooms before we overstay our welcome," Henri whispered in her ear.

She nearly jumped at the sound, not having seen or heard him approach. Some spy she made.

"It's Regan." She jutted her chin at the appalling woman.

"That's my guess as well." He led her away from the court-yard, toward the orchards. "Your stepmother, as the pretend Eira, negotiated with the king to move the wedding to midnight at the ball. Why, is the question."

"She mentioned something about being free before

midnight. Free of the king, and of me." Eira breathed in the scent of apples and paused. "I haven't taken my friend her apples. Do you think we could now?"

The basket was with her belongings in the barracks, so she made a pouch out of her coat to carry as many as she could. Henri shoved several in his pockets and led her to yet another entrance to the dungeons.

"This palace is a bloody maze."

"It's to confuse people. You should see the intricate walkways hidden behind the rooms." He grinned at her and nudged her shoulder. "But then, you already found some of them, didn't you?"

"How does she do it?" She didn't want to think about that morning when he'd grabbed her and she'd been rude to him.

"It's a simple enough spell. All you need is a few ingredients, including something from the person you want to impersonate. Hair, fingernails, a tooth. The spell only lasts a short while, longer if you're more experienced."

"How do you know so much about spells and magic?" She absently rubbed the place where he'd made her skin shimmer with his own power.

"My mother's best friend was quite gifted. She had power like you and me, pure born, innate."

"What happened to her?"

"She died when I was little, but my mother kept up my lessons. We have an extensive library at home full of the history of magic, including sorceresses and their bloodlines."

An entire library full of books that weren't hidden or banned or locked up. What she would give to spend even an hour in such a place. She would certainly find a way to unblock her magic. It wasn't fair that Annah and Regan and Henri could use their magic at will, but she was kept from hers. Now that she knew it wasn't just her own doing, she was determined to discover a way of releasing the ward on her power. And then find a way to never, ever, let that happen again.

She nearly swooned at the thought. "I should like to see your library one day."

"It would be my pleasure."

They made a quick detour to the kitchens, and Eira waited in a dark alcove while he ducked into the noisy rooms. When he retrieved her from the hiding place, she cocked a brow at a bundle of bread, a leg of roasted lamb, and cheese tucked beneath his arm. He flashed a charming smile, but didn't elaborate. He didn't need to. Whatever duties an ambassador did, she was just grateful he had a kind heart and also a tiny bit ashamed she thought he could ever kill her.

At the end of two flights of stairs, they came to a dark tunnel. Henri lit a torch with a square of flint and some straw. They entered the dungeons through the main door, their uniforms allowing them entry unchallenged. The scratchy things were quite useful when subterfuge was in play.

Babbling came from the cell area, and Eira hung back, not wanting to risk being seen by the new prisoner while Henri approached the cells with caution. Sacheen greeted him warmly and looked her way. She waved, but kept to the shadows where she felt safest.

"What's this, eh? The guards taking care o' the prisoners? Well, I'll be a goat's dinner," a drunken drawl said from the opposite cell to Sacheen.

Henri divided their spoils between the prisoners and asked after them both. He bent his head low and whispered something to Sacheen, but it was too low for Eira to hear. When tears leaked from Sach's eyes, she wondered if it had to do with Leon. Sacheen shook her head violently and Henri stepped back, hands up in defeat. Later, she'd ask what the conversation was about and why Sacheen had reacted with anger.

"There's a man dead in the woods, y'know. Theys saying he was killed by wolves." Grubby hands gripped the bars, and Eira saw an even grubbier stub nose peek through. "Din't do it, did they? They wouldn'a tore his face like that. Naw, they wouldn'a at all."

"What did you see? Tell me true and I'll bring more food tomorrow." Henri stood close to the cell, but kept out of hand's reach.

"I seen it all, din't I? But theys don't believe me, do theys? Wanting to kill all the wolves, theys do. For no good reason, neither." His nose and fingers disappeared, and she heard a soft thud. A few moments later, loud snores came from the cell.

"He's been rambling about that all day. He says it's the trackers that killed the man." Sacheen cocked her head and bit her lip. "What do you think?"

Henri swore and planted his fists on his hips, his head tilted to the ceiling. "I think it's none of my business, but if he's not careful, he'll wind up without a tongue to wag." He blew out a breath and arched his back. "I don't know when we'll be able to bring more provisions. Is there anyone you'd like me to get a message to if I can?"

"You've done enough. At least I know I wasn't forsaken or betrayed. Hey snow girl, stay alive, yeah?"

Eira peeked out and waved goodbye before casting a hesitant glance at the huddled man in the other cell. He was obviously drunk, but that didn't diminish the impact of his ramblings. She knew who the "theys" were, and desperately hoped the trackers wouldn't find the dwarves.

Regan had accused Leon of killing the man in the woods, but what if it had been the dwarves? She didn't think they would kill someone, but then, she didn't know them. Her gaze slid to Henri's tight jaw and flared nostrils. The prisoner's words had upset him, too. It struck her that she didn't know him, either.

Yet she did. She knew he was kind and learned and more patient than she deserved. What she didn't know, she hoped to discuss over the coming days and years, if he would have her.

They walked briskly to the barracks without a word. When Henri closed the door behind him, he held Eira's shoulders between a firm grip.

"I must see to something. You stay here. I'll have supper brought to you, but don't leave this room. Do you promise?"

"Where are you going? I can help." She was always left behind. Alone. "Please. Don't leave me here by myself." She hated how weak she sounded, but she hated being discarded as useless even more.

He kissed the tip of her nose and inhaled before speaking. "I'm sorry, Eira. I truly wish you could come with me, but it's just too dangerous. You're safe here." He wrapped his arms around her and squeezed as if it would be the last time she ever saw him. He stepped back and withdrew a dagger from the nothingness of the air. "Take this. I taught you enough today to defend yourself, but if you need something deadlier, this'll do the trick."

She ran a finger along the silver sheath and over inlaid blue marble. The dagger slid from the sheath with a soft swish. Its marbled blue hilt matched the case, and tiny gems sparkled in the candlelight. She drew her finger across the flat of the blade. She knew this dagger. It was the same one from her dream. The very same blade that Henri used to cut out her heart.

Maybe she was wrong. Maybe she really didn't know him at all.

Chapter Thirty-Three

Eira lay on the uncomfortable cot and stared at the ceiling. Shadows from the fire danced across the bland surface with reassuring constancy. Henri had yet to return and her worry grew to insurmountable proportions.

Sounds penetrated the thick walls of her room—birds and other night creatures, but also shouts and cries that she couldn't tell were from pleasure or pain. At one point, she heard muffled grunts and peeked out a window to see two men, heads bent, arms entwined, scuffling on the dirt walkway. Henri had said no one came this way, that they'd have privacy here. From the men's cavorting, they thought they'd have privacy as well.

Drunken sexual brawls, animal calls: these were not things she was accustomed to, and suffering them alone made it all the worse. She sat up and raked a hand through her hair. There were no books, no writing supplies, not even embroidery for her to pass the time. She blew out a breath and held her hand in front of her body.

Concentrating on the words Henri had said in the cottage, she urged her power forth. Just a flicker, something, anything to let her know she could grasp it. Nothing. The place where Henri had stroked her arm tingled still, and she pushed up her sleeve to see her unblemished skin. She traced her finger along where she remembered his touch being and a light-blue shimmer followed in her finger's wake. Her own golden hue quickly replaced Henri's blue. For a brief moment, they glimmered together, brightening before settling beneath her skin.

Excited, she adjusted her shoulders and, keeping a hand over the soft glow, she snapped her fingers. The tiniest of flickers popped and she nearly peed herself. It was true—she had power that was somehow being suppressed. Not that she didn't believe she had the power, but seeing the small spark was confirmation. And it was more than she'd been able to conjure alone in the woods by her castle.

Another snap. Another spark. And another until she could snap-spark with regularity. The flickers were tiny, still, but enough to encourage her. A peculiar little thrill of triumph wound its way through her veins. She had power. She.Had.Power. Her! She wasn't useless or a dimwit. She was a sorceress. Well, one in the making. Her father had been speaking true all along. She said a silent prayer to the goddess and snap-sparked one more time just to reassure herself.

Henri needed to know about this new development, and as soon as he returned, she'd show him. Her heart swelled as she imagined the look of satisfaction on his face. If only he'd come back.

But what if he couldn't? What if he was in trouble and had no way of alerting her to his distress? She should give it until morning. If he wasn't back by then, she'd go looking for him. But nighttime afforded her shadows and stealth. Plus, half the palace would be too drunk to notice a lone guard skulking through the halls. She'd been pushed to the side, discounted, and left alone too often and she was done with it. No one seemed to believe in her, but she could believe in herself.

Without giving herself time to debate or demure, she dragged her boots over her woolen socks. If Henri was out there and needed her help, at least then she'd be doing something, rather than laying here frightened like a little mouse, playing with flickers of light.

The walkway was quiet as she slipped from her room, and she strode briskly toward the orchard. The barracks were on the far side of the eastern wall, and the orchard on the west, which meant she had to pass several courtyards, all of which had groups of courtiers lingering overlong. Some were obviously sleeping, while others gossiped and argued, their half-full glasses sloshing with their gesticulations. Where the bloody blazes did Otto get the money to pay for this indulgence? It was yet another gross display of his oversized ego that made her ill.

Sleepy servants stood at the ready, their hooded eyes immune to the capriciousness before them. In the garden, the king held court, with a jester miming a charade. On the Otto's beefy thigh perched his mistress who looked bored with it all. Otto idly fondled her exposed breasts, a look of contentment on his ruddy face. Lady Annah arched into his caresses and Eira hesitated, suddenly doubting what seemed like good reasons to search for Henri. But she needn't worry. Annah's eyes drooped as she looked toward the stars.

Eira slowed her steps and circled around so that she crept closer to the king from behind. A group of courtiers sniffed petulantly in her direction, but didn't sound the alarm that a pretender had entered the fray. She tried to look as authoritative as the other guards, sneering to the courtiers with haughty self-righteousness while spying on the king and Lady Annah.

They turned their backs on her with subtle huffs, and she caught Annah stroking the king's hair in a comforting, intimate manner.

"Why won't they let me marry you, my love?" He snuggled his face in her chest, and she sighed long and low.

"You know why. Let's not have this conversation again. You will marry the beauty and we shall continue our relationship with or without her permission. It's a simple business transaction."

Eira shuffled closer and strained to hear the whispered conversation. The courtiers moved off, ignoring her as a lesser servant, and she risked getting within two paces of the couple, her heart beating so loud she was certain they heard her in the mermaid kingdom.

Annah held Otto's face between her hands and kissed him softly. "The kingdom needs a queen and you need powerful new heirs who aren't actively trying to kill you or are an ineffectual milksop mired in ancestral strife. With her, you'll be stronger, more powerful, and your heirs will be raised by me."

Eira stifled a gasp and placed a protective hand over her abdomen.

"They can try to kill me, but they'll never succeed. I'm too stubborn to die." The king laughed heartily and shifted his paramour. "I do wish that meddling stepmother of hers would leave off. I shouldn't have to pay for the privilege of bedding my own wife." He stroked Annah's face with such care it nearly broke Eira's heart. "I don't need a virgin. Hells, I don't need a wife. I only need you."

"You do need her, my love, and you know why. Woo her, say all the pretty things, and marry her like we agreed. Fuck the virgin by the light of the full moon and get your silver's worth. I'll deal with the stepmother."

Meanness entered her tone, and Eira shuddered at the enmity this woman had toward Regan.

Despite her breasts being exposed, she wore an expensive gown and gems glittered in her copper hair. Moonlight cast an ethereal glow on her face. She was stunning. A stab of jealousy hit Eira, and she staggered backward, surprised by the pain seeing the king's affections for another caused.

What did she care if he flirted with or bedded other women? But it wasn't that. It was something far more sinister. They'd lied. All of them. The cruel taunts, the threats, the lies. And they'd enjoyed every moment of it. Even this woman, whom she didn't know nor had ever met, was using her—had tried to kill her. To what purpose? To give the king powerful heirs? Another lie. She rubbed the underside of her forearm and choked against a dry heave. She couldn't be sick here, not where she would be exposed.

Eira backed away, her mind scrambled with bits and bobs of information that had yet to coalesce into one coherent thought. Why would all of them enjoy mentally and emotionally toying with her? Was it for pure enjoyment? Did they get some sort of perverted pleasure from seeing her tremble in fear? Or perhaps it was yet another way of keeping her biddable. If she was too wrapped up in anxiety, she wouldn't ask too many questions.

The king bellowed at the fool who was performing a juggling act with two knives and a teacup. Eira froze, terrified she would be recognized. Sweat glistened on the fool's forehead as the shouted another threat. The poor fool dropped his items and immediately went to his knees, begging forgiveness. Otto rose from his chair, nearly knocking his paramour to the ground, and stormed to where the fool prostrated himself.

"Useless! All of you!" The king kicked the poor man and laughed.

The fool's pleas rose in octave and eloquence, but the king ignored him. His face reddened and fists clutched as he continued kicking the man in the sternum, the groin, the face; anywhere his foot could make contact, Otto delivered one vicious attack after another.

Eira stared at the courtiers, who all watched with passive indifference. Even the guards appeared bored. If she ran, they'd catch her, but remaining where she was, a witness to the king's cruelty, made her physically ill. Slowly, she moved to the shadows where she gasped and retched, abusing her empty stomach.

After a few minutes, the man's pleas stopped and his crumpled body lay limp on the bloodied ground. She couldn't see if he breathed or not, but how could anyone survive such a brutal attack?

"Get that piece of crap out of my sight." Otto pointed to the unmoving fool and then beckoned to a servant to clean off his shoes.

Eira turned away in horror, her stomach churning anew. Only moments before, he'd seemed like a kind, loving man, but now she truly saw the beast her stepmother had bartered her to marry.

Chapter Thirty-Four

Eira strode through the orchard with her head low, her heart beating in her throat. Lady Annah's words punctured her thoughts with each stomp of her boot. The prince was trying to kill the king. Not all dynasties were built on love and loyalty. What she knew of Guillaume, it didn't surprise her that he'd vie for the throne through deceit and murder. But what did she mean about Leon? What exactly was ancestral strife? And what was Eira's role in their schemes? They were using her, all of them, but to what end? Was she just a pawn in Henri's schemes as well? Where the blazes was he, anyway?

"Not so fast, duckie." Madam Davina stepped out from behind a tree and stopped Eira with a firm palm to her chest.

She wheezed against the sudden loss of movement and glared at the woman. "I need to find Henri."

"You need to stay in the palace grounds." Davina took in her outfit and grinned. "Got a new position, I see."

"It was Henri's idea, so that I can stay hidden, yet in plain sight." She chewed her bottom lip, afraid she'd given away too much, and equally curious why the woman was alone late at night. "How is it you recognized me on a dark night in an unlit orchard when no one else has?"

"Because they see what they want to see, and I see the truth." Davina turned Eira around and walked her a few steps toward the palace. "Go to your room and stay there. You can trust the huntsman, duckie."

"Turns out, he's not a huntsman. He's—well, I don't really know what he is, but he seems to be good at a lot of things. Keeping secrets, for one."

"We all have secrets, don't we? Some more powerful than others." Her gaze was filled with meaning.

Eira blew out a breath. "Fine. I'll go to my room." She took two more steps and then turned back to the witch. "The woman with the king, Lady Annah, do you know her?"

Davina nodded slowly, her gaze shifting toward the king and his paramour. "Aye, duckie. Tragic, that story, but it's not mine to tell."

Eira snarled at the sky and fisted her hands. "Why is everyone so damned duplicitous around here?"

The witch stroked her arms and made soft tutting sounds meant to soothe her fury. "I know it's not easy, but if you trust in yourself, everything will work out in the end."

Trust herself? Not so easily done. What she wouldn't give for a dose of valerian. If she could sleep for a week, then she'd miss all the drama and could go home to her quiet, comfortable life.

"Do you happen to have any valerian or betane?"

Davina's eyes widened and her lips tightened. "Who gave you betane? Was it your stepmother?" At Eira's nod, she grunted with disgust. "She could've killed you, duckie. Never mix valerian with betane. How many times did you take it?"

"Twice that I know of, but I feel fine."

"It's a miracle you survived." She reached in her pocket and took out several dark-green leaves. She squinted to see in the dim light and used the pads of her fingers to feel each stem. "Make a tea with these holly berries for now. They'll help clear your system, but what you truly need is orinth. I don't have any at the cottage, but tomorrow, first thing, go see the shopkeeper at the apothecary. He'll have what you need. Betane is a powerful herb that should only be used in extreme situations. Once in your system, it's difficult to remove, but orinth should do the trick. You don't want permanent damage, duckie."

Eira slipped the leaves into a pocket and thanked Davina. "What's it used for? The betane?"

"They call it the sleeping death. If enough is consumed, it'll make you appear dead, but you're not quite dead. Your heart slows and breathing becomes so shallow no one can tell you're still alive. Take too much and you'll die for good."

Eira nodded, her mind a murky funk. Sleeping death. A prince wishing to kill his father. The poor fool. Holly berries in tea. A huntsman with a gleaming dagger. She shook her head to dispel the strange images that cycled through her brain as if on a loop.

"Thank you for your candidness. I'll go see the apothecary tomorrow." Apothecary to offset the betane. Yes. Tomorrow. Why was she suddenly so tired?

"Go now, duckie. Sleep. Rest. Don't talk to anyone or stray from your path. That's a good girl." Madam Davina gave her a gentle push and Eira stumbled forward, her mind firmly set on the cot in the small barrack.

She drifted through the orchard in a haze, replaying conversations, trying to find clues in the most insignificant phrases. Regan's, Guillaume's, the king's: they all bumbled and tumbled in her brain, giving her a headache that pinched her skull.

A new, far more dangerous scheme began to take shape, but she needed her writing supplies to plan it properly. She hadn't brought them with her to the barracks, which meant she needed to retrieve them from her rooms.

Stay to the path. No.

Had Regan been in one of the courtyards? Either as herself or false Eira? She couldn't remember, but she had to take the risk that her stepmother would be out. Her mind was too crowded to be trusted to remember exactly what was needed. She used the servants' stairs at the end of the hallway and moved quickly through the quiet palace to the door to their suite. After a moment's hesitation, she tried the doorknob, relieved when it turned.

If Regan was present, it would've been locked.

Inside their rooms, several lanterns gave off enough light she could make her way to her bedchamber unhampered. The room looked untouched, but the hairs on her neck tingled. She scanned from corner to corner, searching for the disturbance. Aside from the tray being gone, and fire cold, nothing was out of place, yet she couldn't shake the unease.

In her wardrobe, the casket with the apple was still hidden beneath a pile of petticoats, and her court gowns hung as she'd left them. She reached beneath her neatly folded wool skirts for her writing supplies, relieved when her fingers touched the parchment.

She was being silly. Everything was as it should be.

Still, she felt as if she were being watched.

Keeping her breathing level, she closed the wardrobe and started for the door. The sound of a boot scuffing came from behind her, and she whirled around, papers clutched to her chest with one hand, the dagger held aloft in the other. She hoped the intruder couldn't see that it was still sheathed and shaking violently.

"Show yourself." A tremble gave away her nerves.

Silence answered, and she backed slowly out of her room,

her gaze darting from one side to the other. It was too dark to see whether anyone hid in the shadows, and she didn't much care to find out whether they meant to cause her harm. The papers slipped from her grasp and she held them tighter, bobbling the quill and ink pot as she did. She couldn't very well traipse through the palace with papers trailing after her, but she'd used her only bag to carry her belongings to the barracks.

She hurried through the sitting room to Regan's bedchamber and paused outside the open door. Snoring came from within, and Eira peeked her head inside to check that the bed was unoccupied. Not only was it empty, the bed looked far too tidy in the crowded room. Dresses were strewn over every surface, save for the bed. Jewelry lay haphazardly on a table, and several feathered hats dangled from chair backs.

A heavy black blanket covered the magic mirror and it was from here she heard the snores. Eira shuddered to think the thing might be alive. That would take enormous magic—dark magic—to make an inanimate object sentient. The how didn't matter as much as the why.

Regan's laughter shattered her musings, and panic whipped Eira into action. She snatched a beaded satchel off the floor and shoved her writing supplies inside before looping the strap over her head. She unsheathed the dagger and held it in her trembling hand.

Voices came closer to the bedchamber, and she debated her options: hide under the bed, in the wardrobe, behind a chair, or make a run for it and hope her stepmother didn't recognize her. Seconds ticked by, but her legs wouldn't move.

Guillaume said something that made Regan squeal, and that broke Eira's paralysis. They were right outside the door.

She leapt to the wardrobe, slipping behind a heavy tapestry that hung several inches from the wall. A cool breeze teased the back of her neck and a moment later, Henri stood beside her, his finger to his lips.

Relief washed over her, just as quickly followed by a terrible dread. There, glistening in the poor light, she saw the dark stain of blood covering his hands.

Chapter Thirty-Five

Henri smacked Eira's arse with the flat of his wooden sword. "Again."

She snarled at him and took up her offensive stance. Since he'd found her in Regan's room, he'd hardly said a dozen words to her. He was angry, she got it, but she had every right to be angry with him, too. Showing up covered in blood and not explaining what had happened? Sure, he confirmed it wasn't his blood, but then said nothing about whose it was or where he'd been. Not that he needed to tell her his every movement, but some kind of reassurance would've been nice.

That was two nights past. She couldn't take much more of his sullen behavior. Something must've happened while he was out, but if he wouldn't talk about it, how could she help?

"Again!" His sharp command startled her, and she lunged forward. "Not a parry, a slice. Dammit, Eira, pay attention."

"Well, it's kind of hard with you yelling at me constantly. I'm tired and hungry, Henri. We've been at this for hours and everything hurts."

"Not until you get this right." He raked his hand through his hair so roughly she was surprised he didn't pull it all out. "Your life might depend on this."

She tossed her wooden sword on the ground and squared her shoulders to face him. "Just because I'm wearing a guard's uniform doesn't make me a soldier. I doubt a few days' worth of training will keep me alive, especially when the people trying to kill me aren't using weapons."

Her boots crunched on the dirt as she pivoted and stalked toward the barracks. She'd had enough torture for one day. What she needed was a hot bath and nice cup of tea. Neither of which she'd get in their tiny room. At least she could continue writing out her plans. That was an activity she enjoyed and had been busy at when he'd rudely interrupted her and told her it was time to train.

Train, train, train—that's all he wanted of late. He truly believed he could make a soldier out of her in only a few days. He was deliriously mad.

He grabbed her by the shoulder and spun her around. "Where do you think you're going? We're not finished here."

"Yes, I am. And until you start being honest with me, I have no reason to stay."

He growled at the sky and shook out his fists. "You're such a spoiled princess."

"Stop calling me that."

Myriad emotions crossed his face, from rage to concern to irritation. But it was the last one that made her stomach flip in the best possible way. His eyes darkened and nostrils flared. Before she could say another word, his lips crashed onto hers. Strong hands cradled her head, and she pressed her body against his, igniting the passion she'd been suppressing ever since their afternoon in the cottage.

She'd hoped for this moment, dreamt of it, but didn't quite

believe they'd ever kiss again. He lifted her and hurried to their room, kicking the door closed behind him before setting her on her feet. His hands were a whir of motion as he unbuttoned her coat, and then her breeches. Her own fingers shook with desire as they unfastened his many awful buttons.

They kicked off their boots and stripped naked, their breathing coming in short rasps. Her nipples ached to be touched and her womanhood pulsed with anticipation. She wanted this—needed this more than she'd realized. After everything she'd witnessed that awful night, and then his anger this morning, she needed to feel his strength inside her. Needed him. Only him. Always him.

He didn't lead her to the cots, but grabbed her hips, lifting slightly, and pushed her against the wall. Instinctively, her legs wrapped around his back, and she bit her lip to keep from whimpering her need. There was no lead up to their lovemaking, no drawn out preparation to ready her and when he entered hard and fast, it hurt slightly, but was a good, soothing kind of pain. This frenzied pace was new and different from their lazy day at the cottage. There was nothing sweet or charming about the way he pounded into her, and she bloody loved it.

His cock filled her, and she arched to take him deeper. His balls slapped her ass, igniting her lust, titillating her in places she'd thought forbidden. The naughty desire spun through her veins with a secret thrill that one day, they would explore even further.

Henri breathed heavily against her neck, his sweat mixing with her own. Their scent filled the room and she inhaled deeply. Raw and primal, she felt like an animal gyrating against the wall and bucking her hips as much as physically possible. The freedom of their fucking broke something loose within her, and she moaned against his neck. Another kind of freedom—to be unabashedly wanton and demand what she needed—lifted a weight off her and she cried out.

"Don't stop, Henri. Ahhh, just there, yes, there. Harder, oh hells, yes." Her pleas were rewarded with Henri's furious thrusting.

His muttered grunts and delicious moans were interspersed with words of devotion and compliments on her bravery, her beauty, her perfection. Yet she cared nothing about those. All that mattered was his gorgeous cock and what it was doing to her.

Tendrils of an achy need tightened in her pelvis, and she closed her eyes against the flashing of stars that began with her quickening breath. The world stopped for one perfect, bliss-filled moment and then exploded with her release. Her body convulsed and quivered; her skin prickled with each brush of air against her nakedness.

Henri made a sort of growling, gruntish moan and then his face crumpled into the one she knew so well and delighted in seeing. Euphoric torment, to be sure. She kissed his neck where veins stood out and sucked playfully on his damp skin. Warmth filled her as he spilled his seed, and she clasped her legs tighter around his hips.

They remained pressed against the wall for several minutes, regaining their equilibrium. When their breathing evened, Henri shifted, but she held fast with her legs.

"I'm sorry, Eira. I should've told you where I went the other night, but I was so angry at seeing you in your room, I wasn't thinking straight."

Surprised, she cocked her head. "That was you in my room? But why didn't you say anything?"

"I didn't want to frighten you. I was, after all, covered in blood."

"Whose was it?" She released her grip, and he helped her to stand.

Their clothes were scattered across the floor, yet she didn't wish to wear the guard's uniform. Instead, she grabbed a nightdress and slipped it over her head.

Henri pulled on his smallclothes and breeches, but left his torso bare. "Not a who, but a what. When I left you, I went to check on the dwarves. The trackers are getting braver, reckless even, and I was worried about them after hearing what the drunk in the dungeon said. I knew if I told you where I was going, you'd insist on coming." He smiled and ran the back of his hand over her breast.

"The blood, Henri...?"

"On my return, I saw the trackers. I wasn't sure if they were following me, so I took them on a merry little chase." Henri's fingers twisted her nipple and she moaned into him. "Turns out, it wasn't me they were after. They shot a doe, not for nourishment, but for sport. I found her lying with the arrow still in her neck." His eyes clouded and lips thinned. "They left her to die, alone, scared, and in pain. I removed the arrow and helped her peacefully transition beyond the veils."

Heaviness settled in her chest. No one should be left to die alone, nor should Henri have had to bear the burden of the trackers' callous behavior. "That was a very kind of you to help that poor creature."

"It's what anyone with an ounce of compassion would've done." His lips tightened with a little shrug. "I was on my way back here when I saw you enter the palace, despite my warning you to stay put."

He sat on the cot and beckoned her to join him. Instead of sitting beside him, she lifted her nightdress and straddled his lap. At his surprised look, she giggled and nuzzled his neck.

"And what of your adventure that night, Lady Cannaid?"

"I have a surprise." She held up her hand and snapped.

A flame larger than any she'd made previously flared, and they both gasped.

"Well done, princess. Well done indeed. How did you figure it out?"

She watched the dancing flame as she made it hop from one finger to the other. "I believe it has something to do with you, but I don't know yet."

That awful night, she'd been touching the place he left his magic, and now, she sat upon his lap. But why would his closeness open her power?

He put his hand over hers and snuffed out the flame. "We'll investigate this more later, but I'd really like to know what possessed you to leave the safety of the barracks and explore on your own."

"I was worried about you. It had been ages since you'd left and I needed to be sure you weren't injured or worse."

She slid off his lap and delayed saying more by getting dressed. Instead of recounting the king's horrible behavior and witnessing the fool's murder, she told him of her meeting with Madam Davina.

"I've been thinking." She buttoned her coat and smoothed it over her chest. "Why can't we just leave this place? Let Regan pretend to be me and marry the king. None of them care a wit about me, so why should I remain and be a witness to their debauchery?"

"Believe me, I've thought of that as well. But the spell your stepmother is using doesn't have lasting effects. What happens when Otto discovers he's been deceived? His wrath is mighty and he'll hunt you until his last breath."

She chewed her bottom lip a moment, unsure if she should tell him of her plan. She'd promised herself she'd trust him, and she did, but fear kept her from fully believing in him. Or believing in herself. Yet she had to stop being so damn afraid. A leap of faith was exactly what she needed if she was going to break the cycle of depending on others. It was more than a baby step, but at least it was a step forward.

"I was afraid you'd say that. Then, in that case, we'll need nine horses, the dwarves, and an antidote, but I've thought this through fully and believe I've found a way out of our predicament."

Henri paused in tying his boots and cocked his head. "I'm intrigued. Go on."

"I die." She shrugged, as if that were the most normal thing for her to say. "I take a healthy dose of betane. It will make me appear dead, and once I've been taken to the crypt, you come along with the antidote—the orinth we're going to purchase from the apothecary—and revive me. Then we, and the dwarves, ride to safety in one of the other kingdoms. You seem to know your way around places. Surely we'll find a suitable cottage to live in. That is, unless you have room in your home. Wherever that is."

"And what if the orinth doesn't revive you? What if the king doesn't believe you're dead? What if your stepmother knows betane's properties and is suspicious enough she drives a dagger through your heart just to be certain? There are far too many variables to your plan. I don't like it."

"The king will be relieved to learn of my passing, trust me. As will his mistress. Regan, we'll have to come up with a way to distract her long enough she loses interest. From what you said, the king hasn't paid her. If she thinks I'm dead, then she knows she's not getting the silver and has no reason to stick around. She'll go back home, and I'll get my freedom."

"You make it sound so simple, even I want to believe it'll work." He held the door open for her and swatted her arse as she passed. "I'm not saying we'll go with your plan, but I'm not saying we won't. Until we can think of something better, let's at least prepare for the worst. Let's go get that antidote."

He was right—there were far too many things that could go wrong, but she couldn't focus on those. The plan had to work. Dying was the only option.

Chapter Thirty-Six

The apothecary shop was located on the south side of town, far from the palace, which suited their needs just fine. As Eira and Henri made their way through the stalls and hawkers in the market, she noticed more than one apprehensive look given to the pair. The townspeople feared the guards, but why? It wasn't that they recognized the pair—their faces could hardly be seen in the low hat and high collar of the uniform.

Then she remembered the guards' passive expressions when Otto beat that poor fool to death. They'd become desensitized to brutality, or were forced to pretend indifference to keep from suffering the same fate. Lawks, they might even be just as brutal as their king. A brotherhood of murderers. It gave their sense of family a new, dangerous, and dark taint. Those kinds of families she understood far too well.

Henri's fingers brushed hers, and her breath caught. He was here, by her side. She had nothing to fear from the townspeople. They didn't know who she was. It wouldn't have mattered if they did—either way, she was the enemy. A pawn of the king.

"The other night," she began, her voice lowered so only

Henri could hear. "Otto did something...disturbing." While they walked, she told him about leaving the barracks to search for him and the awful event she witnessed. She left nothing out and ended with him scaring her near to death in Regan's bedchamber.

He listened intently, never interrupting, but often giving a quick shake of his head. When she finished, she shuddered, and he caressed her back beneath the cape she wore.

"I'm sorry you had to be party to the king's vileness. Be wary of Lady Annah. She appears soft and fragile, but she's just as wicked as Otto. She's been his lover for many years, but cannot marry him because she can't bear children." His jaw tightened and he glanced at her with sorrow in his eyes. "The reason being, she was once beaten by Otto much like he beat the fool last night. The king likes his drink, but never cross him—drunk or sober, he doesn't forget a slight. Rumors swirl of what Lady Annah did to upset Otto, but only those two know the truth. She survived the beating, but he damaged her internally so ferociously, that she was never able to conceive."

"Why does she stay with him?"

"Love. Love will make you do crazy things. The king loves her and sadly, she loves him. It's twisted and vile, but it's their love. After the beating, Otto vowed to never hit her again and begged forgiveness. As far as I know, he hasn't laid a hand on her since, but as you witnessed, he takes out his frustrations on others."

She understood his words a little too well. She once believed she loved Regan, and that if she gave her stepmother enough love, or the right kind of love through obedience and servitude, that Regan would love her in return. But now, she saw the destruction of that kind of codependence. It only worked out well for the person in power.

The impact of what else he said hit her like a physical blow.

She stopped and faced him, her head pounding beneath the woolen cap. "Henri, they were discussing me. Do you think—"

"Don't, Eira. Don't blame yourself for Otto's atrocious behavior. You are not responsible for what others do."

Logically, she knew it was true, but her heart refused to believe she wasn't the reason that poor fool was dead.

"Annah said something about Leon that's puzzled me ever since. She told the king he was, 'ineffectual milksop mired in ancestral strife'. What do you think she meant by that? Ancestral strife could mean she knows he's a wolf shifter since Leon's mother was one, too."

Henri moved her out of the way of a cart and brushed off her cape, but the dirt splatters were too many. "An ineffectual milksop seems harsh. Leon goes with the tide. He doesn't cause rifts or court danger, which is unlike the rest of his family. She could be jealous of his easygoing nature. But you might be right. I doubt there's little that happens at Otto's court that Annah doesn't know about. And being a witch, she'd have access to other means of getting information."

"If Annah or the king know Leon's a shifter," Eira kept her voice low so that only Henri could hear, "then Regan's threats are futile."

Henri ran a finger along his jaw and Eira tracked it like a starved mongrel eyeing a haunch of lamb. It was wicked to think of their sexual romps in the middle of the town, discussing important matters, but she couldn't help it. Every moment, his scent, his touch, his presence consumed her until all she wanted was more.

It was more than that. His presence gave her strength she didn't know she had. She questioned things, and wasn't chastised for her thoughts. In his own quiet way, he empowered her to think, to dare, to do, and yes, to dream. She'd never been around someone so assuredly confident in themselves, nor anyone as compassionate as him. One day, when she was done with the vileness of Otto's court, she would discover who she was meant to be, and at the center of everything, kindness would rule.

"You might be right, clever lass. We'll discuss it more later. First, we dine." He stepped to their right and spoke to a stall owner for a few moments before returning with two small pies. He handed one to her, and held his to his nose.

"There is no finer scent than that of a freshly baked meat pie." He opened his mouth to take a bite, but paused. "I lied. You are the finest scent I've ever smelled, but after you, a close second, is this pie."

"I smell like a goat."

"You smell divine." He took a bite and moaned as he chewed.

Eira hesitated. "Is it, you know, safe to eat? This isn't the most sanitary place."

"A little dirt won't kill you. Come on, be brave. Live a little." He nudged her shoulder and chuckled good-heartedly.

She nibbled the crust and a waft of gravy-soaked meaty goodness filled her nostrils. He wasn't wrong. The pie smelled amazing. She took a bite and matched his moans.

"Oh my. This is delicious. I'll bet you know how to make these." She rather hoped he did, and that he'd bake her a dozen someday.

"Believe it or not, I don't. Baking was never one of my talents."

"Prince Charming has a weakness. I wouldn't have guessed it was possible." She joked, but a jag of disappointment hid behind her words. She could live on meat pies forever. They might even one day be her favorite above apples.

His eyes narrowed, she hoped not out of spite, but a curious glint reflected in his dark pupils. They finished their pies and walked on, with Henri regaling her with tales of his baking disasters. By the time they reached the apothecary, her sides hurt from laughing so hard.

At the entrance, they straightened and smoothed their uniforms, doing their best to present themselves as the king's guards. A little bell chimed when they entered, but the shop was empty of customers, and the shopkeeper. Henri surreptitiously clasped her hand in his and gave a quick squeeze before drifting off to peruse a shelf overflowing with jars and dried herbs.

Eira inspected the other side of the small shop, her heart galloping in her chest. She'd have to ask for her ingredients casually, as if buying a deadly herb was as natural as the sun after rain.

"Can I help you?" An older gentleman tapped his fingers atop the counter, his narrowed eyes belying the tilt of his lips.

It was a curious glance, full of conceit and a pinch of condemnation.

"We need several herbs, two potions, and a tincture," Henri said as he approached the counter.

The man straightened and stared at Henri's uniform. "Have you found my Daria? Is she safe?"

Henri glanced to Eira and then back to the shopkeeper. "I'm sorry, but I'm unaware of any missing persons. We're here on an errand for the king. He needs these potions."

"And what the king wants, the king gets. But what about us poor stooges? What do we get? My daughter goes missing and nothing. I get nothing. But you, you need potions and potions you shall get." Spittle formed at the corners of his mouth and his voice rose and lowered with his rantings. "People are hungry, starving, but the king needs his wine. People have no wood for winter, but the king wears fine furs. Always for the king. Pish. Call me a traitor, what's it to me? I'm old. My daughter's gone and none of your lot care."

Henri waited patiently during the tirade, his face a mask of geniality. When the man took a breath, Henri warned him, gently, to perhaps keep his opinions of the king to himself or he'd find himself in the dungeons and then where would that leave his daughter? After promising to inquire of the missing Daria, he listed the items they'd need.

The shopkeeper glared at them both before storming to the back room.

"What was that about?" Eira flicked a glance to where the man could be heard muttering to himself.

"I'm not sure. There are rumors about the, uh, less than saneness in this family. Could be he's having an episode and is confusing reality, or it could be his daughter truly is missing. When we're back at the palace, I'll make a few inquiries to suss out the truth. If it's as he says, I'll make sure the captain is aware. It's the most I can do for him." Softness filled Henri's eyes.

"You're a kind man, Henri Callan. A good man." She cupped his jaw and stroked his cheek with her thumb.

His lips brushed hers ever so lightly. "And despite your step-mother's best efforts, you are a good woman, Eira Eloise Francis Cannaid."

"All the names? Well then, it must be true." Regan must've given him her full name for reasons not obvious to her at the moment. Not that she minded, but it was a little odd. She chuckled and was about to return his kiss when a shadow passed in front of the shop door. "We should probably not be overly friendly. If, you know, we want to appear to genuinely be guards."

"I'm sure there's mischief between the guards, but you have a point. In public, no snogging."

She put a hand over her heart and looked shocked. "Kind sir, I am offended. I kiss, I do not snog."

He nudged her shoulder with his own. "Well, maybe you should."

The shopkeeper returned with several bundles in his arms. "You have some potent herbs here, sir. Does the king understand their volatility?"

Henri inspected each bundle, unwrapping and rewrapping them in front of the scowling shopkeeper. "Everything looks to be in order. The king is highly aware of what he's purchased, but would appreciate any advice you can give as to the most effective administration, especially this one and this." He tapped two smallish pouches.

The shopkeeper rubbed the top of his nose between his brows and blew out a long breath. "Most people, amateurs, really, like to make a tea out of valerian, and some unscrupulous sorts will even add a pinch of betane. I try to warn them that betane is not a sleeping agent, but do they listen? No."

"I assure you, we understand the delicateness of the herb's properties. When handled correctly, it eases the king's pain, as I'm sure you're aware." Eira leveled the man with a look that brooked no argument. She only hoped it was true.

"Yes, well, fine. As I was saying, to get the most potency, first make an extract from the flowers, then crush the leaves into the liquid and let steep for a good long night. Infuse an apple or fig —some kind of naturally sweet fruit—with the potion. Don't you fools ever talk to one another at the palace? I told this to the woman who came by the shop early last week. She, like you, said she was purchasing nearly the exact same ingredients for the king."

"Did she also purchase orinth?" The hair on Eira's neck stood on end and a chill swept across her too-warm skin.

"No, that one she didn't ask for." He leaned forward and peered closely at Eira. "Though she did ask if there was an antidote and hinted that I might want to deplete my stash. Strange woman. A lady by the looks of her, but I tell you true, she ain't no lady."

"Thank you for your time, and your excellent advice, kind sir." Henri paid the man and pocketed the items before he steered Eira toward the door.

"Most people don't know that holly berries will prevent betane from being absorbed. Raw berries, eaten at precisely the same time as the betane is consumed. Best make sure there's none of them around when you make your potion." He cleared his throat and adjusted his cravat. "Tell the king, of course."

"Of course. Thank you again." Henri tipped his hat to the man.

When they'd crossed the threshold of the shop and were on the street, he exhaled a shaky breath. "Are you thinking what I'm thinking?"

"That Regan didn't give me an apple to enchant the king, but to make it look like he's dead? Perhaps so then later they could actually kill him? Then yes, that's exactly what I'm thinking. This doesn't alter our plans, Henri. All it proves is that I had the same idea, just not for the same reasons. It might need a few tweaks, but we can work with this new information."

"I do love your optimism and enthusiasm, but I think we should come up with a backup, just in case." He strode forward, his head bent as if in thought.

She jogged to keep pace with his long strides and just there, half-hidden beside a shabby building and watching them with a vicious snarl on his lips, was Guillaume. The wobble in her legs nearly stopped her momentum, but seeing him, hiding in the town, obviously following her and Henri, something snapped. She was through with hiding when she'd done nothing wrong. Mid-step, she pivoted toward the prince. The look of surprise that crossed his face gave her that extra bit of courage she was lacking.

Henri didn't see her turn and she dared not risk calling out to him and giving Guillaume a chance to escape. She'd catch up to him in a minute. She had a prince to confront first.

"Has my stepmother sent you to finish the assault you spectacularly bumbled the other night? Or are you just her lacky now, spying on me for kicks?" Eira skidded to a stop close enough to the prince it was scandalous. She didn't move backward or waver in her stance.

Guillaume took a step sideways, closer to the edge of the building. A look of genuine bewilderment settled in his features. "I have no idea what you're talking about. Why are you wearing that ridiculous costume? I could have you jailed for impersonating a guard."

"And I can tell your father that you and my stepmother are scheming to take his throne."

"There's no way my father would entertain your lies. I'm his greatest champion."

Eira stood on tiptoe and glared at the prince. "You're more of an ass than I thought if you truly believe that." She poked him in the chest, aware that her actions might draw a crowd. "Haven't you wondered why your father needs to marry at midnight of a full moon? And why me? Not just a virgin, but me." She jabbed her thumb at her own chest. "And why does he have a dungeon full of magical creatures?" She stepped away, but didn't turn her back on him. "Perhaps you're the one being played, Your Highness."

Before he could reply, she slipped around the building and ran, full out, toward Henri, only slowing to grab his hand and continue to the barracks before Guillaume could call the true guard on them.

Chapter Thirty-Seven

Eira pressed herself against the wall and peered out the window into the darkened courtyard. Her packed bags sat near the door, waiting for the moment Henri arrived. After her confrontation with the prince in the town, there was no way they could safely stay at the palace for the next three days until the ball. She'd been a fool to think they could skulk around unnoticed. Yet with so many guards milling around, it was a good plan until it wasn't.

Her nails cut into her palms as she squeezed them together to block the rampant irritation that pummeled against her brain. She'd been reckless and far too emotional when she confronted Gil. A mistake Regan would never have made. But she wasn't her stepmother and these intrigues were too new for her to have mastered them already. Going forward, she would use her mind as well as her heart before making rash decisions. She shook out her hands and scanned the area for the hundredth time.

She hid in a different barrack, barely able to breathe for the anxiety tightening her lungs. Henri should be back by now. After hurriedly packing their belongings, and making certain not a single clue was left of their presence, Henri had settled her in a barrack opposite and told her, under no circumstances, was she to leave the room, open the door to anyone, or make a fire. And this time, she obeyed.

He was confident Guillaume would be angered by her confrontation and rise to the challenge of not just finding them, but punishing her. Henri hadn't chastised her behavior, but she saw in the tightness of his eyes he wasn't happy she'd approached the prince. The last she saw of Henri, he'd disappeared into the shadows. Whether magic or not, it was a skill she found useful and would love to learn. She'd ask him during their next training session. Whenever or wherever that might be.

He'd left her at just past sunset and she waited anxiously for full dark to descend upon the palace, worry gnawing at her belly.

Voices drifted through the walkways, hushed yet commanding. The rasping sting of swords being drawn cut down her back as if a blade tore her skin. She couldn't move for the fear that paralyzed her limbs.

The door to her room opened, and she shoved her fist in her mouth to keep from screaming. Henri slipped silently into the room and gripped her hand in his, a finger to his lips.

Relief was short lived as they watched a group of four men stalk the building opposite—the one they'd been living in for the past few days. With the shadows and lack of moonlight, it was difficult to see facial features, but Eira knew the arrogant walk of their leader. Guillaume.

Henri was right. The prince wasn't one to let grievances go, but what did he hope to accomplish by surprising Eira and Henri in their room? It would give him proof they were hiding there, nothing more. Yet she knew that was a lie. He'd probably been spying on them for quite some time. Possibly even the entire time they'd been staying in the barracks. She had to assume he overheard their plans, even listened while they made love.

A loud bang startled her, and she bit down on her bottom lip to smother yet another cry. Voices rose: some in anger, others to call out that the room was empty.

"Find them," Guillaume snarled. "Bring them to me when you do." He turned and glared at the barracks, but his gaze roved over where Eira and Henri hid without any recognition.

They waited until the men dispersed, and then another tense hour before Henri led her away from the barracks and through a gate on the west side of the palace. They wore the guards' uniforms and she was grateful for the warmth the woolen clothing provided. The pleasant warm spell had ended and now a chill lingered in the air, with the possibility of snow coming in the next few days.

She rubbed her arms and glanced at the bleak surroundings. "I never wanted to be any trouble."

"You are not to blame for any of this." He wiped away the tears that threatened to spill over her cheeks and pressed his lips to hers.

He never once chastised her tears, despite their frequency of late. In fact, he made her feel as though all of her emotions were valid and respected. His presence brought a sense of confidence —not just that she was outwardly beautiful, but that all of her, from her tears to her anger, and even her confusion was accepted and loved. These faults, as she was led to believe them to be, were not something she should hide out of fear or punishment. He allowed her to be herself without judgement.

In answer, she opened to him, inviting in his warmth and security, giving him all she had to offer in return.

His arms embraced her and she melded herself to his body, wishing for all the kingdom they could be anywhere else but there. It was no use. If they stayed in the palace, they'd be hunted by Guillaume, and possibly even Leon at every turn. Lawks, probably by the king's true guards. Despite her apprehension, they had to leave.

Henri ended their kiss and stroked her face with chilled fingers. "I've made arrangements where we should be safe until the ball. They're a bit rustic, but right now, safety is our biggest concern. We'll need to be vigilant on the road."

Two horses awaited them in the shadows and Henri tied her bags to his saddle before helping her mount her own ride. He truly was a marvel. Stealing the king's horses, finding them accommodation, he didn't seem to fear anything. Is this what being an ambassador entailed? Courage under pressure? Bravery in the face of defying a king?

"That first day, in the king's antechamber, why did you warn me to be silent?" She asked once they were a good distance from the palace.

"I didn't want you to scream and give our position away."

"And you thought sneaking up on me was the answer?"

"I wasn't sneaking. I made no effort to be quiet in my approach." His teeth shone in the waning light of the moon.

A shiver went through her. "The wedding is to take place on the full moon." She looked to the skies with a silent wish that they'd find a solution. Somehow.

"Aye. I've been wondering at the timing, and why Otto would keep so many magic-enhanced prisoners."

Eira gripped the reins tighter. "That day, when you spied on me, I overheard Lady Annah with the king. They were talking about his illness, I believe, and mentioned the full moon and the trackers helping. Did you happen to hear their conversation?"

He shook his head. "I only arrived when you saw me, I didn't have a chance. Did she say what ailed the king?"

"No, but his pain was great, of that I'm certain."

"Otto was once young and full of life, but a jousting accident several years ago changed him. He suffers from gout and other ailments. He's a glutton and full of bile from his impotent rage. I will not mourn him when he passes." Henri touched his fingertips to his forehead and his heart. "Goddess forgive me."

"Nor will I—" Eira's horse reared, nearly knocking her from the saddle. She clasped the reins tighter and tried to steady the beast. "Easy girl. Easy." She stroked the mare's neck, feeling the rampant heartbeat beneath her fur. Eira's wasn't much slower.

Her gaze swept the side of the road, seeing nothing. Then, hulking in the middle of the road fifty paces from them, was a grey beast half the size of her mare. His fanged maw snarled and snapped, his great paws swiped at the dirt.

"Wolf." She breathed, but Henri already knew.

His steady gaze was locked on the wolf as he inched his horse closer. The movement spooked her mare and she bolted to the left, straight for the forest. Eira's yelp was lost to the wind that whipped past her face as her mare galloped wild through the underbrush and low branches that threatened to knock Eira from the saddle.

She clung to the mare's mane, desperately trying to get a better hold of the reins to stop her, but her horse had the bit and wasn't responding to Eira's commands. Twigs tore at her cape as they raced through the darkened woods, and leaves slapped her skin, tearing it. The only sounds she heard were the thundering of her mare's hooves and the blood rushing through her ears.

A branch hung low and she ducked, but not far enough and it caught her shoulder with a blow mighty enough to fell her from her horse. She crashed to the ground and rolled ass overhead several times until coming to a stop against a log. Lights danced before her blurred vision and she swayed violently to one side as if on a swing and she was about to fall off.

The sound of leaves crunching came from the darkness and

she scrambled to her feet. The dagger Henri had given her poked from her belt and she brandished it at her unseen foe.

"Show yourself."

The wolf came into view, its teeth bared, ears pinned back. A growl, low and threatening filled the space between them. It could've attacked, but instead it circled her, its ears flicking forward and back.

Her bowels nearly tuned liquid as she faced the beast. This was not how she had envisioned her death. The wolf sniffed the air and pawed at the ground. A snarl was followed by a whimper. Eira studied the wolf, the way it hesitated when it should strike, the way it flicked its tail in agitation, the way it watched her in an almost human manner.

"Leon?" She dared to hope it was her one-time ally. The wolf snapped and shook its head. "Leon, don't do this."

She listened for Henri, but there was no other sound in the forest besides her labored breathing and the wolf's scratching at the ground.

"What would Sacheen say if she saw you now?"

That got his attention. The wolf made a sort of cry that pierced her heart with pity.

"She's alive, Leon. In the dungeons. I saw her myself. I brought her food."

The wolf shook his head, making his coat fluff up and look more intimidating. Not that he needed to be more terrifying. She was taking a risk that this was the prince and not some other shifter. If it wasn't Leon, she'd just revealed his secret.

Eira sheathed the dagger and put her empty hands in the air. It was dark enough she could only see a short distance from her to the wolf. Each foot she placed on the ground, she hoped her instinct was right and it was Leon she faced. When she was only a pace away, she knelt on the forest floor.

Henri burst through the trees, sword brandished, a look of

venom in his midnight eyes. Where the lawks did he get a sword?

Eira cast him a pleading look and put out her hand. "Stay where you are, Henri. I'm unharmed for the moment."

The wolf snapped in his direction, but did not lunge for him. Henri's jaw clenched, but he did as asked and sheathed his weapon. The wolf swung his head between Henri and Eira, as if confused which to eat first.

"I'm not going to harm you. And I don't think you want to harm me." She drew the wolf's attention and very slowly slipped her hair off one shoulder before tilting her head to expose her neck. Her body trembled hard enough she shook the leaves her knees rested upon. "You're not a murderer, Leon."

Despite what Regan said, Eira couldn't believe the prince was a calculating killer. Enough so, she was betting her life that he wouldn't snap her neck with his powerful jaws. She hoped this one time, she wasn't wrong.

Chapter Thirty-Eight

The wolf drew near and sniffed her neck, growling low in its chest. She could reach out and stroke the beast, it was so near, but she held her hands at her sides, fighting the tears that stung the backs of her eyes. A small cry burst in her throat and she held her lips closed tight to keep from shrieking.

Another long moment passed with the wolf's wet nose scratching her bare skin. She was certain it could feel her quickened heartbeats through the veins on her neck. Or smell her fear. Was that only horses that could sense fear? Or were wolves attuned to human emotions as well? If so, then this wolf surely knew she was close to expiring from a stopped heart.

Henri remained motionless, a shadow in the starlight.

The wolf stepped back, another snarl coming from its curled lips. She closed her eyes, preparing for the inevitable pain that would come with her death. The rustling of leaves was all she heard. When she opened her eyes, instead of the beast, Leon stood in front of her. She blew out the breath she was holding and leaned back on her heels, her head resting on her chest. A rush of adrenaline spiked, and then dragged her energy low, leaving her spent.

"You don't know me, Eira."

She rose on unsteady legs, cautiously accepting his help. Within another breath, Henri was there, his strong arms around her waist. She sank into him grateful for the support.

"Do we ever truly know someone? Perhaps not, but what I do know of you, leads me to believe you are a man of honor. If not, am I to mistake your kindness for manipulation? Your compassion for deceit? Have you been playing a game with me all along as the others have?" She shook her head and reached forward to grip his hands. "I don't think so, Leon. Your family has lied and berated you when you didn't deserve their scorn. In that, we are not so unlike. But we don't have to listen to them any longer. If we don't stand up to the bullies of this world, to the Regan's, Otto's, Annah's, and Guillaume's, then who will? They don't get to tell you who you are. Only you can decide your moral compass. And I'll tell you true—I don't believe you would kill unless it was in self-defense or protecting someone you loved."

His features softened and wetness glistened in his eyes. "Did you truly see Sach? Was she well?"

Eira looked up at him and saw not a powerful wolf or a prince, but a man consumed with heartbreak and dared not hope.

"She thinks you've forgotten her, Leon. That you abandoned her and left her there to die."

"I would never."

"Then tell her. Tell them all who you are and fight for her, Leon." She squeezed his hands before letting them go.

Leon started to say something, but stopped himself. He shared a curious look with Henri that Eira couldn't decipher, but she had the sense they'd spoken about Sacheen before.

"I'm sorry, Leon. Sach forbade me from telling you where

she was. She feared you would be imprisoned or worse if you found her." Henri's shoulders sagged with the confession.

"I've searched all the dungeons. Annah must be hiding her location." Leon growled and Eira felt his hot breath on her neck. She had to keep herself from taking a step backwards, away from the threat.

"We'll find a way through Annah's deception." Henri said. "But I need to get Eira to safety. Gil found where we've been hiding."

"Then you aren't safe at the palace." Leon arched his back and stretched, his face to the sky. "I hate that the kingdom has come to this. Can you get word to Sach?"

"I'll do my best, but do not give up hope."

Eira watched the pair, intrigued by their words, and familiarity. "Has Leon been helping you this whole time? Do you know each other from your ambassador position?"

Leon made a "do tell" face and looked to Henri.

"We have, on occasion, helped one another. These past many days included." Henri turned to the prince. "Can you find Eira's mare and take both horses back to the stables? We've scant time to be searching for her."

Leon agreed and Henri gathered his horse. He removed Eira's bag from the saddle before giving the reins over to Leon. Henri was right, they hadn't time to dawdle. As it was, Guillaume and his men might be tracking them at this very moment.

She hugged Leon tightly before kissing him on the cheek. "What about Regan and my heart?"

"I'll deal with your stepmother. You just stay alive until the ball."

The ball. The wedding. Three days hence. Everything hinged on that night. They were no closer to unraveling the various plots and schemes of their respective families. With no small amount of sadness, Eira and Henri said goodbye to Leon.

Henri wove a path through the forest, every so often stopping to scatter nuts and bread crumbs across their trail in the hope animals would disturb the leaves and soil, confusing the trackers. It seemed like a silly plan, but since she had no experience with this type of subterfuge, she said nothing. Her belly growled and she put a hand to her abdomen, jealous of the food he wasted. Neither had eaten since the meat pie in the market and the longer they hiked, the hungrier she became.

It might've been an hour or four when Henri finally stopped. Her legs had long since turned to mush and her head floated in a hazy weightlessness that would've been welcome any other day.

"Where are we?" She bent at the waist and panted against the crispness cutting her lungs. At some point their path led them up into the mountains where the air was clear and stars bright.

"As long as we're careful, we should be safe here." He set down her bag and dug through a leather satchel to retrieve a flint and piece of curved steel. He bent low and struck the flint while blowing on kindling, igniting a small flame.

"Where did all of this come from?" She shuffled closer to the fire and glanced at the pile of supplies he'd amassed. "Are we to hide here until the ball? Won't we freeze?"

"The dwarves and I brought it up after the man was murdered in the forest. It was meant for their use, but now it'll benefit us. I'm sorry, princess, but no more warm and cozy palace life. At least not for a few days."

"I'm not marrying the king, so you can stop calling me that."

"Of course, Your Highness. Whatever you ask, it is yours." He bowed low and swept his arm out to the side in a mockery of reverence.

She should've been angry, but he was too ridiculous by half. "Please tell me we have food. Or do we have to catch it ourselves?" She rubbed her belly and pouted. "If that's the case, I'll starve before the ball and all of our problems will be solved."

His sharp look pierced her heart. "Don't talk like that. You dying is the worst possible thing that could happen."

"I was only jesting." Except, that was a lie. Or was it? Did she still believe death was the only escape?

In less time than it took to make her court gowns, she'd experienced more living than in the whole of her years previously. She'd conquered her dependence on Regan, faced down an arrogant prince, confronted a wolf-shifter, and lived to tell the tale, as they said. And through all the lies, the betrayals, and the interminable schemes, she discovered a woman she could be proud of. She knew love now. Not the desperate affection she sought from her stepmother, but true love. Perhaps Henri loved her, and after the ball they would make a future together, but the love she discovered on this miraculous journey was of herself.

A flush worked its way up her chest to settle on her cheeks. It was true, she loved who she'd become in such a short amount of time. There was more—she respected herself. Never again would she believe Regan's lies. Never again would she diminish herself at the whims of someone else.

"I don't want to die, Henri. Not now. Not after..." She blushed and wrung her hands. "You've given me hope where before there wasn't any. Our plan has to work."

"I hate that plan. We only have a few short days to think of something better."

After setting up the tent and eating two meat pies from the stash Henri brought, they curled together beneath thick wool blankets. Night animals made mournful cries and every so often the snap of a twig close to the tent would startle Eira, but with Henri's arms encircling her, she felt safer than she ever had in her whole life.

For the first time that she could remember, she slept without a single nightmare marring her slumber.

When she woke the next morning, Henri snored softly beside her, and she eased from the blankets without waking him. The small collection of pots and pans she found were a riddle to her as she'd never so much as made tea. Undaunted, she was determined to make them breakfast.

A shrew scurried between her feet, his sweet little snout foraging in the leaves. Eira bent to watch him, and he paused momentarily to look up at her. His whiskers vibrated and a tiny chirp came from his mouth. He resumed his searching, coming up with a fat earthworm that he laid at her feet.

"Why, thank you, kind sir. You are most generous." She reached a finger to stroke his head and he leaned into her touch. His soft fur sprang up as she petted him and his little body hummed. "What a funny little creature you are. Go on, eat your breakfast." She nudged the worm toward him and smiled encouragingly.

He shook his head and pushed it back to her before running off, his tail sticking straight up.

By the time Henri woke and helped prepare their tea, she had three more prizes added to her collection. And throughout the day, the gifts kept coming. It didn't matter whether she and Henri were training, he was teaching her how to use the myriad cooking utensils, or she was scribbling notes, animals of varying size and stature would approach, leave her a gift, and then allow her to pet them before scampering back into the forest.

With each, Henri would bow to the creature, but it was only to Eira that they brought their treasures. Nuts, seeds, blades of grass, all things found in the forest, and all things important to whichever animal presented it. She received them all with gracious thanks, but was stymied why they singled her out.

"Do they never see women in these woods?" she asked Henri as they readied for bed.

"Why don't you ask them?"

She chuckled good-naturedly, even though the idea was ludicrous. "In the morning, I shall do just that."

"There's an old legend about a Snow Queen, a beautiful woman as pure of heart as the freshly fallen snow. Benevolent and humble, she ruled over all the forests of Savinael."

"Where is Savinael? Is that another kingdom?"

"The seven kingdoms make up the entirety of Savinael. I do not know of other kingdoms beyond Savinael's borders, which leads me to believe this is the whole of our world."

One day, she would see every kingdom of Savinael. "This forest queen, how does she rule over all of the forests? Jura is vast, surely one person couldn't keep them all safe?"

Henri pulled his tunic over his head and her breath stopped for a moment as she admired the contours and ridges of his body.

"I couldn't say, but perhaps she is infused with magical powers that allows her to travel great distances in mere heartbeats."

She slapped his arm playfully, and let her fingers trail along his chest. "You're teasing me again." She cocked her head and grinned. "Perhaps one of my new animal friends could also tell us why Regan wished the king dead."

They'd not spoken of it much that day, mostly because this was her last opportunity to be alone with Henri before the ball. She had no idea what was to become of her, and she didn't want to spoil the day by dragging the others into their private moments.

On the morrow, they would prepare the elixir and set their plan.

"We could live like this. Just the two of us in nature, with no one to answer to but the weather." She looked at him with forced hope.

"And would you be happy? Truly? You were born to privilege. Giving all of that up won't be as easy as you think. You didn't complain today, but what about tomorrow when there are no more meat pies to fill your belly? What about when the snows come and you are half-starved and even more frozen? Will you learn to hunt and shoot one of those hares that brought you flowers today? Do you think you'd willingly learn how to skin a deer and sew a blanket from the hide so that you won't freeze next winter?" Henri took her hand and wiped a tear from her cheek. "I don't say this to be cruel. Living off the land is a rough life and not one easily embarked upon."

"What about your family? Could we live with them? At least, until we find work and can afford our own hovel." She smiled wryly, hoping she conveyed humor rather than moroseness.

"If we run, the king will hunt us down like boars. We must return to the palace and face whatever trials come our way." His grip tightened and he pressed his forehead against hers. "With you, all things are possible. I do not fear the king, nor his sons. What I fear most is waking each morning without you by my side."

She sought his lips and pulled him to the blankets. "Let us think of them no more for tonight. After the ball, we shall live long lives, together."

His warm breath came in shallow puffs against her cheek. "If you dream it, your heart will make it true."

"I dream it, my love. With all my heart." She pulled her nightdress over her head. "The prophecy was true, after all. You have quite stolen my heart."

"No, Eira. You gave it unconditionally. I vow to protect it until my dying breath."

Her reply was silenced by his kiss. As the kiss deepened, her heart beat stronger, pulsing hard and fast against her chest. She ran her fingers through his hair and gripped him to her, afraid to ever let go. In a forest or a palace, she would love him for all time. The heartbeats quickened, becoming louder until all she heard was pulsing, followed by an echo beat. Two hearts beating in rapid succession.

"I love you," Henri whispered as he entered her, and she returned the sentiment with a low moan.

Yes, she loved him. And he her. Together, they could do anything.

The twin hearts pounded once, twice, thrice, and then silence.

Chapter Thirty-Nine

Birdsong greeted Eira, and she stretched beneath the blankets, delighting in the sound. Unlike Henri teased, she couldn't understand them, but imagined they chittered about their nests and seeds, perhaps even about upcoming snow. Thoughts of Henri gave her warm trembles. She ran a hand up her naked body, recalling their lovemaking each night they'd been in the forest. By turns gentle and forceful, and she'd given of herself completely. Whatever happened today, she would at least have her memories.

Three nights and two full days of only Henri. Grateful for the time alone with him, she didn't once complain during their training sessions, of which there were many. More holds, even more releases, sword work, dagger skills, she was positive he was training her to become an assassin. But now, their lovemaking and lessons were over.

Henri was right. They couldn't run from the king, or from time.

Today was the day of the ball. A chill wriggled through her veins, and she stared at the tent roof. Each time she thought she'd solved the puzzle, she spotted a gaping hole in the entire picture. What was she missing? Regan and Leon, Guillaume's cruelty, and Otto's indifference. Three connected yet disparate schemes. Or were they?

What did each have to gain? And where did Annah fit in? What did she hope to gain? Was her only wish to raise Eira's children? Somehow, she didn't believe the witch would stop at that.

The questions swirled in her mind as she dressed, grateful this was the last time she'd have to wear the scratchy guard's uniform. Henri was right—she wouldn't enjoy a life on the run spent living off the land. She wasn't some princess who demanded soft cushions and huge banquets, but she did enjoy comfortable chairs, a nice fire, and books to read. None of which would be hers if they ran. He was also right about Otto. The king would hunt them to their last dying breath.

Each time she thought of midnight, or of her supposed wedding, her nerves frayed and anxiety spiked. The forest critters continued to bring her gifts, for which she still hadn't a clue as to why, despite Henri's charming story. The previous day they'd made the elixir even though Henri swore they'd come up with a plan that was less gruesome.

Thus far, neither had an alternative, although Henri did hint that he had someone working on the inside of the palace who might get them the crucial piece of the puzzle that they needed. With time running out, and their return to the palace imminent, Eira determined that she'd not hesitate when the time came to play her role. One bite of an apple to free her forever. It was a small price to pay.

She exited the tent and squinted against the bright early morning sun. With a hand over her eyes, she shuffled carefully to the campfire, where the crisp scent of stewed apples beckoned. The oaty aroma of porridge followed. Her stomach twisted its unhappiness. Perhaps she was more spoiled than she'd thought. Since seeing the viridian leaves in her breakfast, she was quite turned off by the stuff.

"I've worked out Stepmother's and Guillaume's reasons for wanting myself and the king dead, but I'm stymied by her asking Leon for my heart." She yawned and stretched to work out the last of her sleep.

"We're stumped by the young prince as well, ain't we?" Dorton said, and Eira glanced at him, surprised to see eight jolly faces watching her.

Relief warmed her heart. "You're here. You're safe."

She hugged each dwarf in turn, delighting in the little tickles their beards made against her cheek. When she'd finished her exuberant display of delight at seeing them again, they properly introduced themselves as there were several she'd not yet learned their names. At each, she curtseyed and they kissed her fingers like proper gentlemen.

"Gorse, Dorton, Hamlin, Rosco, Nevins, Treely, and Smith. Phew. It's such a pleasure to meet all of you. I only wish it was under different circumstances."

"As do I." Henri wrapped his arms around her and snugged her close to his warm body. "They're helping me with the elixir."

She noted the hint of sadness in his tone and put her hands over his. "Perhaps our fine friends can also help us with a better plan."

Dorton took his seat on a felled log and picked up a sheet of paper.

She recognized her writing and turned her head to give Henri a questioning glance.

"You take excellent notes. You must've been a good pupil for your tutor. And your handwriting is beautiful." His shoulders hitched with a shrug. "I didn't think you'd mind, especially if your notes give us answers."

"Then let's get to it." She poured herself a mug of Hamlin's special brew and situated her bum atop a lumpy rock. She would not miss that rock one little bit. It had been the most comfortable of her chair options and her arse would never be the same. "What insights do you have?"

"Not many," Henri confessed, "but I think we've made a start. Gil wants to be king, but to do so, he needs both his father and brother out of the way. The king—easy. Dupe a fair maiden into killing him, publicly to boot, and all suspicion is off the heir. The younger prince, as you said, is quite a riddle. If you kill the king, then Guillaume takes the throne. But there's the tricky business of the second son. If Leon is found guilty of murdering the tracker they found in the woods, then he's no longer a threat."

"If I kill Otto in front of the entire court, wouldn't I be thrown in the dungeons? And what about Lady Annah? I'm sure she wouldn't let me—or someone disguised as me—casually murder her beloved. The king is unwell, and she's desperate to save him. We're missing something vital."

"Unless Regan sought to somehow indict Annah in the scheme. Once Gil is king, he can pardon you, and execute both Leon and Annah. It's rather simple, really. Your stepmother's thought of everything. I only wish we had sooner." Henri grimaced and scuffed at the dirt as if it offended him as much as Regan.

"How'n, then, do you think the young lady's heart fits into the scheme?" Rosco filed at his cuticles with a sharp blade, and Eira winced.

A good soak and gentle massage would work better on his nails. But she didn't voice her concerns about his beauty regimen. Instead, she focused on the dilemma at hand.

"If'n it's still beating, it contains all that person's magic, don't it?" The one called Treely asked.

Henri paced the little campsite. "What did Guillaume say to you at the stables?"

She'd tried to block the memory from her mind, but his cruel words were seared into her psyche for all time.

"He said I'd broken a promise. I assumed he meant because I'd been with you, and he somehow knew. But he was so angry. Said I'd teased him, but I haven't, I swear."

Henri held her trembling hands. "I'm sorry to make you relive that horrible event."

"I thought he would kill you. He accused me of having a lover and said he'd do vile things to him. And then he threatened to slit my neck if I cried out." A sob caught in her throat and she coughed against it. "He said by rights I should be his, but I don't know why."

"Broken a promise? By rights his?" Hamlin tapped his cup against his temple and snorted several times. "Was there a betrothal between you and the prince?"

"No, of course not."

Henri held her chin and turned her face to his. "Can you be absolutely certain?"

All warmth drained from her body. "I can't. I didn't even know about my marriage to the king until we arrived at the palace. I thought we were coming for the ball, nothing more."

The realization pinched her skin, and she recoiled from the depths of her stepmother's depravity. Of her own innocence and belief in others' goodness. She slapped her forehead and swore at her stupidity.

"She met with Guillaume just after she told you to take me somewhere safe. He kept banging on about playing a role, but I didn't understand what he meant. He said I played my part of the virgin so thoroughly he almost believed it. Lawks, do you think Regan promised me to Guillaume? She seemed irritated that he'd attacked me and said he almost ruined everything." She kicked at the ground and shouted at the heavens. "That duplicitous witch. In league with one brother and blackmailing the other, with me caught in her trap. She planned this perfectly. Tonight, when I kill the king, it'll be gossiped that I did so out of my love for Guillaume. I'll bet those papers he had were love letters penned by Regan, but signed by me. It would explain why he thought I had broken a promise."

Henri rubbed his chin and walked a circle around the dwarves. "If, perchance, your stepmother has a still-beating heart, in or out of your body, that's full of untapped power, that gives her unlimited potential. For all we know, her plan was to kill you all along and continue the farce of taking on your visage. As long as she's never required to be in the same room as you, no one would be the wiser. She becomes queen and a powerful witch with one fell stroke."

"Brilliant and simple. And utterly unprovable." Nevins smoothed several sheets of parchment. "We need those letters, if for no other reason than to discredit the scheming stepmother."

"Leave that to me," Henri assured them.

A twig cracked and they turned in unison to see a great stag emerge from the thick woods. His antlers barely cleared the space between two great pines. His lush brown eyes watched Eira intently and his nostrils flared with each step.

Eira stood still, unsure what to do. Henri stepped in front of her, dagger drawn. The dwarves made a half circle of defense between her and the stag.

He cleared the trees and stopped several paces before the dwarves. To her astonishment, he bowed, one foreleg extended, one bent, his great antlers lowering to nearly touch the ground.

Each of them—dwarves, prince, and lady—stood, transfixed. Then, as one, they bowed low to the magnificent beast.

The stag snuffled and rose, his gaze locked to Eira. A curious calm overcame her as she threaded her way through the dwarves. Their gasp startled her out of the reverie and she, too, gaped at the sight of a pure white doe stepping lightly from the foliage. Her ears flicked back and forth, side to side, and her pink little nose twitched. A wreath of holly leaves dangled from her mouth.

The stag stepped backward to allow passage of the doe, as if he were merely her guardian. Eira could scarcely breathe, acutely aware of the gravity of the moment. The doe approached Eira with delicate steps that belied her strength and speed. Eira feared moving, feared speaking, for if she did either, the doe would bolt away.

But the doe didn't run. Nor did she flinch when one of the dwarves sneezed behind Eira. Her gaze, like the stag's, was focused on Eira. She reached to stroke the doe's muzzle and was rewarded with the softest fur she'd ever touched. Her fingers ran through the snow-colored tuft between her glossy brown eyes. Her hands swept down the doe's neck. Beneath her apparent delicateness, a strong heart beat a steady pace. She wasn't frightened of Eira or the men.

The doe rubbed her head against Eira's middle and pressed the wreath into her hand. Another gift. She held the wreath, her thumb tracing the holly leaves, her mind crowded with questions and confusion. Why her?

"Put the crown on yer head, lass," one of the dwarves whispered, loud enough even the tiny critters in the trees could hear.

She snugged the wreath against her head, feeling only a little silly. The doe and stag bowed low, but Eira didn't understand. She looked back to Henri, who also bowed, his hand over his heart.

"What does this mean?" She searched his features for clues, but saw only pride.

"It means, Princess, that it's time for you to claim your throne."

When she looked back to the doe, both she and the stag were gone.

Chapter Forty

An air of excitement permeated the town when Eira and Henri returned from their secret place in the forest. Townsfolk danced in the street, raising toast after toast to the king and his good fortune, although Eira suspected they were more grateful for a day off than for their sovereign. Tables laden with food lined the street and she hid her surprise that Otto would give them such a grand feast. She refused to be bitter—especially not after seeing the joy on the townspeople's faces and knowing that tonight, their bellies would be full.

She and Henri hurried through the palace, using the servants' stairs. They'd left their guard uniforms at the camp, along with the rest of their belongings. It was decided they'd confront Regan, and give her a chance to confess before going to the king. Without proof, however, Eira had little hope that her stepmother would comply. If that were the case, Henri ominously claimed he had a secondary plan they could use, but only if absolutely necessary.

"Are you sure you don't want to disclose your secret scheme to me? I know you said if I don't know, Regan can't pluck it from my mind, but it might help if I knew what I was going along with." It wasn't that she didn't trust him, just that she didn't like surprises. Especially ones that might end in either her or Henri's actual, can't be saved by orinth, death. Or imprisonment. Neither sounded like good options.

They stood before Eira's rooms, stalling. The time for planning had passed, and now it was time for action. She didn't fear the future, but her stepmother was clever and a few days of freedom might've lessened the hold Regan had on her, but she wasn't truly free. Not yet.

"It's for the best. Please, have the same faith in me that you've entrusted thus far." Henri squeezed her hand and cocked his head toward the door. "Ready?"

Lawks no, she wasn't, but she nodded anyway. Might as well face the beast and be done with it.

Regan wasn't alone in the sitting room when they entered. She stood before Prince Guillaume, her face a storm cloud of anger. Eira kept her pace steady, her features schooled into indifference.

"There you are. It's about damn time." Regan flung an arm in the general direction of the prince. "His Highness here has been telling me tales that I find rather extraordinary. Would you care to confirm them?"

A slow burn of panic started in Eira's sternum. No mention of Regan's command to Leon, no surprise that she was alive, just condemnation and accusations. Why Eira had expected anything less was a mystery. Seeing Regan and Guillaume together, pretending innocence, broke something in her. She no longer cared what her stepmother thought, or even what she did to her, she just wanted to be done with the scheming.

"I can't confirm what I don't know." Eira gazed at the pair with an air of defiance.

Guillaume's harsh laugh boomed against her hearing. "Such

a pretty liar, slag, but a liar all the same. Tell me, did you promise him your hand in marriage, too?"

Henri remained close, but at a respectable distance, even though she desperately wished she could reach for his hand. Guillaume knew. He knew they'd been intimate and now he'd told Regan. Her gaze whipped to her stepmother, whose countenance appeared more annoyed than angry. Was this their new scheme? Defraud Eira to the king? Her thoughts spun quickly, trying to find all the angles that Regan might play.

Turning to Guillaume, Eira straightened her shoulders and lifted her chin. She channeled as much haughtiness as she could muster. "I assure you, Your Highness, I have not promised myself to marry anyone."

"Lies!" Guillaume slammed his hands on a bureau and glared at her. "You were promised to me, you cunning little bitch. And though we had a signed betrothal, I was willing to go along with your little performance. After all, you were offered a sum you couldn't deny. But to debase yourself with someone who'd fooled you so thoroughly is an insult I can't ignore."

She staggered at the lies he spewed, and by the hurt, confusion, and anger on his face, she almost believed he thought he spoke true.

"Someone has played a cruel trick, I'm afraid." She knew exactly who, but Regan stood with her fingers over her mouth as if she were just as horrified by the news as Eira. "Someone who has the most to gain from these intrigues." And now Eira did confront her stepmother. "All of these lies, these deceptions—why, Stepmother?"

"How dare you." Regan moved as if to strike Eira and quicker than a flash, Henri stepped in front of her to block the slap.

"Do not touch her again, Lady Banworth, or I shall be aggrieved to take swift—and permanent—action."

"You dare threaten me, you insolent beggar? I should never have trusted you."

"He's no beggar, my lady." Guillaume flexed his fingers and made fists that he then rested upon as he leaned forward to glare at Henri. "He's been parading around the palace like a humble huntsman, a nobody servant, when in reality, he's a prince."

"What?" Eira's throat tightened and she licked dry lips. This was too much. Guillaume had lost his mind. "Henri is no prince, I can assure you. He's kind and caring. He's a good man. Unlike you."

Eira cast a quick glance to Henri and the anguish in his eyes struck like a dagger to her heart. Guillaume hadn't lied about this one thing. Henri's gorgeous lips tightened and he looked at her as if seeking forgiveness. He thought he'd failed her in not admitting who he truly was. But he hadn't failed her or anyone else. He'd been protecting her by hiding his identity. She saw it all clearly now, and knew that had he told her who he was, their lives would've pivoted in a different direction. As far as she was concerned, nothing had changed with this revelation. He was still the kind man she'd given her heart to, and would gladly give again for the rest of her life. Beggar or prince, she loved him.

She advanced on Guillaume, noting the curl of Regan's lips as she passed her stepmother. "And even if he is, he's thrice the man you will ever be. I wouldn't dare debase myself to marry you. I assure you, anything you have with my signature is a forgery."

All the names. Henri had known all her names. Something a simple huntsman might not know, but a prince would. That, and a dozen other clues dropped into her thoughts like raindrops on a pond. The clues were there, she just hadn't seen them. Neither had Regan, a cold comfort, indeed.

Guillaume's hand raised, but Regan ordered him to stop.

"You've assaulted her enough, Your Highness. Can't you see, she is not right in the head? This man, this lying, devious usurper has told her lies that have obviously damaged her sensibilities. We wouldn't want to involve the king, would we?"

Deeper meaning roped through her words, but they were lost on Eira. "The only lies told here are from you, Stepmother. Yes, let's involve the king. You can confess your pathetic schemes to him and live out the rest of your lives in the dungeons. If he lets you live, that is."

Regan grabbed Eira by the throat and slammed her against the wall. "I haven't spent that last eighteen fucking years with only your miserable company to live out my life in a dungeon, you stupid cunt. If you think the king will save you, you're even thicker than I thought."

"Lady Banworth, release your stepdaughter." Henri stood behind Regan, a slim sword held against her neck.

"Or what?" She gave Eira a harsh squeeze and released her before turning on Henri. "You don't have the balls. Prince Pathetic is what you are."

Eira wheezed and coughed as stars danced in her vision. A buzzing started in her ears, and she strained to hear what the others said.

Henri sheathed his sword and helped steady her to stand.

"Where'd the sword come from?" A magical dagger pulled from thin air, an invisible sword—what kind of prince was he, exactly? A powerful one with magic just like hers. Except, he could reach his readily and she could not.

Henri kept his focus on Regan, his hand gripping Eira's. Her magic sparked in her veins, straining to be freed.

Henri bent close and whispered, "Not yet."

Was this his plan? Use their combined magic against Regan? She pushed her power down until the spark dimmed, and felt the loss with a swift and immediate ache.

Regan snarled at them, and then stormed across the room and back. "What do you want?" She glared at Guillaume with arms crossed over her bosom; her fingers wriggled against her gown.

"Him." Guillaume pointed to Henri. "And your silence."

"If he is who you say, and you kill him, you'll be responsible for a war, Your Highness." Although her words were grim, to Eira's hearing, it sounded as if that was exactly what she wanted.

"You can't have him." Eira stood in front of Henri and squeezed his hand. "This ends here, Stepmother. The lies, the trickery. No more. We're going to the king to tell him of your ruse. He'll—"

Regan flicked her fingers toward Eira, and she choked on the words she tried to speak. Only a small squeaking came out, like a mouse caught by a cat.

"He'll do nothing because you'll say nothing. You may have the prince in a moment, Gil. I'd like to play a game with him first."

Regan flourished her hand and a simple glass box appeared on her palm. Eira's heart quickened, and she gripped Henri's hand harder. He stared straight ahead as if paralyzed. The warmth of his magic slid up her arm and she tried to reach her own power, but it was blocked. Regan must've tightened the wards the moment she realized they'd been loosened. Again, she reached for her magic, but the spark she'd felt was cold. Where Henri's magic had warmed her skin, only a creeping scratch remained. They were both cut off from their magic. Eira glared at Regan, unable to speak the venom she wished to spew. How dare she? How very dare she?

Regan's horrid laugh filled Eira's ears and then her stepmother began a spell she knew to be from the grimoire, in a section filled with dark magic. Her body trembled even when she couldn't move her limbs. They were petrified, she and Henri, literally.

"You will not remember each other. You will not recall the events of the past two weeks. You will return to what you knew before you met." Regan's fingers curled and wriggled with her spell. She touched first Henri's temple, and then Eira's.

The glass box filled with an inky bluish mist that swirled and undulated. Such a pretty miasma that she didn't understand. A wash of coolness swept from her temple to her toes, invigorating in its chillness.

Eira withdrew her hand from the man at her side, unsure how she came to be so close to a stranger. He was handsome, with a strong jaw and eyes the color of deepest sapphire, so dark they were like midnight, but it was his lips that caught her attention. Kissable. Very kissable.

She put a finger to her own lips and chased a fragment of memory, but it was gone before her next breath.

"Do you know him, Eira?" Regan prodded.

Her throat hurt when she tried to speak, but after a long swallow, the words flowed. "I apologize if we've met before, but I don't recall your name." She curtseyed low, as she'd been taught.

"And you, sir, do you know this woman?"

"I confess I do not, but should like to very much." The man bowed and took Eira's fingers in his own. A tremor of something pleasant, a scent of pine and apples, drifted to her. "I am Prin—"

"That's enough." Guillaume stormed forward and jerked the man away from Eira. "Guards!"

The outer door opened and four guards entered, their faces stern, their steps heavy.

"Take this man to the western dungeons. Do not allow him to speak, for if he does, the words will be lies," the prince commanded.

The guards saluted in reply. They grabbed the man roughly and half-dragged him away.

His gaze didn't leave hers. Even when a guard blocked her view, she saw him shift so that he could see her until they were out of the sitting room entirely. Prince Guillaume followed, his muttered grousing full of threats.

"What did he do?" Eira asked of the young man.

"Never you mind that. Do you recall what today is?"

What a silly goose her stepmother was. "Of course. It's the day of the ball."

And her marriage to the king.

"Can I dance at the ball?" She'd never been to a ball before and it sounded exciting.

"Of course, darling. But first, we must get you bathed. You smell like a rotting corpse." Regan called for servants and spoke low before shooing them from the room.

"Do you still have the apple I gave you? The one to enchant the king?"

"Yes, Stepmother. I shall serve him first, and then myself as you have instructed is the custom on one's wedding night." Her wedding night. It was supposed to be a time filled with joy, but why did her stomach twist at the thought? "Will it hurt, Stepmother?"

"What, darling?"

"The, uh, when we consummate our marriage."

If you're who I believe you are, do not let him consummate your marriage.

Who had said that? An image of a woman with wild grey hair and kind eyes nudged against a wall in her mind.

"Only for a moment. Then all will be well." Her stepmother waved toward the bathing room. "Go on, we need time to prepare you for the ball. After tonight, you shall be queen, just as you've always dreamed."

Yes, she'd always dreamed of being queen.

But had she?

It means, Princess, that it's time for you to claim your throne.

Who had said that? She was a lady, not a princess. There wasn't a kingdom for her to rule.

Images flickered through her mind, confusing in their brevity. Just fragments of memories dashing in and out of her thoughts. She shuffled to her bedchamber and shoved her hands into her pockets. In the right, she felt the smooth handle of a dagger. In her left was the prickly edges of holly leaves. How the hells had they gotten there?

She removed each carefully and placed them inside her wardrobe beside the casket that held her enchanted apple. After a moment's hesitation, she retrieved the casket and placed it on her dressing table beside a gorgeous fan she couldn't remember owning. The wreath and dagger she tucked beneath a tapestry. If tortured, she couldn't say why she hid the items, only that she felt an overwhelming need to protect them.

To protect...something precious. Something forgotten, but not quite lost.

Chapter Forty-One

Eira winced with each tug of the hairbrush, but her stepmother was oblivious. She hadn't stopped talking about what Eira would do that night, who she could dance with, who she had to avoid. Regan acted as if Eira had forgotten all of her manners and protocol.

She'd been raised a lady. Even though this was her first ball, she knew how to behave. Another rough tug made her cry out. That earned a scowl from her stepmother and a swat to her shoulder. They sat in Regan's room in front of the ornate mirror her stepmother refused to be without. Eira had never liked the mirror and she had the sense the mirror didn't like her, either. How could an inanimate object have feelings? Such nonsense. Even so, when she looked closer at her reflection, she could've sworn she saw a ripple across the glass surface, and a hint of green outline their faces.

"If you'd brushed your hair after riding, we wouldn't be in this position, would we?" Regan smoothed Eira's tresses and rested her chin on the silky dark locks. "In a matter of hours, you'll be queen. I'm so proud of you, darling. And to think, your marriage to the king is a love match."

Was it? Eira didn't feel as if she loved the king, but then, it had all happened so fast. A whirlwind romance, Regan called it. She positively adored reminding Eira how, upon their arrival to the palace, the king had been immediately smitten and had wooed Eira with trinkets and words of devotion. Each night they dined together and danced beneath a trellis of fall blooms, with only the moon for company.

The entire court was dazzled by their love.

Everyone except Eira.

"Who did I ride with this afternoon?" She played with a sparkling diamond bracelet, trying to recall memories of the day. It was all a blur.

"Your lady-in-waiting, of course. Now, put those silly nerves away. Tonight is your wedding night, darling. Enjoy it."

Regan pulled strands of hair from the brush and meticulously straightened them before making a tiny braid.

"What's that for?" Eira cocked her head and watched her stepmother tie the braid around her wrist.

"Just a token of love for me to remember my daughter on this very special day." Regan hugged Eira and kissed her on the cheek. "I'm so proud of you, darling. Never forget that. I love you."

"And I you," Eira said. But the words rang hollow in her heart.

"All of this excitement has quite exhausted me. I'm going to lie down for a brief nap. Why don't you go rest as well? We have a short while until it's time for the ball, and you need to save your strength."

Eira didn't understand the cheeky grin Regan gave her. It was full of meaning, but why? What would she need her energy for? Dancing? She shuffled to her bedchamber, her thoughts muddled. The room was empty of servants and she gratefully headed for the bed. A basket of apples sat on the table and she could've sworn they weren't there before.

She paused, head cocked. There was somewhere she needed to take the apples, but where?

Take this man to the western dungeons.

The dungeons. But a lady wouldn't dare go someplace like that, and especially not alone. Yet she couldn't deny the pull of insistency that she take the apples to the dank place. The more she fought the desire, the more insistent and urgent the need became. She couldn't very well wear her dressing gown, but her wardrobe was empty save for her wedding gown. A luscious crushed velvet in deep purple with gold filigree embroidery on the bell sleeves. Her father's colors. What a touching way to have him with her on this most important of days. Her other clothes had been taken to the queen's rooms already. Her rooms after tonight.

She would have liked to wear something plainer, but slipped the soft velvet over her bare skin. The caress of fabric reminded her of a rug before a fire and the kindest, sweetest, impossibly dark eyes she'd ever seen. But that wasn't a memory, only a fantasy. A dream. She'd had many dreams of late. Most didn't make sense; a few frightened her enough she'd wake drenched in sweat.

Rather than let the nightmares ruin her mood, she pushed the dream memories aside and picked up the basket of apples. No sense recalling nonsense that happened while she slept, even if most of her nocturnal imagination involved sweet kisses from a man she didn't know. It was best to focus on the moment, on being young and alive. She was to marry a king tonight and would wake on the morrow a queen.

A secret door she'd not noticed previously stood ajar and she quickly retrieved the dagger she'd hidden, before slipping through the doorway to a dusty corridor lit by a single torch. She unfastened it from its hold and held it aloft to light the way. Which way, she wasn't certain. On instinct, she went left.

At the entrance to a tight spiral staircase, she paused. Then her foot stepped onto the first stair and her body followed. Down and down she went until she came to a small enclave that led to an opening.

Surprisingly, fear was absent as she made her way through the murky darkness. Only a budding curiosity lingered. She stepped from the alcove to a row of cells and paused. The dungeons. This was where they'd taken him—the stranger she'd met in her stepmother's rooms. But who had made the demand? And why was he a scoundrel?

"Who goes there? Show yourself," a raspy voice ordered from the shadows.

Eira stepped forward, her torch and basket held aloft in a firm grasp. "I come bringing nourishment. Apples."

"About fucking time you made it." A dirty nose stuck out from the bars of one cell, and Eira turned toward the woman's voice.

"Take as many as you like, but save some for the others." She took in her skeletal frame and grime-encrusted skin. "Do I know you?"

She felt that somehow, she should, but why would a lady know a prisoner?

"Aye, you do." The woman looked intently at her, as if encouraging her to remember. "We met nearly a fortnight past. You brought me apples then, too."

"I did?" Eira rubbed her temples. "I don't remember, I'm sorry."

"'Tis all right, lass. I can see you're not yourself today." She lifted her chin toward the other cells. "You might want to give that lad an apple. And have one for yourself while you're at it."

She turned around to see two other cells were occupied. In

one, a young man with raven hair studied her. His face was mottled with purplish bruises, as if he'd been fighting. In the other, a shortish man with a round belly and snub nose gripped the bars and pressed his face against them, as if trying to escape.

"Well, well. If it ain't a pretty bird. Come to release me? I tell ya, I ain't the killer. Neither's either of these two louts. Don't have green eyes, do they? I seen 'em, I did. But no one believes me."

Eira approached cautiously. "I'm not at all sure what you're talking about, but I have apples if you'd like some."

"The murder! Gotta be the gossip of court, innit. A man had his face tore up. Said it was wolves, but it weren't." He reached for an apple and bit into it. Drool slid down his chin, and Eira looked away.

"That's...terrible. I didn't know."

Green eyes. She remembered seeing green eyes somewhere, but where?

"I'll take an apple if you have any to spare." The handsome man in the last cell stuck his hand out, and she saw red marks around his wrist, as if he'd been restrained.

"Who beat you?" She placed an apple in his palm. When her fingers touched his skin, a tickling sort of jolt went through her nerves. Her gaze flicked to his face and by the widening of his eyes, he felt it, too. "What was that?"

"I don't know." He looked at the female prisoner opposite. "Perhaps you could cut it up for me, seeing as my jaw is mighty sore. Do you have a knife?"

She was beginning to think coming to the dungeons was a very bad idea. She shuffled the basket behind her, out of his reach of the dagger that rested beside the fruit.

"Share the apple with him. Go on, then. Both of you, take a bite," the woman with dirty hair urged, her eyes darting between them and the dungeon entrance. "Don't be wasting time."

"You promise you won't hurt me?"

His eyes narrowed and then widened. "I promise I will never hurt you."

A fire, spiced apple tea, and soft words spoken. *I'm here to protect you Eira.*

Eira removed the dagger from the basket and exchanged the torch for the apple. The handsome man stared at her dagger as if it were an asp about to strike. With a trembling hand, she cut through the apple, slicing her finger in the process.

"Ouch! Silly, clumsy me."

The prisoner took her hand in his and soothed where blood oozed from her cut. A bluish spark flared around their entwined fingers and a fresh memory, of a blue light followed by shimmering gold, danced in her mind.

"Kiss her, you fool." The woman jeered and Eira snatched her hand away. "Lady Cannaid, search your heart. You know him, just as you know me, Sacheen."

"Sacheen?" An image of a wolf, frightened and fangs bared, scorched her mind.

"Yes, that's it." Sacheen waved her toward the prisoner. "I can't believe I'm going to say this, but kiss the man. True love's kiss will break any spell and looks like you two have a doozy of a memory block. Do it. Now."

Eira glanced at the man, at his bruised skin and tempting lips. "Do you know what she's talking about?"

"I don't, but at the same time, I feel I know you." He tapped his heart. "In here."

"Yes, I feel it, too."

She stepped closer and gripped the bars to rise on tiptoe. This was madness, kissing a perfect stranger in a dungeon, but it was right. In her heart, she knew what Sacheen said was true.

Their lips met between the cold steel of the dungeon cell. His warmth encircled her, holding her in an embrace so loving she never wanted to be with his touch. Kisses so sweet she wanted to cry floated through her memory. Not just kisses, but his gentle caresses, their languid lovemaking.

A rug in front of a fire.

Her blood quickened and more memories crowded her mind of a cottage where dwarves lived, of apple tea, and of a man she loved.

"Henri."

"Eira."

He was the huntsman come for her heart. Her prince charming who hid his identity to keep her safe. She had to die so that they could live.

Chapter Forty-Two

Henri reached through the cell bars, and cradled Eira's head. She swooned closer, longing for what his touch promised. Freedom. Dying was the only way to save them both. She knew this to be true just as she knew Henri in her heart.

The loud creak of an iron door opening startled her, and she jerked backward. Impotent desire and panic raced through her veins and her heart thundered louder than a team of six horses galloping on a dirt road.

The guards couldn't find her here. Alone, in the dungeons. Word would get back to the king and he'd be incensed. She shook her head against the thought. The king wasn't important, Henri was. A hazy push against her mind sought to stamp out the memories that struggled to break free. Someone had manipulated her so that she wouldn't remember Henri. Who would do such a thing? And why? The harder she focused on the questions, the sharper pangs cut into her brain. Only one person in her life would be so bold, yet when she thought of Regan's name, it physically pained her.

Henri. Keep Henri safe. She snuffed out her torch and

crouched low in a corner at the end of the cells as heavy footfalls entered the dungeon. A beefy man, with arms the size of her thighs and grime smeared across his face, stopped in front of Henri's cell, a torch in one hand, iron cuffs in the other.

"Put these on. You've got an audience with the crown prince."

The goaler's gruff tone hinted at the danger awaiting Henri. Eira fought through a fog of memories, trying to pick out which were real and which weren't. Henri's touch was real. She held onto that one truth, for that was all she could carry at the moment.

The goaler opened Henri's cell and roughly pulled him along toward the dungeon entrance. She raced to follow, but he closed the iron door and locked it from the other side, taking all the light with him.

"Go after him, Eira. Remember who you are." Sacheen's voice came from the darkness.

She held out her hands to keep from stumbling and made her way to where she'd snuffed out her torch and retrieved it. The basket she gave to Sacheen. In her other hand, she gripped the dagger. What an odd thing to say. Of course she remembered who she was.

And despite your stepmother's best efforts, you are a good woman, Eira Eloise Francis Cannaid.

Henri had said that to her. He knew her. Knew all of her names. She had to save him.

"I will. Thank you." She curtseyed to the prisoner and smiled warily. Somehow, she'd find Henri.

A torch flared to life near the dungeon entrance and Eira jumped with a shrill squeak, her bowels nearly emptying themselves. A face stepped from the shadows and she backed into a wall to escape the approaching man.

"Leon?" Torment laced that single word and Sacheen

pressed her face through the bars. "I thought you'd forsaken me."

Leon strode to Sacheen and gripped her hands through the bars. His eyes roamed over her, a look of feral rage creasing his features. "I've been searching everywhere for you. It wasn't until I followed the guard just now that I could gain entrance into this part of the dungeons. Annah must have them warded to prevent unwanted visitors." His gaze slid to Eira. "How is it you're able to slip in here unharmed?"

Eira shook her head, too frightened to speak. He was the wolf who'd attacked her in the woods.

"Her memory's not right, Leon."

"Aye, but mine is. Yer the killer, ain't ye? Seen ya, I did." The grubby little man sneered through the bars.

"Ignore him. He prattles on and on all day about the green-eyed man who murdered someone in the woods." Sacheen pulled Leon closer, as much as the bars would allow. She cocked her head, her eyes blinking rapidly. "It was you? He's speaking true? But why?"

"I was searching for you. I was losing my mind with worry since your disappearance and risked running the woods."

"During the day? That's too risky. You should've waited."

"I did wait and when you didn't return, I couldn't wait any longer."

Trackers carrying a naked man on a wooden pole, a forest at night with the great wolf, the king kicking a poor fool to death, those memories swirled in Eira's mind as she kept still and silent against the wall. Eavesdropping wasn't ladylike, but she was trapped.

"How many others are there?" Worry sparked in Sacheen's eyes.

Leon glanced at the other prisoner, a frown marring his handsome features. "Twelve. Their cells locked are warded."

"As is mine. Twelve of us, and I make thirteen."

A circle of thirteen. A page from a grimoire drifted through her mind. A magic circle. Powerful. But to heal or harm?

Leon's lips thinned and jaw tightened as he processed Sacheen's words. He turned to her and his face softened. "Eira, I am truly sorry for that night in the forest. I was desperate for my secret to stay hidden, but I no longer care. My father needs to be stopped. You were right. I need to step into my own power." He reached for the cell lock, but Sacheen stopped him.

"Don't, my mate. It's warded."

Eira put a hand on Leon's sleeve and felt his innate magic calling to her own. He was like her, but she didn't recall having power of her own. Yet she did. It hurt to think of magic and power—hurt her mind as if someone was piercing it with an ice pick. Stabby pricks against her skull, and her heart.

Leon and Sacheen spoke quietly while the other prisoner muttered and wrung his hands, his intense focus on the pair. Eira lit her torch from Leon's and approached the grubby man's cell. He backed away, his eyes wide with—not fear—apprehension. He was afraid of her, but why? She was just a girl, a nobody.

A nobody the king was to marry.

Her gaze slid to Leon and Sacheen. A circle of thirteen, a still-beating heart, papers with a promise of betrothal, what did it all mean?

"Who are you?" She held the torch close to the bars and he scampered to the corner where shadows danced on the stone walls. Her gaze went to a pile of food, uneaten by the man, but presently being enjoyed by two fat rats.

Heat from the torch warmed her skin, but a shiver chilled her to the bone. She stepped back to pull on the cell door and it swung open unimpeded. It wasn't locked. Why would his cell not be locked?

"What's this?" Leon stood beside her, his scowl matching her confusion.

"I..." Eira began, uncertain how to phrase the thoughts spiraling through her skull. "I don't believe he's real."

The prisoner whimpered and crouched so believably, she had a moment's doubt. When he leapt at her, sharp teeth bared, claws reaching for her neck, she screamed and thrust the torch into his face. A blast of Leon's magic rushed past Eira and knocked the man against the wall. The rats squeaked and scattered.

The gurgled cries that came from the man didn't sound male, but as though they came from a woman. An image of a pretty lady with copper curls burned against Eira's skull.

Chapter Forty-Three

Eira stepped toward the man, but Leon held out an arm to stop her. His angry hiss wasn't directed toward her, but she flinched from it all the same. Another powerful blast of his magic and the whimpering prisoner disintegrated to nothing. Not even a mote of dust was left of the man.

Sacheen gasped from behind them and Eira whirled to see her push open her cell door.

"Leon." Eira touched his sleeve and indicated his mate. "She's free."

Leon's magic must've destroyed the wards on Sacheen's cell, too. Whoever was controlling the imaginary prisoner lost control over the other cells when Leon blasted them. Intriguing. But who would do such a thing? And why?

Leon turned toward Sacheen and his face lit up with a smile so full of joy it nearly broke Eira's heart.

"None of us are free, not yet." Sacheen closed the space between herself and Leon and clung to her mate. "That was Annah's doing, I'd bet my pelt on it." She rubbed her temples. "I have strange memories of Annah coming here each day to taunt me. My magic would bristle at her presence, but then I would wake and the memory was but a dream. My magic, however, felt violated."

"A witch who steals magic from others and becomes powerful enough to conjure a believable image? How do we defeat that?" Eira gripped the dagger until her knuckles whitened.

"Together. Eira, go find Henri and bring him to the ball-room." Leon put his arm around Sacheen. "We'll get the others and meet you there."

With her legs trembling violently, traversing the stairs was tricky at best, but she managed to find her way back to her rooms without collapsing in a fit of despair. There were intrigues in play that she didn't understand and each time she thought she had a puzzle sorted, she'd lose a piece and have to start again.

Once in her room, she returned the dagger to its hiding place beside the holly wreath. One look at her gown made her heart sink. The bottom half of the skirt was completely covered in dust. She batted at the expensive fabric to remove any evidence that she'd been outside her rooms. If Regan caught her, there would be recriminations and punishment.

Regan.

Henri.

Eira paused in her batting. Who was Henri to her? She touched her lips, and the memory of his kisses and a forest sprang to mind. He'd taught her how to use her power, and how to defend herself against the prince.

Guillaume.

He'd tried to rape her.

He was holding Henri hostage and most likely was respon-sible for his bruises.

You've got an audience with the crown prince.

The memories flitted through her mind like a hummingbird,

never landing long enough for her to retain for more than a few moments.

A light knock startled her, and she jumped behind the table to hide the dust on her gown. A maid entered with a cup of tea, and Eira relaxed. Exactly what she needed.

"Thank you." She held the cup to her lips, but didn't drink. This was no tea she recognized. "What's in here?"

The maid looked askance, not meeting Eira's gaze. "The mistress bade me give it to you. Said I needed to watch you drink it all."

She sniffed the liquid and swirled the cup. Tiny white flowers danced on the surface.

Valerian and betane. One name she recognized, but not the other. They were herbs, and something else, but it eluded her. Probably to help with her nerves for the wedding.

She drank the tea and handed the cup to the maid. "Tell Stepmother I finished it all."

The maid gave her a solemn nod and left the bedchamber. The sound of a key scraping in the lock sent chills down Eira's back. If Regan knew she'd left her room, she wouldn't have locked that door, but found a way to secure the hidden passage. So, why imprison Eira?

She bent to dust off her gown and peered at the fire. A memory of throwing food and tea into it seared against her skull.

Holly berries. She needed raw berries for...something. It was imperative she eat them now.

Eira grabbed her holly wreath and tore three berries loose. She popped them in her mouth and chewed, puckering at their sourness. A wave of nausea swept over her, and she leaned against the table, breathing through the churning of her stomach. She smoothed the tapestry over her hidden treasures, her vision wavering. Heat prickled her skin, and she stripped off the gorgeous gown. Standing in just her small-clothes, she fanned herself against the sudden warmth in the room.

She could've killed you, duckie. Never mix valerian with betane.

If Regan loved her as she claimed, why would she want to drug her own daughter?

Eira glanced at the mirror and saw not a vibrant young woman about to be married, but a caged soul longing to be freed.

She unfurled her fingers and traced where the dagger sliced her flesh, but there was only smooth skin.

Lies. They were all lies. But whose? And why?

More importantly, who could she trust?

I know it's not easy, but if you trust in yourself, everything will work out in the end.

A woman, the same one with wild hair and kind eyes, had told her that. A seemingly different woman, but Eira realized was actually the same woman who brought the apples. What was her name? When she tried to recall the memory, another sharp pain stabbed at her skull.

Trust herself. She lay on her bed with one hand on her belly, the other on her forehead. What did trusting herself even look like?

Scraping brought Eira out of her reverie, and she lay still, pretending sleep. Her stomach had settled somewhat, but the fever lingered. Whether from the berries or the tea, she wasn't sure, but what she knew for certain was that there were schemes afoot that involved her. And playing docile was her best bet to uncover exactly what they were.

The lock clicked and the door opened with a soft hush. Keys were placed upon a table and a moment later, the bed dipped where someone sat beside Eira.

"Darling, are you awake?"

Eira moaned and fluttered her eyes as if it were the most difficult thing to open them.

"I'm ever so sleepy, Stepmother. Can we talk when I wake?"

"I'm afraid you'll never wake, darling." She smoothed Eira's hair and spoke in a soothing, motherly tone. "You see, I thought I could trust you, but you've proved that you're unreliable. Therefore, I have to do what you cannot."

"I don't understand." Her words held the right amount of grogginess, but her brain was alert. She had to concentrate on keeping her breathing even, her heartbeats slow.

"No, I don't expect you would. You never were the smartest of girls, albeit you are the prettiest. I was once called a great beauty, too. You'll never know how the years will ravage your skin and give you wrinkles where before you were flawless, like fine porcelain."

Her stepmother smoothed Eira's forehead, her nail scratching along the surface.

"The king must die, my darling, and you will be the one to kill him. Once he's dead, I will marry Guillaume and I shall be queen."

Eira nodded as if this were the most sensible plan she'd ever heard. "You will make an excellent queen. Thank you for thinking of everything, Stepmother."

"I always have contingency plans, darling. You should know that by now."

"Will you wake me when it's time to kill the king? I just need a few hours rest and I should be fine." Eira hoped her delirious-sounding ramblings were pleasing to Regan's ears. They hurt her own and internally, she seethed.

Which were the lies and what was the truth?

"I'll handle everything, as I always have. All you have to do is sleep, darling."

They call it the sleeping death.

"Thank you, Stepmother."

Regan lifted from the bed and ran a fingertip along Eira's brow to her jaw. "You truly are the fairest in the land. I shall mourn the loss of your beauty, but will not regret your absence." She placed her fingers along Eira's neck, where her pulse was strong. "I shall keep you in a glass box so that I can siphon your power whenever needed. They say true love's kiss can wake someone from a sleeping death, but your true love doesn't even remember you exist."

Eira curled into herself and nodded with a sleepy, happy smile.

True love's kiss.

Henri.

Regan drew the blankets over Eira and patted them with such gentleness it surprised her.

"Goodnight, princess. Sweet dreams." A harsh, guttural laugh filled the room and followed Regan out the door.

Eira shuddered against the sound and pulled the blanket close to ward off the horrible things she'd heard. But she couldn't unhear them.

There was more to Regan's plan. Memories and conversations drifted through her mind. Yes, there was a sister. Who? Lady Annah? Of course, they were so alike and yet so different. That's why the king allowed Regan's horrid mirror into the palace, because his paramour had wished it. The image of the pair in the sitting room, laughing at something she couldn't hear, came to her and she placed a protective hand around her neck.

Genuine sleep tried to overtake her, and she fought it off. She must stop Regan from killing the king. What did she mean that Eira was to kill the king? But how could she do that if she was sleeping?

A page from Regan's grimoire drifted through her thoughts,

and she sat up, her mind spinning. The bracelet of Eira's hair wasn't a token of love. It was part of an elaborate spell used to conjure someone else's looks.

A flash of memory—of wearing a guard's uniform and watching herself in the courtyard with the king went through her mind. He'd given her the delicate trinket she now wore on her wrist. She unclasped the thing and flung it onto her dressing table. It glided to a stop alongside the fan. The woman in the courtyard with Leon on her arm hadn't been Eira, but a false version of her and she knew exactly who it was—Regan.

She held her head and groaned against the sludginess in her brain. The holly leaves had kept her from falling into a deep sleep, but they'd done nothing to clear her mind. Memories were scant and fragmented, as if she'd lived two lives for the past fortnight.

Henri could help. Yes, she must find Henri. He was brave and smart and...what else? He was something, but it slipped away. She slid from the bed and retrieved her wedding dress. It was the only article of clothing besides her dressing gown that she could wear, yet it somehow seemed appropriate. She strode to the bedchamber door and paused. Regan expected her to be fast asleep. She couldn't very well prance through the halls as herself.

She bit her cheek and paced around the table. If she looked like someone else, then she could go about her mission unnoticed. The maid would work. Maids were allowed everywhere. Except, she didn't have anything personal from the maid.

The only other option was Regan. Her stepmother would be perfect—she was a lady, allowed places even maids dared not go, like the crown prince's apartments. What would it take to pretend to be Regan? Was she actually considering this foolhardy plan? Did she have any other choice?

Chapter Forty-Four

id she dare? Could she pretend to be the very same woman pretending to be her? Eira had to try. It wasn't just her life hanging in the balance if she didn't. Henri, Leon, Sacheen, the magical folk in the kingdom, they all suffered if she didn't do something, anything, to force Regan's hand. Thus far, her stepmother had called all the shots, manipulating her, Henri, the princes, lawks, even the king. Had she'd done it all with the help of her sister, the king's mistress, or were they adversaries vying for the same prize?

The two had probably been scheming for years, waiting for just the right time when the king was weakened. A time like now. It was the night of the ball, a full moon when magic was strongest, and the king was suffering from an ailment that Madam Davina could no longer heal. A flood of memories washed through Eira's brain, dizzying in their intensity. Some made sense, others were puddles of confusion. She hoped they'd all be cohesive when the time came to do what was necessary. She just wished she knew what that was.

Eira scrunched up the blankets and pillows to make it appear there was a sleeping form huddled beneath them.

Adrenaline pulsed through her veins and she felt alive, excited and anxious for what was to come. With torch in hand, she crept along the hidden passageway, counting the steps to where she suspected Regan's rooms would be.

A flash of memory—of Henri covered in blood and leading her away from the very door in front of which she now stood.

Doe's blood. Not Henri's. They'd been here before, spying on Regan. That wicked pain slashed through her skull, and she winced against it. The memory of Henri scattered like skittle pieces struck by a ball.

She set the torch into a metal bracket attached to the stone and pressed against the wall until she heard a soft click. The door swung away from her, and she sidled through the narrow opening into an even smaller space covered by a tapestry. Dust tickled her nose, and she held her nostrils to suffocate a sneeze.

Snoring came from somewhere in the room, and she muttered an unladylike swear word. As quietly as she could, she eased from behind the tapestry. No one slept in the empty bed, and the chairs scattered around the room were draped with clothing, but not people. Her gaze went to a velvet curtain covering a good-sized portrait. It rested on a bureau to the side of the large bed. Snores issued from beneath the black fabric.

Regan's mirror. She took it everywhere with her. Eira had always hated the thing. She ran a finger along the underside of her forearm and thought of the blue and gold shimmering. Magic. She sensed it in the mirror, could feel its pull against her own power.

Her own magic. Yes, she was of the pureblood magic passed down from the goddess. Hers had come from her mother. She caressed the place where Henri's magic had touched her and recalled a cramped room, heated cries, and passion so raw it made her eyes sting from unshed tears. She had to hide from the mirror just as they'd hidden from Regan.

The mirror was the source of Regan's power. Yes, why hadn't she seen that before? Because she was warded. By Regan, or someone—or something—else. And now Regan sought to add Eira's power to the mirror.

She crept cautiously toward the dressing table and retrieved a handful of Regan's rather dull brown hair. She gripped it in her fist and retraced her steps to the hidden door. An unremarkable leather trunk caught her attention and a sudden tug against her heart nearly knocked her off-balance. On a table beside the trunk rested Regan's grimoire, and next to that, a glowing glass square filled with bluish-black miasma.

The amount of magic she sensed from the trio—the grimoire, glass box, and trunk—was incredible. Memories of summer days spent chasing butterflies in a meadow were followed by the sound of a woman's laughter so sweet it gave her goose pimples. Her father's voice echoed in the recesses of her mind and she held the memories tight for one long moment. She didn't often remember her mother, and her father less so as the years wore on. She closed her eyes and was with them again, in the meadow.

They reached for her and she clasped their hands, wishing to never let go. Their love wound around her, comforting in its embrace and she knew without any doubt, that her mother and father had loved her very much. Regan's lies had tried to kill Eira's memories of her parents, but their love was too strong. Her stepmother had locked Eira's memories away, just as she'd locked her parents' belongings out of reach. She saw a door with a keyhole that led to a world of wonder, but she didn't know that door, or what lay beyond. Another mystery to solve, but at the moment, more pressing matters took precedent.

With a sigh full of longing, she reached for the leather-bound tome, her heart aching for what was inside. Never before had she allowed herself to touch the spell book, but she couldn't resist its allure. It beckoned to her in much the way her parents had.

"Mirror," Regan called out, and Eira snatched her hand away.

She leapt to the tapestry and held it taut to hide her presence.

"I need to go out for a few minutes. Alert me if anyone enters or leaves our rooms. Prince Guillaume should be arriving shortly. Watch him, will you?"

"Yes, mistress." A sleepy reply came from the mirror.

"Soon, darling, I shall possess all of Eira's magic and beauty, and we shall be the fairest in all the land, and the most powerful."

"You shall be queen at last."

"Yes, and I shall be queen." Regan laughed that horrid, throaty, wicked laugh. "And all of these fools shall bow to me. How do I look?"

Eira chanced a peek from behind the tapestry. She didn't see her stepmother, but an exact copy of herself. Even down to the glittering diamond bracelet that she'd been wearing.

"Repulsive, but perfect."

"Charmer." Regan leaned forward and kissed the mirror. "You be a good boy while I'm gone and I'll treat you to a show later."

"I am breathless with anticipation."

Eira slipped out of the secret door and held a hand over her chest. She must be quick. There was no telling where Regan was going and it wouldn't do to run into her. The torch cast flickering shadows on the wall, and Eira took a long breath to steady herself. So much could go wrong with this plan, not the least of which was that she'd never used her own power to cast a spell.

If she ended up as a mouse, she'd have no one to blame but

herself. Just to be safe, she shuffled her feet to scare off any mice that might be curious enough to get close.

The page of the grimoire danced in her mind and she spoke the words written in a beautiful hand. Regan's hair singed her skin, and she imagined herself as her stepmother: Hair styled after the elaborate fashions popular at court. Gems twinkling in the curls. A gown of rust covered her body and a pearl choker snugged her neck. Each detail, no matter how tiny, was thought through.

The transformation felt as though a million paper cuts tore at her skin. Too small to cause permanent damage, yet insistently brutal all the same. Her skin warmed and then, without warning, turned molten as her body shifted into Regan's likeness. When the unpleasantness settled, she ran her hands over the velvet gown and took a long drag of musty air. It was too late to change her mind, and too much rested on her acting the part flawlessly.

Eira started for the doorway to her rooms, but turned back and went in the opposite direction. She didn't know whether the mirror could track her through the secret passage and couldn't take any chances.

At the end of the dark hallway, she set the torch in an iron rack and eased open a door, not knowing where it led. She blinked into the sudden light and breathed a sigh of relief that she was in a recessed alcove, away from prying eyes and gossipy courtiers.

After taking a moment to dust off her gown—and to give herself a quick pep talk to remind her she was a lady; she was more than capable of pulling this off—Eira strode to the main hallway and sashayed as if she owned the place. Music drifted to her from the courtyards below. The ball had already started, she must hurry. She passed a mirror and caught her reflection, nearly gasping at the woman who stared back at her. Even Regan wouldn't be able to tell the fake from the real.

She just hoped the spell lasted long enough to find Henri.

The only flaw in her plan was that Eira had no idea where Guillaume's rooms were located. After a discreet inquiry of a page, she made her way as quickly and ladylike as possible to the fourth floor of the palace, where all the royals lived. It irked her that she didn't know such a simple thing, and that Regan surely would know it, but she couldn't let doubt creep in now.

She knocked on the door, admiring the gold painted filigree and decorative moldings. A page answered and she asked to see the crown prince on urgent business. He led her to a small sitting room off the main hallway, but instead of waiting as told, she followed several paces behind. Her court slippers made no sound on the marble tiles, but the soft swish of her skirts were a problem.

The boy didn't seem to notice, or care. He wove through two hallways before knocking once on a plain door at the end of a long row of doors. Without waiting for a reply, he entered the room. This was it. Her life, and Henri's depended on her playing the role of Regan immaculately. If the prince had even a single doubt, it would spell disaster. She took a deep breath and dug deep to channel her inner witch. Whatever waited for her on the other side of the door, no matter how horrific, she couldn't show emotion.

Chapter Forty-Five

The door to Prince Guillaume's office opened and the page who'd left her in the receiving room startled when he saw Eira standing there. She brushed past him with an irritated grunt. The terrifying scenarios Eira had imagined couldn't have been farther from the sight that awaited her. Guillaume paced in front of a huge desk, and seated behind it, his face bloody from his previous beatings, sat Henri. A plate of food and tankard of ale sat atop a pile of papers.

Apart from the bruises, he and Guillaume looked as if she were interrupting an important meeting, neither of which were pleased by her presence. She schooled her features into a show of contempt and sneered at them both.

"What are you doing here? I sent word I'd see you in your chambers shortly."

"Whatever you're doing with Hen—Callan," she corrected herself. It wouldn't do to give away the game in the first few moments of play. Regan never called Henri by his first name. "I need him. You can finish whatever business you have when I'm done." She peered closer at Henri. "Does he remember anything?"

"You mean about that slag? Nothing." Guillaume placed his fists on his hips and arched as if he'd been sitting a long while. "Barely remembers his own name. I suppose a break would be nice. We're hammering out a treaty agreement between Ventoux's kingdom and mine. Once Father is dead and I'm king, you will take your place at my side as my mistress. Not only that, but Ventoux has promised me the negotiated sum for Eira, and the hand of one of his sisters. My choice."

"Your mistress? I had hoped you'd change your mind, Your Highness." Eira put as much bile into the last two words as she could muster. "Lest you forget, you wouldn't be king if not for me, and my stepdaughter." Eira tapped a nail to her tooth and glared at Guillaume. "Don't make me alter our plans. There's still time to allow Eira to continue living. She would make a wonderful stepmother to you, and I would make a powerful queen mother."

I always have contingency plans, darling. You should know that by now.

Regan excelled at duplicity.

If Guillaume's glare was daggers, Eira would be a shredded, bloody mess. "I have papers claiming Eira is my lawful betrothed."

"Yes, as you've often said. But what are papers when I have the girl, and the promise of your father, the king?"

"A king that will soon be dead and then I will take the throne, and you'll be my mistress as agreed. Have you come to a decision about Lady Annah?"

Eira faltered for a moment. If there was a scheme Gil knew about with the king's mistress, she wasn't privy to it, but Regan would be.

"That leech?" Eira sashayed to Guillaume and slid a hand up his chest, doing her best not to knee him in the privates. "I have something special planned for her."

This was the man who nearly raped her, but she couldn't allow herself to fear now. Regan had encouraged him in the attack and, as much as it disgusted her, she had to play the part of his lover. She shoved her own feelings aside and sneered up at him with a seductive purr.

Gil stared at her for a long moment, his nostrils flaring and brows making a straight line across his handsome face. "You promise to kill her as painfully as possible?"

"You'll hear her cries even in this haven of protection. Better yet, why don't you watch?"

He groaned and grabbed her buttocks, pulling her close enough she was certain he would discover her fraud. Don't scream. Don't panic. Swallow the sickness his presence brings. This is for Henri. She repeated the mantra to keep herself from ruining everything. She had to channel Regan. Her stepmother would enjoy this. Lawks, but she fought against the trembling in her heart.

"I could fuck you right here, you devious witch."

Eira wriggled out of his painful embrace and laughed as throatily as possible. They were wasting time. "Now, now, Your Highness. Not with so much yet to be done." Eira leaned over the desk and peered at the papers, wanting to risk a look at Henri, but keeping her gaze lowered. "This treaty, is there any sort of compensation for myself? I am doing a lot of work on your behalf."

Guillaume thrust his half-erect cock against her arse and she swallowed her rage. How very fucking dare he? Such a disgusting, rutting pig. The apple didn't fall far from his father's tree, that was for certes. She gripped the desk and steadied her nerves to keep from shrieking and ruining the farce. His very presence made her itch with revulsion. How did Regan put up with it? An image of her stepmother wiping her mouth after kissing Guillaume ripped through her mind. Regan played a dangerous game, indeed. What was her end game? How did she see herself winning?

The prince ground against her in a swirling motion that made her stomach churn. "And you'll be well rewarded with prestige, jewels, the affections of a king. What more could you want?"

What would Regan want?

"A crown, darling. A mistress is easily replaced, but making me your queen, well, that's something."

Guillaume grabbed her arm and spun her around so quickly, she was thrown off-balance. He held her hands in his, and she shuttled a fission of panic that threatened to make her collapse. She smothered a cry at the sudden memory of being trapped by him, her arms above her head. She breathed through the fear that he'd uncovered her charade and would finish what he started.

"We've discussed this. You know why we can't marry." Was that actual sorrow in his eyes?

An echo of a similar conversation flitted through her brain. A woman had said something similar. It hurt trying to remember, so she let it go, but an ickiness lingered.

"A girl can dream." She raised a brow and half-shrugged. "Fine, I'll let it go for now. You know I can't deny you when you're being devious. I really do have urgent business of my own. If you'll allow me to take this man, I promise to have him returned within the hour. Should I, uh, alter his memories more? Make him more amenable to your," she playfully traced a finger over the papers in front of Henri, "treaties?"

"You devious witch. You know how to get a man excited. Fuck with his mind all you like, and I'll fuck you however you want tonight." His lips crushed against hers, and Eira gagged at the invasion.

She curled her fingernails into her palms to keep from

punching him. Again. She'd punched him? Yes, she reminded herself, she had, and it felt good. So damn good.

"Now, now." She pushed the lecherous cad off her and resisted the urge to wipe her lips with the back of her hand. "Save some for later. You don't want to muss my hair, do you?"

"So vain. Fine. Take Ventoux, but return him within the hour. If you don't, I'll be forced to punish you."

"Your Highness, don't say such things to me. I might dally on purpose."

He swatted her behind and she giggled, a little too much like Eira.

"I like this softer side to you, Regan. I hope it stays after tonight."

Was that a threat that he knew something was off? Eira straightened her shoulders and stood like Regan would. "Once your father and my stepdaughter are dead, I'll be as soft as you like, my lord."

"Go now before I change my mind and take you right here."

"With him watching?" She flicked a glance to Henri, but his head was bowed, his gaze intent on the papers.

"He's so out of it, I doubt he'd notice." Guillaume snapped his fingers in front of Henri's face. "See? Muddled. I doubt you need to do anything more to him, to be honest."

"We shall see." Eira grinned and tried to laugh that horrendous laugh that Regan made, but it came out slightly maniacal. "You, follow me."

She pointed to Henri, and he looked up with a sheepish slump to his shoulders. A moment later, he rose and shuffled to her side. Her heart went out to him. This poor broken and defeated man, and it was all her fault.

She smacked him upside the head just like she'd seen Regan do on numerous occasions to staff, and even Gil once. "Stand up straight. You're a prince—act like it."

Henri stiffened and lifted his chin with a haughtiness even the real Regan would admire.

"That's better. Now, no talking to others, understood? We have precious little time."

Guillaume pinched her arse as she passed and she bit back a yelp. Instead, she glared at him with true contempt. He only laughed and waved her away.

Henri led the way through the myriad hallways and rooms to the main door of Guillaume's apartments. The real Regan probably knew the way by heart and the fact that she had to depend on Henri would've been a sure giveaway to anyone watching.

Instead of taking the main staircase, Henri led them to the servants' stairs, and Eira's heart fluttered.

"You were acting."

He grinned and poked her in the rib. "Same as you, princess."

"But how did you know? Do you think Guillaume suspected anything?"

"You were excellent. True, I'm not happy with that kiss he gave you, but he doesn't suspect a thing. If he did, neither of us would be here right now." He kissed her hand and clasped it in his own. "I would know my Eira anywhere, no matter what face you wore. Even if it was that of my greatest villain."

She held his face between her hands. The desire to kiss him was strong, but not with this face. Not as Regan. The age spots on her hands faded and her true, unblemished skin shone through.

"We need to hurry. The spell I cast is weakening." She tugged him toward the door to their floor, but he shook his head.

"My valet is waiting in the stables with horses. This way."

"She has our memories, Henri. If we leave now, there will always be gaps in our lives."

"We will make new memories."

"No. I mean, yes, we will, but we can't leave any holes to be exploited. The king would hunt us, remember? And if not him, then surely Gil. We can't be responsible for starting a war between your kingdom and Jura."

"Yes, you're right. I—everything is confusing at the moment."

"I know, my love, but we must persevere. I saw Leon, he's expecting us at the ballroom. He found Sacheen and the others. We can't leave them, not now when he needs us most."

"Yes, I remember. We must see that Leon takes the throne and not Guillaume." His jaw clenched and the corners of his eyes tightened. "Such a foul man. He'd be no better a king than his father. He was so sure of my memory-impaired performance, he confessed everything. How he'd been bedding Regan to get revenge on you, but when she started making demands, that's when he made plans of his own. He was going to frame her for the king's—and his new bride's—murder. This was, of course, after Lady Annah dispatched Leon and Sacheen's pack, stealing their magic in the process. Then Regan would kill Annah and Gil would be the sole survivor of a horrible scheme that he, naturally, was innocent of."

"Phwoar, that's some messed-up family dynamics. I think Regan stole more than just our memories, possibly even filled in some of the blanks with what she wanted us to believe. That doesn't matter any longer. I know where our memory box is. We just need to sneak past her magic mirror to get it."

He peeked from the stairs to the main hallway and ushered her through.

Most of the courtiers were already at the ball, or in their rooms getting ready for the night, which meant she and Henri could hurry through the halls without incident. She hoped Regan was still on her errand so that she and Henri could get the memory box as easily as they traversed the palace halls.

Instead of using the main door to their apartments, Eira led

Henri to the alcove with the hidden doorway. He retrieved the torch and made his way to the same door she'd used earlier. It was the one he'd taken her through the night before, which meant he at least remembered some of the past week. Her heart skipped happily, but she cautioned herself not to get overly confident.

"Farther, to my room." She nudged him along until they reached her bedchamber.

She slipped through the doorway and checked that it was safe before waving Henri through. While he squeezed himself into the room, she retrieved the dagger from its hiding place.

"My dagger."

She held it out for him, but he shook his head. "I couldn't remember where I'd gotten it from. Do you recognize this?" She tucked the dagger up her sleeve and pulled the wreath from behind the tapestry.

"I don't, although…" He rubbed his temples and scrunched his face. "Snow comes to mind."

"I don't remember, either. We'll sort it later. Are you ready?" She placed the wreath atop the casket with the poisoned apple inside.

"I can't recall. Am I ready?"

His grin made her belly tickle with little flutters, and she chuckled at his jesting. In the grim situation they found themselves, a touch of light-hearted brevity was exactly what she needed.

They held hands as they crept through the silent sitting room. In Regan's bedchamber, everything was as Eira had left it. The trunk, the grimoire, and their glass memory boxes were all there. Her gaze swept the rest of the room and her heart chilled when she saw the mirror. The black cloth had been removed and two soulless eyes stared straight at her and Henri.

Chapter Forty-Six

A shriek like Eira had never heard and hoped to never hear again punctured her hearing, and she covered her ears to shield them from the wretched screech. Henri doubled over, his hands also over his ears. Moments later, Regan ran into the room, looking exactly as she had before—a perfect replica of Eira.

"God's truth, Mirror, shut up!" Venom lined her words, and she pointed a flawless finger at Eira. "How dare you impersonate me! And a miserable job you've done of it as well. I hope no one saw you like this."

Eira chanced a glance in the only other mirror in the room and blanched. Half of her dark hair hung down her back, with the other piled high atop her head in an ornate style. Her skin fluctuated from creamy porcelain to sun-kissed olive. In the short time she gazed at herself, the spell completely dissolved and she looked fully like herself.

And exactly like Regan, down to the gown and wedding shoes. The only exception was Eira didn't wear the diamond bracelet the king had given Regan, thinking she was the real Eira.

Henri stared from one to the other, his eyes wide. "It's truly remarkable. There's not a mole out of place."

Regan scoffed. "You would know. Ruining my stepdaughter. What did you promise her, Callan? A throne? Money?"

"No, Stepmother, those are only things you're interested in. If you really want to know, Henri denied me when I first asked him to take my virginity."

"Disgusting, the pair of you. Doesn't matter. I'll kill you both and blame the prince. Did you sign the treaty, Callan?"

"That's Your Royal Highness, Prince Henri of Ventoux to you, my lady. And I don't owe you any answers."

Eira stood a little taller, pride for Henri suffusing her with a giddy boost of much needed fearlessness.

Regan circled them, her forefinger rubbing along her chin.

Eira braced for an attack and curled her fingers around the dagger's hilt.

An inky sort of tendril floated in the air between Henri and the glass box. He swooned and moaned, his eyes showing nearly white.

"Stop it, you're hurting him. What are you doing?" Eira reached for Henri, but was blocked by a powerful force that she couldn't see.

Behind her, the mirror hummed a sort of low vibration that made the air agitate. Though the walls didn't move, Eira felt as though they were closing in, cutting her off from the rest of the palace. The air grew thick and it was hard to breathe. Regan's magic scratched along her skin, more irritating than the imagined paper cuts the transformation brought. Henri lost all color in his handsome face and only the whites of his eyes showed. She had to stop Regan or she would lose him for good.

"What are you doing to him?"

"I'm taking all of his memories. They'll help me when I go to his kingdom to destroy everything he loves."

Eira lunged for Regan and grabbed her arm, knocking the pair off-balance. Her stepmother snarled and bared her teeth. For one horrific moment, Eira envisioned her as a wolf, and she backed away, giving Regan the space needed to attack.

Her hands wrapped around Eira's neck, and she squeezed hard enough Eira couldn't get air. She coughed and sputtered, her face warming and pressure building behind her eyes. Henri staggered to his feet, and Regan let go with such suddenness, Eira lost her footing and fell to her knees.

Her stepmother also went to her knees.

"Don't hurt me." Regan said, her voice the exact cadence as Eira's.

It truly was like looking in the mirror. IF their lives weren't in peril, Eira would've liked to study Regan's work out of sheer appreciation. Right then, all she cared about was saving herself and Henri from her deranged stepmother.

"Henri, help me to stand." Regan sneered at Eira from behind a curtain of dark hair and held her hand for Henri to take.

"No, that's Regan. Don't trust her." Eira pushed herself up from the floor and wavered a heartbeat. Stars lit in her vision and her entire body felt like jiggly pudding.

Henri's hand hovered between them, his gaze going from Regan to Eira and back.

"I don't—do I know you?"

No, no, no, nooooooo. Eira's heart sank and hope faltered.

"Henri, it's me, Eira. You love me and I you."

"No, Henri, you love me. I'm the true Eira," Regan countered with a shake of her long, glossy hair. Her deep blue eyes, the same shade as Eira's, blinked against unshed tears. "You must remember me. Please." Just there, snide little snarl raised her lip in classic Regan, but would Henri notice in his memory-stolen state?

Eira reached for Henri, but Regan snatched her wrist and pulled hard. A memory snapped against her mind, and she pressed her hand atop Regan's and swung it around just like Henri had taught her to do. From there, she pushed Regan to the floor.

"Eira." Henri staggered forward, his eyes glassy. But he knew her. Somewhere in his memory, he knew her.

"Mistress!" The mirror shrieked from its stand, deafening both her and Henri.

"Kill them, Mirror. Kill them now."

Regan struggled against Eira's hold, but she jerked Regan's arm across her back, immobilizing her.

The pull of magic struck her like a blow, and Eira fought against it. Blue shimmers ripped from Henri toward the mirror, mingling with her own golden strands. She kicked Regan's back and dropped the dagger into her hand. With all her might, she gripped the hilt and flung the dagger toward the mirror, using its own pull to strengthen the throw.

Regan screamed and tore at Eira's gown, but it was too late. The dagger flew through the air and slammed into the reflective glass. One last shriek pierced the air and then an ominous silence descended over the room. A single heartbeat later, the mirror shattered.

Deadly shards flew at them in a rage and Eira covered herself. A barrier of bluish light kept most of the glass from tearing at her skin. A large shard landed at Eira's feet, and she reached for it at the same time as her stepmother. Henri pushed Regan aside with a dazed look. He was slipping back into not remembering her. She couldn't lose him. Not again, not ever again.

He hunched over the chest beside the grimoire, his breathing labored. Regan sobbed and wailed for the broken mirror. There was no time to argue or debate or negotiate. They had to act now.

Eira grasped the shard and stepped toward her stepmother with only one thought in her heart and mind: save Henri. To do so, she had to break Regan's spell. She'd hoped shattering the mirror would've done the trick, but she could still feel her stepmother's power sucking at her own

Except, it wasn't Regan's magic...Eira tightened her grip on the shard and winced against a slice of pain. She ignored the blood that dripped from her palm and focused on her stepmother. Regan was stealing hers and Henri's power. The question of how beat against her skull. How could Regan continue to steal their magic without the mirror. Her gaze went to the grimoire. She sensed the grimoire's reluctance to help Regan, as if it, too were under a spell. So many questions with only one answer. Regan must be stopped.

A guttural laugh came from Regan's lips, and she shook her head. "You can't defeat me, stupid girl."

Eira didn't flinch as she thrust the shard forward and sliced through the expensive velvet gown Regan wore. The sharp glass tore through skin and soft tissue, embedding itself in Regan's gut.

Regan gasped and glared at Eira. "No." She pulled the shard free and staggered to the bed. The bloodied weapon was clenched between her fingers. "How could you?" She groped for more shards and gathered them into a small pile. "My beautiful mirror. What do I do now?"

Regan's features wavered between hers and Eira's. Her flawless skin evaporated to show the wrinkles and age spots that Regan hated—and feared—so much.

Blood poured from Regan's abdomen, but she paid it no mind. The stupid woman should've died from the wound, but she was too stubborn. It would take something more direct, and more lethal to kill her. Eira retrieved the dagger and pointed it at her stepmother. Her hand trembled like a leaf on a blustery day, but she held strong like an oak. "What you do now, Stepmother, is you die so that you can never hurt anyone ever again."

"I can't die. Not yet. I will be queen."

"You would make a vile, evil queen, Stepmother."

Eira had to stop Regan. For herself, for Henri, for the whole kingdom. She couldn't let Regan's plans come to fruition. She drove the dagger into Regan's chest, plunging as deep as she could. The squelch of blood turned her stomach and the crunch of bone brought bile to the back of her throat, but she didn't stop. Eira pushed harder into the blackened heart of her stepmother.

Regan's eyes glared at Eira as she slumped against the bed and slid to the floor, her mouth opened as if to spew one last angry retort. Her lips hung empty, impotent. At last, her words were silenced. The dagger slid from her body and dangled from Eira's fingers. For once, the tears that rolled over her cheeks to drip on her stepmother's inert form flowed without fear of reprisal. She'd repressed her emotions for too long and she welcomed the cleansing her tears brought. Pinkish foam bubbled from Regan's slack mouth and Eira stared, horrified and fascinated that she was capable of such an act.

She was free. Finally free of Regan's cruelty. Yet she didn't feel exalted or joyful. An overwhelming sadness coursed through her that it had come to this. The price of her freedom came at the cost of destruction of another. There was no cause for celebration for her.

An icky sense of being violated slid into the recesses and hidden spaces of her heart and she realized it was the same she'd felt every time Regan stole her powers. Never again. Regan would never hurt her, or anyone else.

As if from a winter storm, a blast of frigid wind pummeled

her thoughts, releasing memories from years and years of her life. Bits she'd forgotten or never knew existed slammed into her, and she staggered beneath the weight of it all. She saw herself with her parents in the meadow, but in this memory they were joined by a pretty lady with flaxen hair and a little boy with eyes like a midnight sky. His black hair shone in the sunlight. Henri. Her Henri. They'd been friends before Regan came along and ruined everything.

Her heart beat fiercely as she relived those happy days filled with unconditional love and friendship. Days she'd have once more.

Henri cradled her in his arms, taking the dagger from her and tucking it into his belt.

"They're free, Eira. Because of you, they're all free." He pointed to the open chest where dozens of glass boxes, some rounded orbs, a few triangles, and even more squares shattered, releasing the inky black miasma of memories, but they weren't hers. "Regan will never hurt anyone ever again."

She gazed at woman who should've been a mother to her, but was too selfish to help anyone but herself. The deep sadness that flowed through her veins turned to pity. After all the years of abuse, she was adrift, unsure where to anchor her thoughts. Fresh memories bloomed, of Regan poisoning first Eira's mother, and then her father, and gloating about it to her when she was just a child. Regan had believed her confession safe, that Eira would never regain her stolen memories.

Pity turned to rage and her nostrils flared with an unbridled need to kill the woman a second time. To destroy anything Regan held dear. Her stepmother had taken everything from her. She glanced at Henri and her heart softened. Not every-thing. Regan had tried to take Henri from her, but she had her prince, and her future. She would live while Regan rotted.

Her nerves quaked at the enormity of what she'd done. This

wasn't who she ever sought to be, and now, she'd have to live with her actions for the rest of her life.

"I killed her, Henri. I'm a murderer. The king will surely have me sentenced to death."

"Not after we explain what happened." He glanced at the broken glass in the trunk and at Regan's belongings, finally settling on the mirror. "It will not take much convincing. Otto has no honor and, truth be told, will most likely be glad of the favor you did him."

Eira snorted. He wasn't wrong. But still, the king was mercurial at best. She didn't like placing her future in his hands now, any more than when she was supposed to be his bride. "Where do we start?"

"First, we will help Leon claim the throne so that Jura will once more be a thriving kingdom. And you will be exonerated for this nasty business. If you'd like to return to Castle Falkoyn, I will escort you myself. But I would like to take you to Ventoux, my kingdom, where you will be safe. And if you should so desire it, I would like us to marry and one day, we will rule with kindness."

"I guess then I'll actually be a princess."

Henri held her face gently between his strong hands. "My love, you always were. Your mother was the sister of Marguerite, Queen of Morovia. Regan stole those memories from you, but, with time, you'll recover those and more."

A princess. A vision of her mother fussing over her in a great hall she didn't recognize wafted in her mind. Regan had cut her off from not just friends, but family, telling her she only had Regan and no one else. An ache settled in her heart. Why hadn't they tried to visit? Her breathing deepened with the understanding that they probably had tried, but Regan convinced them Eira didn't wish to see them. She had to make things right.

"Yes, someday." Untangling the lies and manipulations

would take ages. And she might never know the real truth of anything. But she knew one thing for certain—she loved Henri, and he loved her. For now, it would be enough. It would have to be. Her entire life was upended and her tether to reality was more frail than ever.

He brushed his hands down her gown and she winced at the many cuts the mirror had made. Blood, warm and sticky slithered from a wound on her forehead, and where she'd gripped the mirror shard a large gash throbbed with every heartbeat.

"Shall I heal you?" Henri held her hand in his and already she saw the skin kitting together. He looked at her, eyes wide. "I'm not doing this."

She stroked a finger across the gash, delighting in the little tickles she made. "I am. I remember how you healed my hand in the dungeons and the grimoire supplied the words."

Her power flowed through her unfettered. Cool and refreshing like a surprise rainstorm in summer, her magic cleansed her of Regan's taint. Her power filled the empty spaces, making her complete for the first time in her life. Invigorated, a sense of invincibility was followed closely by overwhelming vulnerability. With great power came equally great responsibility. She flexed her fingers, delighting in the tingling that bubbled beneath her skin.

No wonder Regan had shielded her from this. Eira breathed deeply and calmed her nerves. No one would ever take this gift from her again.

Henri released her hand to snatch the grimoire from beside the trunk. When he handed it to her, she instinctively recoiled.

"I can't touch it. That belonged to Regan." So why then, did it divulge its secrets? She knew the answer even before he spoke.

"This was your mother's, Eira. I remember it from when I visited your castle as a little boy. My mother and yours were great friends. For a time, you and I were even playmates."

She eyed him with renewed curiosity. "Have you always known who I am, or are you just remembering?"

"I've always known. You're the reason I came to Jura in the first place. I couldn't believe my sweet Eira would marry the king. I came to find the truth."

She took the grimoire from him with shaking hands, but the moment her fingers touched the leather bindings, a sense of calm overcame her. It originated from the grimoire, as if at last, the spell book was reunited with its true heir. She stroked the cover reverently, her love for her mother flowing from her to the book and back. All of its knowledge, even the spells Regan tried to hide from her, crammed into her brain with such insistence, she feared her skull might burst.

The grimoire had waited two decades to share its secrets, it would be rude of her to ask it to stop. She opened the book and lovingly pressed her hand against her mother's handwriting. A flash of her mother holding her with the grimoire laid out before them was followed by another vision of a woman with black hair and a magnificent crown anointing Eira before an alter to the goddess. Her Aunt Marguerite had asked the goddess to watch over Eira when her mother passed.

Both women loved her. She felt the force of their love in those two memories and her heart beat stronger, swelling with emotion. Words from the grimoire rose from the page and danced on the air, startling both her and Henri.

"Your mother was a great sorceress, Eira. Her healing skills were beyond any I've ever witnessed, although I don't recall her being able to self-heal. In time, you will grow into your own strength, whatever that may be." He brushed his lips to hers. "I look forward to the day you claim your birthright."

Eira clutched the grimoire to her breast and led Henri to her bedchamber to retrieve the holly wreath she'd hidden behind the tapestry. When she withdrew her hand, it wasn't leaves, but a silver tiara in her grip. She glanced at Henri, questions bouncing in her mind.

"This was the holly wreath the doe gave me in the forest. You saw it, didn't you?"

"Your sigil is the white doe. When she paid you respect in the forest, she was acknowledging you as the rightful heir to your family crest. This was also your mother's."

He placed the tiara upon her head and stepped back to admire her.

"I feel a little silly."

"You'll get used to it." He held out his hand to reveal a ruby and pearl pendant made with pure gold.

A sob caught in her chest. She stared at her mother's most cherished possession, afraid if she touched it, it wouldn't be real. After seeing Regan wearing it, she believed she'd lost it forever. Her fingers skimmed the cool ruby, and she closed her eyes, remembering her mother's laughter and dancing with her father.

"They loved me."

"Aye, they did, Eira." Henri clasped the pendant around her neck and kissed her bare skin. "And now I shall love you."

To be loved, unconditionally, was all she ever wanted. Their future waited for them just beyond the palace, but they couldn't leave just yet. No matter how much Eira wished they could run away from the mess Regan had made, she and Henri still had business with the king. She tried to swallow, but her throat went dry and scratchy. Not just the king, but his witch of a mistress.

Chapter Forty-Seven

Leon and a group of others, townsfolk and courtiers alike, huddled in an alcove off a deserted hallway. As Eira and Henri approached, Leon's cool gaze surveyed their clasped hands, the rips in Eira's gown, and the dagger she gripped in her right hand. A slow smile raised the edges of his lips and he grinned cheekily at them both.

"You are not the timid girl I first met a few weeks past. You bear the mark of a fierce dragon with a heart of fire."

"Or an alpha female of her pack." Sacheen, her skin glowing, freshly washed hair cascading over a clean tunic, curtseyed low to Eira. "We all owe you our lives, Lady Cannaid."

Henri started to correct Sach, but Eira squeezed his hand. "You honor me, but we've no time for pleasantries. Regan's dead." She held up a hand to stop their questions. "All will be revealed later. Leon, do you have a plan?"

The prince did, but what it amounted to was not much more than storming the ballroom and hoping they survived. The longer Eira listened, the further her heart sank. Leon and Sacheen were angry, rightfully so, but their need to avenge the wolf shifters' imprisonment wasn't the priority. They made a valid point that the king likely wouldn't listen to reason, and with Lady Annah by his side, surprise was their best option.

Eira turned her gaze to the other shifters, noting their unease in the slight twitches, and hasty glances over their shoulders. A circle of thirteen. It wasn't yet ten o'clock, too early for the wedding ceremony, but it was a full moon.

"Is your magic at its greatest strength during a full moon?" Eira interrupted Leon and he looked like a rabbit caught in the sight of a hound. "Shifter magic, I mean."

Several of the others fidgeted and a few even took several steps away from the group.

"It is. What are you thinking?" Leon kept his voice low, measured, but she saw the look of expectation in his green eyes.

"Annah's been siphoning magic from those who have power. I don't know for how long, but Sacheen said it herself that Annah would visit her each day, she'd feel woozy, then wake feeling violated. I know this feeling. Regan did it to me most of my life, but I never knew what it was or why. Since it always accompanied a beating, I assumed it was part of the abuse."

A few murmured condolences, but she waved them off. This was not a time for feeling sorry for herself.

"A circle of thirteen of what I'm assuming are powerful wolf shifters would give Annah plenty of magic, but what does she need it for?" Henri looked first to Eira, and then Leon.

"The king is dying." Eira blurted. "That's why they need me."

Leon glanced at her, surprise crossing his features. A breath later, sorrow softened his eyes, but he neither confirmed nor denied her statement.

"There were rumors," one of the shifters said, "but those who spoke of it aloud were silenced." No one needed to question what he meant.

"I'm sorry, Eira. I did question my father as to the timing, but he was never alone and my concerns were dismissed."

"You had other concerns taking your focus." She glanced from Leon to Sacheen. "There is nothing to be sorry for. As for the wedding," she tapped her sternum and grimaced. "If I'm not mistaken, the plan was, gather you in the dungeons where Annah could siphon at her leisure, then tonight, at midnight when your power is at its peak, slaughter the lot of you."

"Why?" Sacheen bared her fangs and Eira's knees buckled.

"So that she would have enough strength to murder Eira and take her magic as well." Henri put his arm around her and held her tight.

"Or keep me in a glass box so that she could continue sucking my power until I eventually died. That was Regan's plan, I don't see why her sister wouldn't wish for the same."

"Sisters?" Leon and Henri said in unison.

Eira nodded. "And adversaries, I believe." She knew what she had to do, but it didn't make the decision any easier. "I must confront the king and Lady Annah. They don't know Regan is dead, and we can't be certain they know you've escaped, so you'll wait for my signal and then you can attack."

It was the only way. If the king was complicit in Annah's schemes, they could denounce him in front of hundreds of witnesses. If he was innocent, then she'd have to come up with another plan. Henri looked displeased, but he didn't argue. They were in an impossible situation. Every scenario ended with someone wanting Eira dead. Except Leon, who wanted his people to be safe, and for magic to be legal as it had been in the old days.

They discussed the finer details of her ridiculous scheme and when it was clear nothing more could be said, Eira drew a long breath to steady her nerves. She'd already killed one wicked witch, she wasn't keen to do it again, but would if left no other choice.

The group entered the great hall through a side door and

Henri took her hand. She held tight, grateful she wasn't alone. Music sounded from across the massive room and swirling couples floated by in layers of silks, velvets, satins, and brocades. She smoothed her own rather plain looking gown when compared to the confections these women wore. Whether Annah's or Regan's doing, they'd dressed Eira simply as yet another way to make her feel unworthy, an outcast. Her lack of adornment was a subtle way of telling the court Eira didn't belong, she wasn't one of them. But it mattered little now. She was happy for the lack of frippery. Henri stepped to her side and she nodded that she was ready. One more lie among all the others. She'd never be ready for what they'd planned.

They moved along the outer edge of the dancers, avoiding servants with trays of glittering drinks and Eira nearly reached for a flute of tristano. The languid feeling and hazy thoughts it brought would be a welcome relief from the anxiety that knotted in her heart.

On a raised dais, she saw the king sprawled across a massive chair, his bulk spilling over the armrests, his legs splayed as if he were already drunk. To his left, in what should've been Eira's chair as queen, sat a very rigid Lady Annah.

Heat flashed through Eira's veins and Henri slid his hand across her lower back. That small touch helped to calm her rage. The witch was too arrogant. Much like Regan, she thought herself above everyone else, including the king. That was Regan's undoing, but Eira doubted Annah would be an easy foe to beat. She'd had decades as the king's paramour to study her enemies, hells, for all Eira knew, she was responsible for the king's past wives' mysterious illnesses and deaths. In that, the sisters were too similar.

The sobering thought slowed her steps and Eira hesitated only twenty paces from the king. Henri looked at her with concern in his dark eyes.

"What is it?"

"What if Annah killed all the king's past wives? She's strong, Henri, far more powerful than me."

He stroked her arm and lifted her right hand where she still clutched the dagger. "You are not alone, nor are you weaponless. And I don't mean just this dagger. It will fly true to whatever target you wish, but I don't think killing the king's mistress would garner you any favors just yet. Speak to the king. Hear his excuses, then your heart will tell you what you need to do."

"You'll be with me?"

"A dozen war horses couldn't drag me away."

Henri's hand slipped from hers and she mourned the loss, but understood why he couldn't be seen touching her intimately. She was still, in the eyes of the king, his betrothed. Still trapped. Still owned. Still a prisoner in a pretty cage.

Chapter Forty-Eight

I f Eira was going to get out of her arranged marriage, and subsequent murder, she'd have to find a way out herself. She wouldn't rely on anyone else to save her. She was tired of being a damsel, waiting for her prince charming. Although, Henri was quite charming, and, turns out, he was also a prince. But this wasn't his fight and they both understood the cost if he challenged the king. War between their kingdoms. Eira wouldn't have that on her conscience long with all of the other guilt she bore.

No one would ever barter her, or wage war for her, ever again. This ended tonight, either with her freedom, or her death.

She stepped up to the dais, ignoring the sneering hiss from Lady Annah, and curtseyed low to the king. "Your Majesty, I would ask that you give your bride a private audience."

King Otto roused himself and stared at her as if seeing her for the first time. "What in hells name happened to your gown?"

She curled her fingers around the hilt of the dagger that she'd slid up her sleeve. Not yet.

"That is part of what I would like to discuss. Will you grant me my wish? I won't take more than a few minutes of your time." Eira flicked a glance to Annah. "Alone."

Annah stood and glared at Eira. "I won't allow it."

Eira lifted her chin and stared down the witch. "I don't need your permission, neither does the king. You forget your place." She almost added, *whore*, but it was implied.

Annah's fingers began writhing and Eira braced for an attack.

A door banged open and Prince Guillaume's voice boomed from somewhere in the crowd. The music stopped and a nervous hush fell over the ballroom. Fabric ruffled, fans snapped closed, shoes shuffled on the parquet flooring, but no one spoke.

"Father, stop!" Gil ran up to them, eyes rolling as if he were a boar trapped with arrows on all sides pointing at his bare flesh. "She is promised to me. I have the papers." He waved a stack of papers in his hand, sweat poured from his forehead to drip to his shiny boots.

Eira stared from him, to the king, unsure what to make of this new predicament. Guillaume losing his ruddy mind wasn't in any of their plans. She glanced at his rumpled vest, at the spots of blood that ruined the cream-colored satin, and her heart went cold. Had he been to Regan's room? If he told the king what she'd done before she had a chance to explain herself, surely he'd paint her as a murderess and not as the intended victim.

"What are you squawking about, boy?" Otto hefted his belly so that he could reach for the papers. He spent an agonizingly long time perusing them, his face turning redder by the minute. When done, he thrust the pages at Lady Annah, who took yet another life-sucking moment to read what they said.

"How dare you." She threw the papers at Guillaume and he scrambled to collect them. "How dare you go behind your father's back to secure a marriage to the very same woman he's due to marry tonight."

The prince stood to full height, the papers forgotten. "I am the rightful heir to this throne. Who are *you* to sit on this dais and speak in his stead?"

Otto half-stood, his legs wobbling with the effort to support his bulk, or perhaps from his mysterious illness.

"I saw no such signature from the king on those papers. Tell me, boy, if I didn't approve this betrothal, then what gives you the right to believe it's legitimate?" Otto bellowed and the crowd took a step back, a murmur of *ooohs* following.

"I shouldn't need your permission to marry whom I choose, Father."

Oh, that was rich, considering neither the prince, the king, nor Regan had asked her permission to wed.

Annah stormed across the dais as if to smack Guillaume's ruddy face. "I should've killed you ages ago, you magicless teatling welp."

She punched his chest with far more strength than Eira would've given her credit, and it was then she felt the woman's magic singe across her skin. Guillaume fell backward onto his ass, fury razing his features. Leon and Sacheen moved stealthily through the crowd to stand beside Henri, several paces behind where Eira stood trapped between the king and Annah. She slid the dagger down enough she could easily drop it into her grip and brandish if necessary.

"Did you agree to this farce of a marriage?" Annah glared at Eira and pointed to the prince.

"I agreed to no wedding. As you are well aware, I am here for only one purpose, and that's for you to murder me to save your lover. Isn't that right, witch?" A gasp went through the crowd and Eira settled her shoulders. "I won't have it."

"You think you can defeat me?" A horrid laugh, far too much

like Regan's for Eira's comfort, came from the woman's open mouth. "My sister was a dithering fool. You will find I am not so easily overcome."

So, she did know Regan was dead. Probably felt it when the mirror shattered. Eira gathered the sleeve surrounding her right hand and made a fist so as not to lose the dagger in whatever was to come. She dared not draw a weapon on the woman with Otto riled up over his son's bad behavior.

The first wave of Annah's magic slammed into Eira and she staggered against it. She raised her arms to deflect the blast and felt Annah's magic burn against Henri's dagger. The witch swore and shook out her arm, her gaze roving the crowd for the source of the dagger's magic. A ruffling of fabric and feathers came from behind Eira and from the corner of her eye she saw the twittering crowd huddle closer. Their thirst for drama and spectacle kept them rooted to the great hall. If Annah chose to attack them, there was nothing Eira could do to protect them if they chose to stay. Her mind whirled with actions she'd never attempted, and which, frankly, terrified her.

The the grimoire was carefully hidden with Henri's belongings, along with the tiara the doe had given her, but she held all of its wisdom in her heart and mind. She took a step forward, making a show of rebuffing Annah's magic to draw her attention away from Henri and the others. She pushed back with her own power, but not too fiercely. It would do no good to let the witch know Eira was no longer warded, although she must suspect that with Regan's death the bonds would break. Unless Annah herself had placed wards on her, then she was in trouble.

Eira gathered her wits and focused on the woman. It didn't feel like she was bound, but then, she'd never sensed Regan's wards, either.

A soft glowing came from Annah and Eira clearly saw the magical rope that lashed out at her, too fast for her to avoid being caught. The crowd took a step back, giving Eira the answer to her unspoken question. Annah was allowing them to see her magic, to bring it out in the open, unafraid.

The rope wrapped around her body and lifted her high in the air. Eira screamed at being flung so high so quickly and kicked impotently against the witch's magic. Her mind begged for calm, but raw panic coursed through her veins. Annah was too powerful, she was an amateur at best, nothing more than the trapped mouse Guillaume accused her of being. Increasingly more negative thoughts washed through her mind and she faltered in her newfound strength.

Annah's laughter filled the ballroom with Otto's clapping giving his mistress encouragement. Devious fools, the both of them.

The rope tightened, squeezing valuable breath from Eira's lungs. She had to still her racing heart, to not expend all of her energy fighting the rope. She was not a mouse, nor was she a powerless victim caught in Annah's trap. From the edge of her vision, she saw Henri skulk toward Leon. She was creating the distraction they needed—she just hoped they didn't dawdle. The circle of thirteen could be the downfall of Annah as well as the king's cure.

Eira pushed her fear to the far corners of her thoughts and reached deep within herself for the magic she'd always kept hidden. It was there, yearning to be unleashed and she opened herself to the flow of power so pure it brought tears to her eyes as it flooded through her veins. The release was cleansing in its own fashion. Doubt, anxiety, fear, all burned away as her magic filled her, infusing her with confidence she'd never known the likes of before.

Annah continued that horrid laugh, either unaware of Eira's growing strength, or uncaring. She probably thought she could overcome Eira, and she might, but Eira refused to give up. Her hands were bound by the magical rope and she struggled to release the dagger from the confines of her sleeve, but it slid easily into the palm of her hand, steady and true. She focused her gaze on the witch and mentally pushed out with her magic, sending a blast centered at Annah's heart.

At the same time, Eira hacked at the rope with the dagger, feeling Annah's rage with each slice. The woman hated Eira with such venom and bile it nearly made Eira ill. She gagged against the putrid essence that came from the witch's magic. Her blast of power struck Annah full on. The look of shock and surprise on Annah's pretty face gave Eira cold comfort. The witch had underestimated her, to her detriment. The bonds of Annah's magic loosened enough Eira could free her right hand.

A cream and black blur rushed from the side of the dais, just as Eira gave the rope another, more vicious slash. Eira watched in horror as Guillaume ran toward the king's mistress full out, sword in hand. An awful squelch sounded when his sword ran the woman through.

The magic rope released and Eira plummeted to the floor. A scream lodged in her throat, but there was little time for much of anything before she thudded into Henri's arms.

"I've got you, Princess." Henri held her tight.

He'd come from seemingly nowhere. Surrounding him were Leon and the other shifters. They'd moved to the center of the ballroom in the scant moments she'd fought Annah. She clung to Henri, relieved he was unharmed, happy to be alive.

Annah screamed, her curses spewing from her slackening mouth, but they held no power. Otto roared obscenities at his son and waved a rapier in the air with wild abandon. The king reached for Guillaume and grabbed at his heart as he wobbled forward. Eira shuddered to see the king stagger toward his son. His pale lips were coated in foam, his bloodshot eyes rolled dangerously to the back of his head.

The ballroom froze in silence as the king gave one final gasp. The rapier in his hand wobbled, the steel glinting in the candlelight as it stretched toward the crown prince. Henri cradled her close, but she slid from his embrace to stand beside him, ready. She didn't pull her gaze from the dais, couldn't look away. Guillaume cried out and turned toward her, his neck a rivulet of red staining his lovely cream vest.

"You are the fairest in the land. I deserve the best." He pointed an incriminating finger at her and she lifted her chin in defiance.

She would not hide from his shame, nor would she be party to his blame. She'd done nothing to encourage him, yet if he chose to believe Regan's lies, that was for him to reconcile. Never again would she be made to feel less than to soothe someone else's ego.

The king and his son hit the floor at the same time, each rolling twice before they stopped at the foot of the dais steps.

It wasn't the escape she'd imagined, but she was free. Finally, fully, forever, free.

Chapter Forty-Nine

Weeping came from behind them, followed by astonished gasps and calls for the guards. Eira glanced at the men and women who she'd disguised herself as several days earlier. They, to a one, stood transfixed, unsure what to do.

Leon stood with his pack, shock clear in his features. Eira went to him and touched his sleeve.

"Your Majesty." She curtseyed low. "The king is dead. Long live the king."

He stared at her, unblinking, unseeing.

"Now then, duckie, he's had a bit of a blow." Madam Davina stepped from the crowd and indicated Sacheen should comfort the new king before turning to place one hand on Eira, the other on Henri. "I see you took my advice."

"Thank you, for everything." Eira impulsively hugged the woman, clutching her tight to her bosom.

"There now, there, there." She smoothed Eira's back reassuringly. "Like I said, trust yourself, duckie, and it'll all work out." Her silver hair floated above her head, reminding Eira of another older and cryptically crankier woman. A puzzle piece slid into place.

"You were the servant woman who left the apples." It wasn't an accusation, more of an understanding.

"Guilty, I'm afraid." She giggled like a maiden and handed Eira one last apple. "This will sustain you for the long ride ahead."

The sight of the apple made her stomach churn. The enchanted fruit Regan gave her on that first day was still in her wardrobe. Henri took the apple and tucked it into his belt pocket.

"Your kindness won't be forgotten" Henri bowed to the witch. "I'll make sure Eira gets home safely."

Madam Davina inclined her head to both Henri and Eira with a promise to visit them soon. Then she moved to the center of the room and banged a staff three times on the parquet floor. The sound echoed through the grand ballroom, quieting those gathered.

"Tonight was meant as a celebration, but for whom, that is the riddle. You see before us the remnants of greed, gluttony, and tyranny. King Otto is dead. Long live King Leon!" She pounded her staff thrice again and a cheer rose from the crowd.

The witch lifted her staff and waved it high above her head. The candles flickered in their elaborate candelabras before dimming, plunging the ballroom in near darkness. The guests twittered and groused, some afraid of what would come next, others excitedly watching Madam Davina. Eira was firmly in the latter group. Their oppression was at an end. The villainy of Otto and his father was over. She hoped in time those who opposed magic would come to see it as a natural force for good, and not the dark threat Annah made it.

She held Henri close as Madam Davina pointed her staff to the dais. The king's body, as well as Guillaume's and Annah's lifeless forms glittered and glowed as they rose above the floor, appearing to disappear the higher they went until only a column of glittering motes rose to the high ceiling. A fourth column joined the three and she flicked a glance to the witch. Her cheeky wink confused Eira, but then she realized the fourth was for Regan.

Her heart swelled with gratitude for the woman. What a wonderful gift she gave to Eira and Leon. But Davina wasn't done. Next, she whipped the staff upward where the heavy beamed ceiling faded away to expose a spectacular glass ceiling that showed the full moon in all her glory. Stars twinkled around the moon, thirteen in all.

The king's dull gold and ruby banners burned away and gleaming silver banners unfurled to reveal Leon's sigil—a wolf's head.

The crowd oohed and ahhed with each new reveal until their attention came to Leon. He stood in the center of his pack, a look of awe softening his features.

"Take your place upon the dais, King Leon." Davina ordered him to the ornate chair and he obeyed.

Sacheen stayed at the foot of the dais, but Leon bade her forward and she sheepishly stepped beside her mate.

The mischievous witch flourished her hand and a shining gold crown rested upon her outstretched palm. She glanced at Eira, indicating that she should be the one to place the crown upon Leon's head. It was an honor she didn't feel she'd earned, but the witch's insistent stare left no room for hesitation.

She took the steps one at a time, balancing the crown between her fingers. It wouldn't do to trip now and have the heavy gold clatter to the floor. Leon bent low enough she could place the crown firmly upon his head. She kissed him on each cheek and stepped to the side to embrace Sacheen.

"I hope you will return for the coronation." Leon held her hand in his, sorrow mixed with his joy.

"And the wedding." Sacheen added.

"We would be honored to be here for both." Henri bowed to the new king and escorted Eira down the steps.

Leon stood proudly to look out over his subjects. His voice, strong and sure, rang out through the ballroom with promises of a tolerant kingdom where everyone was welcome. Magic would once more be accepted, and even encouraged, so long as it did no harm.

Eira hugged Madam Davina, holding her close and thanking her again for seeing in her what she herself had not known was there—courage, trust, love.

A man called out the name Daria and Eira looked over her shoulder in time to see the apothecary race toward a young woman who stood with Leon's pack. He'd found his missing daughter at last. With time, she hoped all the old wounds caused by King Otto would fade to nothing more than a sometime itch that was soothed by happy memories.

Her gaze swept over the assembled guests, landing on Bryn's sly smile and twinkling eyes. They inclined their heads in recognition and a little thrill went through Eira. She hoped they would meet again so that she might hear the tale of the sleeping beauty who nodded off in orchards and danced with lords.

Leon called for music and the mood shifted. The oppressive subjugation of King Otto was firmly, finally, gone and an air of lightness descended upon the room. Leon took Sacheen's hand and led her to the dancefloor and others followed. Eira blew her friends a kiss and left the ballroom, her heart full, despite her uncertain future.

Instead of leading her to her room, or even his where a delightfully soft mattress waited, Henri took her to the stables.

To her surprise, the dwarves were waiting for her with an older gentleman.

"This is my valet, Bernard," Henri explained and turned to his valet. "Do you have the papers?"

"I do indeed, sir. I'm certain your father will find them most interesting." Bernard patted his coat. "It's a pleasure to meet you, Your Highness."

"Oh no, it's just Eira, please."

"Nay, lass. You be Princess Eira of Morovia. Daughter of the late, and sorely missed, Eloise of Morovia. May you be blessed with a long life," Dorton bowed low to her and the other dwarves followed.

She would have to get used to the new title, and the change in treatment that came with it. Regan had to have known she was a princess, but diminished her to a mere lady so that Eira wouldn't outrank her. The depths of that woman's hatred were too deep to excavate without permanent damage. Determined not to let Regan steal any more of Eira's precious moments, she pushed thoughts of her stepmother aside. One day, she would deal with everything that had transpired in the last fortnight, but for the moment, she wished to be fully present, in the moment with her friends.

"Are princesses allowed to wear trousers?" She pointed to her dress and then to the saddle of her horse.

"You are allowed to do whatever you please." Henri motioned to Bernard, and he pulled a pair of riding pants from a saddlebag. "I had a feeling you'd ask."

She threw her arms around Henri's neck and kissed him hard. His hands wrapped around her back, and she rocked against him. Desire and apprehension mingled in her thoughts as their kiss deepened. For the first time in her life, she was in charge, fully and wholly, of her life.

She, Princess Eira, chose to live her life with kindness each day, and to love those deserving of her affections.

"I want to learn to sword fight and perhaps archery. I want to climb mountains and swim in rivers. I want to see the ocean and visit all the other kingdoms, starting with my Aunt Marguerite's. And I want to do all of that with you, Your Highness. More than anything, I want us to live happily ever after."

"We shall do all of that and more." He kissed her fingers and nipped the skin on her knuckles.

"You're a devious prince."

"And you like it."

"That I do." She didn't even blush when saying it. She liked being a rogue with him, and from the gleam in his eye, he didn't mind one bit.

"It's a long ride to my kingdom. We'll stop at your home if you like, or we can ride straight through to Ventoux."

Castle Falkoyn. Her childhood home and also her personal dungeon. She couldn't put off confronting her past forever.

"A brief stop at the castle to see that everything is in order will suffice, and then I wish to see your home, Prince Henri." A moment's hesitation made her belly pinch. "Do you think your family will like me?"

"They will love you, Princess Eira. As do I." He retrieved the apple Madam Davina had given him and held it out. "This should tide you over for a bit."

She eyed the glossy red skin and shook her head. "Thank you, but I think I've gone off them."

His wicked grin was temptation enough, but then he took a huge bite of her once favorite fruit. Juice ran down his chin, and she squirmed in her saddle. Lawks, but she wanted to lick him. Lick, suck, touch, taste, feel every inch of him until she didn't know where he ended and she began.

"I suppose one bite won't kill me."

She leaned over, but Henri's hand cradled her head and his warm lips covered hers. She grasped his collar, not wanting to let go. There would be plenty of time later to make love. Her nerve endings tightened with the promise of what lay before them. They had the rest of their lives to make new memories.

"Have I ever told you how utterly, delightfully, enchanting you are?" His tongue flicked across her mouth. "From the moment I saw you sneak into the king's antechamber, I was bewitched. Your stepmother had it all wrong, my love. I didn't take your heart, but you certainly have stolen mine."

Eira breathed in his heavenly scent of apple and pine. "I love you Henri."

The simple phrase held deep meaning for them both. He was the first person she'd ever, truly, said the words to and meant them with every fiber of her being.

"Let's go home." He brushed her lips with his and pulled away with a saucy wink. A promise of more later.

The group rode away from the palace with music and laughter drifting from the great ballroom, and Eira sighed with happy contentment. She'd still never danced at a ball, but there would be laughter and merriment in their lives. Forever.

And they would live an enchanted happily ever after.

Chapter Fifty

Weeping came from behind them, followed by astonished gasps and calls for the guards. Eira glanced at the men and women who she'd disguised herself as several days earlier. They, to a one, stood transfixed, unsure what to do.

Leon stood with his pack, shock clear in his features.

Eira went to him and touched his sleeve. "Your Majesty." She curtseyed low. "The king is dead. Long live the king."

He stared at her, unblinking, unseeing.

"Now then, duckie, he's had a bit of a blow." Madam Davina stepped from the crowd and indicated Sacheen should comfort the new king before turning to place one hand on Eira, the other on Henri. "I see you took my advice."

"Thank you, for everything." Eira impulsively hugged the woman, clutching her tight to her bosom.

"There now, there, there." She smoothed Eira's back reassuringly. "Like I said, trust yourself, duckie, and it'll all work out." Her silver hair floated above her head, reminding Eira of another older and cryptically crankier woman. A puzzle piece slid into place.

"You were the servant woman who left the apples." It wasn't an accusation, more of an understanding.

"Guilty, I'm afraid." She giggled like a maiden and handed Eira one last apple. "This will sustain you for the long ride ahead."

The sight of the apple made her stomach churn. The enchanted fruit Regan gave her on that first day was still in her wardrobe.

Henri took the apple and tucked it into his coat pocket. "Your kindness won't be forgotten." He bowed to the witch. "I'll make sure Eira gets home safely."

Madam Davina inclined her head to both Henri and Eira with a promise to visit them soon. Then she moved to the center of the room and banged her staff three times on the parquet floor. The sound echoed through the grand ballroom, quieting those gathered.

"Tonight was meant as a celebration, but for whom, that is the riddle. You see before us the remnants of greed, gluttony, and tyranny. The time of fearing magic is at an end. King Otto is dead. Long live King Leon!" She pounded her staff thrice again, and a cheer rose from the crowd.

The witch lifted her staff and waved it high above her head. The candles flickered in their elaborate candelabras before dimming, plunging the ballroom in near darkness. The guests twittered and groused, some afraid of what would come next, others excitedly watching Madam Davina. Eira was firmly in the latter group. Their oppression was at an end. The villainy of Otto and his son was over. She hoped in time those who opposed magic would come to see it as a natural force for good, and not the dark threat Annah made it.

She held Henri close as Madam Davina pointed her staff to the dais. The king's body, as well as Guillaume's and Annah's lifeless forms, glittered and glowed as they rose above the floor, appearing to disappear the higher they went until only a column of glittering motes rose to the high ceiling. A fourth column joined the three, and she flicked a glance to the witch. Her cheeky wink confused Eira, but then she realized the fourth was for Regan.

Gratitude swelled in her bosom for the woman. What a wonderful gift she gave to Eira and Leon. But Davina wasn't done. Next, she whipped the staff upward where the heavy beamed ceiling faded away to expose a spectacular glass ceiling that showed the full moon in all her glory. Stars twinkled around the moon, thirteen in all.

The king's dull gold and ruby banners burned away, and gleaming silver banners unfurled to reveal Leon's sigil—a wolf's head.

The crowd oohed and aahed with each new reveal until their attention came to Leon. He stood in the center of his pack, a look of awe softening his features.

"Take your place upon the dais, King Leon." Davina ordered him to the ornate chair, and he obeyed.

Sacheen stayed at the foot of the dais, but Leon bade her forward, and she sheepishly stepped beside her mate.

The mischievous witch flourished her hand and a shining gold crown rested upon her outstretched palm. She glanced at Eira, indicating that she should be the one to place the crown upon Leon's head. It was an honor she didn't feel she'd earned, but the witch's insistent stare left no room for hesitation.

She took the steps one at a time, balancing the crown between her fingers. It wouldn't do to trip now and have the heavy gold clatter to the floor. Leon bent low enough she could place the crown firmly upon his head. She kissed him on each cheek and stepped to the side to embrace Sacheen.

"I hope you will return for the coronation." Leon held her hand in his, sorrow mixed with his joy.

"And the wedding," Sacheen added.

"We would be honored to be here for both." Henri bowed to the new king and escorted Eira down the steps.

Leon stood proudly to look out over his subjects. His voice, strong and sure, rang out through the ballroom with promises of a tolerant kingdom where everyone was welcome. Magic would once more be accepted, and even encouraged, so long as it did no harm.

Eira hugged Madam Davina, holding her close and thanking her again for seeing in her what she herself had not known was there—courage, trust, love.

A man called out the name Daria, and Eira looked over her shoulder in time to see the apothecary race toward a young woman who stood with Leon's pack. He'd found his missing daughter at last. With time, she hoped all the old wounds caused by King Otto would fade to nothing more than a sometime itch that was soothed by happy memories.

Her gaze swept over the assembled guests, landing on Bryn's sly smile and twinkling eyes. They inclined their heads in recognition, and a little thrill went through Eira. She hoped they would meet again so that she might hear the tale of the sleeping beauty who nodded off in orchards and danced with lords.

Leon called for music and the mood shifted. The oppressive subjugation of King Otto was firmly, finally, gone and an air of lightness descended upon the room. Leon took Sacheen's hand and led her to the dance floor and others followed. Eira blew her friends a kiss and left the ballroom, her heart full, despite her uncertain future.

Instead of leading her to her room, or even his where a delightfully soft mattress waited, Henri took her to the stables. To her surprise, the dwarves were waiting for her with an older gentleman.

"This is my valet, Bernard," Henri explained and turned to his valet. "Do you have the papers?"

"I do indeed, sir. I'm certain your father will find them most interesting." Bernard patted his coat. "It's a pleasure to meet you, Your Highness."

"Oh no, it's just Eira, please."

"Nay, lass. You be Princess Eira of Morovia. Daughter of the late, and sorely missed, Eloise of Morovia. May you be blessed with a long life." Dorton bowed low to her, and the other dwarves followed.

She would have to get used to the new title, and the change in treatment that came with it. Regan had to have known she was a princess but diminished her to a mere lady so that Eira wouldn't outrank her. The depths of that woman's hatred were too deep to excavate without permanent damage. Determined not to let Regan steal any more of Eira's precious moments, she pushed thoughts of her stepmother aside. One day, she would deal with everything that had transpired in the last fortnight, but for the now, she wished to be fully present with her friends.

"Are princesses allowed to wear trousers?" She pointed to her dress and then to the saddle of her horse.

"You are allowed to do whatever you please." Henri motioned to Bernard, and he pulled a pair of riding pants from a saddlebag. "I had a feeling you'd ask."

She threw her arms around Henri's neck and kissed him hard. His hands wrapped around her back, and she rocked against him. Desire and apprehension mingled in her thoughts as their kiss deepened. For the first time ever, she was in charge, fully and wholly, of her future.

She, Princess Eira, chose to live her life with kindness each day, and to love those deserving of her affections.

"I want to learn to sword fight and perhaps archery. I want to climb mountains and swim in rivers. I want to see the ocean and visit all the other kingdoms, starting with my Aunt Marguerite's. And I want to do all of that with you, Your Highness. More than anything, I want us to live each day with joy."

"We shall do all of that and more." He kissed her fingers and nipped the skin on her knuckles.

"You're a devious prince."

"And you like it."

"That I do." She didn't even blush when saying it. She liked being a rogue with him, and from the gleam in his eye, he didn't mind one bit.

"It's a long ride to my kingdom. We'll stop at your home if you like, or we can ride straight through to Ventoux."

Castle Falkoyn. Her childhood home and also her personal dungeon. She couldn't put off confronting her past forever.

"A brief stop at the castle to see that everything is in order will suffice, and then I wish to see your home, Prince Henri." A moment's hesitation made her belly pinch. "Do you think your family will like me?"

"They will love you, Princess Eira. As do I." He retrieved the apple Madam Davina had given her and held it out. "This should tide you over for a bit."

She eyed the glossy red skin and shook her head. "Thank you, but I think I've gone off them."

His wicked grin was temptation enough, but then he took a huge bite of her once favorite fruit. Juice ran down his chin, and she squirmed in her saddle. Lawks, but she wanted to lick him. Lick, suck, touch, taste, feel every inch of him until she didn't know where he ended and she began.

"I suppose one bite won't kill me."

She leaned over, but Henri's hand cradled her head and his warm lips covered hers. She grasped his collar, not wanting to let go. Her nerve endings tightened with the promise of what lay before them. There would be plenty of time later to make love. They had the rest of their lives to make new memories.

"Have I ever told you how utterly, delightfully, enchanting you are?" His tongue flicked across her mouth. "From the moment I saw you sneak into the king's antechamber, I was bewitched. Your stepmother had it all wrong, my love. I didn't take your heart, but you certainly have stolen mine."

Eira breathed in his heavenly scent of apple and pine. "I love you, Henri."

The simple phrase held deep meaning for them both. He was the first person she'd ever, truly, said the words to and meant them with every fiber of her being.

"Let's go home." He brushed her lips with his and pulled away with a saucy wink. A promise of more later.

The group rode away from the palace with music and laughter drifting from the great ballroom, and Eira sighed with happy contentment. She'd still never danced at a ball, but there would be laughter and merriment in their lives. Forever.

And they would live an enchanted happily ever after.

You are cordially invited to the wedding of HRH Henri of Ventoux, and HRH Eira of Morovia.
Nothing is ever as it seems. When a curious guests arrives to give Eira a gift, it will change the course of hers, and Henri's life forever.
Become a VIP Dragon today to receive my Dragon Dispatch newsletter and you'll instantly get the exclusive short story of their Enchanted Ever After.
You'll also be the first to know when more Daring Ever Afters are released!

Visit Tameri's website at the link below to get your exclusive story.

TameriEtherton.com/EnchantedEverAfter

About the Author

Tameri Etherton is a *USA Today* Bestselling and award-winning author of fierce scorching fantasy and magical ever afters. She grew up inventing fictional worlds where the impossible was possible.

It's been said she leaves a trail of glitter in her wake as she creates new adventures for her kickass heroines, and the rogues who steal their hearts.

She lives an enchanted life traveling the world with her very own prince charming and their mischievous dragon, Lady Dazzleton.

Read More from Tameri Etherton and explore the Aetherverse at
www.TameriEtherton.com

Author Notes

Enchant began as a much shorter story in a shared world anthology. I always knew Henri and Eira had more to offer, so when the anthology was unpublished, I let the characters tell me the rest of their tale. What materialized is a darker story than I set out to write, but one with heart, hope, and the healing power of true love's kiss. I hope I've done Eira justice in presenting her not as a victim of trauma, but as a woman who grew to understand her power.

As always, writing is a solitary endeavor, but along the way I had others who helped and supported the process. My earliest beta readers, Callene Rapp, Lynn Trahan, Dawn Line, Caprice Whitmire, and Kristin Ogilby were wonderful at giving me feedback to that first anthology version.

For this updated and expanded version, Stephanie Rawlins at Rawls Reads did an amazing developmental edit, and Faith Williams worked her magic on all those pesky commas and typos. If, however, you find one or two still remain, they are my errors alone as I often make tiny tweaks after Faith's edit. I would love it if you would email me to let me know where you found them so that I can remove the little buggers.

Thank you to Leigh Cadiente for this gorgeous cover.

A book wouldn't come to life without the love, support, and brainstorming of my fabulous husband David. He's my happily ever after.

xo,

Tameri

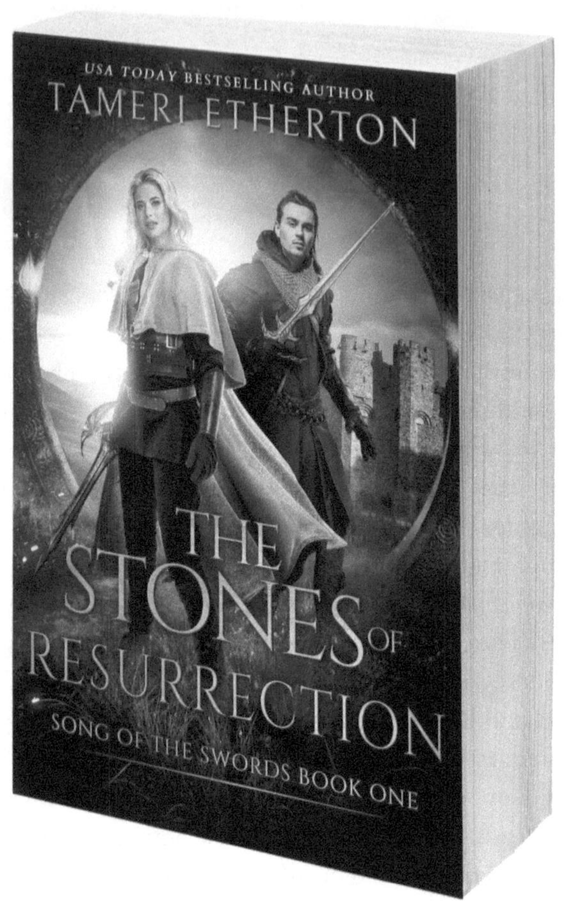

Otherworldly portals. Mysterious powers. Evil hungrily awaits her return.

Taryn's simple life is all she's ever known. Living above a busy London pub with her grandfather, they're ripped from their reality and plunged into a strange world to jumpstart an ancient prophecy. And when he's killed defending her from a vicious intruder's magic, Taryn's left nearly alone... and forced to trust a rugged savior.

Rhoane has one job. Sworn to protect the young woman who has returned to fulfill her destiny, the assassin dare not let his feelings get in the way of her training. But he knows the time will come when she accepts her power and recognizes he's her fated mate.

As Taryn learns her life on Earth was a lie, she must unlock her hidden talents to save an entire world from destruction. And though Rhoane will show no mercy to anyone who stands in her way, he fears her biggest threat comes from the family she has never known.

Will the destined pair rise to stop the annihilation of a vast kingdom?

The Stones of Resurrection is the enthralling first book in the Song of the Swords fantasy series. If you like ensemble casts, intense action, and dark family sagas, then you'll love Tameri Etherton's epic tale.

She's been hijacked by fate. He's running out of time. Can these magically mismatched outsiders find their forever-after before their realms perish?

Rori MacNair has learned to close off her heart. Molded into a spy to follow her legendary family's legacy, the faerie assassin is stunned to wake up in a strange forest and start reliving past traumas. Suspecting mind control, she shatters the spell trapping her only to stumble upon a handsome thief.

Therron Mistwalker is avoiding a cursed crown. Tracking a dark magic-wielder to end her vile acts, the elf-prince-in-disguise is unprepared to meet a captivating fae determined to slay the same villain. And realizing the prophecy he dreads has finally caught up to him, he teams up with his prickly new ally while worrying about the clock now ticking down to his doom.

Pursuing the evildoer through forbidden portals, Rori

worries she's warming up to her mysterious pointy-eared companion far too easily. And a guilt-ridden Therron struggles to set aside his ever-growing attraction as their prolonged witch hunt leaves behind a trail of dead bodies.

Can Rori and Therron bring their foul target to her knees and rescue their worlds?

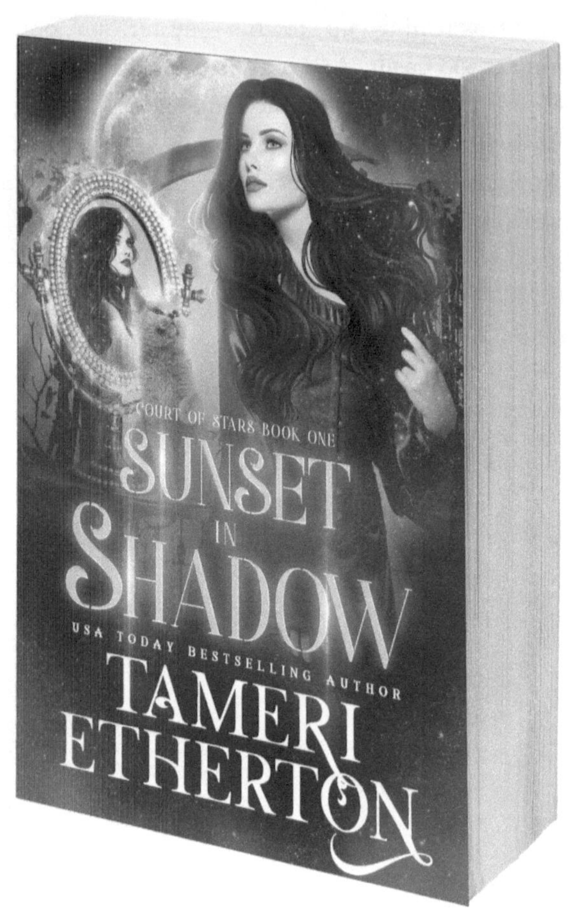

Essence of elegance by day. Rampant with desire by night. Can she keep her deadly secret while she wins a prince's heart?

Lady Rainne Dequette hates her ugly magical curse. Transforming from dignified elf to reckless ogress every evening, she's resigned to dispatching bandits after sundown instead of dancing at magnificent castle balls. But when her epic skills with a blade save a handsome royal from ravenous wolves, revealing her shameful form could get her killed.

Prince Theo Mistwalker would rather be in his grand library than combing the forests for his wayward brother. But after he's attacked, he's smitten by the swashbuckling rescuer who plants an alluring kiss on his lips before vanishing into the trees. Though his loyalty weakens while he heals in a local duchess's home and develops feelings for her beautiful elven daughter.

After Rainne confesses her burden to the noble man she's fallen for, she has no choice but to deal with her self-hatred or risk losing her one shot at happily-ever-after. And to be with the woman of his dreams, Theo must embark on a dangerous quest to break the spell.

Can they find a way to end Rainne's torment and surrender to their destined passions?

To unleash her dragon, she must confront her past.

In the seven years since Amaleigh failed to assassinate her best friend, she's been on the run jumping from world to world. All she truly wants is to stop running and find a place to call home. And maybe be kissed by someone who doesn't leave her feeling indifferent. Love doesn't come easily for her, yet unlocking her cold, dead heart might be a start to unleashing her inner dragon. That would mean trusting another and there's only one person she's ever trusted—the same man she couldn't kill.

Prince Gwilym knows he shouldn't risk Amaleigh's life by asking for help, especially since he's the reason she had to escape Eidyn. Now his life is in peril and she's the only person he trusts. He wouldn't blame her for not daring to return to the city that celebrated the slaughter of her kind and cast her aside.

Can she survive the very place her parents were murdered, or will palace intrigues claim another victim? If she fails Gwilym, she might lose her chance to come to terms with her past, and open her heart.

Forced to make a desperate choice, she must put aside her hatred for the man who murdered her family and sentenced her to a life of crime and loneliness.

To save those she loves, she must become the Dragon Mage the king fears most.